I0563006

From **TANSTAAFL Press:**

CorpGov Chronicle novels by Tom Gondolfi
An Eighty Percent Solution – CorpGov Chronicles: Book One
In a world where corporations suborn governments as a part of good business practice and unregistered humans can be killed without penalty, Tony Sammis, a midlevel corporate functionary, finds himself unwittingly a pawn in a guerilla war between a powerful cabal of business leaders and an elusive but deadly underground movement. His final solution to the biological terror unleashed mirrors Tony's own twisted sense of justice.

Thinking Outside the Box – CorpGov Chronicles: Book Two
Winning one war doesn't seem to be enough. Tony Sammis and the Green Action Militia are once again thrust into the center of a conflict that will change the lives of everyone in the solar system. This time they are allies with the fledgling CorpGov and even the United States government against the ravages of the corrupt Metropolitan Police Force. The GAM and their allies are fighting a losing war with few soldiers and even fewer weapons. Behind the scenes, a humble and unsuspected power block lurks with its own axe to grind.
Self-interest, romance, freedom, and a lust for power are stirred together in this chaotic soup of tension, intrigue, assassination, and war.

Also by Tom Gondolfi
Toy Wars
Flung to a remote world, a semi-sentient group of robotic mining factories arrive with their programming hashed. They can only create animated toys instead of normal mining and fighting machines. One of these factories, pushed to the edge of extinction by the fratricidal conflict, attempts a desperate gamble. Infusing one of its toys with the power of sentience begins the quest of a 2-meter tall, purple teddy bear and his pink, polka-dotted elephant companion. They must cross an alien world to find and enlist the aid of mortal enemies to end the genocide before Toy Wars claims their family—all while asking the immortal question, "Why am I?"

By Bruce Graw
Demon Holiday
Torval, Demon Third Class, Layer Four Hundred Twelve of the Eighth Circle of Hell, has been in the business of chastising sinners longer than he can remember. Delivering punishment is the only job he's ever known—the only job he's ever wanted. After Torval witnesses something unexpected, his demonic Overseer demands that he take time off to resolve this personal crisis. And so Torval, the demon, finds himself sent on vacation...to Earth, the proving ground of souls!

Demon Ascendant
Torval, Demon Third Class, Layer Four Hundred Twelve of the Eighth Circle of Hell, on *vacation* to Earth has managed to find another demon, has dated an angel and inadvertently explored some of the sins of humankind: greed, gluttony and lust. Through all this his biggest struggle involves deciding if he wants his holiday to end or to continue forever.

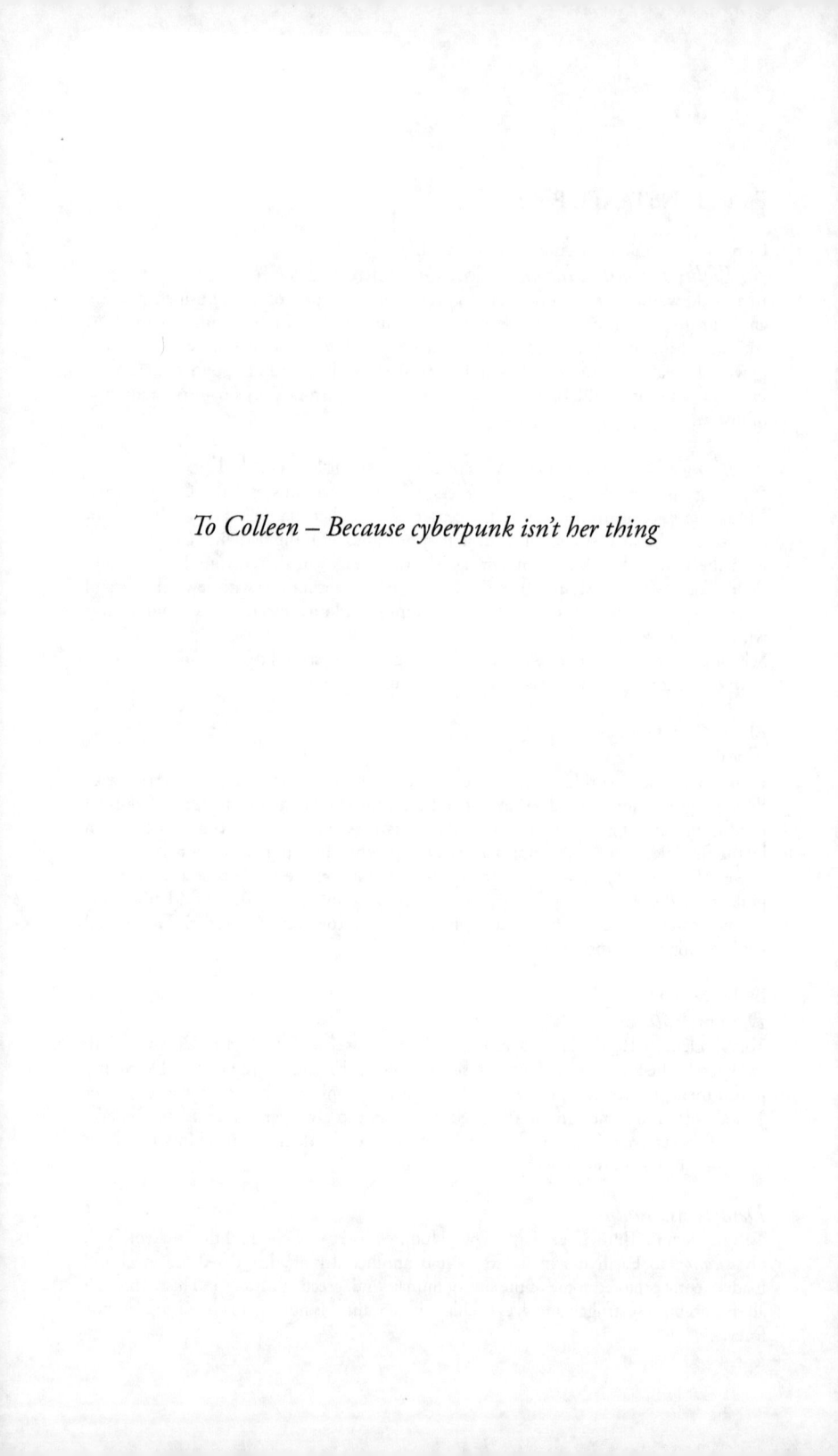

To Colleen – Because cyberpunk isn't her thing

Of Demons and Coal

Monarchy of America: Book 1

Thomas Gondolfi

TANSTAAFL 🧸 PRESS

TANSTAAFL Press
891 PH 10
Castle Rock, WA 98611

Visit us at www.TANSTAAFLPress.com

Of Demons and Coal

First printing—TANSTAAFL Press
Copyright © 2020 by Thomas Gondolfi
Cover art: Kristin Bryant at www.kristindesigns.com

Printed in the USA
ISBN: 978-1-938124-61-7

Book layout by Hydra House Books

1—Friday, February 3, 1888

"'Electric Light Fraud!'" yells a bundled-up huckster waving the newspaper's late edition. The *Boston Herald* never publishes positively about Edison. No great loss. I think the idea of lightning running through my house, no matter how chained, is rather disturbing.

The snow piles up in drifts gray with soot between the ruts of the cobblestone streets and against the red brick buildings. The chill of the light wind cuts through my long cloak, even with the rabbit fur around the high collar. My shiver stifles the yawn that had been poised on my lips. I pull the cape closer. With a long, metal pole bearing a slow wick, an enterprising young girl in dirty overalls lights the gas streetlight in front of me. As she turns to race to the next lamp, she nearly runs me over.

"'Scuse me, Widow Ochoa."

"Out of here, scamp," I say, swatting at her playfully. The little ones can't know how much I hate the moniker, "widow." I always associate it with someone old. At twenty-three I'm not even a spinster. Oh, I'm not young, and definitely not beautiful.

Ten hours of spelling coal byproducts from the gritty Boston skies has me wanting nothing more than to stoke the fire in my room, climb into my nightdress, and bury myself under six layers of blankets for some well-deserved sleep. My pay and the widow's pension from the Royal Treasury of King Frederick II gives me barely enough to live at Chapman's Boarding House. With a two-hole privy and accommodations that boast just enough room to change my petticoats, it borders on livable. On good days, the North End stench of the fish offal and rancid whale oil from the docks doesn't cover up the smell of Mrs. Chapman's pickled-cabbage stew, a taste treat at which even pigs turn up their noses.

The tinny sound of bells pierces the evening air. I wince. Only the Mission Church bells carry that thin tone. Three quick strikes on the higher-pitched bell indicate an alarm meant for my team of hellfighters and me. This is the second time this month they have called me out. The two-tone bells call out a Morse message. Low tone pause—T. High tone low tone high tone pause—R. High pause—E and more before the dispatch repeats itself. Tremont Street about a mile out. Rich neighborhood.

Walking all that way in store-bought shoes doesn't appeal. Corns have already formed on the tops of my feet. My savings would more than cover new shoes or a cobbler to fix them, but if I dip into them every time I am uncomfortable, I'd never be able to support myself in old age.

Hacks don't come down here this time of the night, although I might find one cruising the bars along Prince Street. Stretching my coin is another story.

As fate has it, a streetcar meanders down to the corner at the end of the street. I run over, being extra careful not to turn my ankle on the cobblestones or slip on the ice.

Raising my skirts and undergarments, I climb onto the running board. The vomit and muck on the trolley's floor makes me rethink my decision, but the damage is already done. I envision the scrubbing time it's going to take me to clean some previous drunk's evening from the hems of my dress and undergarments and frown.

The driverless transport waits its prescribed thirty seconds before trundling off again. I don't quite understand all the reasons we don't need a driver. Something about a pair of bumpy cylinders the trolley men call cams that allow the cars to follow set paths. I understand the missing horses. The earth witch in me can feel the energy stored in the massive metal springs in the thick ceiling above me.

The trams are free if a bit finicky. Sometimes they stop and never restart. Once I saw one turn in a circle and keep turning. It took three engineers to get that one stopped and back on track.

The only other passenger, a bookkeeper from his looks, sits across from me. He wears the bare minimum society requires of his station. His black breeches have seen too much lye soap. He wears a leather coat patched eight times more than a stumblebum might wear, and a dress shirt fraying at the cuffs and collar. Turning toward me, he says, "Them bells sound'n' off 'gain. Must be mean'n' 'nother demon on the loose." He runs a finger inside the stiff collar of a shirt that may have at one time been fashionable in England, but nowhere else.

I try and stay out of conversations with men as a general rule, but especially on a tram. Besides, I have my work cut out for me as the person who left the glorious trail of after-excessive-drinking seems to have doused the entire floor. I lift my hem from the mess, knowing the cause is lost already.

"Oh, this here trolley is going right up where the hellfighters is gonna be."

"How do you know about that?" I ask. "I mean, I know, but—"

"I be reckoning that if'n one building in fifty be powered by hellspawn, I gotta learn about them bells. They's installing them right after the Demon Fire of '72. I hears them so much I figures out right quick what they means. That there low bell is a T," he says, making out the bells that continued to ring until all my fellow hellfighters arrive. "And that there is an R. Puts 'em all together an' you got Tremont."

His statement requires no response, so I try to ignore the man so I might get a nap on the way out. I lean back and close my eyes.

"Maybes you lookin' fer a man?"

"What?" I ask, bolting up with a start. I don't need a bookkeeper or anyone else pawing at me if that is what he has in mind.

"Thems hellfighters makes a good livin'. Not like no hack driver or no bookkeeper, neither. I hears some of the high-born ladies say they's mighty fine lookin', too."

"No. I assure you I am not looking for a husband. As a widow, I've had quite enough men for this lifetime and probably the next."

"Youse don't look old enough to be no widow woman. But then the Irish Liberation did chew up lots o' men. Is that where you lost yourn?"

I try not to think about my husband, Aaron, dead only five years. It seems like he just stepped out for a pint, yet five long years separated us. "Yes. He died at Termonbarry."

"Lots of good men went to St. Peter at that place. Did they ever find out who summoned that demon? Survivors tell stories that don't match. English, Irish, American. Me, I think us Americans and the Irish gave them bloody Brits just a bit too much lead to—"

"Will you please be quiet?" I ask, giving just a little too much snap to my voice.

"Sorry, mum."

Aaron, my massive Moor. Had I loved him for even a hundred years, it wouldn't have been enough. My husband's loss in that cauldron of death, Ireland, left a charred spot in my soul bigger than their entire accursed country.

Growing up, neither men nor boys ever held any fascination. Girls around me, especially Karie, giggled and wondered what matching their parents might make for them. At the time, I found the male of our species beastly at best and demonic at worst. I would go a long way around the carriage house to avoid talking to one. My mother, the reigning goddess of all knowledge about the stronger sex, still despairs at my lack of interest. While not part of royalty, my mother always adopts an air eight stages better than her station in life. Back in my youth, she insisted I have a coming-out party and engage with the Boston socialites. Never had so much money been spent on so little outcome. By the end of my fifteenth year, I'd danced with ten young gentlemen, received one young man (who got his instep spiked by my heel when he attempted to put his arm around me in the buggy), and, shockingly, no proposals.

I see the red of fires glowing to the northwest, but still, no definitive location as the tram rolls up the empty street of Tremont past Dartmouth.

A green delivery trailer with gold stencil proclaiming "Dunne's Butchers" flies across the street. I mean flies, not just moving swiftly. It smashes against the side of a brownstone like a china cup dropped on the floor. Splinters of wood and gobs of meat rain down. This is the sign I've been waiting for and pull the trolley's exit cord. The tram rattles to a stop.

"Youse sure you be wantin' to get out here, widow woman?" the bookkeeper says from his hunched-over perch beneath the edge of the tram's window.

"Yes. Thank you for your concern. This is definitely my stop," I say as a horse, minus its head, follows the delivery trailer against the wall with a gory sound of a wet slip slammed against a washboard.

"Go with God then, Miss Widow." Ignoring the simpering fool, I manage to exit the tram without further damage to my skirts.

A steam-wheezing, brass-and-steel, self-propelled monstrosity misses running me over by a whisker. Its wide broom sweeps up the snow and horse apples in front of it. The simpleminded machine puffs and scrubs down the lane. It is oblivious to the chaos it travels toward.

Over the top of the machine, I see the flaming visage of a demon's face, twisted and contorted in rage. With skin the texture and color of a pig roasted overlong on a spit, and beady crimson eyes set deep in its skull, it masses the same as thirty stout men. Its great ram-like horns reach the middle of the nearby building's second floor. I can feel the waves of anger and fury boiling off the hellspawn as bursts of heat.

At least it is a massive beast. That means a short night. The larger the demon, the easier it is to manipulate with its stupid mind. Those brutes have to put a show on about how impressive they are in muscles rather than what damage they can cause by being smart. The ones you fear are those the size of a child—tricky and powerful enough to melt your flesh from your bones at forty paces.

The vaguely human-shaped, horned monster holds a pram like a child might hold a marble. I whisper a prayer to Saint Nicholas that no babe is inside as the evil creature crushes the stroller between its forefinger and thumb. Like all demons, it rejoices in the death and destruction torn from our world. It laughs in a low tone that sends shivers down the spine.

But I am its antithesis.

I bend over and pick up a small bit of cobblestone that has withstood the street sweeper. Popping it into my mouth, I march toward the maelstrom. The earth witch in me feels the orderly structure of the stonework. I taste gritty, acrid clay interspersed with the minute flavors of pig offal, spilled flour, slivers of rust, fragments of store candy, and remnants of manure.

Every time I attempt to describe the symbiosis of witchcraft, I fail. I don't steal another's power. I don't get filled with its essence. Instead, I feel the living entity of the street below me. Its energy and mine merge together in a swirl like that of a baker creating a cinnamon roll. It doesn't fill me, but we share a portion of our spirit. And like that sweet treat, we become more than our components. No longer am I just sugar, cinnamon, or dough. I am more.

A whistle of agony breaks my communion. Two great fists crush down the top of the mindless cleaning machine. Its pressure vessel, dark with tarnish, spews its power into sound and a jet of steam. The evil beast throws his head back from the superheated water with a bellow even though it can't possibly hurt him. After the flinch, it tears the street sweeper into two uneven pieces, stopping the device's death throes. It picks up the smaller piece, only the size of an oxen team, and looks around for a target. Its fiery eyes lock onto mine.

It is now time for me to get into the action, if only in self-preservation. I mentally reach down into the cobblestones and flip them up like snapping a sheet at the end of the bed. A giant groundswell of stone forms a wave thirty feet high. I freeze it in place as it reaches the intersection as a stationary wall. I hear a metallic crash against the rocks and smile at my handiwork.

A loud roar punctuates another crack against the rocks. Bits of brass and wood fountain over the top. I rush up toward my woman-made hill, sneaking through a crack between it and the building, almost knocking over my team lead. Missing him is quite a feat as he is broad as a hogshead.

"Sorry, Carlos. I didn't see you there."

Carlos de Aldana, leader of the *Dos Campanas*, and direct descendant of Martin de Aldana, ex-Duke of Rutland, isn't a man that people flock to. With his acne-pocked face, short stature, and dark skin, many overlook him. His natural charisma isn't in drawing people in. Where he shines is that once you've shed blood with him, you know he will back you with magic, guns, or even politics in even the darkest place of hell itself. He leads. We follow. Even with my superior skills, there is no way I can ever take his place.

Carlos breaks into a rare smile through the heavy pockmarking of his face. "No worries, Stella," he says. "We are almost assembled. We're just missing—"

"I'll bet three *pesetas* that it's Don Alberto," I shout over the beast's bellows.

"No bet. We just need to hold this monster until he gets here." A jet of flame splatters the building next to Carlos, melting some of his salt and pepper hair. Belatedly ducking down, he looks back. "You probably know the drill better than me. I'll have Maxwell set off the signal." Carlos dashes out to take up his position.

On the surface, interning a loose demon is simplicity itself—tease it back to where it doesn't want to go and then imprison it. Two witches take turns baiting the fiend with mild damage spells, getting it to chase them. Three others block the demon's view and access to anything but its tormenters. The last witch heals any of our team who is damaged in the process. In the end, he is also often the one that seals the beast in place. But for all that, every hellfighter has to be on their toes as something always goes wrong.

I get the dirt in the cracks of the cobblestones to take to the sky in a thick cloud. My task as one of the herders is to give the beast nothing but the baiters to see. My work is like putting blinkers on a horse.

The night briefly turns to day when a brilliant white flash appears above the beast like that bloody flash powder used for photographs. The light is the signal that the team is assembled and time to move the critter. Carlos, an air witch, forms a tornado-like vortex behind the beast. Working with earth isn't like air. The components of the ground are almost lazy in their power. They don't want to move. Air, on the other hand, needs to move, and the faster, the better.

I urge my formerly frozen wave forward enough so that I can slide it in front of the buildings and down the street. I am one side of the box and will travel horizontally.

Now I can see the briar hedge forming opposite of me by the nature warlock Raquel Ruiz. We call her Menagerie, or just Menaj, as she always seems to have a group of critters around her. I must be too much of a city girl because embracing nature the way she does seems foreign.

Donny O'Sullivan, one of our two baiters, stings the beast with a small jet of water right in the face. The heat of the creature causes it to erupt into a cloud of steam as the demon bellows. The horned beast lunges for its red-haired antagonist. Donny's slight form easily dodges out of the way. But come to think of it, I've never known a fat hellfighter. I guess that would be just a good way to commit suicide.

Carlos pushes up his vortex into the space vacated by our quarry. Raquel and I slide our walls a couple dozen feet down the avenue. Now, all we have to do is repeat this a couple hundred times.

Massive fists come down on either side of Donny, threatening to roast him between the two sheets of flame. Time for our other baiter to swing into action and draw attention away. Unfortunately, our other baiter, Mateo, had died three weeks past in a bar brawl, of all things.

A new member fills his shoes—Don Alberto Diaz y Serrano de Salamanca. In my book, this prissy warlock knows about as much about demons as a virgin has experience with sex. But, as Carlos says, we all have to start somewhere. Carlos has been training him hard on our methods.

Alberto etcetera, etcetera, also a water witch, forces a bubble of wastewater up from the sewer through the rock. I feel the pressure and pain of the earth being rent apart, so I coax the soil and rock apart like a loosening sphincter. It allows the foul water an easier passage. The bolt of sewage hits the demon from the side. The creature, now ignoring Donny, ineffectively bats at the stream while screaming in rage.

So far, so good, I think.

The hellspawn lurches forward. In the space of a heartbeat, it takes four giant strides toward our backpedaling virgin. A vine snakes out from the hedge and wraps itself around Alberto's ankle. With a jerk, it yanks our new teammate to one side and indecorously dumps him on his arse.

The demon's jaw snaps down on naught but air.

"Side to side, you idiot," calls Maxwell Parker, our dedicated healer and white witch. "They are much faster than you are but about as maneuverable as a train."

De Salamanca's copper-brown face turns the shade of new snow. It shows no acknowledgment of anything but the grinding teeth that had just missed him and the beast's screams of fury.

"Shit," I say. I can see what's coming. Just like any military plan, ours is likely to fall apart at the first contact with the enemy.

Donny sends another horse trough full of water spraying the demon's way all in one glob. It turns on its renewing tormenter, forgetting the sewage and the warlock that sent it his way. Most demons, especially the large ones, have little to no memory and zero follow-through. This is why it is so easy to manipulate them.

It runs forward, banging into the side of a building in a desperate attempt to get O'Sullivan. The side of the edifice crumbles. People fall out, screaming. Debris flies everywhere. I manage to land the six civilians safely in a deep sandpit I form from within the earth and place beneath them. But with too many things to pay attention to, a broken bedstead glances off my right shoulder. Nothing serious, but the bruising and maybe a greenstick fracture will slow me down.

As if summoned, Maxwell Parker shows up at my side. His hands reach down my dress to press on my bare skin. Had anyone else done this, I would give them a brick enema. Max is professional, and it isn't the first time he's touched or seen my skin. I feel the bruises "evaporate"… the only word that ever comes to mind. My bone beneath itches slightly, and the ache disappears.

"Thanks, Max," I say before returning my attention to the fight.

"*De nada.*"

Donny has found himself in a ring of debris with no quick way out. The fiery beast is likely to turn him into pâté if it isn't distracted. Don Alberto seems not to have done anything but sink to the ground and cower under one of the streetlamps.

"Saints preserve fools and children," I say. As I had before, by putting the stone in my mouth, I sample the power around me. I feel the goodness of God Almighty as it flows everywhere. It warms my spirit. God himself seemingly offers a portion of his omnipotence to my command.

"'John saw it rise up out of the sea, having seven heads and ten horns, and up on his horns ten crowns, and upon his heads the name of blasphemy,'" I say, pointing directly at the creature's head. A bolt of distilled goodness lances forward. Where it strikes, it knocks the demon backward onto its fundamentals.

Yes, I am one of the oddities of the witchcraft world. I have more than one talent. While magic is rare, only one person in a handful of hundreds manifests any gift. Then only one in twenty or fifty of those can use it for anything more than parlor tricks. To make me even more different, only one or two witches in a generation can manipulate more than one kind of magic. I don't share the knowledge of my extra skills with many. And while I know white witchcraft, I can't control it with the fine sense that I can use my capabilities with the earth. Instead of merely stinging the beast, I hit him with a massive uppercut. I use white only for emergencies.

Before the beast can recover, Carlos calls out from the back, "Max, take Alberto's place." He knows my white powers can't be trusted for the delicate work of taunting.

The demon shakes his head, glares at me, and leaps to its feet, intent on rending my flesh to goo. Instead, Donny draws its attention with another shot of water. Max gets into position, and our work goes on.

I catch one glimpse of Don Alberto as we move the monster toward its home. The ex-member of our team hides down the stairwell of a brownstone, white as a bleached sheet and eyes the size of dinner plates. No longer a member of our team, he becomes a civilian—someone to protect, but just as likely to get in the way.

Maxwell's brilliant flares of God's gift and the much dimmer streetlamps are the only thing that pierce the night. Grunts and snarls vie with the occasional civilian's scream to rob the night of its silence. Also, without a dedicated healer, we all take some bumps and bruises that we live with. Worse, in a rare slipup, Menaj takes the demon's barbed tail to her chest. I wince, thinking of those spines in her breasts. It will need attention after we are done, but she seals the bleeding with a poultice and a writhing band of vining plant.

A gaping hole blown out from the side of a rowhouse denotes the building the demon escaped from. The orifice is like no other damage. Even a civilian can tell the difference. The brick and lumber have been exploded from within like a boiler with a frozen safety valve.

As we ease the hellspawn into the basement, I break off from the wall team. The baiters stop taunting and form a corral. I go in first to set up the imprisonment. I see a vast rent in the side of the original chalk pentagram, which had held the otherworldly beast, that speaks for itself. With no time to investigate, I brush the dirt floor smooth with a handy broom.

Closing my eyes, I feel the ground. We become one. All enchantments have gone, and the blank canvas is at my disposal. Unlike when first summoned, we don't need all the pomp and circumstance. We merely need to hold the beast until a licensed demon installer can show up and perform the appropriate rituals.

Without opening my eyes, I draw a massive pentagram in the dirt with my right index finger while chanting, "We know that God's children do not make a practice of sinning, for God's Son holds them securely, and the evil one cannot touch them." I pull the stone, the metals, and even the very fabric of the earth itself to my trace in the dirt.

Once the four-foot-wide, five-point star is complete, I call out, "Bring him in."

Snarling and spitting, the demon no longer lashes out at tormenters but claws at the barriers formed by the team. It knows what awaits it now and only wants to escape. It is also our most dangerous time. Those in front are just to keep it trapped while those in back push with their physical and magical strength. No matter how good we are, gaps are always forming between the magicks.

I get smacked by one of the beast's massive fists. A jet of flame starts Carlos's blouse on fire, which Donny puts out with drenching rain he conjures out of the atmosphere itself.

A sound as if a giant child sucked on a sour candy sees the massive creature reduce in size to that of a normal person. I feel the pentagram solidify into an invisible steel prison. The fury of the demon's scream drops in volume to barely be heard.

"In," I say.

"We got it," Carlos announces.

As always at the conclusion of a demon reinterment, we stand there looking at one another in desperate silence. Our blood is up, but the need for activity is gone. And, as always, the building we end up in looks like a massive cannon blew a hole through it.

Stepping outside, we look back at the swath of destruction caused by the beast. Even our skills couldn't block all the damage. A mule lies disemboweled, bleeding out on the street. Corners of buildings have bricks and chunks missing out of them like some child's toys after a tantrum. A barber's pole lies shattered in red, white, and blue glass. A pram is flattened as if the earth goddess herself chose to sit upon it. I emotionally take in the scattering of metal, wood, and stone pieces. The aftermath reminds me of the hurricane of '78.

I turn my attention to the team. The right leg of Maxwell Parker's breeches is burned away, exposing blisters and blackened skin. Carlos's left index finger sticks out at the wrong angle. Each of us is darkened in ash and smoke. I shake like a dog, causing a small cloud.

"*Cacafuego*," Menagerie finally says, breaking the silence.

"You can say that again," Donny agrees.

"*Cacafuego*," Raquel repeats.

Maxwell tends the wounds about the group with his white magic.

"We'll meet up at the Bell in Hand tomorrow night to split the take," Carlos says.

I am too tired to be excited about another reward this month. After a long day of spelling soot and then a demon alarm on top of it, all I want is a meat pie, a pint of ale, and bed. But if I go home, I'll be lucky to get even a bed. I don't remember hearing the seven bells during the fight, but I had other more important things to worry about if I wanted to keep my precious skin intact.

Alice Chapman, my landlady, runs her boardinghouse like something out of the King's Own American Regiment. The doors are closed and locked precisely at eight. Dinners are put on the table precisely at seven and removed at eight after the doors have been locked.

Widow Chapman will not open the doors after eight, nor will she provide any exceptions to the meal schedule. "They promote sloth and loose morals," she says to everything she doesn't personally approve.

The eight o'clock bells from the Mission Church choose that moment to peel off, sealing my hopes and dreams of a meal, a bath, and a bed at home. My waist would thank me for skipping a meal, and my head probably would thank me for skipping the pint. That only leaves lodging. I have my pride. I won't take bed-space.

I remember my best friend, Karie Taylor, and her standing offer of a bed in her apartment. "Gents, I'm going to leave now. I'll meet you at the Bell in Hand tomorrow night."

"Good work, Stella." As an afterthought, I release the spring-loaded earthen wall I'd moved around with my magic. I can feel it sigh as it slumps back to its original shape.

"Thanks, boss."

Now, Karie Taylor's name, otherwise known as Daring Karie, evokes reactions from everyone who hears it. To the upper-crust ladies of town, she is the epitome of all that is rank and disgusting in our world. Other women spurn her, even those in her own profession. To children, she is a horror that mothers invoke to frighten them into behaving. To every man over the age of thirteen, she embodies all that is sensual and sexual. Karie is one of the highest-paid, ahem, ladies of the evening in Boston, and perhaps the whole of the Kingdom of America.

As my friend, I love her to death. She is funny, irreverent, and all that is genuinely charitable and good. She practically pays for the running of the Boston Orphanage by herself and contributes to at least six other organizations for philanthropic works that I know of.

Karie and I went to Harbor Primary School together. We made an odd pairing, but once we compared lives—her the daughter of an absentee fisherman whose wife died in childbirth and my mother being the highfalutin' bitch that she is—we became inseparable.

The years went by, and we each took different paths—me with my Aaron and her with every man who would pay. She took to her chosen profession like a duck to water. Karie isn't a classic beauty like Lily Elsie or Maude Fealy, yet her clientele sings her praises almost in church mass itself. The reason they come back to her bed as often as they can afford it is simply because Karie likes sex in all of its infinite varieties. She loves men, women, thin, fat, and everywhere in between. My friend isn't a nymphomaniac, in that it is not only her vocation but her deeply loved hobby as well. She enjoys everything about sex and passes that joy onto her customers.

I don't look down on her profession. I often feel wives, in general, are whores that aren't paid very well. So what is there to look down on?

Actually, because of the neighborhood, our demon hunt took us to, I am quite close to her home. If I have any difficulty in my decision, the thought of a two-hour walk back to the docks area and casting about for a hotel on a Friday night decides me.

Ten minutes later, I'm at Karie's classy red door. She once confided in me her two-level joke in that color. Red is the color to show that you own your own home. Add to that the red-light-district method of paying for her house. She chuckles every time she leaves the house. A brass plate announcing, "*Casa de* Taylor," and a large brass knocker adorn the door. I use the knocker twice, hoping I'm not interrupting.

The door opens to an older man in a butler suit with a lordly nose that has been broken probably more times than the number of demons I've interned. I understand he used to be a boxer before his hair turned gray. "*Buenas noches, Vdo* Ochoa," Alejandro Sanchez says. "I'm very sorry, but Miss Taylor is engaged."

"I was afraid of that, Alejandro. Is Miss Taylor's offer to use the Blue Room still good? It appears I've been locked out of my boardinghouse."

"*Absolutamente, señora*. That has never been rescinded, and we keep the room fresh just for you. Please, let me take you there."

"Thank you, Alejandro."

"Will miss require a bath or a dresser?"

"Alejandro, how many times do I have to tell you that I am of common birth, no matter what airs my mother puts on. I'm just Stella."

"Yes, Miss Stella," he says, with a playful wink.

"And no, Alejandro, despite my disreputable state, I am exhausted. I'll strip out of these things and be on my way in the morning."

"Very good, Miss Stella."

He leads through the foyer of what appears to be an upper-class home. It bears no resemblance to the velvet and gilt of the bordellos and cat-houses that Karie used to work and live in. A tasteful Monet, *Spring*, hangs at the landing of the stairs. I don't think much of the frogs and their Emperor Vilhelm Bonaparte, but they always export the most wonderful artists.

"Here you are, Miss Stella. Will you want breakfast in the morning?"

"Oh, goodness, no. I have work in the morning. I should be out of here well before the staff is up."

"Very good. Sleep well, miss."

I douse the single candle in the room. The sliver of moon shining through the curtains gives plenty of light. I slip off my dress and hang it on the dresser's chair, hoping the stench of brimstone would air out enough that I don't have to make my way back to the boardinghouse in the morning. The soot marks I can live with as they happen to us filter girls all the time in spelling the filth from the air.

I begin to undo all of my female underpinnings. While my waist is far from thin, my barrel hips and beastly bosom allows me to skip wearing a corset. That doesn't stop the need for a six-hook brassiere. I sigh as the heavy weight of my breasts come off my shoulders. Also, as a working woman, I am exempt from a bustle, so I just slip out of my bloomers.

A silk nightdress, a gag gift from Karie last Christmas, is the only nightclothing available. So slim and form-fitting, the fabric makes me feel even more naked than any time completely bare as with my own husband. Hobson's choice, I think. Sleep in my clothes or the decadent nightshirt.

At least this way my clothes would get the chance of a good airing, I think, climbing under the covers in the filmy nothing from the Orient. I revel in the fresh sheets for about the length of a lightning bug flash before falling asleep.

2—Saturday, February 4, 1888

I drift up to that unmistakable feeling of being married. Aaron's body presses its heat across my back. His hands reach around to tease my nipple through my nightshirt. He kisses softly under my long brown hair at the nape of my neck. It surely must be Sunday morning for him to be getting after me randy like a goat. Fingers find the hem of my gown. His sharp fingernails rake up the back of my thighs. Telltale dampness grows between my limbs in that womanly location. Oh, tarnation, now I am getting randy.

I reach back to show Aaron my appreciation, but between his thighs, I don't find his manhood, hard or limp—

Wait! My husband is dead, my mind screams.

I roll over in bed faster than a dolphin in the open ocean to see my attacker. Through the brocade curtains, the bright morning sun lights up the beaming face of Karie; her crooked smile seems fit to slap on an invisible cat.

"Jesus!" I exclaim, realizing Sunday's confession ought to be interesting.

"Nope. Not even the Madonna," Karie teases, reaching for my breast again. Her auburn hair flounces like a new petticoat.

"More like Mary Magdalene before her conversion," I say, slapping her hand away.

She forms a very sultry pout on her face. "Not even for taking you in last night?" she teases. I levitate out of bed. Her eyes go wide, and a smile sketches across her face at my revealing attire. I remember the old saw of frying pans and fires.

"You are insatiable," I say, pulling my slip off the dressing table in at least a token visual defense.

Karie stretches out like a languid feline showing off her even more prurient bed wear and most of her lithe figure. Everything she has is tight and trim, unlike my beastly bosom or barge hips. "Maybe a little. Say, what's with the coy act?"

A single chime from the hall clock announces the thirty-minute mark.

"Some of us have to work during the day. By the way, what time is it?"

"Too early for anything but playtime with my Star," she says, using her private nickname for me.

"Well, put that on the back burner until Sunday afternoon." After I fasten my bra six ways from Sunday, I duck into my slip. To my surprise, it has been freshly laundered and pressed.

A knock at the door interrupts my thoughts. Alejandro comes in loaded with a silver tray of breakfast goodies, including *pan dulce*, and, by the smell of it, heavenly Columbian coffee.

It isn't as if Alejandro hasn't seen me in a slip before, so I refrain from diving behind the dressing screen.

"Alejandro, what time is it?"

"Twenty-eight to eight, Miss Stella."

"Good grief. I have to fly!" I drop on the bed to pull on freshly shined boots.

"You sure you don't want to be my kept woman?" Karie says, petting my unbound hair.

"Lay off, woman. And don't tempt me. I might just say 'yes,' and then where would you be?

"Alejandro, I need a button hook." He produces one out of his pocket so deftly he must have anticipated my haste. Karie takes the opportunity as I bend over to tease the top of my bloomers through my slip.

"OK, temptress. If you will just lay off long enough for me to get dressed and out of here, I'll come over tonight for dinner. You can ply me with liquor to convince me toward any debauchery you might have in mind."

"You're a witness to her offer, Alejandro," Karie says with a giggle.

"Yes, miss."

Standing, I slide my dress over my fundamentals, noting the lack of either stain or smoke. Alejandro has been busy. Mentally I make a note to do something nice for Karie's staff. I lean over and smack a kiss on my friend's cheek. Before she can grab me and pull me to the bed, I snatch a sweet roll from the breakfast tray and bolt out the door.

"'Edison Arrested for Sorcery without a License!'" calls a news vendor across the street from me. Good riddance to Mr. Edison. But I mustn't dally over the headlines. With no time for a streetcar and definitely no time for walking, I hail the first hack that comes by.

"Where to, miss?"

"East gate of the coal yards. There are an extra two bits in it for you if you get me there before the first of the eight bells."

The jerk of the cab throws me backward into my seat. In my hurry, I'd left my *peinetas* on the table beside the bed. Ignoring the wild driving of the cabbie to get his bonus, I dig into my purse for my spare. Using the teeth, I comb out the worst of the tangles from my long hair. I give it a quick braid, rolling it up into a bun. Pushing in the *peineta* holds it in place. "Whew," I say, as I achieve a minimum of respectability.

I often wonder about my friendship with Karie. The Blue Room has been, since the purchase of her home, Karie's carrot to get me to move in. She isn't kidding when she offers to make me her mistress. It is an offer that is regularly renewed.

Since my Aaron was killed in Ireland, the last thing I want is to be chattel of another man or, for that matter, woman. I loved and still love my brawny Moor. I don't even dislike men, as a general whole, but I crave my freedom more. With the losses in the Irish War of Independence, there seems to be two women for every able-bodied man. The strutting cocks get their pick. Besides, with the marks left on me by Gazzunreep, the very first demon I summoned, I don't have all the attributes a man desires.

The thought causes me to absently pull a few strands of my hair out of the bun to cover the scars over my left ear and neck.

The cab lurches to a halt. "Here you go, Miss. Fare is forty cents." I smile. I wouldn't be late, after all. I hand the hack driver, a man missing his right arm to the elbow, a *duro*.

"Keep the change."

"Miss, this is too much. Even with a tip and the bonus, it's only six bits."

"Where did you lose your arm?"

"The siege of Strokestown fighting for king and country."

"I lost my husband at Termonbarry. So if you won't take it all, give me a quarter and drop the other two bits into the veteran's box the next time your regiment has a reunion."

"That I can do, miss."

The first of the eight bells are ringing. "Goodbye, and God bless," I say, racing in through the gate. I manage to punch my timecard just before it clicks to eight-oh-one.

"Jesus, Mary, and Joseph!" screams the foreman, Mark Carlton. "God certainly didn't give you promptness as a virtue, did he, Mrs. Ochoa."

I just smile and retort with "Ecclesiastes 7:9—'Do not be quickly provoked in your spirit, for anger resides in the lap of fools.'"

Mark is one of those rubes who gets to where he is on nothing more than the merit of being born to the right family. Oh, don't get me wrong. The Crown and royal family of our monarchy belong in their place. They protect us and deserve every bit of loyalty we can muster, but then there are those other malfeasants.

As the second cousin to Bruce Jasperson, leader of the Coal Syndicate, this job gives Mr. Carlton a comfortable income and the ability to be a tin-pot dictator. And like many who achieve rank without merit, he can't do, so he feels he can teach. He wouldn't know *aether* from ale even if poured all over him.

My superior biblical knowledge stings the fool, and he seethes, waiting for a time when he can take it out on me. Fortunately, his dignity is protected by the fact that none of the other witches is present.

My station, if it could be called that, is a large open area with the remnants of soot and cinders lying about. It links with similar other areas where my coworkers already coaxed the air around them. I walk out onto the grimy surface, stopping just long enough to run my finger over the filth. Sticking it in my mouth, I taste the gritty, bitterness that is what remains of the burned coal.

To the north, the great bins of black fuel, ready to be loaded onto barges, sob as the earth no longer cradles it. Fortunately, the mines themselves are too far away for me to feel the anguish as men rip the coal seams from the earth itself. The smaller depots of coal for local deliveries shriek as great steam-powered shovels scoop it up and into waiting wagons. The remnants of the black stone float above us as apparitions to their once rich lives.

"You belong not among the clouds," I call to them. "You harm others there. Come and rejoin your earthly family. Return to the earth where you belong."

Out of the gray sky, a dark fog coalesces. Soot, ash, and cold cinders all drift down like a steady winter snow, if black. Piles of it form around me like the ring of a doughnut or the caldera walls of a volcano. This is my job. Ten hours a day, I mentally sing a song of longing to the ghosts of the earth that, through man's greed, live in the sky.

By the time I have a hollow cone, my height on all sides, the lunch whistle sounds. The others together, air witches all, haven't forced a total among them to match mine. And that is the difference between us. Air witches must force the air to give up the earth, I coax the earth back to where it belongs. My mother always says you get more with honey than with vinegar. At least in magic, it is true. I can manipulate water and air, but only by getting the earth to force it—very difficult.

My stomach grumbles just as I realize I have brought no lunch.

"Twenty minutes, girls," Mark says, looking into my eyes. "Don't be late."

I hustle off to the food carts. I prefer the Spanish foods over the Irish. I get in line where they are selling piping hot *tortilla de papas* or Spanish omelets. I pass over a nickel and two pennies to a Spanish girl no more than nine years old and get a quarter wedge of steaming egg and potato over corn tortillas. I splash some salsa over the top as I leave. Most of the women want to talk during lunch, but I prefer to eat. I find a nice quiet place just outside the gates and bite into the delicious fare.

"Ping. Ping. Ping." Go the high-pitched bells of Mission Hill. "Oh, for mercy sake," I mumble around my food. "Again?" I can't remember ever having two demons loose in two days, nor the last time one happened in the daylight hours. I cram the food into my mouth as fast as I can while spelling out the Morse message from the bells: "Comey's Wharf."

It is only a few blocks east. I look over but don't see any flames or smoke.

I walk over and pull my timecard from the rack, stuffing the last crumbs into my mouth. Mark Carlton interposes himself between me and the timeclock.

"Don't you dare, missy."

"Excuse me, sir?"

"I know you are one of those hellfighters. I also know that bell was calling you. Well, we don't support that kind of social effort. You stay here and do your work."

"Sir, if I don't go, not only will people die, but likely the entire Boston docks will go up in flames, especially this place with all of the flammable coal dust about."

"There are other hellfighters. Let someone else do it. You have a job."

"Yes, sir. And if it came down to a choice, even as intermittent work as being a demon hunter is, it still pays much better than you do. Now please step aside."

His eyebrows furrow. "You punch out, and you are fired."

"OK," I say, moving around him and put my card into the clock.

He grabs me by the arm. "I am not done with you yet."

Very quietly, I think about the ash in the pits beyond him. I wonder what he would look like at the bottom of it all, something well within my power. Softly, I hiss, "Sir, you will release me immediately and never touch my person again."

He matches my eyes with his. Some semblance of intelligence flares in his pea-sized brain. His hand unclenches. "Thank you," I say with the barest civility I can muster. With not a little sadism, I add, "Good luck meeting the royal soot removal quotas without me."

As I walk out of the Coal Syndicate gates, I hear the voice of bluster behind me. "You'll never work here again, bitch!" It might have been "witch," so I decide to give him the benefit of the doubt.

With no obvious signs of destruction, I decide to walk the eight blocks. I will still arrive before the rest of my team. It gives me time to think of my indecorous exit and probable state of unemployment. I may have been hasty. Every day ships dump more Irish and German immigrants on the Boston docks. That is why the companies get labor so cheap, even us witches.

I hadn't been bragging in that hellfighting pays better than the Coal Syndicate—significantly better. If I even get one call every six months, it would be more than what my job pays, or should I say, had paid. I exercise draconian control over that money every time we get our rewards. It goes, in its entirety, directly into one of several bank accounts to save for my dotage. I will not be beholden to anyone nor will I accept the charity of the kingdom's poorhouse.

That leaves me back to figuring out how to eat and how to keep my room. If I swallow my pride, and anything resembling morality, I could take the path my mother and most earth witches take. I could reclaim land. Whenever a noble, or anyone else, appropriates (let's not mince words—steals) property, that earth still feels it belongs to the previous owner. If nothing is done, the earth can, and often does, rebel against the new owner. Both of the first two European settlements in America were swallowed by the land they stole, with no trace of them ever found.

Earth witches can "convince" the land to accept the new tenants.

It is rarely easy and involves the equivalent of a donnybrook, witch vs. earthen spirits. The work is hard, but with substantial pay. Similarly, earth witches are used to soothe the ground from which minerals have been removed. This is even more difficult and usually ends with severe injuries to the witch or warlock as the land always takes its pound of flesh. In either case, the work takes the morals of an English dragoon or maybe even a pirate. I've dodged the reclaimant career for most of my adult life.

Another option for an earth witch is one I shun—summoning demons. Any witch can put up protective wards and summon a demon, but only an earth witch can bind it permanently to the earth to be a heat engine. Just thinking about it makes my scars ache. Once burned, twice shy.

I've done some construction where I'm convincing dirt and rock to reshape. That level of work is only needed by large companies and even then rarely. Because it is easy work, most witches who favor the earth use jobs like that to fill in the gap between slugfests or summoning. Competition is fierce for rare opportunities. Pay is, therefore, rather dismal.

I can always go back and beg for my old job back. Goodness knows that Carlton would love to have something over me. Not to mention the fact that his air witch coven isn't going to come close to the tonnage of soot removal required by the Crown. Maybe the best choice would be to wait and see. Patience is a virtue. *Psalm 37:7 Be still before the Lord and wait patiently for him; do not fret when people succeed in their ways, when they carry out their wicked schemes.* But contravening this is the ever-popular *Proverbs 16:27 Idle hands are the devil's workshop; idle lips are his mouthpiece.*

Being a good woman of the church isn't easy. I guess that is why they have priests. My confessor, Father Juan Dubois y Cantonio, explains well and helps me with moral quandaries. *I don't always listen*, I think, with a mental chuckle.

My thoughts come to the immediate. People are running toward me now, a sure sign of something ahead. Still, I don't see any devastation. I see no smoke or fire. "Damnest demon hunt I've ever heard of."

A ring of spectators, with the combined intelligence of a clam, surround the street end of Comey's Fishmongers Dock. Double- and triple-wide, the wharf serves not only for the fishing boats to unload and dock but also as the local seafood market. I would often come down for cheap fish to make into lunches.

"Excuse me," I ask as I reach the back of the lookie-loos. At sixty-eight American inches, I am not short, but the big fishermen and marketers have me at a disadvantage. "Excuse me, sir, but I need to get through."

"Shove off, battle-ax."

I let him live, although I sometimes think that some rude behavior should be an automatic death sentence. Instead, I move over three people and ask again. "Sir, I need to get through."

"Sorry, ma'am, but it ain't safe up there. They've evacuated the wharf."

"Yes, I know. I'm a hellfighter."

"Go peddle your soap elsewhere, ma'am."

I count to *veinte chimpancés*. I take one step backward and reach down to find a bit of grit on the ground. Lifting it to my mouth, I lick it. This rough sand spoke of the years of solidity in the bedrock as water crashes against it. I feel the compressed layers of stone demanding everyone else pull down against it in what we call gravity. Working in cooperation with the earth below, I push up a wall of rock right through the middle of the crowd. Several bystanders squawk as they get bustled aside. One has to jump, for he found himself on the upward growing apex. I stop the wall's growth at a bit over six feet high. Splitting the wall down the narrow edge right in front of me, like Moses parting the Red Sea, I form a corridor free of even a single idiot.

I hear a murmur in the crowd, "Hellfighter." The words had equal parts fear, reverence, and vileness.

"Thank you," I say with as much sarcasm as I can muster.

Moving down my stone walkway, I tune out the crowd to focus on what faces me. Out toward the end of the pier, a horned figure, no bigger than a year-old babe, stands bathed in an unearthly blue glow. It hovers at the center of an eight-foot, blacken-edged hole in the boardwalk. The intense heat of the figure ripples away in a corona of turbulent air. To somewhat insulate his destructive power, which I can feel from a soccer field distance away, he perches on the stone pillar that at one time supported the wooden wharf. The stone itself glows as if it might run like lava. Likewise, all signs of winter and snow are gone from well outside the radius of the gawkers.

"Oh, shit," I mutter to myself. What idiot would summon a ranking lord from hell? This bastard must have powered most of the waterfront.

"I AM LORD SALMARISH. COME MORTAL MINIONS OF AN UNCARING GOD. WHICH AMONG YOU HAVE THE STRENGTH TO TREAT WITH ME?" They aren't words, but rather concepts shoved into our heads. They aren't shouted but rather carry the power of the most enormous horn ever built times infinity.

If this bastard goes berserk, all of Boston might go up in flames, just like what happened in Chicago nine years ago. I can't stop him alone, but maybe, just maybe, I can keep him talking long enough for my team to show up.

"I am Stella, a witch of the good earth. I would negotiate with you."

"GIVE ME YOUR TRUE NAME, WORM."

"Stella Romero, widow of Aaron Ochoa."

"AHHH, STELLA. I SUSPECTED YOU WOULD APPEAR IF I HAD BEEN GIVEN THE RIGHT LOCATION ON THIS MISERABLY FROZEN GLOBE."

"And why would you expect me?"

"LORD GAZZUNREEP WANTED ME TO DELIVER A MESSAGE."

I involuntarily put my hand to the scars across the left side of my face. I can feel them ache as if they still are burning my flesh all the way down to my left foot. "And what could that formless chaos possibly have to say to me?"

"HE WILL RETURN FOR ANOTHER TASTE OF YOUR FLESH AND THIS TIME MAYBE YOUR SOUL."

"Bloody unlikely. I'm not that naïve little girl of years ago. I'm not likely to be stupid enough to summon a ranking overlord nor give him the opportunity to burn me."

"NO MATTER. HE WILL COME FOR YOU."

"So what about you, Salmarish. Why do you treat? Why not destroy before you have done with this world like all your kind before you have done?" I feel the soft touch of Carlos at my back and the reassuring presence of Maxwell.

"I AM BUT A MESSENGER, BUT NOW I TIRE OF THIS FREEZING PLACE. I WANT NOTHING MORE THAN TO RETURN TO MY FIERY HOME."

"Not going to happen, Your Lordship. We are going to harness you back to power the machines of this world."

The child-sized demon laughs. "I SHALL NOT MOVE ONTO

EARTH WHERE YOU CAN ENTRAP ME AGAIN."

I can hear my fellow four partners whispering behind me and making plans on how to skin this cat. Carlos taps my shoulder to start us off. The others fan out like gunfighters at the OK Corral.

I coax the seabed behind Salmarish to rise up and form a wall blocking his retreat to the ocean. Raquel gets to work by having the boardwalk sprout a wall of briars to form a dense thicket to the creature's right. Carlos forms a water spout within a vortex of wind opposite the verdant hedge. Donny fires a spout of water that hits the boxed demon right in its wrinkled face.

The demon pushes his hands into the flow. The blue heat from his hands flares up, turning the water to steam. "YOUR SIMPLE TECHNIQUES OF ANGER AND FURY WILL NOT WORK ON ONE SUCH AS MYSELF. YOU WILL BE FORCED TO DESTROY ME OR RETURN ME TO MY PLANE."

"Max, smack him and see if we can change his tune."

I feel the love of God increasing in Maxwell's person. Witches and warlocks are only sensitive to those magicks we can manipulate, which is why I can feel the power of heaven in his conjuration. Max glows with divine energy. He focuses it forward in a single brilliant bolt, striking the creature in the shoulder.

"OW. THAT STUNG," the demon says, brushing at the wrinkled hole in his upper arm as if clearing dirt from his lapel. "UNLESS YOU HAVE SOMEONE MORE POWERFUL THAN YOU PATHETIC FIVE, YOU DON'T HAVE THE STRENGTH TO DESTROY ME.

"LET ME FORCE YOUR HAND, WORMS."

His head pulls back like he is planning a humongous spittle. Then he throws his head forward, vomiting a mass of flame. Donny reacts in time to bring the seawater up in a shielding wave. The fire turns the water to superheated spray that is reflected over our heads.

"That's all I had, folks," Maxwell says in his squeaky voice, like a teen boy going through puberty.

"Anyone have any suggestions?" Carlos offers.

"Send him back," I say, knowing our fee will be reduced. "We can't hold him here if he wants to move. We don't want this to turn into another Chicago!"

Donny shakes his head negative, his cropped red hair shaking back and forth. Raquel just raises her eyebrows.

"Do it," Carlos says to Maxwell. "Everyone else plays defense. Be on the lookout for surprises."

As Maxwell chants, I become dizzy. He literally rotates the planes of physical existence and those of the supernatural. I can feel them move inside of me and stagger half a step. Carlos looks at me. I shake my head to indicate that I can continue.

I feel matching holes in the planes lining up, right underneath the demon. The red hot stones there cry out to me as they fall to be interned forever into the abyss.

"AH! THE FEELING OF HOME. CONGRATULATIONS, MORTALS. YOU *CAN* ACCOMPLISH SOMETHING," the demon says. "REMEMBER WHAT I TOLD YOU, STELLA-CREATURE. GAZZUNREEP WILL COME FOR YOU."

The tiny creature falls into a black, wavering pit hanging within the hole in the boardwalk. As far as I can tell, the blue-hued demon falls directly away from me, shrinking until I cannot even determine him as a dot.

I become dizzy again as the dark gateway wavers like the mirage of water on a great desert. It fades and disappears without a sound. The crowd behind us makes up for the sudden silence as they erupt into cheers.

I mop my sweaty brow. Oh, that's right. My mother taught me that ladies don't sweat. We perspire. Either way, I wipe away the wetness. It is a lost cause as my dress is soaked through. I shiver as the demon's heat dissipates, and the cold of Boston winter closes in.

A coat covers my shoulders. I thank him for his gallantry. "Thank you, Carlos."

"You're welcome, *señorita*, but I am not Carlos."

The fatigue of two demons in less than twenty-four hours has left me wrung out. I suck up every bit of energy I have left to find out who offered me such kindness. I turn to be greeted by the charismatic smile of Franklin Cardiff. Technically, Cardiff is the Baron of Snowdonia, although his umpteenth grandfather had been exiled by Martin Luther during the Reformation. He also happens to be one of our competition. Baron Cardiff runs another team of hellfighters known as the Cannons. They use an obsolete ship's artillery piece to route members of their team.

"*Buenas tardes, Señorita* Ochoa," he says, his eyes glittering and his smile bright between his salt-and-pepper beard and mustache.

"Good afternoon to you, Baron. What brings you here today?"

"I was in the neighborhood when the alarm went out. I decided to drop by and offer my assistance. I heard you were down a man, again. I could have told you that Alberto-fop was a coward."

Franklin is a powerful ice witch who runs his team with military precision. He also is one of the most eligible bachelors in all of Boston. I can't turn around at work, or at least what had been my work, or even my boardinghouse without one of those bimbos twittering about what a well-turned-out catch the baron is.

With a strong forehead, shoulder-length silvering hair, and clothes that had to cost more than my entire keep for a month, I can see the surface attraction. But his arrogance shuts down any feelings I might have developed for the man.

"Well, thank you for your chivalry, Baron. The air is bitter cold after that blast of hell itself."

"Yes, I'm sure. Since things are under control, I'll be back about my business."

"Then you better have your coat back," I say, not wanting to leave its warmth.

"Nonsense, *señorita*. Return it to me as you get the opportunity. As our bishop might say, 'Thy necessity is yet greater than mine.'"

"Martin Luther?" I ask about the quote.

"Philip Sidney."

"I thank you again, Baron. I will return it at my first opportunity."

"Just leave it at McGreevy's 3rd Base Saloon."

"I know the watering hole you and your Cannons frequent. I'll get it back to you promptly."

"Have a good evening." The baron bows deeply before turning away.

The crowd is finally dispersing as the show is over. Carlos is in conference with the rest of our team. I edge over to listen in.

"Well, our reward for shipping that bastard back to his home isn't going to be as much as last night," Carlos says.

"Even for a ranking lord of hell?" Menagerie asks.

"Raquel, you know how it is. First of all, the only reward we will get other than from the Crown is from the locals. In this case, the locals will primarily be comprised of the company that lost the beast. Demon lord or not, businessmen are notoriously stingy."

"Very true."

I offer up a question. "Folks, to change the topic, I have a question. Do any of you remember another month where we had three callouts? Much less two in one day?"

"Well, we had two last month."

"And two the month before," Maxwell agrees, his voice breaking.

"But I don't remember even three. Nor do I remember anything during the daylight hours. 'Course, I've only been doing this for two years. What about you, Carlos?" Raquel asks, riffling a leaf across the back of her hand like a professional gambler would with a poker chip.

"I've seen three in a month before, once five years ago, but since then, never more than two, but I've had my ear to the ground. The Cannons took down two this month and four last month, and Los Lobos took down six over the last three months."

"Carlos, remember when you recruited me? You said maybe once a month, more like once every six weeks," I point out.

"True. I remember saying that."

"So, what's going on?" I demand.

"What do we care? It's money in the bank," offers Donny.

I scoff. "You ain't put your money in the bank since you started. More like drink and those floozies you run around with."

"If that ain't the pot calling the kettle black," he fires back in jest.

"Olé, Donny," I rally. "But, at least I don't buy my playmates."

"Ouch," Maxwell whispers *en sotto voce*. "Donny, you want a cloth to staunch the blood, or you want to give up now?"

"I think I will call it a draw," the redhead says, thrusting his skinny chest out like some bull stud. Everyone laughs.

"But seriously, if demon escapes keep going up, will the three hellfighter groups in the area be enough?" I ask. Several shrug. "Anyone care if I look into it?" Four shaking heads give me their approval.

"Well, I don't know about you all, but I'm freezing," Raquel says, breaking any continuing discussion. "I want a warm pub, one of Miss Marion's piping hot meat pies, and a pint of heated mead."

"Damn, but that sounds good," Donny agrees. "What about you, Stella?"

"I have an engagement this evening."

"What's her name? Or did you fancy that Cardiff clown?"

"Shut up, you," I say, playfully swatting him with my purse while I feel the heat in my cheeks that had to bring their color up at least three shades of pink. "Besides, that oaf is...well, an oaf, no matter how much he spends on clothes."

"Folks, can we get serious for just a moment," Carlos interrupts. "I'll be late tonight. I need to see what the good corporate gentlemen will be willing to cough up as a reward."

# # #

My boardinghouse is conveniently located eleven blocks from the docks and my former place of employment. The walk rewarms me beneath the baron's coat. The foot traffic thins as the Mission Church bell sounds off one o'clock. As the peel of the bell dies, I feel a tug at my arm. I look down to see a cut cord as the only thing left from my handmade purse. In front of me is a young man with a sandy mop of hair running for all he is worth, clutching the flowery handbag in his fist. I sigh. The trials of living in a city filled with poverty. He whips around a corner into an alley.

Stepping into the intersection, I bend over and press my hand firmly on the cobblestones. The soft earth under the manmade surface seems eager to comply. I mentally shove, compressing the ground like one might a giant marshmallow. The cutpurse finds his next running step over a fifteen-foot deep hole in the shape of my hand but twelve feet across. He tumbles forward and lets out a squawk as he lands.

"Troubles, Widow Ochoa?" asks the cobbler whose shop is on the corner.

"Not at all, Mr. Kraus," I say as I walk forward. The cutpurse writhes at the bottom of my hole, clutching a leg which is bent in a place no joint occurs naturally. I squat down and touch the earth again to release the compression I'd placed there. The hole rises up to disappear.

I pick up my purse. The boy, not man, has tears streaming down his face. He grimaces in order not to cry out in pain. His clothes don't look like they've been washed in a pair of *meses*. His sunken face didn't look like he'd eaten in longer than that. I'm no healer, but I know what must be done, or he would walk with a cane for the rest of his life.

"Hold still," I admonish. "This will hurt. If you faint you need to know that the cast I'm going to put on you will fall away after your leg is healed, probably in six weeks." I kneel to touch the earth with both hands. I feel the strength of the stone bits and the sandy grit between. I reach through the compression of the soil just beneath and bring forth two tendrils of rock and clay. They wrap around his leg above and below the break. Like a circus strongman straightening a horseshoe, I force the stone tentacles to pull.

There is a yelp. The boy's head lolls over, but his leg is once again in its natural shape. Letting the straightening coils go back to their natural form within the ground, I replace them by summoning up gypsum, water, and sand from the earth below. I mix them like dough without quite touching them. I mentally coat the leg forming a plaster cast. Just before leaving, I tuck a *peseta* into the boy's closed fist for when he wakes.

Standing, I brush off my skirt. I continue heading home, where I find my landlady sweeping blown snow off the stoop.

"Look at what the cat dragged in," Alice Chapman says, wrinkling her nose at my disreputable state.

"Yes, Widow Chapman," I say, pulling on her tail just as much. Despite her proper English upbringing, the turkey-necked cow had never managed to turn the eye of any prospective suitor after her husband passed at the age of twenty-two. Only her family's wealth bought her a living with the boardinghouse.

She blocks my way with her broom, looking me up and down. "Isn't that a gentleman's coat over your own?"

"Yes, ma'am," I say, giving her the minimum for her rumor mill. The English battle-ax lives to spread gossip.

"Are you dating? It would be about time."

"No, ma'am," I deny, pushing her broom gently out of my path.

"Say, what are you doing home in the middle of the day? Shouldn't you be at work?"

"I got fired, Mrs. Chapman." I chortle as I walk by her.

"Fired?" She turns three shades of umber. "Fired? How do you expect to pay the rent?"

"Worry not, Mrs. Chapman. You will get your rent on Monday, the same as any other week."

Ignoring me, she goes on, "I won't give you any leniency, Widow Ochoa." I ignore her ranting as I go up the stairs toward my room. She delivers as a parting shot, "Maybe you will have to find a husband now!"

I close the door to my eight-by-ten luxury digs. I need peace to map out my future. My door and the deadbolt I throw ensures at least a modicum of that. Mrs. Chapman saves a few coppers in coal by not feeding the furnace as diligently as she might. I usually don't mind, but as I strip off my soiled clothing, right down to my stockings and boots, the chilly air raises goosebumps on my flesh the size of bunions on a farmer's foot. I am not going to make them any happier.

I pour a splash of water in the basin and wet a washcloth. With the sliver of soap I keep in my room, I give myself a sponge bath. One thing I really regret with my occasional bouts with hellspawn is not having my own bath. The stench of ash and brimstone tends to put some people off.

My mind does come to the conclusion that this isn't the time to worry about how to make a living. I will collect my fee at the Bell in Hand and have a drink with my team before I take off to an evening that is sure to be full of drunken debauchery with Karie. "Enjoy yourself," I whisper to myself as I wipe down my thick thighs from my hips down as far as my stockings will roll. While I don't have to wear a corset with my figure, I still think Karie got nature's best with her svelte form. I'll bet she never needs to lift her boobs to wipe away the sweat that gets sticky underneath.

I take the time to examine the scars that cover the left quarter of my body as I wash them. With a housepainter's brush, draw a broad, single stroke of ripples and creases of caramel-colored skin from my left ear, down to my foot. It creeps up under my armpit and spreads across my *gluteus sinister*. Demonfire burns and no two ways about it. The reminder mars my otherwise unblemished skin—never had the pox.

The memory of Gazunreep's summoning brings the heat of shame to my face. I remember each and every mistake I'd made as if they are the scars etched into my body. My embarrassment slowly turns to anger. I hadn't been prepared. I hadn't been ready. My proctor, my own mother, let me follow through in not only summoning a ranked demon but also in allowing it to escape my poorly prepared pentagram. I'd spent three months healing from that episode. She could have stopped it at any time but felt I needed a lesson. I look down at the results of my lesson and seethe.

I loosen my hair out of its bun and unroll it. With a double handful, I bring it up to my nose. I catch only the vague hint of brimstone. I'll worry about washing my hair later. I slip into some underthings, intentionally pulling my petticoats on without any bloomers underneath. I slip on a naughty garter of green lace as well, which proclaims, "Open at all hours." Might as well give my gal pal a treat.

It reminds me of the night I treated myself to *Carmen*. I look at the playbill I still have attached to my wall. During the play, Karie didn't give me a moment's rest. Her fingers, hidden beneath my gown, assaulted me all evening. I almost bit my lip through trying to keep myself quiet. *Am I going too far?* I ask myself. I know some call my relationship with Karie sick or unnatural. I don't see it that way. I have only four ways to curb my natural...urges. The church will have you believe that abstinence is the way of things. From experience that just makes me crave loving that much more. Self-pleasure is cold and lonely. That doesn't keep me from doing it, but I need the closeness of human contact.

Men. Well, that about sums it up. I can lust after a man, but if I want to keep my independence, that is completely out. And let's be honest, most of them lack even the basic social skills of an adolescent dog... humping anything they can wrap their paws around. The men that could come close to the qualities of my dearly departed Aaron numbered close to a big...fat...zilch.

That leaves women. Unlike many other of my sex, I find the feminine form exotic and attractive. I can get just as excited, and often more so, by catching a glimpse of a woman's ankle than the entirety of a nude man.

So do I love Karie? Yes and no. I love her as one would a close sister or a dearest friend. I wouldn't want to be her partner. She's too flighty for my tastes. She takes things as they come. I want to plan. She wants sex all the time. I just need it two or three times a month to keep me happy and functioning at peak efficiency.

I pull my church dress over my underthings. While far from provocative with my hem dragging the ground a good half-inch, the breeze over my nether region certainly has my motor running. I hope I don't make too much of a smell before...well, this evening. Maybe I'll attack Karie tonight instead of the other way 'round.

I check my rear in the mirror. My dirigible-sized derriere will be fine without a bustle. I stuff some fresh underthings, a toothbrush, another hair-comb, and a working dress into my carpetbag. As an afterthought, I reach into my stocking drawer. I rummage through six bankbooks. The one with the lowest balance, I drop into my carpetbag and return the others.

I take the time to brush some paint on my lips, in moderation. Not only is the stuff expensive, but I don't want to look like a *puta*. As my olive complexion doesn't take to cake powder without looking like a frowzy actor, I dab just a tiny bit of crimson on each cheek and rub it in.

I put on some enamel, oversized flower earrings, and added my best neck chain of gold plate with a matching floral pendant.

Looking in the mirror, I admit, "*Coqueto,* but not *puta.*" Just for good measures, I squirt some rosewater on my hair and dab a bit under each ear. I am going to enjoy the evening.

Picking up my purse and bag, I unbar the door. *Señora* Chapman waits for me at the base of the stairs like a guard dog waiting for its prey to come in range. Slipping on my coat, I advise, "Mrs. Chapman, I won't be with you for dinner and won't be home tonight. I'll return sometime after church tomorrow night."

"Don't be late. You know when supper is. I don't hold it for anyone who can't get her lazy tail home in time."

"Yes, Mrs. Chapman. Seven PM, Mrs. Chapman," I temporize as I scoot out the front door to avoid any additional lectures.

Having rarely been home from work before six in the evening, I never realized just how busy the streets are during the day. A fishmonger guides his horse past me, pulling a steam-powered refrigeration cart. Based on the size of his coal cart, he is probably on his way west to service Worcester—I mean New Seville, it having been renamed just last year. Kids, fresh out of school, run about playing those loud and noisy games that only children know the rules to. Two men in suit-coats ride bicycles past. The dry goods merchant across the road pulls in products off the boardwalk in anticipation of the early winter dark. A trolley dings its stop at the nearby corner. The billiard parlor lights the gas lamps inside, shining the brilliant colors of the stained glass out onto the denizens of the street.

A *Boston Herald* wagon kicks newspapers off its tailgate. The newsmonger scurries out to pick up the late edition. Before the twine is even cut, he yells out, "'Killer Blizzard Strikes Iowa!'"

"Why'd ya do it, mum?" I hear behind me. I turn to see the little cutpurse standing there with my cast on his leg.

"Why did I do what?"

"Why'd ya fix me up? Why'd ya leave me this?" he says, lifting up the coin I'd put in his palm. "You ain't no charity sister."

"No, I'm not. But I'm not cruel, either. What's your name?"

"Tommy."

"Just Tommy?"

"Ain't got no other."

"Well, Tommy, do you have a home?"

"I sleep down under the storage at the steel plant."

I think twice. I'm not a nun or one of those Salvation Army ladies, but I may be able to help, some. "How would you like a job, Tommy?"

"You'd give me a job? After'n I tried to steal from ya?"

"Yes. Since you know where I live, I want you to come round here every morning at seven AM. Wait fifteen minutes. If I haven't shown up, you can go. Either way, I'll pay you a dollar a week."

I can see the greed in his eyes. "Yes, ma'am!"

"Oh, and you can knock off the ma'am stuff. I'm just Stella—Stella Ochoa."

"Yes, Stella."

"I have your first task. I want you to take this coat to Baron Cardiff at McGreevy's 3rd Base Saloon. You know where that is?"

Tommy nods vehemently.

"Good. Don't leave until you put it in his hands personally."

"I won't, Stella," he says, limping away faster than I would have thought possible. I shake my head.

You're too soft, Stella, I say mentally. Time to move on with my afternoon.

I nod to the greengrocer as I walk past. I look longingly at the pickle barrels in front of the deli but decide that I'll be having more than my figure really should warrant tonight. Karie always sets an incredible table. Besides, I can always get a pickle at the public house. I stop, however, when I see some bright-yellow fruit with the fine fuzz of a peach but only a quarter the size.

"Mr. Bascom, what are these?"

"Fresh shipment of apricots from Damascus, Widow Ochoa." He takes one and rings it with a sharp knife. He cuts off a sliver and hands it to me. "Try it."

The mellow sweetness spreads throughout my mouth halfway between a peach and a melon. "How much?"

"Thirty-six cents a pound."

I whistle at the high price. Then I think of how nicely Alejandro and the rest of Karie's staff have treated me. "Three pounds for a dollar?"

Mr. Bascom piles up the fruit on his scale until it registers just over three pounds. He wraps it carefully in a brown paper bag. As he takes my dollar, he says, "Please be careful. They bruise easily."

"Thank you, sir. Have a great day."

While they are quite distant, I can hear cannons sound. The regular beat tells me that they call out Baron Cardiff's team of hellfighters. Another demon has found its freedom.

Oddly, I remember when demons were first used as power sources. They were touted as being more powerful, much cheaper, and infinitely safer. Advertisements for demon installations scream how safe they are in contravention to the evidence to the contrary over the last months. I know how these beasts are bound. I know it's safe. But why are these chaos machines getting lose?

I wave at Guardsman Paterna, the Royal Constabulary for this beat. In his blue and white overcoat, he gives a stern nod in return. He stops at one of the bright red police boxes to call in his location. I hear that Bell Telegraph now installs those phones in houses. What a swank. Maybe one day, our *Dos Campanas* would have a completely different meaning.

The Bell in Hand Tavern is no different than any other local pub near the waterfront—a bit rough and more friendly than any highbrow establishment. Really our patronage started as nothing more than because of the word "Bell" in the title—*Dos Campanas*—two bells. It seems obvious. After four years, we are regulars. In fact, the proprietor, one Michaeleen O'Flynn, painted a placard with two bells that hangs over our table. Anyone sitting there when we arrive must vacate.

To my surprise, I'm not the first arrival. Maxwell, Raquel, and Donny are playing cards while Donny's girlfriend, a redheaded tart who works in Mrs. Swanson's Meat and Fruit Pies shop, tries to keep her boyfriend's attentions on her. From the sad stack of his chips, she seems to be succeeding.

"Stella," bellows Bill Mattingsly, a regular and a fisherman from the whaler *Jumping Nelly*, "You all dressed up and purdy. Didn't know we had a date tonight."

"We don't, salty. I'm way beyond your price, chum."

Several of his *amigos* laugh. "I'll bid, *senorita*. I got two-bits says you are all mine," another one jibes back. The group laughs again. Michaeleen joins in on the joke with a chortle of his own while he draws a pint for one of the patrons.

Ordinarily, I'd scorch anyone so vulgar, but these are friends, and we often play fast and loose with our teasing. "Oh, that will get you my left stocking," I say, wiggling my boot his way.

"Oh, there is a price!" another one adds. "I bid two *pesetas*."

"Un *duro*," another chimes in.

"Enough, you seadogs. You want to pay, talk to the adventuresses over at Madam Connie's establishment."

"You're no fun."

"To the right person, I am quite fun," I say, rubbing up against Bill like the worst cockchafer I'd ever want to even try to be. In play, he reaches for me. I duck and move back to my table but lift my skirts to give all of them a flash of my ankles. It is all in fun. They are good men, one and all. They also know I have no interest in any of them.

Donny's girl, Anna I think, looks me up and down and sniffs. She has nothing to worry about. I can't give two mackerels about Donny other than as a solid teammate.

"You sure are looking nice tonight, Stella. What's the occasion?" Raquel asks. "I'll take two," she says, discarding two cards and getting two in return.

Maxwell looks up from dealing the cards to give me a once-over. "Dealer takes one." His voice cracks in the middle of the first word.

"I'm celebrating being fired from the Coal Syndicate."

"Really?" Donny pipes in. "Didn't like you walking out in the middle of the day?"

At that moment, Carlos's rumbling voice behind me says, "Good. You shouldn't be working at that sweatshop anyway."

Carlos tosses four individual linen pouches on the table. They jingle quite happily as they hit. Unlike coal, precious metal is happy to be free of the earth. It is pleased to be pressed into service as some of the most valuable things in the world. It almost sings as people handle it and exchange it. Max grabs his up and starts counting the gold coins right on the table.

"You all know the score," our leader continues, "but I never want there to be any mistrust between us.

"We each get one share. I get an extra share for recruiting, collecting, and Royal Taxes. With that coward out of the way that makes six shares. For the one up in Tremont, I collected four hundred fourteen dollars for returning the demon to its steam plant. The locals gave up a citizen's reward totaling two hundred four dollars. The miser companies on the dock only coughed up a pathetic sixty-two *doubloons* for a ranking demon from hell. The dock crowd parted with another six hundred *pesetas*. Add to all of that the Crown's standard reward of three hundred dollars per demon totals up to eighteen hundred seventy-six dollars. Split six ways is a tidy three hundred eleven dollars and change. I rounded it up to three twelve, leaving me with six twenty."

Without bothering to count my take, I slip the pouch down between my cleavage. Carlos would never cheat us. I've heard that the baron sometimes forgets to add all the citizen awards to his totals. I don't have to worry about that with my brethren.

"Three jacks," says Raquel.

"Straight," Donny proclaims with a broad smile.

"Sorry, boy. All red, ten high," Maxwell offers, exposing his heart flush. Donny loses another stack of coins. His girl whispers something in his ear that makes him blush.

"Deal me in," Carlos says. "Hey, Michealeen. Wanna bring me over a pint of your bitter, please?"

"And red wine for me," I add, taking the last chair, unfortunately adjacent to Donny's flamboyant arm candy. "To bring up the subject again, any of you bothered by all of these demon calls? I heard the Cannons called out just a bit ago."

"Yup. Over on Eagle Hill," Carlos confirms.

"Never really thought of it," Raquel says. "I just put them away. It's a good living. With more demons going loose, it's an even better living. Might even buy me a buggy."

"But no matter how good we are, people are dying; homes and businesses are being destroyed," I add.

"We didn't do it," Max says. "We are just cleaning up the mess."

"Yeah, but what caused it? Why so many more?"

"More installations than ever before?" Donny offered.

"We've had three times the number of calls in the last three months. You think there are three times as many demons trapped in just the last three months?"

"I'll bet two bits," Carlos says, chipping in a pair of coins.

"I detect a distinct lack of caring from our team. Aren't we dedicated to protecting those around us just like the Royal Fire Brigade?"

"Yeah, but we get paid a damned sight better. Raise four bits," Raquel adds.

"Call. That demon lord this morning had only been summoned last week," Carlos says, laying a bombshell on the group.

"A week? Anyone powerful enough to summon one knows you have to double and triple up on the protections on a beast that powerful," Donny says, leaning forward out of the grasp of his girl.

I jump back in with, "As I see it, there are only really three reasons more demons are getting out. One—lack of education of those who might be tending the furnaces. Perhaps they scuffed a break in the pentagram by accident."

"No one is that stupid," Donny's girl says, in a rare display of intelligence. Everyone looks at her. "What?"

I muzzle my shock and continue, "I agree, Anna, but accidents do happen. In the past, that was most of our business. Some parents didn't keep the door locked, and a kid skipped through the holding spell. Resulting in one dead child and a huge damage bill.

"Two—shoddy installations with potentially substandard materials. With the bloody English's near-monopoly on some of the stuff, prices are through the roof, especially when they are boarding Italian chalk vessels and declaring them forfeit as war materials.

"And three—outright sabotage."

"Stella, lovely lady, as much as I hate to throw a monkey wrench into steam pipes, you missed one—coincidence."

"Yeah, we've been busy before, and we've had dead times before." Donny says before turning his attention back to the game. "Call."

"Remember Occam's Razor: one should not increase, beyond what is necessary, the number of entities required to explain anything," Maxwell says.

"Maybe so, but it doesn't feel right to me," I say, getting a shiver down my back at the same time. I sip on my wine, realizing I'm not going to get any help from my comrades on my theory without something more. With that realization, I settle back and enjoy the rapport of good friends. They even drag me into the game, where I manage to lose only a couple of *pesetas* over the afternoon.

As the lamplighters ply their trades to brighten the streets, it is time for me to go. I wish my compatriots good fortune until our next adventure and walk out. I drop a dollar on the bar for my wine and a big tip. Michaeleen breaks into a big smile.

With a bit of luck, there is a hack just sitting down the row. I flag him over. "Royal Bank of Boston, please." Three short blocks away, the hack delivers me to an imposing marble building. "Please wait."

"Mum."

I walk inside to the bank of tellers with one conveniently ready and waiting for me. "Yes, madam, how can I help you?"

"I'd like to make a deposit," I say, handing over my bankbook.

"Madam has a sizable account with us already. Have you considered an investment portfolio?"

He frowns as I dig around in my brassiere to pull out my bag of coins. I shake my head vehemently. "I've seen too many investments die. I'll take the slow and steady return in your savings plan, sir."

"As you will, madam. How much would you like to deposit?"

"Two hundred ninety dollars," I say. I mentally keep out twelve-fifty for my weekly rent and enough money for spending in case those cheats at the Coal Syndicate don't pay me my wages.

He scribbles in my passbook and a ledger with a quill pen. "Thank you, madam, that brings your account balance to two thousand, one hundred and thirty-three dollars and eighteen cents." I do the math in my head and come up with just over fourteen thousand dollars I've saved. I need another fifteen years of being a hellfighter before I can choose to no longer be dependent on work.

Back outside, I climb back into my cab. "Ferdinand Street and Cedar."

All afternoon the unaccustomed breeze on my damp nether regions proves that I am not a moral woman. It feels glorious, and each airy touch grows my need even further. Now, a school of sardines leaps and splashes about in my gut, pressing and kneading on the knot of my desire. A balloon of lust inflates in my belly. It feels good and is uncomfortable at the same time. "And hurry."

"Yes, mum."

The black Morgan takes me quickly through the cobblestone streets toward my assignation, and I can scarcely wait. The coach pulls up to Karie's red door about the same time as my slip feels just the teensiest bit wet beneath me. Alejandro must have been watching for me as he opens the door before I even knock.

"Welcome, Miss Ochoa."

"One of these days, I'm going to show you that I'm anything but a lady, Alejandro."

"As you say, miss. The mistress is waiting for you in the Blue Room."

"The Blue Room?"

"Yes, miss. She is expecting an early caller and thought that you might want to sleep in. May I take your things?"

"Absolutely. Oh, and I have a present for you and the staff." I hand over the bag of apricots I picked up at the greengrocers. "Thank you for all you have done for me."

Alejandro pulls out one of the fruits and eyes it as if he were a man in the last stages of scurvy. "Thank you, miss. I will share these. We very much appreciate it."

"You are welcome," I say, inching away without trying to look like I am escaping. Alejandro takes pity on me and lets me go without further discussion.

I barely manage to keep my ladylike composure as I climb the stairs. I enter the Blue Room to find Karie presiding over an intimate table set for dinner. A sheath dressing gown forms to her slender figure and delicate curves.

Without a word, I walk forward. Hiking my skirt, I straddle her leg. I take her hand in mine and press it up to cup the heat between my thighs. Her pretty brown eyes go wide. This evening there will be no slow seduction. No coy glances. No fingertip brushes over wine. My needs demand satisfaction by pouring out in a liquid fire. I lean over and press my lips to her neck, nibbling ever so gently.

"Alejandro, hold dinner," she calls out of the room.

"Yes, mistress," comes the distant and discrete reply from beyond the doorway.

"I'd rather you hold **me**," I whisper in her ear as I lick up the crescent. The last syllable catches in my throat as her stockinged knee presses against my dampness. Inflaming me even more, she starts bouncing her leg on the ball of her foot. I bite gently on her neck, panting harder with each rebound. "Oh, not with the door open, Karie. You know I'm not quiet." My voice breaks again.

"He has to be shown you aren't a lady," Karie mocks me as she unbuttons my bodice and places a kiss just above my brassiere line. "Wouldn't now be the perfect opportunity?"

# # #

I gently drag my fingertips over Karie's bare shoulder and delight at the shudders I produce. Her dreamy eyes can't possibly match my wellbeing. My friend elicited great volume in my cries of passion, many times over.

With no false modesty and something of a Cheshire cat grin, I wonder if her shouts had been louder than mine. And now she stuffs me with Spanish delicacies.

How Alejandro and his staff had kept the food piping hot but not dried out for two hours, I'll never know. Karie and I lounge in candlelight over the remnants of *arroz a la marinera*, and fried eggplant with molasses. The smell of spicy seafood doesn't quite cover the reek of our rut.

I breathe a deep, contented sigh. She runs her hand down my leg over that silk nightdress I'd pulled on just before Alejandro served. Somehow I feel better about wearing it than my slip or even trying to get fully dressed.

"Better, *niñita*?" Karie asks. I must outweigh her two to one, but she somehow gets away with calling me a little girl.

"*Si. Muy bien.* I haven't felt this *bien* since Aaron, God rest his soul, left for Ireland."

Karie's throaty chuckle sends shivers across my belly right down to—*Stop that.* I remonstrate myself. *I've been pleasured many times. I don't need more.*

"I'll say that you definitely even sated me," she says.

"Hooey. I don't think any one person can satiate you, *mi amiga*."

She reaches over to pick up another piece of eggplant, causing her dressing gown to fall open, exposing her modest breast and skin well down her belly. She bites the sweet treat in half—the food, not her gently curved flesh. "No, darling, that isn't soft soap. But you are one of very few that can. I'm beginning to wonder if I shouldn't call off my morning customer."

This new revelation of my prowess definitely brings to light her offer of the Blue Room to me permanently.

She wrinkles her eyebrow and frowns as she thinks. To hide it, she grabs my loose hair and tugs enough to make me moan. "I smell brimstone, *querida*. What have you been up to today?"

Arching my head toward her gentle pulls, "Another demon got loose today—a ranking demon. We had to send him away."

Brushing aside my dangling flower earring with her nose, she nibbles on my stretched neck. This is the way our nights usually start—with Karie slowly and gently pushing me into a corner of lust. "Speaking of working too hard."

"All work and no play makes Stella a very needy girl," I offer in a low voice with a whimper thrown in.

"Well, I can tell that," she says, letting go.

Curbing the reawakening cauldron in my belly, I go on. "Yes, this is the third or fourth escape this month that we've dealt with."

"That seems like quite a few."

"More than quite a few, *querida*, it is more than I've ever heard of in the lustrum that demons have been leashed to this work."

"What's causing it?" Karie asks.

"That is something I want to find out."

"I assume this is no accident?"

"I don't think so," I offer, shaking my head.

"*Cui bono?*" she asks in that famous Latin phrase we learned in school, "To whom is it a benefit?"

"I've thought about it some and the three obvious winners are hellfighters as we get more escapes to put down, the Coal Syndicate for making the demon installations look dangerous, and the demon installers themselves by using cheaper substandard materials."

"Did you know Count Helms is a regular of mine?"

Viscount Henry Helms runs Forever Power, a demon installation company that does ninety percent of the internments in the northeast. Forever Power has branches from Maryland all the way north to Newfoundland.

I perk up. "Really?"

"Yes. Poor bastard is in a marriage of power. His wife, the Viscountess Adrianna Helms, comes from the very wealthy Astor family. It let Henry set up his business to make them even more powerful. But for all of that, he tells me that his wife is a frigid cow. She might as well be neutered."

I smile and know exactly why Count Helms desires Karie's company. "Could I get a letter of introduction? I've got connections with all of the hellfighters and even can probably get to the Coal Syndicate leader, but didn't know how to start with the demon installers."

"Certainly, dearest, but there will be a price," she says, getting down on her knees in front of me. She runs her hands up my limbs.

I tuck my negligee between my thighs in mock defense. "Oh, no. Anything but that!"

Karie's eyes light up. "Anything?" With her repertoire of diversions, she is throwing down the gauntlet.

"Yes, anything...And that!"

3—Sunday, February 5, 1888

My smile makes me wonder if my face is going to crack. Last night Karie took my garter's motto literally. We woke each other up so often that I need to pinch myself from time to time to keep awake. My freshly laundered Sunday dress and slip feel like new, and the contentment underneath makes the long walk to mass seem trivial even in these damned store-bought shoes. I'll be sleepy in church, but what better place to just float in a blissful haze?

"'Death Toll Fifty-Seven in Midwest Blizzard,'" calls out the newsmonger, if a bit quieter because of the Sabbath. I've already read the paper over the morning feast Alejandro served us, including ham steak with heaping mounds of fluffy yellow eggs and an endless supply of almond croissants. I think I'll gain forty pounds. No one in the fourth estate seems to have twigged yet to the excessive demon escapes. Maybe I am making a mountain out of a molehill. By now, I expect they would be screaming their heads off.

I look around at all the families walking in their Sunday best. Immaculately currycombed horses pull shiny buggies filled with more well-dressed folk. If I am paranoid, then let it be on the side of protecting all of these good people. I owe it to them, paid or not, to make sure they aren't in any unnecessary danger.

St. Leonard's Church is definitely a work in progress. On the order of Pope Leo XIII, construction started in eighty-five to serve the growing Irish population in the north end. So far, all we have is a basement serving as our sacred space. I don't fault Bishop Murphy. He fights, ecumenically speaking, with Boston's Archbishop Mendel Mrak for the funds to build and open. The bishop has no love for the Irish and makes no pretense of hiding it.

Father Murphy consecrated the nave of our basement space a little over a year ago. As a direct result, the locals flock to services and pour their money directly into the building fund, rather than the coffers that the archbishop controls. Individually our neighborhood may be poor, but when you multiply the few coppers we can each afford by our numbers, it is a substantial sum. We have seen more construction in fourteen months than in the previous four years combined.

Father Juan Dubois y Cantonio stands at the door, greeting the parishioners. He is a short Spaniard with flowing black hair that I envy. Even in his fourth decade, his ponytail disappears across the man's cassock without a strand of silver.

"Welcome, Mark and Felicity

"Good Sabbath to you, Maria.

"And a *buenos dias* to you, Stella. You are looking very chipper this morning."

"*Gracias*, Padre. I feel particularly well in being, thank the Lord."

"Any special reason?" Father Dubois says, needling me. I have never been able to get anything past him. I'm sure he already suspects my dalliance of the night before. It has been a regular topic of my confessions.

I smile. "I guess that is a topic for later this morning."

"Ah, confession of the soul is a good thing, my daughter." He winks at me and shoos me off to the nave.

I take my place on the back pew as always. After only twenty or so decades of witches' known existence, the Church hasn't decided what to make of us yet. Until they do, they segregate us from the rest of the congregation as if we are a disease that mere distance will keep the rest from contracting. Many witches have become disaffected with their religion as a direct result.

"Hello, Elizabeth," I say to a young girl just learning how to control her own air magicks. Her parents sit in with the rest of the congregation, which I think hypocritical. Who am I to condemn? With the loss of my Aaron, I likely will never be a parent, so I can't imagine the rigors.

Elizabeth wears the frown and crossed arms of a good sulk. "Hi, Auntie Stella. My daddy just put bars on my window."

I'm not a real auntie. My mother became barren after my birth. One of the reasons she gives for whomever-my-father-is leaving. "Oh? Is he worried about burglars?"

"Well, that is what he says, but I overheard him and Mommy talking about keeping me from flying. I just learned how and like it."

A third-floor bedroom likely will keep even the most adventurous young woman from trying to climb to the ground, but when she can take to the winds whenever the feeling takes her, that paints a new problem for a parent.

"Well, you get plenty of practice during the day, don't you?"

"Yeah, but I wanted to fly over to the Royal Zoo."

"Heck, that's in Philadelphia next to the American Palace."

"Oh!" she says, covering her mouth. "Father Juan says you can go to hell for saying bad words in church."

I make a sign of the cross. "Forgive my blasphemy, my Lord." I turn my attention back to Elizabeth. "But that's a long way for a young girl to fly alone."

"I know. I can't fly very long yet anyway," Elizabeth pouts, playing with the hem of her dress as she dangles her feet off the pew.

"Hello, Dermot," I greet a fire warlock whose weak talent allows him to light the furnace without a match on most mornings.

"*Buenos dias, señora.* You and the young *señorita* are both looking lovely on this God's day."

I greet others, witches, and warlocks all. None of them with the power to even get the attention of a demon, much less destroy one if necessary. And all of us in the back row as second-class citizens.

Father Juan delivers a sermon based on Matthew 22:39 "…Thou shalt love thy neighbour as thyself." Unlike his high, tinny voice in person, the padre's proselytizing voice pierces every corner of the vast room even with the low, makeshift ceiling. He speaks of a benevolent God who welcomes all people into his loving arms, whether they be Spanish, Italian, Polish, English, French, Russian, or even Irish. His voice cuts hard on the last nationality. Throughout the sermon, he continues to refer back to those refugees from Ireland as examples of whom to be good to. We all understand his continuing feud with Archbishop Mrak, but even this seemed a bit strident.

After the final prayer, I join the queue for confession. Because of construction, the confessional is near the back of the church, and it makes me first in line. Sometimes being shunned has its advantages. The young Elizabeth Lopez waits patiently on her knees in the booth for Father. How many sins can the young girl have on her soul? I wonder if they even warrant her entrance into the booth. Elizabeth skips out to kneel in front of the marble statue of the virgin.

I enter, pulling the curtain behind me. "Forgive me, Father, for I have sinned. It has been one week since my last confession."

"Hello, my daughter Stella. What sins could you possibly have to confess in only a week?" Father Juan says with a chuckle.

"Many more than that innocent young girl that came in earlier. But be that as it may, I have to confess to the sin of lust and lying with someone outside the state of wedlock."

"Jesus, Mary, and Joseph, Stella. You need to find a man and get married to curb that. Or skipping that, marry your girl. While we don't shout it to the rooftops, the book of Ruth is as clear about same-sex marriages as others are against it. However, the pope has made his feelings clear to support any union that is founded in God's love."

"I'm sorry, Father. I do want to do better and become a good woman of the Church, but I won't become chattel of another man or woman except for love. I've found none worthy."

"Then curb that hot nature of yours."

"I do try, Father."

"My child, say ten Hail Marys and four Our Fathers. God, the Father of mercies, through the death and resurrection of his Son has reconciled the world to himself and sent the Holy Spirit among us for the forgiveness of sins; through the ministry of the Church may God give you pardon and peace, and I absolve you from your sins in the name of the Father, and of the Son, and of the Holy Spirit."

I walk out of the confessional with both a lighter and heavier heart. I have been given absolution by my priest. But at the same time, I worry about the next time. If I work very hard, I can probably curb my lust. That would lead me to end up a shrew—like my landlady, poking my nose into everyone else's business and being holier than thou.

I kneel in front of the Virgin's likeness, and whisper, "Hail Mary, full of grace, the Lord is with thee…"

# # #

I have to at least ease my own mind that there are or aren't more demon escapes recently. Baron Cardiff, of the Cannons' hellfighters, seems to have experiences matching my own, but two could just be a coincidence. That's why I've walked three miles to confer with Red Hawk.

Los Lobos's hellfighters have a friendly commune in the Fens. One longhouse of log, covered with growing grass, makes one side of a loose, open square. A three-hole privy and a smokehouse make up the other two sides. Patrick McDonald, wearing a handmade deer-hide jacket and store-bought denim pants, stirs a cast iron pot hanging over an open fire.

The onions and the meaty smell of venison stew waft an aroma I can smell even from a hundred yards away. My stomach grumbles in response.

"Hey, Pat."

Standing up, Patrick slicks back his long, inky hair. "*Estrellita—* Star—Stella! Haven't seen you in a coon's age."

"How long do coons live?"

Patrick laughs. "About six seconds before they wind up in the pot." I give a chuckle. "Is Red Hawk around?"

A deep voice behind me jokes, "No, but I might be square."

I turn around at the pun to the face of an aging Powhatan native with a high forehead and cheekbones that could be used as chisels. His leathery skin sports more wrinkles than Karie's bedsheets in the morning. He wears his trademark wolf's skin as a cloak over slender shoulders.

"Do you just spend all day thinking up new gags?"

"Only for you, Star. So what brings you out into the wilds?"

Despite the furs of rabbit, fox, badger, and even a deer drying on the walls of their lodge, there are still many farmers that live in the area, and not a few industrialists, who have made large mansions west of Boston proper. They aren't exactly living in the sticks. I sit down on a log in front of the fire. "The wilds of Boston—there isn't any such thing."

"Well, we manage without bumping elbows with anyone," Red Hawk says, sitting across the fire from me. In a wooden bowl, Patrick serves me up some stew without even asking, as part of the native lifestyle he's embraced. "So let's chew the fat, sister. What's brings you out this far? You and your Bell People are city folk. We hunt *el diablo* on the outskirts of town."

The aroma of the stew doesn't do the heavenly taste enough credit as I take a mouthful. "This is excellent, Pat. He must keep you around for your cooking."

"He certainly can't do magick worth a damn," Red Hawk teases. We both know it is a tease. I've seen Pat bury a demon under a twelve-foot drift of snow with his skills.

"To business. I just have a question. Are there more demons to hunt lately?"

"Maybe if you Bell People and Cannon People wouldn't make so damned much noise, we wouldn't have that problem." All eight of the Los Lobos live in the longhouse, and no more than two are ever off-site at any time. They don't need a signaling device.

"So you have?" I don't know whether to be happy or afraid.

"Yes. We've had five this month and four the month before. Also, several of *mis brujos* have been injured. This hasn't happened, but once before. *Los serpientes* are getting smarter. I personally wonder if *Okeus* is stroking his war drums.

"And, *Señora* Stella, the bones warn of a large *serpiente* in your near future. You must take care."

I want to tell him that his pagan gods have nothing to do with demons, nor could they predict their movements or plans, but that wouldn't be fair or polite. "Thank you, Red Hawk, for your wisdom."

"Oh, p'shaw, Stella. Wisdom, if you can call it that, comes from age. Live a few more years, and you'll have it, too."

"Maiden, mother, crone," I offer from my earliest teaching of witchcraft.

"That is so and in that the feminine will always be more powerful."

# # #

I make it home for Sabbath dinner only by hiring a cab halfway home. My three-bit fare got me in the doors a full thirty seconds before Mrs. Chapman puts her Sunday dinner on the table. I receive a lecture for my trouble. Both are of dubious value.

"Just made it again, missy. If you keep consorting with men in public houses, then soon you will be nothing more than a trollop. You'll never catch any real lady in those dens of iniquity."

As I haven't been anywhere near a public house in over twenty-four hours, I just give her a lewd smile as I settle into my seat. Let the old biddy think what she wants. As long as I don't fail to pay my rent on time and don't bring a man into the house, both a sacrilege according to my landlady, she has no hold over me.

"Did you see that the Crown is imposing a tax on spirits?" Alice says as she ladles some form of casserole into my dish. "Best thing that could happen. Make those drunkards pay for their antisocial habits."

I look down at the lumps of rutabaga in a foul red sauce. I think I might see a tiny sliver of fish in the oily liquid. The sour smell coming from the serving dish makes me wish I'd asked for a second portion of Patrick's venison stew. "So that means your sherry will be taxed as well, Mrs. Chapman," I say, unable to resist sinking a barb in her tough hide.

One of the younger girls down the table titters.

"Oh, I'm certain that the Crown will understand the difference between rank spirits and an honest aperitif."

"Oh, I'm sure," I offer, with as much sarcasm as my voice can deliver. I then notice that one chair at our table is empty. "Where is—" One of the women shakes her head. Another tries to wave me off. "Where is Maria?" I am never accused of being subtle.

"Maria Marin has been evicted from her room. I will only have ladies in my home."

"You mean she had a penis?" I ask, with a measured bite of the food before me.

"Mrs. Ochoa, please remain civil. I'm talking about the fact that she traded her virginity for motherhood."

I look around at the stricken faces. "That's wonderful!"

"No, Widow Ochoa, it isn't wonderful that she is a common slut. She got caught with child and without a husband. She can't stay here and corrupt the morals of all of my other charges."

"Now wait just a moment, Alice," I say, intentionally using her Christian name. "None of us is *your* charge. You are our landlady, not our moral compass, not our guardian, and certainly not our spouse. I think I speak for all of us when I say you should get Maria back immediately."

The dowager gives me a cold look over her food. She slowly takes a bite. "As you say, I am your landlady, and that gives me the right to choose who I want to have in my home. Maria isn't welcome." She stared into my eyes. "Don't do anything to make yourself or these other ladies unwelcome."

Homelessness doesn't scare me. I have more than enough people willing to keep a roof over my head until I get a new flop. But the rest of the women here border on the edge. One wrong turn, and they will become lost. Despite my anger and desire to cause a spike of earth to skewer her from bowel to mouth, I do nothing. Maria will have to fend for herself, for now.

4—Monday, February 6, 1888

I avoid Widow Chapman as I leave the boardinghouse. My hatred of the woman still rages even after a night of sleep. I don't trust my restraint. I hurry down Stillman Street as I hear the Charlestown tram bells chime at the end of the block. I'm going to take the lazy way to pick up my last wages. While I'm at it, I'll use Karie's letter of introduction to visit Lord Helms, especially as he lives all the way across the Charles River in Cambridgeport. I climb onto the trolley just as the paperboy calls out, "'Archbishop of Boston Segregates Irish. Claims Souls Are Questionable.'"

The bastard has finally gone and done it. Archbishop Mrak has been angling this way for years. Now he openly defies the pope. The audacity is that of a schoolboy bullfighting. I grant you that the pope is an ocean and a continent away. However, I don't see the pope standing still for this one, no matter how many times he's pulled Mrak's chestnuts out of the fire.

The tram is standing room only. The vast majority of the people are heading to the North End station to take the Philadelphia Flyer to the capital. I'd seen the Philadelphia Palace once as a young girl. Someday maybe again, but only if I somehow secure another job.

"Nice morning," offers an older woman with a marketing basket. She lifts it off of a seat to offer it to me.

"Thank you. Yes, it is a lovely day," I say, smiling in the morning sun. For winter, the temperature didn't even warrant a coat. The crisp air is just enough to keep me cool through my brocade dress and cotton underthings. Although by lunchtime, I probably would be sweating beneath them all.

"We'd better enjoy it. We're supposed to get a storm tomorrow night," the woman says.

"Oh? Did the papers say something?"

"Oh, heavens, no. They are wrong more than they are right. My daughter has a way with the weather."

An untrained air witch in all likelihood. "I'll make sure I'm home."

"Oh, and make sure you have stores in for a few days. It is supposed to be a nasty storm. Remember that one that hit the Midwest?"

"Yes, I read about it," I say.

"That's the storm. Going to be really bad."

"Thanks for the warning." My mind whirs on ways to stop the conversation, but the woman has that rare quality to know when she is overstaying her welcome. She instead turns to look at a garish billboard advertising balloon rides.

In the open square, the market is in full swing where produce vendors offer lettuces, broccoli, cauliflower, potatoes, apples, and fruit preserves in mason jars. The Masterson and Sons butcher's box wagon is open with hanging chicken, ducks, and even a side of lamb from the eaves. His helper stokes his tiny furnace to keep the distinctive three-tone calliope playing. The butcher carves off some ribs for a woman, wrapping them in brown paper. A tin peddler is polishing up some of his wares to attract more attention. A woman is selling brightly colored, heavy quilts. I think of how nice it would feel to have an extra layer at night but put it off again for want of a steady income.

Eight more stops sees me to my place of former employment. Dismounting, I thank the lady with the basket. I march through the gates, giving a nod to one of the guards, and continue straight to the paymaster's cage.

"May I help you?" asks a man with a narrow face and twitching nose. He's new, and I arbitrarily allocate the nickname Squirrel to him.

"Yes, I'm here to pick up my final pay."

"Name?"

"Stella Ochoa."

The Squirrel consults his books before looking up at me with pursed lips and wrinkles across his nose as if he'd smelled something unpleasant. "I'm sorry, Madam Ochoa, but our books say that you owe us fourteen dollars and seventeen cents. I can collect that now if you would like."

"Excuse me? I have five days' pay coming and never purchase from the company store."

"Your pay for that period was ten dollars and ninety-three cents. It says here that you damaged work equipment to the tune of twenty-five dollars and seven cents."

"I didn't work with any equipment. I spelled soot out of the air."

"I'm sorry, ma'am, but I'm just following company policy. Now, will you please remit the fourteen dollars and seventeen cents?"

"Only on a cold day in hell, sir."

"In that case, I will have to call security," he says, reaching for a bell.

"You do and someone dies, starting with you, weasel nose," I growl. The Squirrel stops. Up to this point, he has maintained the upper hand and felt protected behind his cage bars. Now I can see the fear in his eyes for the first time. "I'll have my ten dollars plus change, and I'll have it now."

"Mr. Whipple?" he blurts out. The regular paymaster steps from a back room.

"What now, Renardo?"

"This lady is demanding her pay even though the books say she owes money. In addition, she has threatened me."

Whipple pulls down his glasses and peers over them at me. "Stella? What's going on?"

"This bilge licker is keeping me from my final wages. I won't stand for it."

"Let me see." Whipple looks down at the books through his round spectacles. He chuckles. "I'm sorry, Stella. It's not funny to you, but someone decided that your leaving merited a penalty. I'll see to it that it is removed from the books. Renardo, pay the woman now before she gives you a stone enema while I hold you still for it."

The new pay clerk's face changes from fear to loathing. I'd made him look bad to his boss. As a result, I twice recount every penny he gives me to make sure it is right before signing the ledger.

"Thank you, Mr. Whipple," I say, ignoring his underling.

I walk away, wondering just how close I'd come to witches' prison. Provoked or not, the Crown takes a dim view of people abusing their powers. I shudder under the damp sea breeze. I've only heard rumors about what is done to keep people from using their magick in those jails. None of them is pleasant or survivable for long.

The next trolley along isn't for almost another hour. Still, I find the presence of the Coal Syndicate yards too oppressive for my tastes. I decide to walk for at least a few blocks through the laborers, messengers on bicycles, porters, teamsters, and even naval men with their smart uniforms. However, the military men tended to stay over in Cambridge nearer the naval yard. Shouted conversations, the ever-present roar of steam escaping, the clopping of shoed horses on the cobblestones, shopkeepers hawking their wares, and piercing whistles—both human and steam made—all melded together to form a cacophony that is only tolerable because I'm inured to it from birth. I can sleep through a hurricane and wake up wondering why my bed is floating and the roof over me is missing.

"Stella!" I hear shouted toward me. I look around but see no one I recognize. I figure the noise has made me imagine it.

"Stella!" I hear again. This time I stop and look around. The Baron of Snowdonia strides through the crowd like a ballerina dancing around but never touching the horse apples. Franklin's steel-gray suit with matching blouse and tie would have stood out as exceptional even at a royal banquet. But he went even further by accenting it with a golden tie tack and watch fob. A peacock, red shell, and star, the symbols of his lost title, surmount his ebony walking stick.

"And how are you doing this morning, Baron?"

"Quite good, Stella. Thank you for returning my coat so promptly." Mr. Cardiff falls into lockstep with me as I turned onto Cambridge Street.

"You are welcome, Baron. Tommy is a good kid. And thank you for its loan in the first place."

"So, what are you doing off of work on a Monday?"

"Actually, I was fired because I took the liberty of going to stop a demon rather than remain loyally at my post."

"I empathize, Widow Ochoa. Sometimes I wonder if that fool Karl Marx might have the right idea—the haves oppressing the working classes."

"Somehow, I don't see you as a communist, Baron."

"No, I'm not, but I also am not sure I agree with the rampant capitalism in this country." He shakes his head as if bothered by a fly. "Be that as it may, where are you off to on this fine morning?"

"I have an introduction to meet Lord Helms."

"So, still pursuing the thought that the demon escapes lately are not chance?"

"Yes."

"Well, I've come to believe the same thing. One of my people was hurt last night, fighting a nasty little beast across the river on Bunker Hill, just outside the naval base. Some fool of a captain got in our way, messing up our coordination."

"Hurt bad?"

"Just a couple of ribs and a leg were broken. He'll be at it soon enough. I killed that beast right then and there."

I can't quite bring myself to believe the baron could summon up that much emotion for one of his people. Despite his protestations, all the rumors say he looks out for number one, first, last, and always. *Maybe I judge him too harshly?* I wonder. "Well, that is a blessing. Do you have enough people to fight again if necessary?" In spite of his less than sterling reputation, the baron always has barrels of witches hovering around him for the chance to be on his team. I never know why.

He just waves it off as unimportant. "So would you mind a little company? I'd like to dig into this mystery with you."

Maybe I do judge him too harshly. "Why not. The more, the merrier."

Two young women walk by, craning their necks to stare at the baron's radiant presence. He smiles directly at them and doffs his hat with a small bow. The two women titter, turning around and whispering together. I sigh. *I'm with a strutting rooster,* I think.

"Shall we catch the tram on this side of the Longfellow Bridge?"

He didn't quite wince at riding such plebian transport. "I have a better idea." He waves his hand, and miraculously his coach pulls up. It must have been pacing us. I guess there is a benefit to having a well-heeled man around. What would have taken a good two hours by trolley and foot takes only thirty minutes of wending through the thick traffic.

The Helms Estate stands on a wooded hillock with an uninterrupted view of the Charles River. Its modern, art-nouveau style seems to clash with the brownstones and clapboard buildings I see every day downtown. A sweeping stairway from the crushed shell roadway leads to a double portal. Each door is inset with what can only be a Tiffany window: the size and depiction of a male peacock in full bloom. I find it rather tasteless and an ostentatious display of wealth. Maybe the baron feels at home because of his own fortune. Franklin just pulls the announcement cord—a sash made of blue silk, I might add.

I hear the gong go off and then slow, regular steps. The door opens to a stiff-necked butler in full regalia. "May I help you?"

"I have a letter of introduction to see Lord Helms," I say, handing over my letter from Karie.

"Come in," he says in a deep, sonorous voice. The hallway looks big enough to host the World's Fair. Mirrors cover most of the walls, with white marble in a convoluted starburst pattern making up the floor. "Please wait here," he says, placing my letter, unread, onto a silver tray. He strides with a cadence like a metronome down one of the many exits from the foyer.

The jewelry on the woman that attends us could have bought me three brownstones in the best part of town. The centerpiece, an amber stone the size of my fist set in gold, floats between her ample bosoms and makes her honey-blond hair all the more yellow. Her blue, Lanvin-designed dress gives her the dignity that her short stature doesn't.

She turns away from me like she would a cow patty deposited just in front of her with its attendant smell. She addresses the baron. "Sir…?"

"Baron of Snowdonia, Lady Helms," he says with a low bow that belongs in the Spanish high court.

The dumpling smiles from ear to ear. "Baron, what is this in reference to?"

I interrupt. "We've come relating to some concerns about his business, Lady Helms."

She doesn't quite ignore me. "Baron, I'm sorry, but my husband is at his place of work right now. I'm surprised you didn't try there first."

The baron throws me a look. *So I'm not perfect,* I think.

"We were led to believe he would be here, m'lady," I offer.

"I suggest you try at Forever Power. The address is Sixty-Two Pinckney Street, Boston. Normally I would assume you'd need an appointment; however, with such a letter of introduction, you should have no trouble," she says, handing the letter back to me as if it is a snake that will bite her.

Until that moment, I never considered that I might be accidentally telling tales on Lord Helms. I smile at Lady Helms as I take it, but I can feel the heat in my cheeks. I never promise to know everything.

"Thank you, Lady Helms. We will do that." The baron steers us back out the way we came under the glare of the lady of the house. Somehow the butler has found his way to the door before us and holds it open.

After giving his driver the new destination, the baron asks, "What is in that letter? I thought she was going to have us served up skewered on a spit and *flambéed* on the spot."

"I didn't think this through." I offer him the letter. He scans the three almost formal lines of introduction until he comes to the signature.

"¡*Dios Mío!* Did you just rub Lady Helms's nose in the fact that her husband has visited the most famous prostitute in Boston? No wonder she looked ready to shoot fire at you."

"Like I said, I didn't think it through," I offer sheepishly.

"This is what I get for teaming up with a commoner," Franklin remarks to himself. I mentally chastise myself with a reminder to seek penance for my blunder. I certainly didn't mean to hurt anyone, but that doesn't change what seems to be the reality.

The baron stews in silence through the rest of our ride, almost back to where he picked me up. At only a half-block long, Forever Power is an unassuming building for the size of its impact on American life. The large wrought iron gate with the sign "Deliveries in Back" had a brisk business of teamsters and steam engines through it. A bright yellow dirigible with the slogan "Moorcroft's Rare Earths" moors to the building's roof. Its entire carriage is lowered through a series of pulleys and ropes that disappear out of view. As a young girl, I used to delight anytime I could see blimps with their gay colors and disregard for the wind. I'd run to follow them wherever they traveled, sometimes to the point of missing dinner.

The business front of Forever Power seems barren by comparison. I see an accountant come out, but no one enters.

"Can we keep this one a bit more professional?" the baron asks.

"Well, I don't see much of a way of getting the attention of the owner of the company unless we use this letter," I offer.

"I could use my station."

"That might get you to see the special assistant to the secretary of the greeting committee," I joke.

"OK, then my charm."

I bite back my first response as too caustic. "I think we will have to settle for the letter."

The driver opens the carriage before I can even reach for the handle. I'm not used to such niceties. Between the baron and Karie's staff, I am getting used to the good life and not looking forward to Mrs. Chapman and my dark closet.

# # #

The outer office of Forever Power is much busier than the street. People move back and forth throughout the large, open room. A trolley with coffee service trundles here. A pair of architects talk as they walk side by side. Boys are taking mysterious messages to god only knows where. A pool of women type as fast as their fingers can fly.

An ornamental receptionist with an icy demeanor sits behind a marble desk. With her gold-rimmed eyeglasses, she catches my eye but then addresses Baron Cardiff. She seems the type that earns her job by flashing her ankles as often as possible.

"May I help you?"

"Yes, miss," Baron Cardiff says, proffering one of his patented smiles. The woman's coolness warms at least twenty degrees. "We have a letter of introduction to speak with Lord Helms."

I step forward and offer the letter, still in its envelope.

"I take it you don't have an appointment?"

The baron picks it up again, "No, ma'am. We hoped that we could see him as soon as possible. It is a matter of some urgency."

"Your names?"

"Baron of Snowdonia, Franklin Cardiff, and Stella Ochoa."

She snaps her fingers, and a teen boy shows up as if teleported to her side. She quickly types up a message and hands it to the messenger along with Karie's bit of parchment. "To Lord Helms, now," she says to her runner before turning to us again. "If you and your companion would just have a seat, I'll let you know when Lord Helms responds."

We take two straight-back wooden chairs against the wall. "What do you think our chances are?" I whisper to the baron.

"Excellent. Worst case, we have to wait a day or two for an appointment opening."

I count to twenty in Latin. The boy returns so fast I thought he must have flown. The secretary gets up and comes over to us. "You are quite lucky. Lord Helms has made an opening for you immediately. If you will follow Bartholomew," she says, pointing at the runner, "he will take you to Lord Helms."

Franklin smiles at her with his perfect teeth. "Thank you very much, Miss—"

"Vazquez. Karen Vazquez."

"Karen," he says with a wink. "Thank you very much. I'm looking forward to seeing you again."

"Yes, m'lord," she replies, coated with honey that could easily turn to dinner and a romp in whatever horizontal surface presents itself.

As we walk away, I whisper, "Could either of you be more obvious?" With a smug little grin, he replies, "I don't know what you are talking about, Stella."

Lord Helms's double desk stands so far away from the doors that you could play soccer in the open floor space. Cabinets line the walls with papers overflowing the top and sometimes open drawers. "Lord?"

"Please come in," waves someone from behind several large stacks of files on the desk. "Bartholomew, you may return to your duties."

"Yes, m'lord."

Franklin and I walk forward. The lack of décor amazes me—no rugs, no wall paint, no statues, and no curtains. Only two small, utilitarian lights brighten up his side of the room. If it weren't for the size of the room, I'd assume we were meeting with an underling—a not terribly important underling. Lord Helms stands up, and all I can think of is five broomsticks in a cheap suit. He reminds me of Irving's description of Icabod Crane—tall, angular, and about as much weight as a small puppy.

"Miss Ochoa, I have to admire your metal. Not many people would have had the character to bring this to me," he offers, waving my letter of introduction.

"I do apologize about that, Lord Helms. And before we bring up our business, I have to also apologize for something more. I believe I may have exposed your liaison with Karie Taylor to your wife."

The man stands there with a sour expression until, suddenly, his gaunt face breaks out in a radiant smile. "Thank you for being honest, Miss Ochoa, but I'd be surprised if my wife didn't think I have dozens of mistresses. Ours is not a love match. You've done me no harm."

"*Gracias a Dios.* I'm really sorry, m'lord," I say sincerely.

"Really, it is nothing. But you did come here for something, Miss Ochoa." He motions for us to take a seat. "Can we please get to the point?"

"Yes, Mr. Helms," the baron says, breaking in. "We're both members of—"

"Hellfighters. Yes, I know. If I am correct, Miss Ochoa is a member of *Dos Campanas,* and you, Baron Cardiff, lead the Cannons." He smiles broadly again, looking like a cross between a skeleton and the Cheshire cat. "I keep track of most things in my business purview."

Franklin continues, "Good, so we don't need an introduction. We are here because we've detected a larger number of demon escapes than normal."

"That doesn't surprise me. I wondered when folks would begin to notice." He turns around and pulls the cloth off an easel. The graph entitled "Demon Escapes" shows an increasing upward trend. "As it is a part of my business, I have to keep track of all escapes."

"So, you are aware?" I ask, my eyebrows raising.

"I'd be a fool of elephantine proportions if I didn't know, Miss Ochoa. I've been spending more resources than you can imagine trying to find out why."

"Oh?" I try to make that simple exclamation sound nonthreatening.

"Miss Ochoa, I assure you I want nothing more than this all to go away. I've built this business from the ground up. And while my marriage may not be a loving relationship, I assure you that Forever Power means everything to me. Anything that hurts it drives a stake through my heart."

Sincerity, real or fake, oozes from every word and from every grandiose gesture of his skinny arms.

"See this stack here?" he says, patting a pile of folders two feet high. "This is a list of all suppliers I've used over the last five years. I'm examining each vendor and change of dealer to see if there is a problem with any of them." He slaps yet another pile. "Here are the chemical tests of everything we use in our business from chalk to silver. And here," he slams his fist down on another pile of paper, "is a list of everyone working for me from that decorative creature at the front desk to branch manager to installer to salesman." He collapses back into his seat as if the entire experience has exhausted him. "I can't find a bloody thing wrong.

"Oh, don't get me wrong, I found a service girl who was stealing coffee. I even found a branch manager in New Murcia who was embezzling. But nothing that would impact the safety of our demon installations."

The baron looks at me with a blatant question…What's next.

I shrug. "Lord Helms, would you consider some outside help?" I ask.

The man's chest inflates to almost twice its normal, narrow size with a deep breath before answering. "What's in it for you?"

"Despite popular opinion that hellfighting is a glamorous and exciting profession, it's *pinche* dangerous," I offer in the way of explanation. "And while we do get paid for each demon we inter or retire, I for one don't want to do any more than necessary. Ask a fireman how often he wants to fight a fire. People die every time one of those beasts get loose."

"So you don't believe in demons as a power source? Maybe we should ban their use?" he says, bristling.

"*Señor*, that is not what Stella said or even implied. I don't know of a single hellfighter who is against demon power," Baron Cardiff says in defense of my honor. I nod.

"My apology, *señorita*. This problem has me strung tighter than a wire. I haven't eaten in three days, nor slept in longer than that. Although these are still not good reasons to be rude to a lady." He stands and bows.

"No apology is necessary, Lord Helms."

"Please call me Henry. I never liked the stuffy formalness of court titles."

"If you will call me Stella," I reply. I look at the baron, knowing his propensity and love for titles.

"Ah, Lord Helms, if we could get back to the question at hand. Could you use another pair of investigators?"

"*Sí*. Yes. *Da*. *Oui*. If you are involved, at least when it comes out, then no one can say I am trying to whitewash anything." Lord Helms—Henry—pulls out a fresh piece of paper and scribbles something on it. He opens his drawer and pulls out a red wax candle and lights it. Dripping the wax onto the document, the viscount forces his signet ring into the cooling wax to form a seal. "Here," he says, handing me the paper. "This will give you access anywhere in our corporate sphere—anywhere."

Stella Ochoa has the right of access and the right to question anyone equal to my own. <signed> Lord H. Helms.

"That is most generous, Lor—Henry."

He finishes yet another sealed paper and hands it to Franklin. "I'm trying to protect my baby, Stella. No thanks are necessary. I don't think I need to tell you that I will be most grateful if you succeed."

"We obviously aren't doing this for personal gain, Lord Helms. We want to be good peers...and citizens of the American Monarchy," the baron interjects.

"You will have my thanks regardless," he says. "Now, I don't mean to be impolite, but despite my fears, I still have a company to run."

I can't think of any more questions. The rest must be investigations. "Good day to you, Henry. We'll be in touch if we learn something."

# # #

"Stella, can I drop you someplace?" the baron asks as we get back to his carriage.

"Eh?" I answer with the adroit word choice of Longfellow himself.

"Sorry, but I have a lunch meeting I must attend across town."

"Oh, I'm sorry about my presumption, Baron."

"Think nothing of it, Stella. I'll be in touch as my schedule permits, and perhaps we can coordinate some more inquiry.

"Driver, to the barn." I watch the immaculate coach mingle into the traffic.

A buckboard carrying sheet steel rolls through the delivery gate. I'm here, and so is Forever Power's raw materials. I might as well find out if there is anything fishy going on at the base of things. The flurry of activity is noteworthy enough for a king's visit.

The balloon's ship-sized basket is now on the ground with people dragging the boxes out with draft horses. Older boxes obviously filled with broken stone are being dragged back on as ballast. Rivet manufacturers are dumping tons of the little connectors into underground cellars. The bass thumping of a steam hammer shakes the ground, and the matching shriek of escaping, superheated water pierces the air.

I wend my way between vendors rolling huge barrels of grease out of the back of a wagon, and ironically a load of coal.

"Hey, you!" yells someone above the din. "You, missy!"

I realize he's talking to me. "What?"

This burly man with more hair on his arms than a bear says, "You want to get killed? You don't belong here. Now go in through the main door on the street."

I hold up my pass from Lord Helms and bark over the noise, "I do belong here."

He snaps his fingers and waves me over. I weave through the chaos to show him Lord Helms's pass.

"Well, isn't this a pretty nothing," the man says. "Been Forever Power's dockmaster since it opened and ain't seen nothing like this.

"It says here you are Stella Ochoa. Well, Miss Ochoa, what do you want to see? Even g'damned micks got more horse sense than a woman, so I better give you some escort or you going to be nothing but a red stain on the ground."

I bite back my first, second, and third responses as all counterproductive. So I count to ten in Latin before I answer.

"I didn't catch your name, good sir."

"Cecilio Delgadillo." He almost puffs up his chest like it should mean something. Cecilio pronounced the double ell as *y* as a good Spaniard would, not like an American or Brit. Most Spaniards were overtly proud of their ancestry.

"Thank you, *Señor* Delgadillo. Specifically, I'd like to see your chalk, holy water, and silver stores." These are the three critical ingredients in binding any demon.

Cecilio puts two fingers in his mouth and gives off a trilling whistle that tears the top of my head right off. A lad, maybe a year older than Tommy, appears promptly.

"Yes, sor," the boy says in a strong English accent.

"Take the *mujer* to the stores' rooms. Her safety is your responsibility."

"Yes, sor. Ma'am, if you will come this way."

He leads me past a row of automated blacksmith hammers, each driven off the same motive shaft striking one after the other. Skilled craftsmen use the automation to cold-rivet sheet steel steam vessels so fast it astonishes me. The boy pulls me to one side of an aisle when I hear a goose horn behind. A powered loader lumbers by in a puff of smoke and steam carrying a pallet of wooden beams looking like the few squared-off telegraph poles I'd seen on the outskirts of the city. As our trek goes farther into the building, the traffic and workshop noise reduces.

"Here are the storerooms, ma'am."

"Thank you. I think I can take it from here." After the boy leaves, there is only one other person in a room the size of the entire soot extraction bins I used to work in. She is collecting materials out of various areas and adding them to a handcart on big, pram-style wheels.

My boots make a clicking sound on the concrete floors as I walk. I pass a pile of the great wooden beams I saw earlier, stacks of sheet steel of various thickness, eight-foot on a side, and a bin of white powder sand from Bermuda, before running into my first target—pecks of silver-nibbed pens.

The alloy, to be viable for use in summoning demons, must be no less than ninety-two percent pure silver. Typically it is alloyed with copper to strengthen it. It also can't have any brimstone and no more than one percent trace elements. This is where an unscrupulous manufacturer can skimp and save a good deal of money. Each basket holds maybe a hundred pens, each costing at least ten dollars. By cutting the silver content even to ninety percent, you might be able to save a hundred dollars per peck; multiplied by, well, a lot of woven baskets, it would work out to a small fortune.

I bend over to pick up one of the pens when a woman's voice interrupts me. "Excuse me, ma'am, but what are you doing? And who are you?" The statuesque redhead, who had been collecting for the cart, questions my presence. In one sense, this heartens me as I doubt anyone who isn't a known worker for Forever Power could get here and do any sabotage. Abandoning the pens, I smile. I walk toward her with my hand out. "My name is Mrs. Ochoa." With some suspicion, she takes my hand in a firm, male-like shake. "I'm doing some investigation for Lord Helms."

The fiery-haired woman takes her hand back and says, "I am the stores manager, and I don't know you, Mrs. Ochoa."

"One moment, ma'am." I pull out my already used letter and pass it over. "Lord Helms gave me the authority to make these examinations."

She wrinkles her little button nose. I find it cute, but a wedding band on her ring finger shuts down any thoughts I might have in that arena. Her voice comes with a bit of frost, "Well, Helms did sign it. What are you investigating?"

"Could I at least have your name?"

"Sorry, my name is Mrs. Smith."

I smile. "Mrs. Smith, Lord Helms has some concerns about the quality of the materials Forever Power is receiving."

Her snarl twists her face up, including that cute little button nose. "What proof? I sample every lot that comes in. I don't let even a single ounce of anything out of here without a work order. I—"

"Hold up, Mrs. Smith. Neither Lord Helms nor I am accusing you of inefficiency, skullduggery, or any other horrible thing. We are only doing some checking. It may be utterly nothing."

Her brows knit together and she purses lips. I see her corseted chest go in and out in the biggest breath she probably could take. It didn't make for a very impressive sigh. "What do you need?"

"I'm just going to test a few of your materials."

"You won't take any, will you?"

"Only if necessary, and I'll let you know if I do."

"Then, help yourself." She turns back to her work, and I return to my examinations.

I take a pen out and stick the nib in my mouth. The silver and copper speak to me like a long-lost friend. I roll the tip around on my tongue. The copper is five percent, and the trace elements are virtually nonexistent. This pen is better than minimum requirements by a large factor. I wipe off the scribe and test one from another basket and another and another. Each of thirty random pens that I test similarly exceeds specifications.

"Harrumph." I walk over to a huge bin, eight foot on a side, filled with pulverized chalk.

"Ma'am, don't touch that, you will infect it with impurities."

Mrs. Smith doesn't know I'm a witch. I point to a gallon-sized scoop hanging from a chain. She nods. The dipper was hand-forged of silver alloy to prevent contamination. I use it to stir the contents and pour a tiny amount into my left hand. The Italian chalk of the purest quality almost sings an operetta in my mind. I could imprison a demon with just the fraction of an ounce in my hand. I return the scoop.

The holy water to my right is in a silver font, although at six feet across "silver swimming pool" might be a better term for it. It correctly bears the mark of a single cross. Some idiots think more crosses are better, but there is only one Jesus Christ who died for our sins. I lift the solid oak lid and find the silver lining unbroken. At hand is a stack of small glass bottles. Using a silver ladle, I pour no more than a finger of the precious liquid into the bottom of one. I upend the liquid into my mouth. Each priest involved in creating holy water leaves his signature on it along with that of the Holy Spirit. I've never tasted this person's work, but the quality is at least that of a bishop—more than adequate for housing any demon.

I don't have to look for a holy water sprinkler because each witch has his or her own. They don't need to be replaced, ever.

I take a sniff of the myrrh incense, and the fragrant resin, a gum of a thorny tree, fills my nose. So concentrated is the smell that I sneeze. I manage to do it into the crook of my arm to prevent contamination of anything nearby. The myrrh hasn't been adulterated and is from North Africa. I put the stick back in its oilskin wrapping.

From just a touch, I can tell the censers, the ball-like device that produces smoke at the end of a chain and is usually swung by an altar boy, are of exceptional alloy. Because of the heat of the burning offering to God, they needed to be replaced often.

Looking around, all I can see and test are top of the line materials. Everything says my initial guess of a company cutting corners is falling flat, at least at the corporate level.

I glance over at my hostess. I'm sure I can come up with a more dramatic version of impatience than the one she shows, but I'd be hard-pressed. Mrs. Smith stands, arms crossed, tapping her foot at the room's entrance, unable to leave her duty station until she can lock it up tight.

"Mrs. Smith, I have to commend you on your well-organized, high-quality stock," I offer as an olive branch as I walk toward her. Her demeanor softens by at least five notches.

"Thank you, Miss Ochoa. I'm sorry I'm so testy. To prove myself, I have to work three times harder as the only woman on the dock."

"No, Mrs. Smith—"

"Please call me Patty."

"Absolutely, Patty. I do understand. One of my jobs has me working with *matones. ¡Madre Dios!*" Patty laughs. I continue, "I see that you are getting ready for another installation."

"Yes, Miss—"

"Stella. It would be rude of me not to reciprocate with my given name."

"Stella, I am getting ready for corporate installations. Along with being effectively a supercargo on this dock watching every sliver of tin, ounce of chalk, and inch of solder, I have to create install kits for our witches."

"May I?" I ask, pointing at the cart she seems to be protecting with her body.

"Certainly," she offers now that I've taken the time to ingratiate myself.

"Two?" I ask, holding up two fingers to inquire if she is preparing for two installations. Patty nods. I look over the quantities of each kit, and everything is as it should be. Just to be sure, I watch her face as I put my tongue on the stylus. She looks interested but not concerned. My taste buds came away with the same percentage of silver as before, well above minimums.

"You do good work. Are you a witch?" I ask curiously.

"Heavens, no. I am good with figures and seem to be able to memorize pages of text at just a glance."

"'As each has received a gift, use it to serve one another, as good stewards of God's varied grace.'"

"Peter four, verse ten. But that is much too easy. Many people have memorized the Bible."

I think for a moment, "'Vengeance is in my heart, death—'"

"'—in my hand, blood and revenge are hammering in my head.' Didn't care much for *Titus Andronicus*. Not one of Shakespeare's better plays."

I smile. "Well, if I ever need a person with the memory of an elephant, I'll let you know, Patty."

"So, can you tell me what this is all about, now that I have a clean bill of health?"

"Sorry, Patty, but I'm bound only to share details with Lord Helms. I would tell you if I could."

"That's alright. I'm used to secrets by now. My husband works for the Ministry of Defense. He can't tell me anything about his day even if, like now, the stinking British keep testing us. It is eating away at him. The dockworkers never confide in me, but I hear a great deal at lunch as I sit and eat quietly."

"They ever say anything about someone spraying money around?"

"Not that I can think of. If I do hear such a thing, how can I get in touch with you?"

I no longer have any reason to suspect Lord Helms. I might as well use him as a confidant. "Just tell Lord Helms...in person. I'm sure he'll get it back to me if it fits in with our investigation."

Patty nods. "Thank you, Stella. I've enjoyed having someone who sits down on the privy to share with today."

"Not a problem. By the way, how do I get out of this maze? I need to see Lord Helms one more time before I leave today." Still one more thing to check out before I call it a day and head to the pub.

"Follow me. I'm heading in that general direction anyway." She pushes her cart along, talking as she walks. She wants to take advantage of our girl time. She tells me about her husband as a junior functionary working on new ship designs, how hard they try to have children, but God just hasn't yet gifted them, and even about the new dress her husband bought her for their anniversary. I listen politely and interject only the occasional nod or confirmation. "Front lobby is through that door there," Patty offers after we weave our way through a web of passages that I couldn't retrace if I were being chased by Gazunreep himself.

"Thanks."

"Have a great day," she says as she pushes her trolley off down another hallway.

Miss Ankles is still at her desk. I go right up to her. "I need to talk to Lord Helms briefly."

"I'm sorry, but that isn't possible."

"Oh, please, Karen. Do we have to go through this again?" I wave Lord Helms's free pass under her nose.

"Miss Ochoa, I don't demur because I don't wish to. I do it because it isn't possible. Lord Helms has left work early to prepare for the opera with his wife."

My cheeks flush, and I feel about the size of a sugar ant. "I'm sorry I jumped to conclusions."

"It happens frequently. I have even been referred to as Miss Ankles, for the belief that I do nothing but flirt and provide men with inappropriate views of my body. There are times I wish I'd been born homely. Those times are few because beauty does open some doors, but I prefer to be judged on merit."

I keep getting smaller, and my cheeks get hotter as she describes, to a tee, how I imagined her at our first meeting. "Well, I won't judge you that way again. Thank you for the information." I hustle out the front door of Forever Power as quickly as my embarrassment will take me.

Putting aside my discomfort, I figure if the Helmses will leave for the opera, it won't be until at least five. My Aaron's pocket watch that I keep in my purse says two thirty-three. Somehow I'd missed several of the afternoon bells and even the noon whistle. I do get caught up in a project. I have to hustle if I'm going to make the two forty-five trolley into Cambridge.

Three blocks later, my blisters decide for me that as soon as I have another job a trip to the corner cobbler is in order, cost or no. You definitely get what you pay for, and cheaper, store-bought shoes just won't do. With my sores in mind, I pick my steps onto the self-guiding car with care.

The last half mile I do on foot, wondering each step if I should just have sent Tommy in the morning. *No*, I tell myself, *that won't do.* I pull the announcement rope for the Helms's home as the sun is setting behind the mountains in the west.

"Good evening, ma'am."

"Good evening. Is it possible to see Lord Helms before he is off to the opera?"

Before he can answer, Lady Helms, in a yellow chiffon gown that makes her short-form look taller, pushes past her servant. "You are bold as brass, missy. I'd think someone of your profession," she barks, screwing up her face at the word, "would be more discrete."

"Lady H—"

"I don't care what you have to say, and you can have nothing that my husband wishes to hear. Now get lost, madam." Lady Helms even manages to twist that honorific into a slur with her tone.

Before the door closes, I shove my boot into the crack. I bite my lip as it slams into one of my sores. I push through the opening to the white face and wide eyes of the viscountess. Her butler looks equally shocked.

My righteous indignation flares. "First off, madam, my virtue is not for hire. It never has been and never will be. Second, I'm here at your husband's behest to deal with his business. Third—"

Lord Helms's voice interrupts from the stair's landing. "Adrianna, dear, Mrs. Ochoa is doing a job for me, although I didn't expect her here this evening, or I would have so informed you."

The lady of the house purses her lips and frowns at me. The look she shoots her husband is barely less scathing. She picks up her hems and storms out of the foyer deeper into the house.

Resplendent in his tuxedo bearing the orange sash and the rampant eagle of his house, Lord Helms strides toward me with remarkable grace considering his lanky build. "I'm sorry for that, *Mrs.* Ochoa. What news do you have?" I can tell by the conspiratorial glance over his shoulder that his wife can be counted on to be listening.

"Good news so far. I've tested a number of your stores, and they look exceptional," I say loud enough to ensure his wife hears our conversation.

"Cutting corners when you are dealing with something as intrinsically dangerous as demons is silly," he remarks in kind.

"I can't agree with you more, sir. I also looked at a couple of the kits set up for installations, and they look in exceptional shape as well. What I came here for was to request that we witness at least one of the installations tomorrow."

"What an exceptional idea. I try to visit at least a few every year. Why don't you meet me at Forever Power at ten tomorrow morning, and we will go and watch some internments: a commercial one and a residential one."

"My thanks, *Señor* Helms. *Buenas noches.*"

By the time I limp off the Helms's property, I realize I need some assistance, cost or no. It still takes another half mile before I can flag down a cab.

As a pleasant surprise in exchange for my fare home, Mrs. Chapman has prepared haulupture—pickled cabbage rolls stuffed with rice, barley, and fried pork crackling in a creamy tomato broth. Somehow she manages that dish exceedingly well. I eat until the overfull feeling in my belly rivals the throbbing of my feet.

"Widow Ochoa, you received a message delivered here today."

"I did?" I ask, thinking I want to get out of these shoes.

She hands over a gaping envelope with my name on the outside. It doesn't take a constable to see that the envelope has been steamed open. Sometimes I really hate my landlady. I don't have any real secrets, but it is the principle of the thing.

Within the plain paper, a bland message has been typewritten but has no signature.

> The Coal Syndicate, Air Remediation Division, would be willing to reconsider its decision to terminate your services and discuss your returning to your position if we can assure loyalty to our company and not abandoning your post.

I fold the paper and put it back into the envelope. "Hand-delivered, Mrs. Chapman?"

"Yes, just this afternoon."

"Thank you. I think I'll retire now. Thank you for a lovely supper."

Alice looks at me with her mouth half-open. Oh, I can read her the riot act for opening my mail, but fatigue is fogging my eyes. Besides, the note gives me a bigger dose of happiness than half a bottle of laudanum. I let her slide if for no other reason than one of my mother's favorite aphorisms: "Smile at your enemies; it makes them paranoid about what you are up to."

5—*Tuesday, February 7, 1888*

The next morning comes too early with piercing bright light. My poor feet complain about supporting even their own weight as I put them onto the floor. I soothe them best as I can with some cold cream I have on my nightstand before rolling my stockings onto them.

Also on the nightstand is the note I got from the Coal Syndicate. I read it again. By interpretation, if I go bonnet in hand, I can have my old job back, at a fraction of my previous pay, subject to good behavior. I smile. I pick up a pencil and write, "I wouldn't return unless you publically beg my pardon.

"I remain faithfully,

"Stella Ochoa"

I smile again at the thought of Mark Carlton apologizing. He's too big of an ass to have ever said sorry for anything. It is time for him to learn the pain of being a misogynistic Neanderthal with a dash of anal sphincter thrown in.

As I enjoy my response, I can hear the newsmongers outside my window. "'Tesla Announces Pilotless Airship.'"

I frown at the breakfast Madam Chapman has laid out for us. With no eggs or meat, I choose a piece of cold toast and slap some blackberry preserves on it. I dig through all of my roommates' outer clothes to find my heavy winter coat. I pull the fur neckline tight around myself before stepping out into the cold.

A new layer of snow, a bare inch thick, covers the ground. *Can't forget about the blizzard.* I think about the woman I met on the trolley yesterday. Fine flakes of white, the consistency of flour from a sifter, continue to fall. Tommy, good as his word, stands on the porch puffing out little bouts of steam and stamping back and forth. Looking over his threadbare clothes, I understand why. He has sixteen-odd layers on, but the best of them looks not even good enough as a discard from the rag bag.

"Hello, mum."

A little respect is a good thing, runs through my head. "I've got two errands for you today, Tommy." As I hand him the envelope I had slipped my response to Mr. Carlton into, I realize I hadn't addressed it. *Not going by Crown Post*, I assure myself. "Take this to the east gate of the Coal Syndicate. Deliver it to Mark Carlton. He is one of the managers. Put it in his hand yourself, don't give it to anyone else to deliver."

"Yes, Stella. I'll do it."

"Oh, and when you do, you might want to make sure you aren't within arm's reach of the man. He's likely to be sore when he reads it."

Tommy smiles.

"Next, I want you to meet me at the Bell in Hand tonight between three and five."

"Absolutely, Stella. Anything more?"

"Nope. Get on with you!"

At least he has shoes, I think, as the youngster speeds off, remarkably fast with the splint on his leg.

It's time for me to get on with my errands of the day. It is so much more convenient not having a day job sometimes. I pull my shawl over my *peineta* and the rest of my head before stepping out in the flurries. The cold soaks right through my shoes and stockings to numb my sores, helping me walk without limping.

The greengrocer is setting out his daily wares. I catch a glimpse of a sale sign on a hogshead he rolls out by tilting and rotating it. It reminds me that I have a dearth of materials to make my lunches. I cross the snowy street and slip under his awning.

"Morning, Stella," he greets me, stacking up the apples in the barrel.

"That's a right good price for apples, Mr. Bascom. Worms get in them?"

"No, but they only have another week or so to go before they turn. I don't have good storage for them."

I admire Mr. Bascom as a person. He doesn't hide anything from his customers, and he doesn't cheat on the weight. He might charge a penny higher than I might get things from elsewhere, but I know that it will be good quality.

"Why don't you give me five of those apples, a bunch of those carrots, a pound of cheddar cheese, and oh, give me a dozen pears. I'll take one of those with me. Can you please have your boy deliver them to my room? I don't want to carry them around with me today."

"No problem, Stella. On account?"

"No, I'll pay cash." I never charge anything. By always paying cash, I know what I can afford.

I make similar stops at the baker and the butcher, having a loaf of bread and a large stick of salami sent back to my flat—lunches for a week at least. I also tuck a roll and pepperoni stick into the bag with my pear for lunch.

The snow continues to fall but not heavy enough to erase the marks left in it by footprints, carts, or horse apples. The chuff of a steam-powered, snow-removal auto-train alerts me. I wait as the car and its connected coal carriage rolls by obliterating the white covering by blowing live steam at it. With a handkerchief, I daub at the worst of the brown splatter it throws in all directions. *Effective but messy.*

The trolley is almost empty by the time I climb on. The workers are already on duty, and the housewives wisely stay out of the weather. I undo my shawl and shake it free of the tiny flakes clinging there.

I have one errand before I meet with Lord Helms. My good fortune is that they are near one another. The Coal Syndicate has its main offices three blocks from Forever Power.

I exit the trolley in front of the black-granite edifice proclaiming "Coal Syndicate—Home Office." Bands of white and gold swirl through the façade, setting off the giant gold-colored lettering. It seems more like a castle from Frankenstein on a stormy night. I have to keep reminding myself that bad guys rarely wear a black hat as a sign of warning. People flow in and out of the conglomerate like ants to and from their hill. Businessmen in suits, bundled messengers, a pair of tradesmen carrying a ladder, a trio of naval officers, and more make up the continuous traffic. *Why not one woman in a gray rabbit-collared coat?* I ask myself.

I get into the queue to go through the revolving doors. Some adventurous person takes the close quarter's opportunity to pat my derrière. I whip around, but lucky for him or her, I can't identify the culprit. Just because I don't wear a bustle doesn't give anyone the right to paw at me. My glower must have set the blackard off. I get no other inappropriate advances.

The main floor looks surprisingly like the Forever Power offices, except there is a bank-like cage on the right where people line up to pay their coal bills. A janitor spends his time mopping up the snowmelt in the foyer.

Shaking my shawl out again, I walk up to the receptionist. This woman could be a clone of Karen Vasquez at Lord Helms's business. I will not make the same mistake I did with the other worthy. "Excuse me, miss. I'm looking to secure an appointment with Mr. Bruce Jasperson."

The woman looks me up and down as if counting every penny I spent on my clothing. "Your business?"

I fumble for a moment. She asks a great question. Do I just barge in and ask if he is behind the rash of demon escapes? Not very good form. "Competitive research," I offer. My conversation will have to revolve around motive rather than opportunity. Goodness knows that a man of his wealth could hire any number of intermediaries.

"Let me see if Mr. Campbell will meet with you. Mr. Jasperson is too busy to be bothered with such trivia." I swear she managed to say it with a sniff.

"Never mind, miss. Mr. Campbell won't be able to help me. If you can't schedule me in with Mr. Jasperson, then I will take a different approach."

"I'm sorry, ma'am, but without Mr. Campbell's approval, Mr. Jasperson will not see you." She emphasizes the final pronoun as if I am unworthy.

"Thank you for your time," I say with unceasing civility. No need to make her job more difficult. Securing my scarf again, I venture outdoors.

My mind spins, thinking of the step I didn't want to take. I know I can get an audience with Jasperson, but it means engaging with the one person I don't want to be around, much less ask for a favor—my mother. With many thanks to God above, I have more urgent tasks, not to mention seeing an acquaintance leave the Coal Syndicate building less than a minute behind me. His impeccable dress and coiffured steel-gray beard and mustache are unmistakable.

"Baron!" I call out as he moves toward his carriage. "Baron Cardiff!" I repeat when he doesn't pick me out immediately.

"Stella! How wonderful to see you here. I was just on my way over to Forever Power for our installation observation."

Mini alarm bells go off in my head. "How did you know about that?"

"Lord Helms sent a messenger to me last evening. He told me of your exceptional idea. Would you like to ride over with me?"

And all of the alarms shut off. I'm becoming paranoid. "And miss the joy of walking in the snow in heels?"

"No wonder your mother can't ever find you a match in society. Your sarcasm seems to know no bounds, nor station."

"It's one of the tools I keep sharp in my demon-fighting kit, Baron. I didn't mean to slice you with it," I say as he hands me into his coach.

The baron laughs. "Well, the damage is well and truly done. Just don't twist that knife." He bangs on the ceiling of his coach, and we set off. "So what brought you into demon hunting?"

I'm thrown by the sudden change in topic. "I didn't want to steal."

"Excuse me?"

"My mother makes her living convincing the earth that it belongs to someone else," I offer, pulling the travel blanket up to my chest to counter the chill.

"Ah, yes. *Doña Josephine Romero.* I believe I've met her."

"Possible that you have met, Baron. She spends a good deal of effort to rub shoulders with those at court."

"But what does stealing have to do with your mother?"

"I almost define theft as taking land titled to one person by right and custom, and giving it to another by magical means."

"I understand your feeling, *señora.*"

I can tell from his tone that he doesn't exactly agree, however. "So what brought you to demon hunting, Baron?"

"That's easy, Mrs. Ochoa. Money. After my father spent the entire family fortune trying to regain our English position, I inherited an empty title and an even emptier family coffer.

"Now I won't claim that the American Monarchy is the land of bread and honey that everyone touts, but it does offer economic opportunities that I could never have had back in England. I find that money is close to a substitute for power, so I have accumulated every dollar I can get my hands on." I'm saved the need to respond by the coach stopping. "After you, *señora.*"

I climb out from underneath the blanket and out the door. The snow has renewed its assault on the town. I stick out my tongue to catch an extra-large flake.

"Which reminds me, Mrs. Ochoa. This snowstorm will hit historic proportions late tonight. Make certain that you are well and truly in a safe, warm place with stores for several days."

"Really? You are the second to warn me."

"Yes, the storm will be severe," he says, taking me by the arm and leading me toward the entrance of Forever Power. "My powers as a witch and the leg I broke back in seventy-eight insists that it will be quite brutal."

"I thank you for the warning, Baron."

To my surprise, Lord Helms is discussing something with Miss Ankles...I mean, Miss Vasquez. "There you two are," Lord Helms says with the youthful buoyancy of three or four of Tommy. "And early, thankfully! This snow is going to cause some delays."

"Good morning, Lord Helms," the baron offers.

"Henry," I add in greeting.

"Yes. Let's not waste a moment. I have my staff preparing my poderabile."

"Huh?" I say.

"It is a mouthful. As you know, *poder* is the Spanish word for power. Maybe I should just call it a power coach?" Henry says, leading us into the maze of corridors. "It's something I invented. Edison and Tesla aren't the only ones to have ideas. Fortunately, I have the means to have it made."

We exit onto a second dock, a much quieter one than the loading area. Standing in the center is what looks like a tradesman's cart but with no traces to hook up a horse. It is painted a conservative gray with large gold lettering proclaiming, "Poderabile by Henry Helms (Inventor)."

Workmen are busy loading metal cylinders six feet long and eight inches across into corresponding holes in the back of the cart. There are an even dozen of these metal bottles in a grid. Only the stubs of their round ends stick out.

"Behold the poderabile," Henry says. "Come. Climb up. They will be done powering us up in just a minute or two."

I climb up into the seat to find no reins but rather two levers, both coming up through the carriage floor. "Baron if you will climb up the other side. I have to operate this beast in the middle."

"Lord Helms, you are loaded," one of his crew says.

"Thank you, George. I'll let you know how she handles."

"Is this safe?" the baron asks as he climbs into the seat beside Henry. He eyes the mechanics with trepidation.

"Hasn't blown up yet," Henry says, with a smile and a wink in my direction. He pushes both levers forward, almost like letting the reins of a horse go slack. A hiss like a steam engine releasing its pressure through a safety valve provides a backdrop. The carriage begins to ease forward smoothly, unlike the lurching start of a train. The hiss fades to a lower pitch and then suddenly a higher tone again, like the chuff of any steam engine before repeating. Henry pulls back on a lever, again like steering a horse, and it turns into street proper. The contraption turns to the right and gathers speed, the chuffing frequency increasing as we do.

"So I can tell you aren't using an earth spring to drive this," I say as we reach the comfortable speed of any other carriage on the road.

"No, too expensive. Also takes too long to tension the spring. I wanted something that could be recharged and ready to go on a moment's notice. Also, a spring constantly held in tension deforms and loses its strength."

"So you built a steam engine? Nothing more than a train without tracks," Baron offers.

"Not at all," Henry replies. "There is no fire in this vessel. No stoking required. The bottles you saw loaded are pressurized canisters of air that release gas, by virtue of these levers, over a special gearing mechanism of my design, and that propels us. Besides, the piston system used by trains is woefully inefficient." Henry pushes the lever further forward, and the van leaps forward to the speed of a galloping horse, and he still hasn't moved the lever beyond halfway.

"Are you planning on selling this in lieu of horse-drawn carriages?" I ask.

"I've thought about it, but the process to fill the pressure bottles is very large and bulky. I'd also have to create the infrastructure to support them. It just won't pay."

"Here we are," Henry says, pulling the levers back toward him. I'm thrown forward as our conveyance slows. The baron stays on his seat only because he leans on his cane that is braced against the dash. "Sorry. I don't use this enough to have perfected the finesse to operate these controls."

Picking myself up, I find that we are in South Boston, Dorchester Street. We have traveled across the city in a time I'd not thought possible. I can't remember crossing the Dexter Street Bridge. A Forever Power trade wagon with a normal brown mare at its front waits before one of the brownstones.

The baron looks a bit green, climbing down from the driver's box, but clenches jaws tight. The muscles at his temples work back and forth.

I hop down. I breathe hard in excitement. I take the time to adjust my hair and reseat my comb with a smile.

"We have a simple residential installation here. The summoner, Michael Christmas, has been working for me since we opened our doors."

As a trio, we walk up to the porch. Lord Helms knocks. A young woman, a babe suckling her breast, opens the door. "May I help you?"

"Yes, ma'am. I'm from Forever Power."

"I don't understand. The warlock is already in the basement, and the steam vessel has already been installed."

"I'm sorry, ma'am, I should have explained more fully. My name is Lord Helms, and I own Forever Power."

"Really?" She turns back toward the house and calls out, "Johnathan! Johnathan! We have Lord Helms here to install our demon personally!" The child lifts away from her breast and begins wailing.

"No, no, ma'am. We're just here observing."

She tucks the baby back down and bounces on her toes. She adds, rocking back and forth before murmuring, "Oh, well then, they are down in the basement. Take those stairs."

"Thank you, ma'am," I whisper as we walk past. "You have a fine-looking little one."

"Nice of you to say so."

The basement looks as they always have for decades on end, maybe centuries, with dirt floors and walls under rough-hewn beams. The only difference is the asbestos pad around a square metal water box strapped to the ceiling. Five lanterns light the space.

Any demon installation requires three basic components: a steam vessel, a capturing pentagram, and a summoning. I care not at all for the first, and honestly, the last one only matters with how powerful the defenses are. Fortunately for us, the water boiler and protective asbestos blanket have already been installed above the location. I need to watch the crafting of the pentagram.

Michael Christmas didn't live up to his name. His skinny body, almost a twin of Lord Helms's, might have made a hundredth of Saint Nick. He sees us come down the stairs but doesn't break his stride.

The man I assume to be the husband, Johnathan, gently swings a smoking censer with the pungent aroma of myrrh spilling out. Michael chants softly. I can just make out the Lord's Prayer. He flicks his holy water sprinkler, the size and shape of two serving spoons taped together, to splatter a large piece of butcher paper. "…And the glory forever and ever. Amen," he finishes.

I personally use Psalm 23:4, but to each his own.

Michael rolls up the tube into a cone. After dipping his thumb in holy water, he places the digit over the narrow end. Christmas pours the Italian chalk that Patty had packed into it. He walks to the smoothed earth and begins, "The angel of the Lord encamps round about them that fear him," as he pours the chalk from his spill. I watch closely as this is a mistake many new witches make. I rub my scarred ear. I didn't move slowly enough to draw a complete line, but this warlock knows better. He poured out a good, steady line. I can also feel the earth embracing the chalk, claiming it as its own.

"Put on the full armor of God, so that you can take your stand against the devil's schemes." Michael does know his scripture, moving with ease from one quote to the next. Also, I feel his control over the earth, binding the very core of the ground to the lines he draws. "But the Lord is faithful, and he will strengthen you and protect you from the evil one." After five repetitions, one for each line, he ends his pentagram at the starting point.

This starts another crucial step. Many novices stop the pour, but it must be continuous. Michael shows his experience and continues to circle the tips of the star. "You believe that God is one; you do well. Even the demons believe—and shudder!" The witch finally ends his pour and begins the second circle, the safety net in case all goes wrong, surrounding the first. "To you, it was shown, that you might know that the Lord is God; there is no other besides him."

Doing the slow, continuous pours take a steady hand and a patient witch. It may seem simple until you've cramped up arms and shoulders every day from just practicing. I roll my shoulders at the memory.

The warlock picks up his holy water sprinkler. "In the name of the Father," shake, "the son," shake, "and the holy spirit," shake. "Amen."

I don't approve of this last unnecessary flourish. I know many who use it, but those droplets can break the chalk lines. I at least give the installer credit for checking to make sure they haven't been disturbed.

Drawing the runes isn't especially tricky. You just have to know not to draw across the entire width of the chalk lines. Warlock Christmas used the silver-nib pen with the care of much experience. The strokes were crisp, deep, and easily readable to those who had studied Latin. One biblical quote of love for each line of the star.

"The Lord loves righteousness and justice; the earth is full of his unfailing love."

"May the Lord direct your hearts into God's love and Christ's perseverance."

"We love because he first loved us."

"Let all that you do be done in love."

"Anyone who does not love does not know God, because God is love."

And one each for the enclosing circles.

"Love is patient, love is kind. It does not envy, it does not boast, it is not proud. It does not dishonor others, it is not self-seeking, it is not easily angered, it keeps no record of wrongs."

"There is no fear in love. But perfect love drives out fear, because fear has to do with punishment. The one who fears is not made perfect in love." In all the writing, he never once breaks the outer edges. I usually choose Psalm 103:8 and 1 Corinthians 16:14, but that is only personal preference. Christmas's choices are perfectly valid. Surround the evil with love, and he is forever caged unless he learns to love, at which time he is no longer evil.

I have been so engrossed that I've forgotten my comrades. The baron looks bored. "Exceptional job," I whisper to Lord Helms, starting a hushed conversation. We don't want to interrupt the summoner's concentration. "No issues here," I say, dipping my fingers into the spare chalk just to double-check its purity.

"You don't need to see the summoning to be certain?"

"That circle would hold against anything short of Lucifer himself," I reply.

"Then you're satisfied?" I nod. "And you, Baron?"

"Personally, I think looking this over is silly, but I agree with Stella. This circle has been professionally spelled and should hold anything less powerful than a prince of hell."

"Then let's make our excuses to our hostess."

After polite noises to the nursing mother and her now sleeping babe, we exit. Outside, we climb into the power coach. "We'll be heading to a commercial installation next," Lord Helms says as he pushes the lever forward and merges into the regular traffic.

"Are we sure this is necessary?" the baron tosses in.

"I'd like to see one more," I say. "I want to make sure that the procedures are uniform across all setups."

"By all means," Lord Helms says, pushing his lever forward. The increase in speed forces me back into my seat. Henry has no fear as he races around obstacles, avoiding people on foot and dodging horse-drawn vehicles. He honks his horn as often as he pulls and pushes the levers forward and back to change speed and direction.

The baron leans out the side halfway through the trip. From the sounds I imagine he coats a goodly section of the street with with his breakfast. Smiling, I lean forward into the breeze like an air witch flying on the wind. I could ride this way every day.

Henry's reverse lever brakes us to a halt just in front of a Forever Power trade van. The bay mare looks up at us and whinnies. The building is Fredrico's Pizzeria, an establishment I know well, it being just eight blocks from my mother's home. This will be convenient as I need to talk to the wicked witch, literally.

"The installation here is a bit tricky. The demon will be heating the entire block of buildings and firing the pizza ovens. Because of the size, we need a more powerful demon."

Baron Snowden struggles down to the ground and snatches his kerchief to wipe up the remains of his lack of control. Even before I married, I learned never to push on a man's machismo, ever. I actually direct our host's attention away from the baron's discomfort.

"So, Henry, this entire block will be powered by one single demon?"

"Yes. Our demon finders have identified something similar to a viscount, or their equivalent lower-order noble. We feel that not only will this power the entire block but actually may be able to power all of the surrounding blocks if adequately vented. This will allow for future expansion, even without a new installation. Venting steam pipes is easy by comparison to summoning fresh.

"But that reminds me, we need to hurry if we are going to see this. Baron, are you coming?"

Lord Snowdonia had regained his dignity and about three-quarters of his facial color. "Absolutely, Lord Helms."

We walk down a narrow alley between buildings to find a stairway down.

"Our warlock here is John Quarrels. He's been with me for the last two years. One of my most expert installers," Helms says as he opens the rusty iron door. Its hinges are no better than the rest. The portal squeals like a schoolgirl with her pigtail dipped in an inkwell by a bully.

The witch, with his dark Spanish face, looks up from his preparations. His eyes go wide at the three of us coming through the door. He smiles and says, "Hello, *Señor* Helms. Coming out to do your random installation check?"

The hair on the nape of my neck stands up, and I have the urge to run away from John Quarrels as fast as possible. I have absolutely nothing to base it on. It isn't his appearance because, barrel-chested and swarthy, he actually reminds me of Carlos, the leader of my coven. But my deep-down feeling dares me to ignore it.

"Absolutely. Please don't let us interrupt, John." Henry begins checking out the piping, vent stack, and protective thermal break, leaving me in the spotlight of the man who sends chills racing up my back. He doesn't undress me with his eyes, as many men do, but rather he eyes me as a cat might eye a feather on a string.

"And to what do I owe the pleasure of a famous hellfighter attending me today?"

Franklin, possibly more pale in the face than he'd been on the street, jumps in with, "Oh, Stella Ochoa is known far and wide for her skill. I am not as well known. I am Baron of Snowdonia, also known as Lord Cardiff and leader of the Cannon Coven."

I have never seen the baron so humble, nor so effusive with his praise.

"My apologies. Two famous hellfighters are gracing my presence," John says.

"We're just observing, *Señor* Quarrels," I offer, hoping that the man will prove my instincts wrong.

"I encourage it," he says, handing me his card. I consider his hand about equivalent to the filth found in a public privy. I take the introduction by its very corners.

Master Earth Witch John Quarrels
Summoning, Casting, or Dispelling Demons
Earth Reclamation, and Construction
9A Seneca Way, Boston

Quarrels continues without noticing my reluctance. "Summoning a demon is a terrific rush. Having an audience heightens the sensations. But then I should get back to work."

"By all means," the baron says.

"*Señorita* Ochoa, would you care to hold the censer?" Quarrels offers.

"Perhaps Lord Helms would be more appropriate."

"Quite right," Henry says, climbing down from his inspection. "I haven't done that since our third installation." He loads the bottom half of the silver ball with charcoal already gray with heat. He pours salt over the surface before dropping a handful of the myrrh resin atop the salt. The smoke and teasing smell starts almost before he has completely sealed the censer back together. Swinging the ball on its chain like a clock pendulum, he nods to his installer. Quarrels has already laid out the butcher paper and loaded his holy water sprinkler, a massive ornate mace with enough runes on it to make a monk go blind. The gold cross on its front bears a mass of gaudy scrollwork.

No part of God's love requires ostentation. *He hath swallowed down riches, and he shall vomit them up again: God shall cast them out of his belly.—Job 20:15.* More reasons not to like this witch.

All that being said, his technique using the skull-buster and his knowledge of scripture prove sufficient to anoint the paper. I watch closely as he uses his christened-parchment cone to lay out his pentagram. I want there to be something wrong. I mentally beg for him to make a mistake. In the end, he performs with a skill I would have trouble matching. Likewise, his biblical quotations and writing in the chalk are flawless.

"That's that," Lord Helms says.

"Wait a moment, Henry, I'd like to see the summoning of this particular demon," I say.

"As you wish."

The hard part of installing an unholy beast is the wards. The relatively easy part is calling the demon you want by his true name.

Part of a witch's instruction is the tedious process of finding those names. Like fishing, you cast your name into the water of hell, and then you pull back on your line until it snags something or you get it back empty. An experienced witch can tell by the tug on the spell the size and power of the demon at the other end. If empty, you hook another name and cast again. Lord Helms has an entire cadre of witches devoted to sniffing out these names and providing them to the installers.

John steps high over the chalk rings into one of the voids between star points with a single page of paper in his hand. He kneels down and runs a bit of the raw earth through his fingers. I feel the earth respond as he begins to cast.

"By the Lord God, our Father, I call forth Seresphinix." The room shakes. Dust filters down from the ceiling. "Seresphinix, I demand you appear before me. Take form on this plane."

The ground within the pentagram center vomits forth as a slight, serpentine form that vaults upward where it clings to the ceiling. I can feel the heat roiling off its scales. A pair of six-foot-long tails lashes out, slamming into the barrier of goodness, which will be its cage.

John Quarrels steps out of the circles.

It's crocodilian mouth hisses, "RELEASE ME, HUMAN, OR SUFFER IN FIRES OF MOLTEN SUGAR POURED OVER YOUR BODY. ENDURE THE AGONY OF ACID DRIPPED INTO YOUR EARS, AND ENEMAS OF GLASS SLURRY FOR ALL ETERNITY."

"No. You are bound to serve the needs of humanity."

The form jolts forward to slam itself against its invisible cage. "LET ME GO, OR I WILL LIQUEFY YOUR ORGANS AND FEED THEM BACK TO YOU. I'LL PIERCE YOU WITH A STALACTITE COVERED IN THE FECAL MATTER OF A GOAT. I'LL GOUGE OUT YOUR EYES WITH MY FINGERS, AND WHILE YOU CAN STILL SEE, I WILL URINATE ALL OVER THEM."

"No.

"There, all done," John says. "What do you think, boss?"

The demon gently tests its new confines. "HUMAN! ATTEND ME!"

"Will you shut up," John barks.

"ONLY AFTER YOU ATTEND ME!"

"What do you want, spawn of evil?"

"I MUST GET A MESSAGE TO A HUMAN NAMED STELLAOCHOA. WILL YOU GIVE A MESSAGE TO IT?"

I jerk back from the door I'm about to leave through. Three sets of human eyes snap to me. I shrug, but now my innards are deciding whether or not to vomit.

"We would consider it," I offer, swallowing the vile taste in my mouth and moving closer to the protective wards. "What is the message?"

"GAZZUNREEP SAYS THAT HE COMES TO TASTE HER FLESH."

"Who in the hell is Gazzunreep?" Lord Helms asks to me rather than to the demon.

"We can talk about it later, Lord Helms," I say, tossing my head toward the door. He scowls at me but walks up the stairs. "Demon, I will ensure Gazzunreep's message is delivered."

"THEN ALL IS AS WELL AS IT CAN BE IN THIS FROZEN WASTELAND," the beast screeches in its high voice.

"Welcome to our world," the baron says from the doorway. "Hope that we never have to meet again."

John Quarrels winks at me as I push past Baron Snowdonia. Even the thought of Quarrels touching me makes me shudder. I have no time to waste on such thoughts. Black clouds circle Lord Helms's head. It takes fewer than moments before thunder rolls from his mouth.

"Mrs. Ochoa, would you now please explain why a summoned demon knows you by name?"

"Yes, do tell," Baron Cardiff adds, as he makes it to the street.

"Lord Helms and Baron Cardiff, I'm almost as surprised as you both are. First, Gazzunreep is a ranking demon from hell. As a thoughtless apprentice, I summoned him as my very first solo effort some years ago. The wards of an apprentice naturally didn't hold him." I lift up my hair on the left side of my neck, exposing the scarring. "This, all down my body, is the legacy of my carelessness. My proctor dismissed him back to his own hell before he could do more damage.

"Other than that, and a comment by a demon we fought just Saturday last, I hadn't given that demon more than a passing thought in the intervening years."

"Another demon said what?" Lord Helms asks, crossing his arms.

"He offered that Gazzunreep wants to taste my flesh and soul."

"You haven't made any pact with a demon?" Henry asks.

The baron chortles.

"Did I say anything funny, Baron?"

The baron comes to my defense before I can speak. "As you aren't a witch, you don't have our training, Lord Helms. Back in ancient times, witches tried to harness demons in elaborate promises, blood pacts, and even the promise of the witch's soul. It never worked as there is no such bond on the evil creatures. Only modern science has learned how to harness the beasts for the simple task of being a power source. In short, pacts or bonds with demons, in modern time, are a myth."

"Oh," Lord Helms says, his arms dropping from his defensive posture, and the righteous indignation fading from his face. Turning toward me, he offers, "Please accept my apologies for my manner, Mrs. Ochoa."

I throw him my brightest smile, "No harm done, Henry."

"Thank you, ma'am. In way of compensation, would you like to try my poderabile?"

"You mean to drive it?" I try to keep my schoolgirl enthusiasm down, but I think I bounce on the balls of my toes.

"Absolutely. There is nothing magical in it that requires more than a little instruction."

"Then, yes, please!"

Another Forever Power wagon behind its tired mare rolls to a stop. "Excellent timing, then. There are the firebox fitters to finalize the installation. Let's be off, then."

I can't get into the wagon fast enough. "Baron, are you coming?" I ask.

"No, thank you, Mrs. Ochoa. I will take a handsome cab back to my own carriage, so I don't...delay you, as I am traveling in the other direction," he offers weakly. I worry not for the baron's dignity.

"Certainly, Baron. Have a good day.

"So how do I make this work, Henry?"

"First, we put this belt around your chest," he says, lifting a belt from beside me.

"Excuse me?"

"My apologies again. I hadn't considered women when I put it in. It buckles through the loop on the other side."

I eye the leather belt. The height puts it right across my breasts. "Are you sure this is necessary?"

"Quite, Stella. It is essential if there are sudden stops."

I am not going to let a little discomfort take away this experience. I strap myself in just tight enough to call it buckled. "There."

"Now, we turn on the pressure lines with the two switches over your head."

On the roof are two knobs labeled with on and off. I turn both to the on position.

"That's the easy part. Now each of the levers controls the power to that side of the cart. Push it forward, and it goes faster. Pull it back, and it tries to go backward." Now I am not sure who is the excited kid as he eagerly explains his handiwork.

"So to turn, I pull back on the side I want to turn to?"

"Or push forward on the opposite side."

With some trepidation, I pull back on the left lever and forward on the right to move into the street. The wagon turns in place. In shock, I let go of the levers as they center themselves.

I can hear the smile in Henry's voice as he says, "Yes, that can happen. This cart can turn on a penny and then give it back to you in change."

I will conquer this, I think. I push both levers forward the tiniest amount, and the wagon starts forward, followed by its distinctive chuffing sound. The mare behind us snorts as we pull away at about the clip of a one-legged man without anywhere he particularly needs to be.

"Now straighten into the street."

I ease back on the right lever turning us back into the regular flow of traffic.

"Excellent. Give it a little more," Henry encouraged.

I ease the throttles forward enough that at least pedestrians aren't passing us. Two blocks in front of us, a hay wagon turns out of an alley in front of us. Panicked, I yank all the way back on both levers. We both lurch forward, Henry into the dash and me against the leather strap. My bosom bruises with the force of my body against the restraint. I now realize the purpose of the safety belt. Had I not been held, I would have fallen against both levers and shot us forward at a ridiculous speed. Instead, now we start backward. I let go of the levers, and the cart slows to a stop.

I twist my mouth to one side. "So, small motions are best?"

"Yes. Try again."

I experiment, slowly increasing the poderabile's speed. Every moment I puzzle out new idiosyncrasies of the vehicle. I fly by my mother's home like a goshawk chasing a crow. Too bad, but even if not strapped in, leaping off the carriage at this fantastic speed likely would have broken bones.

I find that changing directions while traveling faster is natural. Just the tiniest of tugs on one of the levers causes a horse-like turn. I turn left twice, taking me back toward my mother's. I make a final turn onto Chester Square, with mansions on either side of the extra-wide street. With some skill, at least I think so, I slow us down right in front of my mother's door.

I wince at the bruises I've earned as I reach up and turn off the pressure valves. "Thank you, Lord Helms. This has been more exciting than my first train ride!"

"You are quite welcome, Stella. Was there some reason we are stopping here?"

"This is my mother's home. I'm here to see if she can get me an audience with the head of the Coal Syndicate."

"Bruce Jasperson."

"Yes."

"You think he may be releasing demons intentionally?"

I snort as I unbuckle. "Are you that naive, Henry?"

"No, but I'd rather assume the best of person, even a competitor."

"He probably has even more to gain than us hellfighters, so naturally, I have to wonder."

"True enough. If your mother can't secure a meeting, let me know. In my position, I may be able to make it happen."

"Thank you, Henry, and thank you again. This was a treat."

"You handle this better than I do. Maybe I can hire you as a coachman...er, coachwoman."

"Don't tease. I am unemployed. I may just take you up on your offer. Have a good rest of your day, Lord."

"And you, Mrs. Ochoa."

# # #

I bang on Mother's door with the gilt, not brass, knocker the shape of a walled castle and only a bit smaller. The door opens to a short, swarthy man of dark hair in the traditional traps of a butler.

"Good morning, Miss Stella."

"Good morning, Ozias. Is Her Highness receiving?"

"Likely, miss. Can I know your business?"

"Demons, I'm afraid. I have some questions Mother may be able to help me with."

"Give me a moment, miss. If you will just step inside."

The foyer is tasteful in an overstated way, with Greek columns up each wall. A fiery fresco of the Earth's birth in volcanos and molten lava covers the ceiling. It is the last work of Thomas Gambier Parry. Several antique urns, purportedly from Pompeii hold dried ferns and grasses.

Ozias returns back to the hall. "Ms. Romero will see you in the solarium, Miss Stella."

The sunroom, as I call it, holds a small serving table amongst the growing greenery and the silver winter light. Even though nearly noon, the goddess of all sits in a flowing brocade dressing gown over her nightclothes. Even so, her blonde pixie-cut hair and makeup are as perfect as if she has just stepped from a salon. Adding to her wake-up outfit, she wears earrings of sapphire the size of my entire flat.

"Good morning, daughter," she says over the top of her tea.

I walk over and kiss her on her offered ivory white cheek. "Almost afternoon, Mother. Did you have a late night?"

"Count Anderman and his wife, Countess Anderman, had a party to celebrate their son's tenth birthday. Of course I had to attend. The adults stayed late playing whist and sharing information about the Royal Winter Ball."

"So wasting time and gossiping," I say, sitting at the chair pulled out by Ozias. He then sets a cup and plate in front of me. Toast, currant jam, and butter are on the table. My mother pours tea into my cup and then offers milk and sugar, which I decline.

"Dear, when will you learn that these sessions are rarely a waste of time? You learn so much."

"Probably about important things like who is taking whom to the dance." I roll my eyes.

"I detect your sarcasm, daughter, but knowing who is courting whom can foretell a shift in the winds of power."

"Of which I care nothing," I say, liberally spreading my toast with the red preserves.

"I know. I worry about you regularly about this and your lack of suitors."

That my vain mother would spend one minute about my wellbeing, beyond how it impacted her social standing, seems as unlikely as ever. "I'm assuming you already have a date. You never seem to have a dearth of men prancing about."

"Very true, daughter. I have my choice of paramours. This week Baron of Snowdonia has agreed to take me to the ball."

Coincidence seems to be stalking me. *And why wouldn't the baron have mentioned it to me?* Fourteen years separate them. My mother is definitely robbing the cradle. "Baron Cardiff? He's young enough to be your son."

"True, but he is one of the most eligible matches in Boston. Who am I to pass up any of his attentions?"

I try to unimagine my mother sweaty and disheveled in bed with Cardiff. "I'm sorry I brought it up. It's none of my business."

"So what about your prospects, young lady?" she says, picking up a piece of toast between immaculate, copper-colored nails. "Have you looked at finding a suitable match? I'd like to see you have some social standing and maybe even with some children of your own. I'm willing to help."

I smile about half as much as I might be able to if I really am happy. "Mother, we have this conversation every time I come over. If it is a way to keep me from visiting, it is working exceptionally well. I've told you before, I have no interest in becoming another man's property, so just put it out of your head."

"Perhaps," she halfheartedly agrees after clearing her mouth of the dainty bite she took. Feigning indifference, she asks, "What were you doing with Lord Helms?"

"Oh, no, Mother. Don't you even think of such a thing. Lord Helms is married. He is a business acquaintance only."

"So much indignation. Wasn't it Hamlet that said, 'The lady doth protest too much, methinks'?"

"No!" I say emphatically.

As skillful as any battlefield general, in the parlor my mother reigns supreme. She tactfully changes the topic. "Did I tell you I am to receive an OAM for services to the Crown?"

"Order of the American Monarchy? That's impressive for an English born woman, Mom." Still with a bit of steam built up, I needle her, "What did you do to get it? Take Prince Frederick the Third's virginity?"

"Stella Edwina Romero!"

Oh, all three names; I probably pushed it a bit far, I muse.

"I'm not a whore like that strumpet friend of yours."

"Sorry, Mother," I say, bowing my head in contrition.

"That's better. Forgiven. Forgotten. I'm getting my OAM for services to furthering witchcraft in our kingdom."

I choke on the bite of toast in my mouth. I'm sure the king is ecstatic with the dent she's making in stealing the Canadian lands from the English. "Excuse me. Must have gone down the wrong way."

"What is new in your life, daughter?"

I assume she doesn't want to know about my tryst with the "strumpet." "I got fired."

"Really?" I can't tell if her voice is hopeful or sad.

"Yes. The Coal Syndicate decided that taking off in the middle of the day to intern a demon wasn't in the corporate spirit."

"I think the filthy job was way beneath you anyway. Are you ready to join me in reclamation?"

I decide not to pick another fight. "No, Mother. I'm looking at other options."

"Demon hunting is a dead-end, dear. You can't rely on it forever. It won't be long before Edison figures a way to hold a demon indefinitely with no risks."

"Edison is in jail. He isn't going to figure out anything."

"You must have missed the late edition. He's been released, and all charges dropped."

"Goody," I offer with a good deal of sarcasm.

"Anyway, it is your business. I know you are talented in so many ways.

"So, this brings me to why you have visited me today; as you so rightly pointed out, you avoid my presence."

I feel the heat in my cheeks. Open mouth and insert foot, boot, and all. "Well, two things actually. First, I have had two demons in the last three days call me by name. Both wanted to give me the message that Gazzunreep is looking to come and have more of me. Have you ever heard of anything like that?"

"If it weren't you saying this, daughter, I would probably say, 'Poppycock.' But as it is, you, then I take your statement at face value."

A compliment? I wonder what she is planning.

"I've heard of demons becoming attached to people they have tortured, but never to the point of sending messages—threatening or otherwise. You might check with Professor Xena Xavier at the University of Boston. She is a demonologist and likely will have a more complete answer."

"Thanks, Mother. That helps. It was unsettling the first time, and the second I thought I might start my time of the month early."

"Don't worry too much about it. Gazzunreep can't reach you, and you won't go there, so it is a tempest in a teacup."

"OK, next, I need a letter of introduction to meet with Bruce Jasperson."

"The Coal Syndicate? Why? Please don't tell me that you are trying to get your job back."

I giggle. "Not likely, Mom. But what I do need is to talk to him about the increase in demon escapes."

"What would *Señor* Jasperson have to do with demons at all?"

"Mother, everything I've seen and discovered says that more fiends are getting free than in the past. They are hurting people."

"Daughter, I know you were traumatized by your accident as a young woman, but the welfare of the masses is not your purpose. You need to dedicate your life to improving yourself, not saving the little people."

"I promise you that I'm not sacrificing myself." I know my mother. She will not help unless there is something in it for her or me. "I'm working with Lord Helms on this. He's indicated he'd be quite appreciative." I manage not to lie.

"I would hope he would be. Ozias, please bring me my writing supplies."

"Thank you, *madre*."

As she stamps the request with her seal, she looks me in the eye. "Don't embarrass me, Stella."

"I'll make you proud."

# # #

With some confusion still rolling around in my head, I pick up the trolley on Tremont, just half a block from Mom's house. Ms. Ice Queen complimented me. She has always ridden me to excel. I can't remember a single warm word, and quite a number of bitter ones, about my dating and eventual marriage to Aaron. There must be something in it for her, but I can't figure the angle. My mind is occupied for the full forty blocks back downtown. I am so distracted that I notice the trolley stopping at Union Street just in time to hop off.

Pinhead-size snow drifts down in a fog as I step off the streetcar. It is melting as soon as it hits my hair, reminding me that I left my scarf at my mother's house. I only have to endure it for half a block. The gold light and raucous laughter beckon me to the Bell in Hand. Just as I am about to reach for the door, it opens in front of me. One of our regulars, Inspector Second Antonio Guizzetti, has Fisherman Bill in an arm lock and is walking him out.

"Mr. Mattingsly, you've had too much fun for this afternoon. I suggest you go home and sleep it off."

"Bu' I only wanna make swee' love wi' her."

"That's nice, Mr. Mattingsly, but she declined your advances. Go home."

I walk up and pat Bill on the shoulder. "Bill."

His head swivels too far before coming back to face me. His eyes take several seconds to focus. "S'ella! C'mon an' have a drunk wi' me."

"No, Bill, you have to go home. We'll have a drink another time."

Inspector Guizzetti smiles at me and loosens his grip on Bill's forearm.

"Ya. 'Nother 'ime. Le' me go, ya big dummy." He rubs his right wrist eying the inspector.

"Go home," I say, and I give him a gentle shove in the direction I've seen him leave most evenings. He stumbles off down the street, mumbling to himself.

"Thank you for your help, Widow Ochoa," Inspector Guizzetti says, offering his arm. "Shall we go in and enjoy ourselves, just not as much?"

"I'd be delighted, Inspector." If I were ever interested in getting married, Antonio would be in a tiny pool of candidates. He has intelligence, empathy, and, well, I'm not afraid to say it, he looks pretty. His bright hazel eyes, rimmed in black, set off his sharp Italian features, not to mention his tight, firm ass. All that being said, the thing that tickles me the most is his big hands, so out of proportion with his five-foot-one body. I take his proffered arm.

A Spanish guitarist playing in one corner has the rapt attention of half the patrons of the Bell in Hand. "Thank you, Widow Ochoa," he says, depositing me at the *Dos Campanas'* table.

"Antonio, will you ever be able to call me Stella? I deplore the moniker 'widow.'"

"And miss the chance to tease you? Where is the fun in that?" Antonio says with a broad smile. "You have a great evening." He releases my hand to meander back to a table with his own regulars. I watch his tight ass walk away.

"Forget about him and come snuggle with me, wench," Karie says.

Turning, I say, "Karie, what are you doing here?"

Karie sat in the booth with the only *Dos Campana* member there tonight, Donny. "Slumming. I had a rare night off, so I thought I'd come down to your watering hole and reintroduce myself, at least to Donny-boy here."

Donny's fair skin doesn't hide the blush that creeps over his entire face, about three shades less red than his hair. Rumor has it that Donny had something of a crush on my best friend back in the day. Sitting, I throw my comrade in arms a bone by changing the subject. "Hah! Is there a bar in town where you don't know every owner, barmaid, and regular in it?"

"Maybe in my misspent youth. But Donny has always been a special one," Karie teases mercilessly as she runs a finger over his shoulder. Donny looks to me for help. I shrug. I tried. For Donny's sake, I hope his girl doesn't show up while Karie is having her fun.

"Stella?" comes a tentative voice from over my shoulder.

"Tommy! Glad you are here."

"Sorry I weren't here when you showed up. I didn't think that barman would let me loiter 'round."

"And that is true and smart of you." I catch Michaeleen's eye and hold up two fingers.

"And who is this likely lad?" Donny asks in desperation to take Karie's attentions off of himself. Our bartender puts two pints down on the table.

"Everyone, I'd like you to meet Tommy. He runs errands for me now and is doing a bang-up job of it." Tommy pushes his chest out.

"Your boy Friday, eh?" Karie tosses in.

"Something like that," I agree. "So, Michaeleen, could you let him come in from time to time? He'd only be here if it is for me."

Michaeleen looks the boy up and down with something akin to a scowl. "You one of those steel plant boys?"

"Yessir." I see Tommy's Adams-apple bob, even if he does answer forcefully and keep his eyes on the Irishman.

"Ya willing to work?"

"Always, sir."

"Well, with Stella's permission and 'cause she spoke for ya, if'n ya wash dishes and clean up, I got a cot in the basement ya can sleep on."

"Really?" Tommy looks at me, and I nod. "Yes, sir! I'll clean good!" He looks at me somewhat suspiciously.

"I didn't set this up. Michaeleen has his own mind of who he gives work to." Tommy smiles from ear to ear. I continue, "But don't run off for the dishwater just yet, Tommy. I called you here for an entirely different purpose." I reach out and finger the threadbare fourth-hand cloth of his coat. "If you are going to be running errands for me, I want you well-dressed. Before the real dinner rush gets in, I want you to go to Roberto's *Ropero* on Portland, just north of Sudbury." I hand Tommy a letter that I'd written and sealed earlier. "This will tell Roberto what I want for you and that I will be responsible for the bill."

"Thank you, Stella," he says, snatching the note from my fingers.

"Scamp," I bark at him as he runs out the door. I turn to Michaeleen. "Thank you. I think you are doing a good thing."

His white skin can't hide his blush. "Blarney for all of that, woman. Me last dishwasher ran out on me. I'm gett'n a bargain if he be willing to scrub for just a warm bed."

I hand him payment for my drinks and turn back to my people to save the man more embarrassment over his generosity.

"So, what did you think about Her Highness?" Karie asks me while twirling one of Donny's short red locks with her fingertips.

"Who?" I ask, my mind still thinking about my mother.

"Lady Helms."

"Cold," I say, trying to keep my comments as charitable as I can.

"Really? I thought she might warm up to you."

"Why is that?" I ask, taking a pull of my ale.

"She's a known member of the seamstress's union."

"Huh? I get all my clothes from Paula Simpson. She's fast and cheap, and I don't think she belongs to any organization."

Karie sits up away from Donny to get closer to me. "Seriously, Stella? Boston marriage. Tribade. Invert. Fricatrice. Sapphos. The love that dare not speak its name—"

"Oh?" I say, finally getting her point. "I didn't get that impression. What about Lord Helms?"

"I told you before that theirs was a marriage of power and convenience, not love." Karie takes a sip of her brandy. "He visits me regularly, and she tips the velvet with any number of women in the Boston area and beyond."

"But then why does she act so damned jealous?"

"My dearest Stella, even though you've been married, you just don't understand the dynamic of those kinds of relationships. Lord Helms is her pathway to wealth and power. Any woman, or man for that matter, that might jeopardize that link must be dealt with all due haste and ferocity."

"Even say that you are right, and supposing that I did have designs on her husband, there is no way that the church would grant a divorce."

"My Star is so bright in many things and falling down in others. Let me play two scenarios out for you, mind you not the only ones, but two that have commonly been used.

"What if Lord Helms were to get his mistress pregnant? Then, as his frigid (at least with him) wife has given him no progeny, he declares the bastard his heir. His lover now becomes part of the household, at least obliquely. When the master dies, his son inherits everything, leaving his wife out in the cold."

"That's reprehensible," I spit out. Even hearing it makes me want to wash all over.

"Oh, there are much worse. How about the husband that goads his wife into public tantrums and fights over months. Then with a doctor, in good standing and an excellent reputation, declares her mentally unstable. The pair of them put her in an asylum, usually drugged so badly she can't speak coherently. A discrete amount of time later, his lover moves in and takes over the household as the new, wink, missus. This works exceptionally well if the husband moves because of the embarrassment of having a mad wife. The new neighbors are none the wiser, and if they do somehow find out, they understand the deception."

"Please tell me you are kidding," I say, shivering in my seat.

"I've seen each of those more than once, my dear friend. Oh, there are more and variations on the theme, mostly in the upper class. And we won't even talk about the abuses that are heaped upon women of lower station. This is one reason I buy my protection both publicly and secretly."

The table becomes quiet despite the raucous surrounding. My desire to never be owned grows about three sizes with this conversation. I will remain my own woman, period.

"I'm sorry, I guess that was something of a downer. I think I need to go back to nuzzling Donny-boy to brighten things back up."

"Ahhhh," the youngest O'Sullivan says with the intelligence of a youngster who hadn't quite made it to the bathroom in time.

Karie's eyes turn to the doorway. "Uh-oh. Here comes the party pooper."

I turn partway around to see Anna, Donny's girl, walk through the door, swaying her bustle like a streetwalker advertising. I swear Donny teleports three feet away from Karie.

Whatever venom I receive from her implodes on itself and focuses on my friend. "And who, may I ask, is this?" Anna asks with a hand on each hip.

Just brazen it out, Donny, I urge with all my thoughts.

"Ahh, ahh..." he trails off.

That's done the trick, my mental sarcasm replies.

"Get your paws off my boyfriend, strumpet."

"Oh, you can do better than that, m'dear," Karie fires back. "Bitch might be appropriate. I'd revel in the epithet whore, but strumpet? I just don't think you are doing yourself justice.

"But I can see I've worn out my welcome," Karie says, getting up. She changes her tone to a conciliatory one. "Donny has behaved himself. You can check with Stella. I was being a cockchafer just for fun. Be nice to him. He is a good kid." Karie struts over to the bar and inserts herself between two big men.

Anna's expression of pursed lips, drawn together brows, and narrowed eyes fall off of her face. She looks at me like a coon caught by a lantern.

"She really was just teasing him. Don't you know who that is?" I ask.

Sitting down next to her boyfriend, she replies, "No."

Donny looks uncertain. He starts to put his arm around her but then pulls back.

"That's Karie Taylor—"

Anna interrupts with, "That is Karie Taylor? The most notorious whore in all of Boston?"

"The same, and also a good friend of mine. And don't you go making any associations there. I am not a flat-a-back, nor do I have any designs on your man," I add as her confusion turns rapidly to loathing in my direction.

"Yes, she wants me," Maxwell Parker says, throwing an arm around my shoulder. He bends down and kisses me on the cheek like a brother might. The hair on the nape of my neck stands up as I feel the love of the lord flow off of him. I appreciate the timely distraction by his arrival.

Drops of snow fall off his shoulders onto me, giving me a shiver. I push him away.

"You're supposed to shake off in the vestibule, not on me, you *chocho*."

"And your mother, too," he says, his voice breaking in the middle.

"I can hope," I add.

As far as I can tell, Anna chooses to let things go. She snuggles right up to Donny. When I catch his eye, he rolls his eyes and lets out a sigh of relief.

The table chats and listens to the troubadour. He winds through some saucy Spanish tunes and some more liberal American music. Long about an hour later, we welcome Raquel when she arrives, her wavy black hair seeming to flow everywhere. It hides the baby opossum on her shoulder, but I've learned to look closely for her furry friends. I can also tell she has something moving around in her handbag. I pity the idiot who tries to nick something from her purse.

The young rake that enters the bar looks nothing like the scamp I chased out just ninety minutes ago. He looks like a young teamster in loose denim overalls, a thick cotton undershirt, and a greatcoat that just brushes the ground as he walks. I smile at the choice as he will grow into them. It also seems Roberto had lent the boy a comb.

"You look splendid, Tommy," I say as he walks up.

"I ain't had no fancy duds like this before, ma'am. Why are you doing this?"

"Doing what, Tommy?"

"Why are you spending money on me?"

Before I can answer, Raquel speaks up. "Tommy, is it?"

"Yes, ma'am."

"Well my name is Raquel. Before Stella answers your question, can you answer a question for me?"

"Sure, ma'am."

"What would you do for her?"

"Dang near anything, ma'am. Wouldn't kill nobody, if that's what you are asking."

I chuckle, and Raquel continues. "No, Tommy. She's not asking for you to kill anyone. But why would you do things for her? If I remember her story, just a few days ago, you were trying to steal her purse. So are you doing it just for the money?"

The boy blushed. "Well, some. I won't lie. But mostly because she treats me good."

"Now, can you answer your own question?" Raquel asks.

Tommy stood there with his mouth screwed up and one eye closed.

"Oh, don't strain the boy's brains," Maxwell says, "or you'll let all of the steam out."

"So, she does it to be good to me?" Tommy asks, not fully sure of himself.

"Got it in one," Max says with his voice muffled as his face is almost fully in his stein.

"Without expecting anything back?"

"An honest day's work for an honest day's pay," I say, smiling.

"Enough of twenty questions. I do have work for that pay I give you."

"Yes, Stella."

I fish out Mr. Quarrel's card from my handbag. "Can you read?"

"No, Stella."

"OK, there is a Spanish gentleman of the name of John Quarrels. He lives at 9A Seneca Way. Can you find that?"

"Ain't that south 'tween Dexter and Royal bridges? In them cheap flats up above the Forestall Cannery."

"Sounds like you know it better than I do, Tommy."

"Lots of us...I mean, lots of the steel plant kids would go there in the mornings 'cause they sometimes threw out fish that weren't good enough to put in cans."

"Good, you know it. I want you to go there and follow the man from 9A. Find out what he does, where he goes, who he talks to, and what they talk about if it doesn't get you into trouble. Report to me every morning."

"Yes, Miss Stella."

"Now, off to scrubbing pots with you."

For whatever reason, I feel tired. Even with not pulling a shift spelling soot and the sun just having dipped over the hills less than an hour ago. I stand up. "Folks, I'm calling it an early night. And don't forget, we've got some nasty storm coming in. I'd button yourselves up soon as well."

My crew, Anna included, wishes me a good evening. Karie seems to have taken off somewhere without letting me know. *More like taken off with someone,* I think. The woman can't go half a dozen hours without sex.

The white flakes are coming down hard enough that the streetlamps barely shine bright enough to see from one to the next, and certainly not enough to see unlit storefronts ten feet away. There is no street beneath my boots, only a thick carpet of white already halfway up my boot. I stumble over a loose pavestone I can't see. The combination of white of the lamps followed by the dark of night is disorienting. I almost miss my turn onto Stillman Street. It's made even worse as three of the lamps seem to have burned up their mantles. As only tiny flames that flicker in the sky like anemic lightning bugs, they don't give off enough light to illuminate even the ground beneath them.

While not so cold as to freeze mother's milk, the temperature does chill me even through my coat. I'm not unpleased to see a light shining through the parlor window of my boardinghouse. Inside, I find that I'm all white. To borrow a bawdy expression my husband used to use, I'm covered from bosom to buttocks. As I am relieving myself of my wet burden, Mrs. Chapman bursts into the anteroom, filling it with her sense of self-worth and brass.

"Widow Ochoa, I am not your answer service," she says, handing me an envelope. "And make sure you clean this mess up before joining us for dinner." With a "harumph" and a toss of her head, she storms away as fast as she had arrived.

From the wrinkling of the paper and the water stains on the envelope, I presume it has been steamed open. I must do something about that woman's incessant snooping. More than once, I've found items disturbed in my room. Nothing ever goes missing, but I feel like I live in a glass bowl.

I extract the message from within the envelope.

Mrs. Ochoa,

There seems to have been some misunderstanding between us. I would look favorably on you calling on me at the Coal Syndicate to discuss clearing the air and returning to our previous status.

Yours Faithfully,

Marcus James Carlton

I head for the dinner table. To ensure Mrs. Chapman doesn't miss any of it, I hold off tearing up the note and its wrapper until I enter the dining room. Without any pretext at subtlety, I slip the remnants into the glowing hearth and don't wait for them to blaze.

6—*Wednesday, February 8, 1888*

The morrow comes in bitter. I shiver under my covers, and my breath smokes white in the air. Mrs. Chapman must have let the central hearth go out. After two years, these lodgings kept getting worse and worse. My own fireplace is cold as I rarely light it. A banked fire downstairs is usually enough to keep the upstairs rooms warm enough to sleep.

In my nightgown, I crawl out of bed and wrap my dressing gown around me as goosebumps form. I set up some kindling in a teepee over a paraffin starter cone, and around them both I dribble coal I scoop from a small personal stash. My hands shake as I strike a long match and set it to the makings. The kindling sputters and deigns to fire, but the paraffin does its job and blazes up.

As I wait for the coal to light, I look out my tiny window, which under normal circumstances has a scenic view of the privy. Today, through the panes frosted from the outer edge in, I see nothing but white. I don't mean that metaphorically but rather literally. I can't see the row of houses behind us. I can't see the privy. I can't even see the hip roof five feet beneath the window. I see snow coming down in a steady cascade of chiffon, all but hidden within a thick, soupy fog. Peering carefully, I can catch, now and again, glimpses of the ground. The Chapman's robin-egg-blue privy looks like someone had poured a bucket of salt over a shot glass. Nary a peek of its blue paint can be seen.

Nothing happening today, I realize. I climb back into the warmth of the bed and watch the fire until I drift back off.

# # #

I wake to the muted sound of the piano downstairs playing "The Entertainer." I decide to stop being a slugabed, but the floor is still cold beneath my feet. I must have slept longer than I thought as there is naught but ash in my tiny hearth. I pull on my stockings and boots before anything else. As I pull my dress over my head, I notice that the snow continues to fall. After all my fastenings and a brush through my hair, I make my way downstairs.

Susan plays the "Maple Leaf Rag" as I come into the parlor. I can see only white out the windows beyond the porch. The sun manages to penetrate the snow and ice covering and light it up like a weak candle behind a frosted glass window.

"Buried up above the first story windows. I figure by dinnertime it will reach the second story," Susan says, stopping her play. She is wearing her winter coat and a sweater underneath that.

"Why isn't there a fire going?" I ask.

She responds in a prison whisper. "Her ladyship doesn't have a stock of coal. She claims her normal delivery didn't show."

I consider a few choice expletives and choose to keep them to myself. Instead, I collect my own coat. After that initial period where the cloth seems colder than the air, it helps make me marginally comfortable.

"Any bet our hostess has the last of the coal in her room?"

"I wouldn't doubt it," Susan admits as the clock on the mantle chimes twelve times.

My nap had reached epic proportions. My husband once told me after I'd fallen asleep subsequent to making love all morning long, "You must have needed it, Star." I guess the same applies here, if not in the same wonderful way.

"I take it no one has been able to get out?" I ask as Susan launches into some classical music I don't know the name of.

"Nope. Even though we can see out onto the porch, we can't get the door open."

"How about going out a window?" I ask.

"We never thought of that. How naughty. I used to sneak out the window on summer nights to go watch the boys skinny-dip. But Mama caught me one time and tanned my bottom so hard that I couldn't even wear bloomers for three days."

I smile at her story. "Well, I think trying to dig our own way out would be a last resort. Besides, I've got a small bit of coal in my room that should last me a day or two."

"Oh! Can I come share your hearth?"

"Sure. In fact, pass the word that tonight after dinner, we will all squeeze into my room for the night. Tell everyone to bring any coal or wood they happen to have to keep the fire lit."

"Should we include our landlady?"

"Should we include our landlady in what?" Mrs. Chapman asks as she comes out of the kitchen.

Susan's eyes are wide, and a flush comes to her pale skin. I think fast, "We are going to get together for a stocking darning party after dinner. Would you like to join us?"

"Thank you, no."

"So on a new topic, Mrs. Chapman, I assume we will get a refund of part of our rent? I mean, you are out of coal, a necessary ingredient to keeping us warm and alive."

"Heavens, no, Widow Ochoa. That is not my fault."

"The Duchess of Massachusetts may feel otherwise," I counter with a calm that should earn me a sainthood or at least count as one miracle toward canonization. "As the landlord, you are required to maintain emergency stores. It is a royal edict."

Susan, not saying a word, seems most interested in not being noticed. I know I can't count on any of the other women in our house to raise any objections because they are likely on the ragged edge of society. They are digging in their fingernails to hold onto what little they have.

"Well, I try, but the high price of coal makes it quite impossible. I don't even know why it is so pricey with all of those micks to dig it out of the ground."

I glower at the wrinkled woman who doesn't stop moving, fluffing pillows, brushing curtains—all the things that really don't matter. "If coal isn't in the budget we actually pay for, why not install a demon?"

"What!" Mrs. Chapman screeches as if she'd been stung by a whole nest of yellow jackets. She stops and hugs a pillow to her breast. "I'll not have such a filthy, ungodly, and unholy thing under this roof."

"I don't know how you would be able to tell with as infrequently as you attend mass," I toss back.

"I am a good Christian woman, Mrs. Ochoa. I would not have you slander me in my own home."

Maybe I did go a bit too far. I'll do the one thing the dowager never would. With a deep breath, I let out much of my anger. "I apologize, Mrs. Chapman. That was unworthy of me." I didn't duck my head in repentance, but I put the olive branch out. The woman's face looks like she had sucked out a green persimmon and intends to spit it out on me. Instead, she returns to her useless fussing.

"Well, I still don't know why the Coal Syndicate needs to charge so much when they have all those bogtrotters digging it out. Shouldn't be more expensive than a handful of sand."

"Well, I'll pass on your commentary to Mr. Jasperson when I meet him."

"You don't know the head of the Coal Syndicate," Mrs. Chapman accuses me.

"You are quite right, but I do have a letter of introduction to meet with him as soon as this blessed storm clears out."

"Well, it will be nice to have your poisonous tongue out of here," the old biddy barks at me. "You really don't know how to be a proper lady, now do you?"

"No, I don't, and obviously neither do you."

Ignoring a retort that I don't hear, I take the opportunity to turn in place and storm up to my room. *The moment I find a job, I'm going to find new accommodations. Swear to Jesus.*

#

I hadn't lied to the old bat. Hours later, I still am darning my stockings. With white thread in my hand, I poorly sew together holes in my leggings, now old enough to be just short of gray in color.

I oft wonder if I would have made Aaron a good wife. We'd only been married for a scant few months, and only weeks of that together. My cooking manages not to poison, but nothing better. Cleaning doesn't come naturally. I can barely throw a stitch. And I dress only well enough not to be stoned by other Catholics. My only natural talents seem to be sarcasm, witchcraft, and sex. In the long run, I truly wonder if that would have been enough for my husband. I will never know.

I take a bite of the salami sandwich I'd put together as I refuse to eat whatever dreck that crone puts on the table for dinner. Probably cold canned-beet soup and bread with no butter. A tiny tap on my door catches me in mid-bite. Not wanting to put my feet on the cold floor, I manage a muffled, "Come in."

The door swings open, and behind it is a full bevy of my other flatmates, all bundled in coats and wrapped in blankets. "Can we come in, Stella?"

"Absolutely, ladies, but don't forget your mattresses. That floor is bitter cold." Three of the five dart off to collect theirs. Susan Montrose,

Carmen Rodriguez, Pamela Atwell, and the sisters Isabella and Felicia Wolfe all manage to find spots on the floor in front of the cheery if low fire. I am rationing the coal to keeping the room above freezing but not much more.

"Thank you, Stella."

"Yes, this is most kind, *señora*."

What I know about my housemates can fit in the thimble around my finger. Often finding out about them seems to be more trouble than it's worth. Carmen is a schoolteacher. At twenty-nine, she is the eldest and the most prosperous of the five, although that isn't a high bar.

The two Mexican sisters work in one of the canneries down on the dock. They only make do because they share a room. Pamela works as a clerk's assistant at one of the mail-order stores.

"It is no trouble at all, ladies. Doesn't the good book say, 'You shall freely open your hand to him, and shall generously lend him sufficient for his need in whatever he lacks'?"

"Amen," several of the girls say quietly.

After another bite, I put down my sandwich and pick up my stockings as the women get settled.

"Here, let me do that," Susan says, reaching for my pile of work.

"I can handle it."

Susan holds up one of my mangled attempts. She cocks her head and opens her eyes wide.

"Oh, bother. I don't have this talent," I say, shoving it to Susan.

"Whereas I do. It is little enough payment for a warm room to sleep in."

Before I can say, "Darn," the five had divided my stockings, and all are mending my undergarments.

"Stella?" Felicia asks with her adorable Mexican, not Spanish accent.

"Yes?"

"What makes you brave enough to stand up to *la capulla*?"

The other women titter at her profanity.

"It is as simple as I hate bullies, Felicia."

"We don't like them much, either, Miss Stella," Isabella says before biting off the end of the thread, "but we can't fight her. If we—"

My tone changes to something much more serious. "I understand, Isabella. Ladies, if something happens to you, come to me, and I may be able to help. I make no guarantees, but I will do my best."

"You see, I have means beyond my salary. I choose to live here for economy, rather than necessity, so *chocha* doesn't hold any whip over me." Several more giggles punctuate the room.

"What about Maria?" Pamela asks.

"That goes for Maria as well. If any of you know where she is—"

"Last I heard she was at the Appleseed Inn." I shudder. Compared to the Appleseed, Chapman's is the Parker House.

"I'll make it a point to see her as soon as we all can get free from our white prison."

7—Thursday, February 9, 1888

"Look, the snow has stopped!" one of the girls squeals while jumping up and down. No decent human being should be awakened in this way, especially this early. At least five more bodies in the room warmed it up.

The extra-bright, winter sun streams through the window showing the messy disaster our impromptu sleepover created. The smell of day-old chamber pots of six women definitely gives the air a twang.

"And someone is outside with a shovel! We're saved."

Such drama, I think. I get up and look. It is like our city doesn't exist. Mounds of rippling white are almost all you can see in any direction with only one movement to give any indication of life. Below me, a youth digs his shovel into the drift piled against the back of our boardinghouse. I rub the sand out of my eyes and look down again. It's Tommy, and he is at the drift like a dachshund digging for a badger.

"Alright, ladies, let's get dressed and meet our savior."

Easier said than done, I realize belatedly. My room is the only habitable room. Six women all trying to get on petticoats, boots, and over-gowns turns into laughing chaos. Swirls of lace, brocade, and cotton cover nearly every cubic inch of my undersized lodging. At least we aren't freezing while taking eight times longer than usual to get presentable. Fortunately for us, Tommy continues to dig even after we have all our buttons fastened.

"Mrs. Chapman, we have a guest about to join us," I say as I enter the kitchen. Our landlady wears six extra layers of clothes and a quilt over her shoulders like a second robe. Medusa herself had dressed the woman's hair.

"What!" she screeches. The harridan rushes into her first-floor room off the kitchen.

While bitter cold, the face that emerges from the hole sweats profusely. Damp, sandy-brown tangles fall below a roughly knitted cap on the head that pokes through a small hole in the piles of white. His Cheshire cat grin greets me.

"Tommy, you are a lifesaver."

"I just did what I could, ma'am. It was Michaleen's idea. He give me the shovel and told me I could make some money diggin' folks out."

"I believe you will. C'mon and finish that hole big enough so I can greet you properly."

Tommy spends another fifteen minutes, making a hole big enough to walk in. His reward from me took the form of a massive hug and a kiss against his sweaty forehead. I think he manages to get a real kiss from a couple of the girls.

"Mrs. Chapman, I think the boy should be paid for his labors," I say to our landlady, who rejoins us in a day frock and a scarf covering her unkempt hair.

"I should think not! I didn't hire this—boy."

"No thanks for an entrepreneurial young man that has saved you grief?"

"Coal and kindness—you must think me made of coin, Widow Ochoa. I have no pension to keep the gold coming in."

I can't get over the woman's intransigence. An unchristian part of me hopes that the hottest part of hell has a seat with her name on it. "Do you want to be able to use the privy? I suggest you hire this young man to dig it out."

"No chance. We will move the snow ourselves."

"With what? Brooms? Look at it this way, Mrs. Chapman. There are seven full chamber pots. If you don't get a path cleared to the privy, your mixing bowls and china are next to be filled. Or do you expect the ladies to squat in the parlor? Or maybe out in your backyard?"

I can see the horror on her face at each option. She turns to Tommy. "Two bits if you'll dig a path and uncover our outhouse."

Tommy smiles and looks at me. I give him a fractional shake of my head. With him looking at my face, I roll my eyes upward without giving the *chocha* any idea of my communication.

"Four bits, mum," Tommy counters.

"Three, and that's my final offer," she barks.

"Thank you, mum. I'll get started right away." As he passes me out the back door, he shoots me a smile that I thought would crack his face.

"Tommy, after you're done, I'd like to talk with you."

"Yes, Stella."

It takes the rest of the morning to clear a wide path down through the snow almost six feet deep. It looks like a shaved-ice Grand Canyon. The girls draw lots to see who will go first. I give up my second place in line to chat with my young friend. I stand out in the cold with my arms wrapped around myself.

"I'm sorry I didn't get here yesterday, Miss Stella."

"Do you think I'm angry? Far from it, Tommy. Going out in that storm would have been close to suicide. Be smart rather than following any letter of the law. You did the right thing."

"Thank you, Stella," he says with a blush as he looks down.

"Now, I think you need to go make a few *pesetas* shoveling other folks out. Don't worry about Quarrels until tomorrow. That end of town won't be getting any clearing out anytime soon. In fact, I doubt anyone will be getting out anytime soon."

"I've already taken care of it, Miss Stella. I got Mikey to watch him for a nickel."

"Really? You shouldn't take advantage of your friends like that."

"Heck, Mikey thought she was fleecing me for the nickel."

"Something to think about."

"Miss Stella?"

"Yes."

"Who is the brown-haired girl with the green eyes that lives with ya here?"

"Felicia? The Mexican girl?" I don't think, I just answer.

"Thank you, ma'am."

"Why do you ask?"

Tommy flashed as red as he's ever done in the past. "She done kissed me like she wanted to eat my tongue."

I think about it for a few minutes. "Be very careful, Tommy. Felicia is a lady. You can be a gentleman if you work hard at it, but you need a few years to grow into it. I'll even help you at it if you want."

"Thank you, Stella. You know, stealing your purse was the smartest thing I ever done."

# # #

So I was wrong. I am big enough to admit it, at least to myself. I figured the snow-removal auto-train couldn't possibly cut through even the standing snow, much less the depth of drifts. In that part, I commend myself for being right. What I haven't considered is using fire witches to knock the rest down.

A throaty roar and a sizzle, like on a teapot about to boil, first alerts me to my mistake. Still unable to see anything from the ground floor, I go upstairs and look out the upper windows. From almost two hundred feet away, I can see flames lapping at the snow and gouts of steam over on Charlestown Street. The condition travels east to west in a very methodical manner, about the speed of a walking woman. As it reaches Stillman Street and some of the snow melts off the top, I actually see a fire witch blasting the snow into water and even more into steam with controlled jets of flame. Very tricky. Yet another use for a fire witch.

It makes sense that they will clear the major streets first. I wonder how long it will take before they clear off a little pug of a road like Stillman. With a bit of scouting, I see two more fire witches doing clearing, and a small army of young boys, each armed with a shovel, dig out the privies of many houses in the neighborhood. After freezing my tail this morning on the frozen wood of our two-holer, I envy those who have indoor plumbing.

I decide not to wait for someone to clear out the road. If the major streets are open, then likely the larger businesses will be as well. I need to get my letter of introduction to Bruce Jasperson. There is no chance the trolleys are moving, so I'll have to use shank's mare. Fortunately, walking can take less time than waiting for trolley connections.

My optimism seems to be misplaced. Just getting out of the trench Tommy dug to the latrine takes multiple tries. I have to get on top of the snow to make my way to those cleared streets. Even worse, when I get to the top, my boots sink into the ivory surface all the way up to my nether regions.

Upon extricating myself, I find only two ways to travel. I could roll like a kid might on a small hill. This has issues in that control of my direction seems haphazard, I get dizzy very easily, and I can't roll up drifts. Or, I could crawl on all fours like a small child or someone imitating a dog. While humiliating, this proves the most effective.

I crawl the two hundred yards to Charleston, thinking my ordeal over. I slide down the Stillman Street drift onto the surface of the road, only to find my feet without a purchase. I skitter across the ground on my fundamentals. Lying there with my buttocks bruised, I realize the snow melted to water by the fire witch has frozen into a solid layer of ice. The few people around don't laugh at my situation. More than a few are sliding on their own backsides along the ground. Others spend their efforts in a struggle to stay afoot.

With skill few people have, I call the earth up to me, shattering the freeze with a loud report. The now rough surface allows me to stand, just in time to feel what seems to be a mist. It puzzles me until I put out my hand to find it being covered in sand. A dirigible, a mere dozen feet above the nearby buildings, drifts up the street, sending a shower of grit down. No matter how smart covering the slick surfaces with sand is, I am cold and covered in snow and earth. I'm not a happy camper. I take a deep breath and then two more. The blimp, farther up the street, no longer drizzles me in grit. *I can deal with this.*

I lick the sharp, tiny bits of rock off the back of my hand. I then urge all of their brethren to depart my person for the safety of the earth below. Like insects escaping a dog being immersed in flea dip, the tiny bits of rock jump off of me and land on the ground at my feet. Some, like those who had gone down my collar and others into my brassiere, take more circuitous routes to the ground that tickle. A short shiver, and I am free of the pestilence. With my dignity and mood restored, I continue on my way.

As expected, the major thoroughfares are clear of snowdrifts, but only those required for the basics. My ordinary cross streets, Haverhill or Beverly, look like a scene dreamed up by a cartoonist of Santa's Village at the North Pole.

I don't know how the newspaper managed to produce an edition. Still, a boy stands on the corner of Charleston and Causeway calling out, "Read all about the blizzard. Seventeen known dead." I give the boy two cents for the penny paper whose headline, with no great surprise, reads "BLIZZARD" in a garish font that fills the page above the fold. Walking even on sanded ice requires a good amount of concentration, so I tuck it into my marketing bag to look over what the muckrakes have to say later.

With great care, I make it to the offices of the Coal Syndicate, only falling on my arse one more time. With the bruises that promise to purple nicely, it is a good thing I don't have a husband, or he might wonder who is beating me.

I come through the revolving door and into the warmth. I close my eyes and luxuriate for a moment as senses return to my limbs and fingers. I stamp up and down to remove the excess snow that coats me like confectioners' sugar on a donut.

I recognize the man behind the receptionist's desk and wonder if

I should just leave. It is the Squirrel. I forget his name, but it is that officious bumpkin that didn't want to pay me my final wages.

Without looking up from his something on his desk, he says, "I'm sorry, ma'am, but there is no coal available here or for delivery until at least next Thursday."

"Well, then it is a good thing I'm not here for coal," I say. The receptionist looks up and wrinkles his long nose like he smells a garbage scow. I am not my own best friend as I twist the knife with, "What? Demotion to reception duty?"

"For your information, madam, because of the storm, we are shorthanded. We are all filling in where we can." He does manage to mangle the honorific into something you might scrape off the bottom of your boot with distaste.

"Ah, I see then that you have found a job befitting your skills—one that even a woman could do."

He turns red enough that I expect a steam safety valve to pop open on the top of his head. "Madam, I am certain you didn't come here to insult me. What can I do for you here today?"

"Oh, trust me, the abuse is just a nice bonus. I'm here to see Bruce Jasperson."

His demeanor changes, and he guffaws. "I'm sorry, madam, but Mr. Jasperson doesn't just invite in an ex-employee that wants to bend his ear. So if you will just leave now, I can get back to legitimate business."

"I'm not here as an ex-employee, weasel-nose. I have a letter of introduction from Senior Mistress Witch Josephine Romero." The poor bastard's ego has to be on the verge of shattering. I've beaten it with several sledgehammers. A senior mistress or master is not someone to cross. They hold not only power in magic but also almost inevitably have pull at court as well.

"May I see the letter, please?" He eyes it for a few moments verifying my story and the implied threat. Handing it back, he continues, "In that case, I must inform you that Mr. Jasperson is completely booked today."

"I expected so with the crises this weather has created," I offer, letting up on the sod. "Can I please get on his calendar tomorrow?"

"There is exactly one opening in Mr. Jasperson's schedule tomorrow. It is a fifteen-minute appointment at eleven o'clock." He looks like he'd rather be swallowed by a whale than give me the slot.

"That would be fine, sir." I watch him write my name into the appointment book. With the options of the icy wind outside or the chill I've received from the Squirrel, I choose the elements.

# # #

Despite the cold, I have one additional responsibility on my way home. I all but promised to look after Maria Marin, the woman Alice Chapman threw out for the crime of being pregnant.

Charles Street is major enough to be cleared but hasn't been sanded. I walk in the snow under the eaves of the buildings, where possible, to get some purchase on the ground. Where there is nothing but ice, I call for tendrils of the earth beneath it to crack through to give me a walking path.

The hotel that sits catawampus from the city jail is the most run-down building in town, if you ignore the old hand canneries on the south side. Fortunately, the snow camouflages it in a veneer of respectability. I walk into the lobby, expecting to need a delousing afterward. The aged gentleman behind the desk has enough soot on his forty-year-out-of-date frock coat to be a chimney sweep. On the desk is a long chunk of blackened pipe. "Excuse me, sir, but I'm looking for one of your guests."

"Shore, missy. Who you after?"

"Maria Martin."

He reaches for the ledger with hands as grimy as his coat is dirty. He stops short when I give the name. "Oh, that one! She already done left."

"Oh? Couldn't she pay her bill?"

"Naw. Nothin' like that there. That Maria girl left and happy of it."

"I'm confused." Now, I can imagine being happy about leaving this place. I can't wait to leave now. Did she have another option?

"Twern't none of my never-mind, but she seemed right happy. Some feller showed up with flowers and went to her room. They come down, oh, 'bout twenty minutes later. I be thinkin' I saw a shiny ring on her finger when they climbed into that fancy rented rig he done brung with him."

Her man did right by her. It is about time something went well for Maria. "Thank you, good sir."

I make haste back to home as the chill starts to get under my coat.

8—Friday, February 10, 1888

Even with five other girls warming my room, I shovel the last of my coal and dust on the fire as the Mission Church bells strike four AM. It is enough so that morning is almost comfortable.

"Blizzard shuts down city! Coal orders go unfulfilled! Trains buried!" I hear through the windows. All of this I actually already read in yesterday's newspaper I splurged on. What the voice tells me is that our street at least has been cleared.

Tommy waits actively for me. He's cleared the rest of the porch of the storm's white carnage. "Good morning, Tommy."

"Morning, Stella."

"How did you make out yesterday?"

Tommy gave a grin that could engulf an entire pumpkin. "I definitely lined my pockets, ma'am. 'Course those fire witches made even more, chargin' twenty dollars to clear a block. But I ain't unhappy, miss, atall."

"Are you so rich you don't want any more from me?" I tease.

"Ma'am?"

"Well, I've not heard word one of what I asked you to do for me and that you farmed out to one of your mates."

"Sorry, ma'am. Mikey says that Quarrels dug himself out and visited the privy. None of them snow-melting witches came anywhere near his place. Then he spent two hours in line at *Cocina de Salchicha*, it was the only place open, where he had a chorizo breakfast sandwich with egg—"

"That is extremely detailed, Tommy."

"Mikey wanted me to get my nickel's worth, and I want to give you everything you need."

"This is exceptional, Tommy. Keep going."

"Thank you, Stella.

"Quarrels then went directly to McGreevy's 3rd Base Saloon where he gets a beer and plays some billiards. Mikey says he played with some dandy of a nobleman, pretty as a new dollar bill."

"Must have been the baron—Baron Snowdonia. He is the noble that calls that his hangout."

"Probably, ma'am. Quarrels won a big bundle on that one game. Mikey said she seen at least four twenty-dollar bills in the stack. But they only played one game. Quarrels went down to the Black Sea. That's a place where—"

"I know what a brothel is, Tommy."

"Yes, ma'am. He went into three of them houses before staying in Big Bertha's for eight hours. Mikey says she couldn't go in 'cause they might make her a whore. It's about the only thing Mikey is afraid of. She don't want to be no whore."

"That's good thinking."

"So she waited outside. When Quarrels come out, he stumbled drunk back home and probably went to sleep as the light in his apartment went out.

"How was that, Stella?"

"Excellent. Now I want you to stick on Quarrels for now. Oh, and here," I say, handing the youngster five one-dollar coins. I even wonder why I am being such a spendthrift. I usually make every penny count twice. Now I'm not even working, and I seem to be spraying money around. I need to figure out who is releasing this chaos onto my city.

"Miss?"

"I want you to go back to Roberto's and pay him for your clothes. I'd guess it will be about a dollar. The rest is just in case you have to do something for me that takes money. Like what would happen if Quarrels got in a hack?"

"Prolly do like Mikey done, jump on the back of the cab, and hang on. We do that sometimes to get places quick."

"Well, use your judgment. I'm not made of money. Just let me know when you use it."

"Yes, Stella."

"Now, off with you before Quarrels wakes up from his hangover."

"Yes, ma'am."

So, Quarrels met the baron, eh? There are few enough witches. That the baron and Quarrels know one another is meaningless. I still have nothing that proves anything. I have a hunch I need to follow up on.

Aaron's pocket watch says I have enough time to visit Lord Helms if I don't dawdle.

#

"I'm sorry, Miss Ochoa, but Lord Helms isn't on site today. As is his regular schedule, he doesn't come in on every third Friday," says Karen Vasquez in the lobby of Forever Power. Something niggles at my memory about every three weeks.

"Bullocks," I curse. "Maybe at home?" I mutter under my breath. The thought of encountering Helms's wife doesn't appeal to me. But this is too sensitive to leave in the hands of someone who isn't privy to Henry's concerns. I'd be breaking a trust.

Karen cocks her head at me as I sit there, mumbling under my breath. She leans over the desk and whispers, "I would bet a good portion of my salary that he is home sleeping off a late night."

"Oh?"

"I think he has a mistress that he visits on those occasional Thursdays 'cause on the following Saturday, he always comes in with a big smile."

Lightning strikes when I remember Karie telling me that Lord Helms is a regular.

"That's more helpful than you know. If you are ever at the Bell in Hand, I'll stake you to a drink or five."

"I may take you up on that. Is there anything else I can do for you, Miss Ochoa?"

"Nope. Have a great day!" I call out as I bolt out the door. It takes me less than three minutes to hail a cab. I give him Lord Helms's address.

#

"Good morning, Miss Ochoa," the Helms's butler greets in a manner that seems to indicate he has all day to offer the salutation.

"Good morning. I'd like to speak to Lord Helms if I could."

"I'm sorry, madam, but Lord Helms is still asleep. I would be glad—"

"That's alright, Bastogne," I hear Lady Helms say from behind him. "Please let in Mrs. Ochoa and see her into the solarium."

"Yes, madam.

"Mrs. Ochoa, if you would follow me?"

"Thank you, Bastogne."

He leads me through a segment of the Helmses' home that the Chapman Boarding House would rattle around in. The candle budget to keep the house illuminated must be more than I make a month, or used to make. The orange light gives way to the brighter gray sunlight I just left. Glass proves to be the only roof and also encompasses an entire wall. The moisture in the air and the greater warmth in the room I find luxurious, but the tropical plants everywhere catch my breath.

I love gardening, but never had a place to do it. I gawk at everything, totally missing my hostess and her guest, both seated on white wicker chairs across from me.

"Mrs. Ochoa, would you join us for tea or perhaps coffee while we wait for my husband? I've sent Bastogne for him."

I nod, taking one of the other chairs.

"This is my good friend, Miss Ruby Cartwright. Miss Cartwright, this is Stella Ochoa, a business associate of my husband's."

"Very pleased to meet you, Mrs. Ochoa."

"Likewise." Ruby is an attractive woman in a tall, willowy package. Her skinniness makes me think of a refugee from the potato famine. But her designer dress, immaculately-coiffured, black hair, and jewelry, assure me that she definitely belongs in high society, not in third-class on an immigrant ship.

I really am not trying to snoop, but I can't help but notice a smudge of dark red lipstick on Ruby's neck just under her right ear. It isn't her own shade, but it does match the color worn by Lady Helms. To make it even more clear, a long blonde hair peeks from beneath Miss Cartwright's collar.

"Tea?"

"I'd prefer coffee if you don't mind. Black."

"Certainly." With the dignity of a woman of her stature, Lady Helms pours me a cup from a silver set.

I can't stand it any longer. My eye keeps going back to that smudge. "Miss Cartwright, if you will excuse me." I stand up with the napkin from my place setting and I move toward her. She flinches at first but then relaxes as I gently wipe away the misplaced color from beneath her dark black hair. I draw the hair out, too, letting it fall to the floor. I show Ruby the color I'd removed. To hide the evidence, I wrap it up in the center of the napkin that I wad into a ball.

Ruby's pale skin goes four shades of red. Lady Helms's turns a bit more crimson.

"Ahem. Blueberry scone?" my hostess offers, trying to cover her discomfort.

"That would be nice."

Ruby gathers herself. "What business brings you here today, Mrs. Ochoa?"

I sip on my coffee and luxuriate in the richness I only get at Karie's. "I think I may have some good information for Lord Helms's investigation."

"Really?"

"Yes, but it would be imprudent to share his secrets."

"That is a good course, and I can tell you would make a good friend," she says, looking me right in the eyes. I smile.

"As I have some of my own, I find that keeping people's secrets is the best course of action."

Ruby's shoulders settle down from around her ears. Both ladies relax as I don't seem to have a problem with their evident liaison. More important, they feel that I likely will keep my mouth shut.

We exchange some small talk. Lady Helms is quite the horticulturist, giving me some background on some of the plants around the room, most from out of the country. Ruby is knowledgeable about the theatre, giving me a review of the comic play "The Schoolmistress." Her description and Lady Helms's quoting of lines cause me to laugh enough to make my sides ache. I wonder why I'd ever feared my hostess.

Lord Helms comes into the room, interrupting our fun. While properly dressed, his narrowed eyes look like someone lined them with a mostly burned twig. His hair looks like a haystack. His gritted jaw reminds me of the occasions my husband had imbibed too liberally from the Bell in Hand. "Mrs. Ochoa, may I ask why you are here at this ungodly hour of the morning?"

"Actually, my husband, it is well into middle morning." As if to punctuate her statement, a clock somewhere chimed ten.

"My apology for showing up so early, Lord Helms." I give the other ladies a knowing smile. "I have some news and a question about our joint project. Is there somewhere we can talk?"

"Come with me, Stella." He walks something like a zombie.

"Thank you for a nice coffee," I say to my hostess. "And nice meeting you, Miss Cartwright."

Lord Helms leads me to a library and closes the door after me. "It is quite soundproof in here, Mrs. Ochoa. What have you learned?"

"Well, first a question, if I may. In your research into finding the original problem in your company, did you collate demon escapes vs. installers?"

"Partially. As soon as I found three different installer names, I figured it was random. I never even got close to finishing."

"Was John Quarrels one of the three that you found?"

"Yes, but only one of them. What do you know, Stella?"

"It is little more than a hunch right now, Lord Helms. His manner set my teeth on edge, so I had him followed." I relay what I'd heard about his encounter with Franklin Cardiff, Baron of Snowdonia.

"Hmmm. It does sound a bit off, but playing devil's advocate, it could be nothing more than a friendly encounter with a high stakes billiard game. I've been known to indulge in the sport myself."

"True. I'll be following up but want more information from your records."

"I'll go in today and complete the comparisons. Would you like to help?"

"I am sorry, Henry, but I can't. I have an appointment with Mr. Jasperson."

"Head of the Coal Syndicate."

"That's right."

"OK, if you will wait just a few minutes, I'll drop you by there."

"That would be very kind of you, Henry."

# # #

Lord Helms remains quiet on the carriage ride in. I try to puzzle out if it is because of the hangover or if I have somehow done something wrong.

"Do you think Jasperson may be behind this?" Henry asks out of the blue.

"I don't know. He has something to gain if demon installations go away. He could gain a great deal even if he just embarrasses your industry. But do I think he is orchestrating this? I don't know and won't speculate other than I want to investigate the possibility."

Henry lapses back into a silence that holds for the rest of the ride.

When his driver opens the door for me, Henry says in a melancholy voice, "Thank you for all of your help, Stella."

"While I didn't do it for you, Lord Helms, I do find it pleases me that I'm helping a good man."

"Not so good as I'd like to be."

"The only man that managed that feat was our savior, Jesus Christ. Try to be the best person you can be."

I still can't puzzle out what is going on in Henry's mind, but that isn't my problem. He isn't my husband, father (and I scoff at that thought), or my employer. Let his wife deal with the man's mood. I have other fish to fry.

I once again enter the Coal Syndicate's corporate offices. Fortunately, the Squirrel is no longer at reception, and instead, a woman in a man's dark suit sits there.

"May I help you, madam?" she asks as I come forward.

"Yes, I have a meeting with Bruce Jasperson at eleven o'clock. I'm a bit early."

She opens her planning book before looking up at me. "I'm sorry, madam, but there is no one scheduled for eleven."

"Excuse me? I saw the Sq...I mean, the receptionist yesterday write into that very book."

The woman is fair. She turns the book to me, and amazingly the spot for my appointment time is empty. I look a little closer and see the abrading of the smooth paper fibers. "If you look closely, miss, you will see that someone has erased it."

"True, there is an erasure here, but that could be for any number of reasons." I do understand her point. My anger isn't directed at her but rather the pathetic excuse for a man I dealt with yesterday. "Are you alright, madam?"

"I'm angry at an officious little *idiota*. But that has nothing to do with you. Maybe I should just start at the beginning." I rummage around in my purse and draw out my mother's message. Handing it to her, I say, "My name is Stella Ochoa. I have a letter of introduction from Senior Mistress Earth Witch Josephine Romero to Bruce Jasperson. When would it be convenient to meet with him?"

She unfolds the paper and reads the entire note and even examines my mother's seal. "If you would take a seat a moment, Mrs. Ochoa, I'll see if Mr. Jasperson can see you at eleven." She waves to a runner, this one a young girl. She whispers in the girl's ear. The runner sprints away. My mother would be appalled at the lack of ladylike decorum.

Even with that, my mind is swimming on something in the receptionist's ledger—Franklin Cardiff, Baron Snowdonia, next Tuesday afternoon. What does it mean? It could be totally innocent, but with what I already suspect, it raises the stakes. My mental processes flip from one extreme to the other—guilty, innocent, proof, circumstantial.

"Mrs. Ochoa?" the receptionist says. "We've cleared your appointment for eleven, so Amy will take you right up."

"This way, Mrs. Ochoa," the young runner says, leading me back to a baroque split marble staircase with gilt handrails. "Watch your step on the stairs, ma'am. They get mighty slick with the melted snow."

Even with the warning, one of my boots loses purchase on the white stone for a brief moment. I prudently place my hand on the railing. Amy brings me not to Mr. Jasperson, but rather to another waiting room, thirty feet tall with proportional redwood doors accentuated by drab gray stone streaked with black. The name Bruce Jasperson is in gold, twenty-inch-high letters. "Mrs. Ochoa, for an eleven o'clock appointment, Mrs. Conover."

"Very good, Amy. Welcome, Mrs. Ochoa. If you will have a seat, Mr. Jasperson will be available in a moment."

I honestly think each of the banks of six embroidered, gilt chairs are worth more than Mrs. Chapman's entire boardinghouse. Pulling my dress up underneath me, I perch on the forward edge. I don't even get the chance to really work into a good thinking session when the great doors open, and an accountant hustles out.

"Mrs. Ochoa? Mr. Jasperson will see you now."

I think I'm going to need help opening the door, but the massive thing opened easily, if slowly. The room beyond seems six hundred feet long, but it is an optical illusion. Fluted columns of gray rock veined with black, each a little smaller than the one before, seem to grow out of a floor covered in the same material. They line the green, velvet-covered walls, which aren't square but rather angled to give the illusion of depth.

A painting twenty feet tall is covering the vast majority of the far wall. In the canvas, the portly subject wears full black-and-white court regalia. The desk is monstrous, at least as wide as I am tall and at least twice that long and made of shadow-colored teak. I mentally contrast this ostentation to the Spartan office of Lord Helms and wonder what Mr. Jasperson is compensating for. And then I see the man. He does stand out in a bright yellow suit. I guess that he might top five feet until I see the sloped floor, and then I lower my estimate. If his short stature isn't enough, he is likely half as wide as he is tall.

Without saying anything, he waves to a pair of plushly padded chairs in front of the desk. When I sit in one, I find myself a few inches lower than any other chair I've sat in. Conversely, his chair seems to be on lifts, making him appear to tower over me.

"Good morning, Mrs. Ochoa." If his figure is short, his voice belies it with a deep, sonorous baritone. "Your letter of introduction from Senior Mistress Witch Romero is quite impressive. How do you know her?"

"She is my mother, Mr. Jasperson."

"Really. You picked an exceptional lineage. I've used her services more than once."

I give him a smile that would be the right size for a horse. "I wish I really had a choice, Mr. Jasperson. My mother and I don't see eye to eye on many matters."

"Isn't that true of most parents and offspring? I find nothing unusual in that. I have two sons and a daughter. Half of the time, I wonder if they are plotting for my power and fortune."

"I'm sorry to hear that, Mr. Jasperson."

"Well, that is often the way of things when you are wealthy," the pudgy man says, pulling a cigar from a silver case. With a cutter from his vest pocket, he snips off the end, letting it fall to the floor.

"I never considered that, sir."

With an ivory lighter, he fires the end of his Havana, puffing out a pair of clouds. With some effort, I don't cough. "Yes, well, be that as it may, Mrs. Ochoa, what can I do for you today? The letter is rather vague. Perhaps you are here to find employment? I don't have any work for a witch—you are a witch?—at this time, but in the future—"

"Yes, sir, I am a witch. In fact, up until earlier this week, I did already work for you, in your soot remediation bins."

His friendly demeanor changes to dark with the rapidity of a summer storm. "So, you are here to complain?"

"No, sir. While I did have some issues with your foreman, Mark Carlton—"

"A bumptious man, that one, but if he misses the royal soot removal quota, he will definitely get an earful. He is family; what can you do?"

"Ah, yes, sir. Actually, my business has nothing at all to do with that. I am a member of the *Dos Campanas*."

His calm, cheery façade has returned. "Ah, a hellfighter. You surprise me, Mrs. Ochoa."

"It takes all kinds, Mr. Jasperson."

"That it does."

"I wonder if I could ask you some questions about demon escapes."

"Well, you may ask, but I'll be blunt in knowing less than nothing about demons or how they are caged. I focus on my products, not those of an insignificant business that likely won't even be around in a fortnight." He sucks on his cigar and then blows out a smoke ring.

"Really, Mr. Jasperson? You don't worry that they might dig into your business?"

"Not at all. Look at this," he says, standing. He actually loses height as he takes to his feet. He slides open a wooden panel on the wall to reveal a chart with several lines on it. He points to the dark line, which, with a few minor dips, is moving upward rapidly. "This is our demand. It is almost growing out of control. I've had to go to three shifts in the mines to keep up. In fact, I'm about to open three new shafts, blessed by your mother, in Centralia, Pennsylvania."

"Congratulations, Mr. Jasperson. It sounds like your business is on solid footing," I say, not mentioning the other curves on the graph. I play the dumb female to put him at ease. One line, net profit, seems to be dwindling despite the upward growth of the gross sales. I may not have learned much at Harbor Primary School, but Mrs. Hogarth did teach us to read a ledger sheet and graphs.

"Yes, now if I can only get the trains running again, I will actually be able to bring in product."

"I can see that the storm really impacted you."

"Yes, we only have room for about three days of stores in town. Everything else needs to be brought in by train from our storage lots in the Duchy of Connecticut."

"I can see your problems, sir. I know neither your time nor patience is infinite when you have a crisis to solve, so I want to redirect our conversations to demons."

I think I catch a glimpse of irritation. The president of the Coal Syndicate quickly covers it as he says, "Well, I don't believe I've ever seen a demon, nor am I interested in their impact on our business."

"Well, in confidence, Mr. Jasperson, the number of demon escapes has increased dramatically lately."

"Another reason the demon industry won't be around too much longer. Why risk death and destruction when you can have safe coal delivered to your home at a fraction of the cost."

"As you say, sir. But there will be those who would think that as the direct competitor of demon installations, you would have the most to gain by having their names smeared with bad press."

Bruce laughs. The quivering of his flesh under the banana yellow suit distracts me. "I won't even get angry at the implication, Mrs. Ochoa. As I mentioned, I have multiple transportation issues, which we may at least mitigate by purchasing the Boston & Providence Rail company. I'd be pleased if you would keep that quiet, Mrs. Ochoa. The deal is penned but could be affected by an increase in stock prices."

"I have zero interests in railroads, sir, and even less in investments, so your secret is safe with me."

"Thank you. As I was saying, I have multiple transportation problems and a labor dispute with my mining workers. They threaten to put down their tools unless...Well, just say that they want more than we are willing to give. These are real problems, Mrs. Ochoa. Honestly, demons and Power Unlimited don't even raise up to the level of a nuisance."

"I see your point, Mr. Jasperson. Do you have any idea who could or would be behind something of this nature?"

"While I know little of the issues, two things come to mind. First is that the entire concept of permanently trapping a demon is in itself flawed. Or, if you would excuse my return impudence, that hellfighters themselves have a vested interest in the escapes of demons." He leans back in his chair. The smugness as he puffs on that foul cigar sets my teeth on edge.

"That's fair, Mr. Jasperson. I definitely had considered both. I have only one final question for you, sir. How do you know Franklin Cardiff, Baron Snowdonia?"

"I don't recall ever hearing his name, Mrs. Ochoa. I mean, it is possible as I know a great number of people, but it doesn't dredge up a face."

Do I detect a slight change in his arrogant visage? I have caught him in a lie. Mr. Jasperson is one of the few self-made men in high finance without a title. To get there, he had to have schmoozed everyone in high society, and the baron can't be ignored or missed. "Thank you for your attention during this trying time. I hope your issues get resolved to your satisfaction."

He smiles. "Never forget that removing difficulties just leaves room for others, Mrs. Ochoa."

# # #

As I walk back toward home, I ruminate over what I just heard. I don't know what to think about Bruce Jasperson other than he feels like someone selling patent medicine. He tells you the truth on one hand and inflates what it will do with the other—all the while picking your pocket. I have to assume that the charts he keeps in his own office are the God's honest truth. He carefully pointed me to the line of total sales. He then failed to mention that even with significantly higher sales, his company's profits seem to be falling. He also faces a possible labor dispute of some kind. Those can be nasty as the ironworker's strike of '79 showed. These indicate that the Coal Syndicate well and truly isn't in the robust shape he touts. If I add the appointment of Baron Snow—

So lost in thought, I don't immediately react when the basement of the building a hundred feet in front of me fountains upward into the street. The roar of an explosion, the report of shattered glass on both sides of the road, the clatter of fractured stone blasting off the walls and ground, and the high-pitched scream of a demon threatens to deafen me. This is a first for me, a demon escaping in my lap. It is a first I would rather not be involved with.

Talons grab the edges of the newly created hole. They thrust a pointed-beaked, red visage, roiling with heat, into the breach. The malevolent yellow eyes look both ways as it tries to wriggle its shoulders through. When they don't fit, it screams again and tears fifty score or so bricks from the masonry wall to widen its escape.

Finally, my brain kicks in and spurs me to action. A teen is standing next to me, gawking just as I had been. I grab his coat while digging into my purse. "Boy, I need you to run for help." He still gaped at the scene, I assume with the same surprise I had experienced. I cuff him stoutly across the head. I pull out a silver dollar and press it into his hand. "Get to the Mission Church and tell them to ring the hellfighters with 'Prince Street.' Take a cab and tell the driver to hurry. Lives are at stake."

Wide-eyed, he looks at me in earnest, "Yes, mum!"

He's a good lad. I see him waving at a nearby cab just on the large Causeway Street square. I turn back to the disaster unfolding in front of my eyes. The birdlike demon rips his eighteen-foot body free of the building. It turns, screeching at the building as if it alone had been its captor. Showing strength that belies its skinny arms, it shoves the three-story stone structure over into a dust and snow billowing heap. I see people struggling within the wreckage. The monster leans over with its head and plucks up a woman in its beak like a robin might a worm. Blood cascades over her dress and body. Her mortal shrieks join the general chaos everywhere around. The beast swallows her in a quick gulp, petticoats and all.

I have to do something to mitigate the insanity, but without my team, I am not sure what. I remember Carlos once telling me that any action is better than no action. I pick up a bit cobblestone from the ground and lick the icy bit. I can feel the street beneath me hibernating in the frozen winter. I wake it from its slumber with apologies and commands.

Like a conductor, I raise the stones and earth up around the gigantic, humanoid demon. I form a deep bowl, almost a tankard, to surround it. Moving enough earth to fill a four-story building is a strain that makes me feel as fragile as my creation. The creature proves me right as it punches through the thin wall, tearing a rent in the side the size of a trolley car. Stepping through, the bird-like beast eyes a fleeing victim. The man bleeds through his suit pants as he hobbles away from the center of the disaster. Without someone else to block for me or tease away the beast when it focuses on me, I can't afford to direct its attention toward me and live. One of the creature's four great talons slams down on the man as if crushing nothing more than an insect. It picks up the tattered remains and flings it into its beak, putting shut to a life with a clack.

I set aside the guilt of letting these people die to come up with a plan. *Anything is better than nothing,* rings again in my head. I ease a path through the earth beneath the creature toward the nearby harbor. The earth transforms from solid ground to a sticky, liquid-like mass.

The demon snaps the chimney off an adjacent building and tries to eat it. Its squawk indicates its displeasure. It regurgitates the clay and stone onto the ground as if it is feeding its young. As it gets a look at people running away to the south, it turns, lifting one claw from the muck I'm creating beneath it. My efforts will take more time. I can think of only one thing to keep it in place.

In a clear voice, I call out, "For we wrestle not against flesh and blood, but against principalities, against powers, against the rulers of the darkness of this world, against spiritual wickedness in high places." I point one arm focusing the feeling of my lord and savior into my open hand. The bolt of love, weak compared to those that I've seen Maxwell summon, shoots out and strikes the beast in the back of its feathery head. It hisses as it snaps its head around to face me.

Instead of running away, I run toward it to keep it in place. "Repent, then, and turn to God, so that your sins may be wiped out, that times of refreshing may come from the Lord." I feel the heat roiling off its feathers and skin as I get closer.

As one claw slams down on the ground, I don't find myself jelly, but rather between two of its toes. Backpedaling, I dodge to one side as its beak streaks down to make me its next snack. Duck and weave become my only means of survival. Seconds, minutes, or even hours pass before my muscles burn with every move. I pant and wheeze. Every action is forced upon me to give the water time to turn the ground into more than a mud puddle. But how long has it been? My energy is failing me. My adrenaline burns off enough to allow a claw to barely miss me. So close does it come that it rips my *peineta* from my hair; I know it is time to retire. This time I dodge out instead of aside. Two more evasions get me far enough from the creature to take in the scene without risk of imminent death. It is waist-deep in a growing pool of quicksand, and I am out of its reach.

I bend over and rest myself with my hands on my knees, head hanging down. I am knackered.

"What the hell, over?" calls the voice of Raquel. I hadn't even heard the Mission Church bells ring. I still don't know how long I'd danced with the beast. I don't have enough breath in my lungs to answer.

"What the hell?" asks Carlos.

"What in the great wonder of God?" Maxwell says, his voice breaking halfway through. "We won't ever get it out of that!"

The beast roars as it claws at the earth to escape his gooey imprisonment. I stand up. "I bloody had to do something," I shout. "It was slaughtering people."

"Looks like he didn't do too badly on you, Stella," Maxwell says, pointing to at least three places where my skin stood agape and blood flow liberally. I start to feel the pain of wounds I never knew I'd received. "I'll take care of it." The warmth of God's love flows over me, and the pain eases to a manageable level. Max manages to patch my skin down to just some minor scars. They join the rest I bear, but can't do anything about the rent down the left side of my dress, nor my ruined underthings.

"Damn," I say, pulling the ragged edges of the bloody fabric together under my arm. I let them drop. "Nothing I can do about it now."

"Well, what do we do with this mess?" Carlos asks as he walks around the flailing demon now sunk up to its chest. "I don't see any way we are getting it out of there and put back."

Raquel says, "Normally, I'd say just send it back to hell, but if you do, you are going to leave one hell of a gaping hole, effectively blocking Prince Street."

"I think that only really leaves destroying the thing."

I nod my head. "I'm good with that."

The now fully assembled *Dos Campanas* stand in a circle and link hands. "Shall we use Psalm ninety-four twenty-three?"

"I always liked that one," Maxwell says.

"That is an exceptional choice, Donny," Carlos agrees. "Donny, if you will lead us, please?"

Donny starts us off, although, like everyone in our profession, we all know our Bible from front to back and in reverse. "He has brought back their wickedness upon them and will destroy them in their evil. He has brought back their wickedness upon them and will destroy them in their evil." As we chant the verse, the parts we can see of the creature become less tangible and smeared, like a chalk painting in a downpour. It screams and claws toward us, but even more now can't reach.

After six repeats of 94:23, we all hear a sound like a hoof stepping into a deep puddle of mud, "Glop!" The demon disappears, and the muck closes in on the place he vacated.

Destroying a demon has different effects on different witches. Some it mightily fatigues. Others, like me, it fires up like a shot of pure adrenaline. Despite my earlier exhaustion, I'm now ready to take on a whole army of demons. However, like the drug rush I mentioned, there will be a reckoning. Long about six hours from now, I'll crash, and crash hard.

"We'd better see what we can do for the victims," I say to Maxwell.

"Agreed."

For the rest of the afternoon, I move earth to expose the injured... and the dead. A horde of volunteers shows up now that the demon is no longer a threat. I don't blame them for remaining out of sight during my battle, as none of them have any skill against the unworldly. They all show their bravery and heroism. Even with my assistance with the larger pieces of stone, the rubble is a dangerous place. Cutting edges of metal and even superheated steam lurk for the unwary.

The only coward here is me. I feel the weight of each body we lay out on the street for the coroner services. I manage not to cry or fall in on myself, but I don't know how.

Shortly after sundown, Carlos takes me by the shoulders and cups my chin until he is looking me directly in the eyes. "You saved a lot of people here today, Stella." I don't say anything. I can't with the mass of my guilt. "You didn't kill them, Stella."

"But I could have saved them."

"I've looked it over. The only way you could have saved those people would have been to sacrifice yourself."

I start to leak tears. "I could have—"

"At which time," Carlos forcefully interrupts me, "it would have killed dozens or even hundreds more. You saved people." His tone softens. "I know you, Stella. I've fought beside you. You are no coward. You had no choices."

I wrench my face from his hand and look at the ground, more tears dripping from my cheeks. "I…"

"Stella, you need to talk to your confessor. Let him know what happened. He can tell you if you were right or wrong. In the meantime, you need rest. Go home and get some sleep. We will finish up here."

#

I don't remember stumbling the seven blocks up Prince Street to St. Leonard's in a numb haze. Father Juan shovels snow on the steps of the church. Dropping his shovel to the ground, he rushes to my side. "Stella? What's wrong?"

An analytical portion of my mind decides I must look worse than I even feel. "Father, I…I don't know, but I sinned so horrifically I don't know if God can forgive me."

"Come with me, child. We need to talk, but first, let's get you out of the cold." Father Dubois puts his arm around me and my torn dress. He leads me inside, bypassing the nave and into the rectory. The walls are lined with dark wood, giving it an ominous feel until it opens onto a whitewashed kitchen. "Mrs. Caledon, please bring this poor child some of the soup that's been simmering on the stove."

A dark, heavy woman curses him in Spanish, but soon I have a mug of a hearty, steaming tomato soup in front of me.

"Drink it," he commands, shrugging off his heavy coat. Somehow, he's also gotten my tattered overcoat off and hangs them both up to dry near the cast iron stove. I choke back a whimper and drink. The warmth I didn't know I've lost flows into my chest, breaking up the emptiness that has taken up residence.

"Now, daughter—keep drinking—" my confessor says. I drain the mug in several more gulps. "Now tell me what happened, daughter."

A stream of Spanish invective comes from Mrs. Caledon. I still can't focus enough to even translate.

"Quite right, Mrs. Caledon. If you would be so good as to take her to one of the spare rooms. And if possible, get her some clothes to cover her."

The older woman all but picks me up out of my chair and leads me away.

9—Saturday, February 11, 1888

Sharp morning light pierces my eyelids as if it were an icepick wielded by a crazed lunatic. Moaning, I flinch away from it. Irritation from grit in the corner of my eye won't let me bury my face in the pillow for more sleep. My head is pounding like the morning after my sixteenth birthday. I'd been toasted too many times in absinthe the night before. I never touch the stuff anymore. I ease myself into a sitting position dabbing at the dried-on crust on the corner of my mouth.

As I wipe the sleep from my face, I start in the realization I'm not in my own bed. The bare brick walls, tiny room, and lack of any adornments at all identify my location in a broad sense.

I don't remember disrobing, but an outer dress lays over a simple straight-back chair with my boots underneath. The bells of St. Leonard's chime half past some hour as I struggle to connect to my last memories.

As a leaden block might fall to crush anything beneath it, images of the dead laid out along the street, filthy from rock dust and smeared blood, mash my spirit. My responsibility hangs on me. I dress into the strange gown without enthusiasm. It hangs on me like a tent, but I don't care. A portion of me just wants to wallow in my own guilt, but I can't be that selfish. I must accept my part in the tragedy and perform some penance for my failure to put others before myself. I don't know what service could lift me up to redemption, but Father Juan certainly will.

I follow the smell of frying bacon and find myself in that kitchen that on further reflection is rather cheery, with herbs, garlic, and onions drying from hooks in front of a crucifix. A fire crackles in the hearth. The beginnings of what looks like beef brisket are being assembled on a butcher-block counter.

"*Buenos dias, Señora* Ochoa. I trust you feel better this morning?" says the Hispanic cook, with her hands spreading the rub over the brisket in sure motions.

"Some, yes, ma'am."

"Sit. Breakfast is just about ready. Father Juan will be here as soon as I signal him."

"I'm sorry I've forgotten your name."

"*Señora* Caledon, but just call me Maria," she says with a smile. She is a whirlwind. She pours water and tosses in a bay leaf before covering it. She flips the bacon on a cast iron griddle. She puts the big pot of brisket over the hearth fire instead of in the perfectly good oven. Wiping her hands on her apron, she sits beside me.

"*Dime.*"

Odd that I should have to pay for breakfast at a church, but I don't flinch. I dig into my coin purse and pull out a pair of nickels.

"No. I mean, tell me. What has you in such a bad way, *señora?* I see many people visit Padre Juan, but they seem *débiles*—weak. You are a strong woman."

I look at the floor before mumbling, "I did something horrible, and people died."

"*Murió?*"

"*Si, señora.*"

"I don't see it. You don't have the look of *el diablo.*" Without malice or accusation, she stands and goes to the stove. She rings a dinner bell. Maria scoops dripping hot bacon onto a plate she pulls from the oven that is already heaped in pancakes. "Set places for Father Juan, yourself, and me, *señora.* Plates are in the cupboard there," she points with her elbow. "Coffee cups over there, and silverware in that drawer beside you."

I make myself at least moderately useful by setting places. I even take a vase of flowers from the windowsill and place it betwixt the three settings. To finish, I put the pot of coffee on a dishtowel on the table.

Father Juan saunters into the room. "Smells wonderful as usual, Maria."

"Smells can be deceiving, Padre. Eat first."

Father Juan smiles at me as we sit. "Blessed be these gifts so that we may stay strong in your service."

"Amen."

I'm thankful neither the padre nor Maria are meal chatters. My inner voice still hasn't fully made up its mind what it wants me to feel. I think talking right now would make me feel nauseous. Both my hosts dig into the food with a gusto Karie applies to sex. I guess I will just pick at my meal, but after my stomach rumbles and a hollow ache defines my need, I eat with enthusiasm. Before I know it, I'm looking at an empty plate.

Father Juan leans back in his chair. "Thank you, Maria. You've stoked my fires so that I might muddle through another day."

"*Gracias, Padre.* Now take this poor child off and fix her broken spirit." She genuflects as she says it.

"Yes, ma'am," Juan says, motioning for me to follow. Somehow he makes me feel like a schoolgirl taking my first communion, in awe, but still hesitant. The guilt in me wants to be let out, but I fear the cost to my mind, body, and soul.

The padre doesn't take me to the nave, but to a messy office with books and paper manuscripts occupying every horizontal surface. He scoops up a stack of them from the only guest seat and tries to add them to another tower on the floor. The new chimney teeters over onto the floor. Father Juan shrugs. With a contented sigh, he flops down into an overstuffed chair that has to be at least twice his age.

I stand in the doorway like a girl called to the principal's office. "So tell me about it," he says, waving me to the chair.

I sit, but perch on the very edge like a gazelle on the alert for a predator. I recount the events of yesterday, not sparing myself in any way. My confessor leans in, soaking up every detail. As is the point of confession, I unburden my sins in every way so that Jesus Christ might take those up for me. I manage not to blubber, nor leak tears, and not to bemoan my fate like some hot-bloomered wife who'd jumped into the hay with a sexy man who wasn't her husband. Despite being completely candid, I somehow make a hash of it. After I finish, Father Juan offers, "Stella, my child, I don't see as if you could have done anything else. You have nothing to be penitent for."

"But Father, I let them die."

The padre sighs and rubs his temples. "Let me ask you a few questions to make this clear to you, my child. Did you release the demon?"

"Definitely not, Father."

"Good. Did you personally inter the demon that got loose?"

"No, Father. I don't summon demons."

"Good. So, you bear no guilt in its escape?"

"I don't believe so, sir."

"Next, did you know the demon would escape at that time?"

"How could I, Padre?"

"How, indeed. So, you were surprised by the incident. Now, if you hadn't been in presence, would the same or more people have died?"

"Likely quite a few more, Father. That demon thirsted for blood."

Father Juan barks out, "So why, in Christ's name, do you feel guilty about saving lives!"

"But I could have distracted him...I should have distracted it."

"And ended up going to visit Saint Peter yourself, leading a mob of the Prince Street residents in the queue behind you."

"But I failed them," I say, feeling the tears welling up in the corner of my eyes. I want penance. It will make me feel clean again, and the padre isn't giving it to me.

"God called those thirty-two home as surely as I sit before you. Nothing you could have done would have saved them, Stella Ochoa.

"Aren't you a good woman? Don't you teach the orphan witches to correctly use their powers? Don't you give of your time and coin to those less fortunate than you?" He doesn't give me a chance to answer but continues. "You are all that and more, Mrs. Ochoa. You saved uncountable lives that will never know just how lucky they are that you are smart, quick, and skilled."

I open my mouth to speak, but he interrupts. "Now, I will give you penance for your real sin—pride—in thinking that you can thwart the fate that God himself decrees. I want you to do five Hail Marys, and you shall be cleansed of your sins. Go to the chapel now, my daughter. Not another word."

# # #

I feel marginally better when I leave St. Leonard's until I hear the newsboy cry out, "Escaped demon slaughters thirty-four. Demons rampage!" Two of the injured must have gone to God. My heart sags again. I bolster my spirit with the words of both Father Juan and Carlos. It doesn't banish the feelings, but it does harness them enough to keep my composure.

Even with the hour at prayers of redemption, I can still make it back home before Tommy leaves if I put a good foot under me. I would have made it if it weren't for the vast blocking snows that still dominated most of the smaller streets. To my good fortune, I see Tommy climbing down the snowdrift that I need to climb up to go back home.

"Ma'am, I'm sorry if I left early. You been crying, ma'am?"

I ignore his question. "You didn't leave too soon, Tommy. I'm just running late. What news do you have for me?"

"Well, first, that old biddy running your house is on the warpath.

I heard her this morning talkin' something about being a messenger or some such."

That gives me my first smile of the day. It may be unchristian of me, but anything that offers that bat heartburn gives me joy. "Got it. What about Quarrels?"

"Well, he went to three places where he met up with folks from Power Unlimited; their wagons were out front. I am thinkin' that he might be putting more demons in them buildings."

"Good guess."

"Well, after that, he went and had a pint and a pizza pie at Johnson's Pub, the place right across the street from his house. Then he went home."

"I've never been in Johnson's. Does it have a billiard table?"

"Yes, ma'am, two of them."

"Did he play?"

"Naw. Just ate and went home."

I think for a bit. "Tommy, do you know anyone that plays billiards?"

The boy grins under his mop of hair. "Yes, Stella. George Feller—he calls himself that 'cause he ain't got a last name and he is a feller—is a shark. He makes plenty o'coin playing."

"OK, you think he might intentionally lose if I give him enough silver?"

"Damned straight, he would."

"OK, find George and tell him I want him to play both Quarrels and the baron. I want his assessment of how good each of them is. I'll pay him two dollars for each match."

"That'd do it, Stella."

I hand Tommy some coins from my purse. "Tell George I'm in a hurry."

"Yes, ma'am."

"And you stay on Quarrels."

"Excuse me for my intrusion," interrupts a third voice. I turn to find Lord Helms's coachman.

"Mr. Marsden, what are you doing here?"

"Looking for you, m'lady."

"It looks like you found me, then. With what business do you call?"

"Lord Helms bids me to invite you to his home for a discussion of mutual interest."

I look at the coach, matching Morgans, and the pair of beefy footmen behind him. "I think it is more than an invitation."

"Not at all, ma'am. If you demure, I am to return and report the reason as I see it. I am not to attempt any form of coercion. To the best of my knowledge, Lord Helms has never employed physical compulsion or duress. My companions are only for your protection as things might be getting dangerous."

The image of the two beefy types trying to protect me against a demon flashes across my mind. It stirs up memories that are still too raw. "Mr. Marsden, I'll be more than happy to go with you and your friends if you will allow me to finish my business with my associate," I say, pointing at Tommy. "And change out of this bag of a dress at my lodgings."

"Very good, m'lady." He retreats to a discrete distance.

I lower my voice to a whisper. "OK, stay on Quarrels, Tommy. And don't forget about the other thing, too."

He flashes the coins I gave him and winks before running off as fast as he can stump. It reminds me I should have Maxwell look at how Tommy's leg is mending.

#

I'm not even in the door when Mrs. Chapman starts rounding on me. "I told you, missy, that I'm not your messenger service," she bellows while shaking a note in front of me. Even with the radical motions, I can tell that it is on Coal Syndicate letterhead.

I snatch the note from her hand.

"I never!" she snaps.

I flip it open and find a note from Carlton offering me a fifteen percent raise if I'll come back to work. I crumple it up and toss it in the fireplace to light on the cheery coals. Some delivery or another of coal must have arrived.

"Mrs. Chapman, if you wish to no longer be an intermediary, you have my permission to tell any delivery person to leave it in the post box next to my room. That way, you will not be tempted to snoop."

I turn up the stairs with a tirade of indignation following me. I slip out of my loaned dress and underthings. I give myself a mental reminder to have them laundered before I return them. Looking at my available options, I give myself another remonstration to buy some new clothes— it is no longer an option. Of my two remaining unshredded sets, one is for church, and the other is nearly rags. As I'm going to the home of socialites, I pull out my good clothes.

Ignoring the shrieks of the harpy, I walk back out the door in my Sunday best.

"I'm all yours, Mr. Marsden."

He gives me half a grin and helps me into the carriage. "I doubt it, m'lady, but I think I take your actual meaning rather than its full value."

# # #

The Helms's dining room seems big enough to hold a bullfight. Darkwood wainscoting covers the lower half of the walls. The upper plaster half is painted in a rich red that promises more plum than blood. The table holds more square footage on its surface than my apartment has on its floor. Covering a good deal of it is a magnificent silver service heaping with nuts, meats, and fruits, many of which I've never seen before. A mountain of grapes, most definitely not in season, acts as a centerpiece for the entire smorgasbord.

"Please, Mrs. Ochoa, help yourself," Lady Helms says, presenting me to the feast. She is resplendent in a light blue dress bearing a cobalt-blue print of bluebonnets. Even this early in the morning, she has matching blue painted nails and subtle makeup that is highlighted by the daylight streaming in through a pair of glass skylights. "Our Saturday brunch is a very informal affair."

As hosts, the lord and lady wait to allow me to fill my plate. I cringe at the cost of this informal brunch. I take a little of this and a little of the other, not paying attention to even what I've collected. I sit in one of the three chairs closely grouped at the other end of the table, only a pair of leagues down the room.

"Thank you for this invitation, Lord Helms," I say as he sits. His wife folds her dress and petticoats beneath her as she perches on the edge of her seat to prevent damage to her bustle. It is an undergarment that, with her ample derriere, is superfluous.

"You are quite welcome, Mrs. Ochoa," Lord Helms says, getting excited enough that he looks like a dancing scarecrow. "So, with the news in this morning's paper, it is quite obvious we can't—"

"Excuse me, Henry, but this is brunch. No business during meals, my dear."

Chastened, the viscount says, "Quite right, my dearest."

"So, Mrs. Ochoa, tell me more about yourself. For someone who has been so intimately involved in our affairs of late, I know so little about you."

I scoff internally. If Lady Helms hasn't already hired a man to ask after me, then I'll eat my bloomers with fish sauce. But, as my mother continues to remind me, formality must prevail in such a setting. I can't call her a liar in her own home. Instead, I pop one of those oversweet grapes into my mouth. It even tastes purple. Chewing my mouth clear and chasing with a sip of coffee, I reply. "My life is pretty much an open book, Lady Helms.

"After I manifested earth witch powers, I apprenticed witchcraft under my mother. I tried, without much success, to follow in her footsteps. I married my Aaron three weeks before he was sent to fight in the Irish Liberation. He died there. With his survivor's pension and my work… or should I say former work for the Coal Syndicate, I can live modestly."

"But you left out the most interesting part—about being a hellfighter." Lady Helms grins like a cat about to pounce on a dove. That brings out an interesting, if disturbing thought. Can all of the demon escapes be a subtle attack on her philandering husband? It doesn't exactly fit on the surface, so I file it away for further thought.

"That is a story that likely would take most of the morning to do justice. Let's just say that I met Carlos, the leader of *Dos Campanas*, when an apprentice witch accidentally released a demon she tried to bind. That was a right mess."

"But meeting isn't joining," she says. Lord Helms eats heartily as he lets his wife dominate the conversation. Lady Helms picks up a sliver of plum. Her fingers and wrist are so delicate compared to the rest of her robust figure. I watch the fruit all the way into her mouth, wondering how those plump, carefully painted lips might feel in other places.

I grit my teeth. Bloody body of mine. I have serious work to do, and it is flitting off onto flights of fantasy about a woman I don't particularly care for. She seems to embody all of the bad things about the aristocracy and none of its virtues. I put my fancies as firmly aside as one might a naughty child. "I started hanging out with him and his friends, witches all. They had already formed the *Dos Campanas*. One day when we were all together in the pub, they were called out. I went and observed. The destruction appalled me.

"A month later, Carlos offered me a position in the team when one of their members decided that they'd had enough of endangering life and limb. We all found I have a talent for the work. The rest is history."

"That's fascinating. Lord Helms and I have often wondered what fighting a demon is like."

I narrow my gaze at her. Her green eyes are dilated like that of an opium addict chasing the dragon. *Can this be a game for her?* I ask myself. *Can she be just someone who thrills at hurting others?* More questions. I mean, I have a potential suspect—a likely suspect. Or, can I be blinded by the fact that I just don't like the pompous baron? Or even that he is a rival to the *Dos Campanas?* All things I have to be sure of before I make any accusations. How could I possibly investigate my so-called partner's wife?

I realize my introspection has left the discussion hanging for a few moments too long. "I know the papers and magazines paint it as massively romantic, but it is dirty and severely dangerous work." Outside of any etiquette, I pull my hair and the collar of my dress away from my neck to expose some of my burns. I could show them any number of scars I bear, but disrobing in polite company fails acceptability in any manner. "This is what happens when you fight demons. Just one of many, many injuries that mar my flesh." Lord Henry looks only for education. If I have to guess, I'd say that Lady Helms is sexually aroused as her gaze lingers long beyond politeness. *Maybe she's a sadist?*

The viscountess gathers herself together with a deep breath and says, "So if it is so horrible, why do you support my husband? Why wouldn't you fight against him so there would be no more demon releases?"

"Dear, that could be a terribly personal question," Henry says in my defense.

"No, Lord Helms. Not at all. Lady Helms, I believe that demons are no different than anything else man has harnessed. Power of the wind to send ships across the oceans—but how many sailors die every year? Fire to heat our homes and many other uses—but how many people die in fires that escape to burn?

"What about the workers that slave in the mines to extract the coal for a pittance? Or the earth itself that cries out to be left alone and not be robbed of its soul and body?

"Of course I believe in what Lord Helms does. Properly summoned and shackled, the evil of our world can become a force to eliminate even more corruption and evil." It all comes out in a rush, and I'm left without breath in my breast.

"Goodness, gracious, Mrs. Ochoa. I never knew you were quite so vehemently in favor of my husband's activities."

After a couple of deep breaths, "Don't misunderstand me, Mrs. Helms. I do not have any hero-worship, or any other similar emotions, toward your husband." I continue with my reassurance of Mrs. Helms as if Henry isn't even there. "I respect him and his work. I hate destruction and chaos. Right now, our aims are running neck and neck. At worst, we are allies, at best business partners."

"Well said, Mrs. Ochoa," the viscountess says. "I'm sorry I've been… difficult in your interaction with my husband. I won't be in the future. You are welcome in our home anytime you require it.

"Now, I've interfered with your business long enough this morning. I will head off to my solarium. I have guests coming this morning for tea."

The viscount and I stand as she gets up. "Thank you for your wonderful hospitality, ma'am," I say. She nods as if it is her due before regally departing the room. I catch myself watching the way her bustle sways. Maybe I could get to like her in some ways. But then I remember I still need to examine her as a suspect—and a married woman!

"Shall we go to my study, Mrs. Ochoa?"

I motion for him to lead the way. He takes me through seventeen different twists and turns until we end up in a smallish room, well-appointed with books, charts, and a chalkboard. The writing on the chalkboard catches my attention immediately.

"Ah, I see you have seen my data."

"Only four?" I ask incredulously.

"Yes, eliminating those of obvious contrition and single releases, all of the demon escapees in the Boston area have been installed by only four different conjurers—that's four of over thirty."

I read the list of names in decreasing order of their demon escape totals: "Francois Perrier - fourteen, Johnathan Quarrels - thirteen, Waning Moon Erickson - nine, and Fana Samejo - eight. Holy Mother of God. I didn't think data would be this obvious."

"Mining data is one of my key functions. I'm good at my job, Stella."

"Wow!"

"Yes. And if you notice, Fana works for one of my largest competitors, and Waning Moon is a freelancer working for all three of the demon installers in the northeast. This is not an attack on me personally, but rather on using the hellions as power sources at all."

"This data certainly implies the Coal Syndicate, you know."

"I agree, but it is never to be proven, Stella. Jasperson has too much wealth, power, and influence. Not to mention, he is quite cunning. Unless he knifed the guts out of a virgin on Boston Commons in front of the king himself, he will remain untouchable by the law."

I catch the last phrase, and it sticks in my brain. "Are you thinking of doing something illegal against Jasperson?" I ask with no little amount of trepidation in my voice. While the law is often an ass, as Samuel Clemens is wont to say, I don't desire to be associated with messy and pseudo-legal shenanigans.

"Heavens no, Mrs. Ochoa. There are ways to attack his base, his wealth, and business that are one hundred percent legal. But to do so, I must first extricate myself from this jam. With the papers now making it front-page news, this now strikes at the heart of *my* business.

"So, another thing I've learned is that the releases from demons in the installations of these four have started in just the last four months."

My mind recreates the charts I saw in Jasperson's office. The downturn in profits started five or six months ago. I share this with Henry. "Again, not proof, but very convincing circumstantial data nonetheless."

"It is both, Stella. My plan of action is to sack the two that work for me. I'll also share our data with my competitors on all four of them, in effect blackballing them from ever working in the industry again."

"Oh, no, Henry, don't do that," I interject.

"Why not? I won't have them ruin the entire field of demon power."

"True, but it tips our hand. If we do that, the scum will crawl under a rock, and we will have no proof.

"We are very close to breaking this wide open. We still don't know how it is being done. The why, and the high-level perpetrator, we *think* we have a handle on but aren't sure yet."

For the first time since I met him, the viscount seems unsure of himself. I see written on his face the two warring concerns—protect his baby or apprehend the criminal and prevent it for all times. "How much longer? There are practical concerns on my side as well," he offers.

"I think I can nail it down by Tuesday latest. I mean, you can't sack them until Monday anyway. So, give me a list of the installations by each of these scumbags and three days. I think we can get enough to go to the constables."

"I think that is fair. Three days then."

#

I get more than the three days and a list. Lord Henry also assigns his driver and second-best coach to my needs. I definitely am not going to object. Just my short walks in this snowy he…heck has already formed blisters on my heel and insteps. I'll never again get store-bought shoes!

Instead of getting into the carriage, I sit up next to Jimmy Marsden, who says, "Where to, miss?"

"Here is the list of locations Lord Helms gave me. Closest first, I guess. Want to hit as many of them as possible."

As the gray and white Percherons pull us out of the carriage house, I ask, "Married, Jimmy?"

"Naw. Never found the time nor the right girl, miss."

"Oh, bloody heck. Do I have to go through this with everyone? I'm Stella. Just Stella."

"OK, miss."

I roll my eyes. Jimmy can't see it because his attention is on the road, as is proper. But, I'm sure he heard it as his cheeks dimple. Not a bad-looking man in a rugged sort of way. He sports broad shoulders, a thick, powerful chest, and a gluteus maximus that has, I'll bet, been forged from iron. His hazel eyes complement his dimples and kindly face. If I have to say anything negative about him, it would be a slightly weak chin. But his big, pouty lips look like they are made for kissing…all night long. I feel a familiar tickle in my belly and dampness in my underpinnings. *Jesus H. Christ, woman. Keep your mind off of your fundamentals and on your task!*

"So never been kissed, then?"

"I means there be lassies that set their bonnet on me, but I never felt the spark that made me know it were right. I dunno, maybe I am not the marrying kind."

"It takes all kinds, Jimmy."

"That it does, Miss Stella." I can see by the dimples again that he is pulling my chain.

"So, how long you worked for the Helmses?"

"Nigh on forever."

"Is that because it is onerous?"

"No, quite the contrary. Lord Helms is great ta work for. I just meant I can't hardly remember not working for them. I started as a stable boy when Lord Helms caught me pinching apples from his trees when I was about this tall," he says, marking himself about his waist. That, unfortunately, reminds me of what is under his breeches. I force my mind to focus on my search for the scum who have killed people. That cools me down quickly.

His background reminds me of Tommy. "What about Lady Helms?" I ask, sneaking in my real reason to start the conversation in the first place.

"All in all, a good woman, if you can avoid thinking about what her and her women friends get up to."

"You know about that?"

"Stella, you can't be in that house without knowing about it. Sometimes I drive the women home, and sometimes I take her ladyship to places in areas of the city that best not be talked about in polite company."

"So, she doesn't love the viscount?"

"I wouldn't say that, miss. I think she is tender toward him, but I think they never slept abed together. I've seen her round on one of the servants that didn't treat him proper even if the master weren't gonna say nothing about it. Also seen her go out of her way to make sure he don't see her lady friends nor know about 'em. I'd say she likes him alright."

"Is she harsh?"

"She can sometimes be a bit of a stickler about what she expects from a servant, but I got no cause to fault her none. She never called me out, nor nobody else in the household, that we didn't deserve."

While it doesn't prove innocence, his statements definitely seem to indicate that Lady Helms doesn't have a motive to want to hurt Lord Helms. Such a small thread to pull at when I have leads the size of ship mooring ropes to follow.

"What do you do for fun, Jimmy? Billiards? Rugby?"

He blushes. He actually blushes clear down to his shirt line. "I'm learning the art of bullfighting."

I find my eyes opening wide of their own volition. "That's an interesting choice," I say, leaving my comment noncommittal.

"I always wanted to be a matador since I saw Guerrita, I mean Rafael Guerra Bejarano, become a professional in the ring here in Boston Downs. The crowd cheering him on and all the *señoritas* throwing flowers at him. I dream, but I don't think I'll ever be able to be one. I didn't start training early enough."

"I hope you are wrong, Jimmy. I think you would make a brave and true matador."

Our conversation continues with a discussion of favorite pubs, best tamales in town, and other such until we reach the first place. Jimmy double-checks the list.

"Cadiz Imports, miss. First stop."

Cadiz Imports is a warehouse in a district of warehouses. A security guard barely bothers to put down his newspaper to look over my authorization from Lord Helms. He shrugs, pointing at the door to the basement. This time of year, with the weather so chancy for cargo ships, the large warehouse is nearly empty.

Some newly built stairs, probably as a prerequisite to the installation, lead me down to a rather large demon who looks more frog than man. He eyes me as I approach, hoping I'll be stupid enough to damage the warding pentagram. I get down on my knees and crawl around, looking at it closely.

"WHAT IS IT YOU SEEK, FEMALE?" it says in a voice that half sounds like it is gargling. I choose to ignore it. "I OFFER INFORMATION TO BE SENT BACK."

I've heard it before. Bluster and lies if they can't use brute strength. "GAZZUNREEP COMES. I CAN SAVE YOU IF YOU SET ME FREE TO MY WORLD."

My mind slips the reins of concentration. *Why does his name keep coming up? What have I done to warrant this?* It is a mystery for another time. I say nothing and return to the task at hand. The chalk pour is continuous and undamaged in any way. This should last decades, if not more.

I walk away, but at the last moment before mounting the stairs, I turn and ask, "What is your name, foulness?"

"FARNAMBULO."

"Farnambulo, when, sometime in the far distant future, you return to hell, please give Gazzunreep a message for me. 'I will pray for him and his soul.'"

The demon hisses and gives a warding sign.

The guard grunts to my thanks as I leave.

# # #

"Young's Hotel, Stella," Jimmy says at our fourth stop. The second, the Boston Athletic Club, and third, the Ragged Pinto Bar, also show no signs of tampering with the containment. A small part of me now wonders if this is a fool's errand.

Young's has a reputation as a gentlemen's club. Their billiard room is larger and posher than any in town. They also don't allow women in the main areas or in the hotel rooms. From Karie, I know that doesn't apply to working women or the maid staff. But Young's does have a women's dining room. I enter through the Lady's Entrance off of Court Street.

A man in a smart suit and white gloves offers to take my coat. "May I help you, ma'am?" He asks after he hangs up my garment.

"I'd like to see your power installation as a secondary inspection," I say, handing him Lord Helms's very well-used permission. The man opens it carefully and reads every word.

"Just one moment, Mrs. Ochoa. I will need the manager's key to show you to the power room."

"Not at all."

Two ladies come in while he is away, and I assure them that the maître d'hôtel will return momentarily. They both look down their nose at the dusty mess crawling around in the basements has made of my good dress. I just notice it, so I give them a big smile and mentally command the dirt to leave. All of it drops to the floor in a ring at my feet, leaving my dress a bit more wrinkled than proper but pristinely clean.

One woman puts her hand over her mouth. The other genuflects. Both retreat back out the way they came.

The maître d' returns with a rotund, balding gentleman with a massive walrus mustache. "Ah, there you are, Madam Ochoa. My name is J. R. Whipple, owner of this establishment."

"I didn't mean to take up your valuable time, Mr. Whipple. I just wanted to spend ten minutes inspecting the demon containment."

"Certainly; let me lead the way."

The man is a talker—one of those who are incapable of companionable silence. "We are so happy with our new power installation. It has allowed us to put up the new electric lights—Tesla's, of course."

"They are dandy," I say with a repressed shudder. Having that lightning roaming around seems too much like having an uncontained demon in your building.

I suffer through a history of the hotel, lists of famous guests, and more as he unlocks several doors along the way. The fourth portal seems like something I'd see to a bank vault rather than in a hotel. As it opens, the sound behind is horrendous. The clatter of machinery, escaping steam, and more. It smells of whale oil and mud.

We make our way around all of the pumping pistons and rattling gears to a smaller door. He unlocks it with a unique round-ended key of a type I've never seen before. Inside, with the door closed behind us, the cacophony dies to a point where I can hear myself think. A small demon, probably ranking, sits cross-legged on the earth, his sixteen-point antlers taking up most of the space in his confinement. With his eyes closed, he looks like some swami from the subcontinent of India. More's the better, so I take the time to investigate the spelled chalk lines.

It takes less time to cough than it does for me to spot an issue. Tiny rings, no bigger than the head of a pin, and grouped all in one area of the chalk. Salt contamination. The salt crystals wick moisture out of the air and muddy the white dust, growing larger and larger. When the weakened rings meet one another and form a path, the spells fail. The chalk then has all the strength to keep a demon in as ordinary sawdust— that is, none.

This is one of the reasons for the old wives' tale of throwing salt over your shoulder if you should spill some. The myth is that demons follow the salt away from you, leaving you in safety. Bunk, but at least somewhat understandable.

I count no fewer than thirty salt crystals. From my purse, I pour some additional chalk to cover the voids. The demon, no longer passive, rams his antlers against his invisible prison. He swears improbable things in his native tongue at me. He curses me and my lineage for the audacity of keeping him imprisoned.

I ignore him and his protestations to examine my patch to the line. It will keep for several weeks.

"Mr. Whipple, I've found a small issue. I've made a temporary correction that will let you continue without concern until Forever Power can come back and do a more significant repair." I hand him one of my cards. "I will report this to Forever Power. However, you should do the same. No one wants a patched demon containment."

It is difficult to tell in the white electric lights, but I believe the man blanches. "Thank you, Mrs. Ochoa. Thank you very much!"

# # #

Jimmy drives me to five more installations, two of which have salt contamination, one only days, or maybe even hours from failing. As with Young's Hotel, I patch the damage. In addition, I begin to notice a pattern. All of the places where I find problems are all highly visible or would cause great loss of life—Young's Hotel, the Boston Opera House, Boston General Hospital.

If I had any small doubts that the demon escape was artificial, these corruptions drive them away.

"Jimmy, I'm tired and need to get sleep before church in the morning. Could you drop me at my apartment?"

"Absolutely, Miss Stella." On the short drive there, I write out a note to the viscount. I say that none of the installations I checked today were those of Quarrels. To the relief of my aching body, Jimmy stops right at our front door.

"And would you hand this to Lord Helms. He'll know what to do with it."

"Yes, ma'am."

"Thank you, Jimmy. You've been a dear." I give him a peck on the cheek before I climb down.

10—Sunday, February 12, 1888

Sunday wakes cold. I can tell from the goosebumps I have, even wrapped up in my bedsheets, that I'll need to wear my warmest underthings. I don't want to expose myself to the tortures of a frozen floor or the drafts through my not adequately caulked window, but church service waits for no witch.

Before abusing myself, I at least grab my stockings, which are within reach. Summoning my inner strength, I draw back the covers and shove my leggings on with the speed of a rattlesnake striking. The rest of my dressing routine is done with dispatch. By the time I have my *peineta* in place and a shawl around my shoulders, I'm no longer shivering.

Mrs. Chapman, conspicuous by her absence, has left a pot of porridge over the coals for breakfast. I gobble down a bowl liberally laced with brown sugar and a big, steaming mug of bitter coffee before welcoming the warmth that's come back to my toes and fingers. I finally feel ready to start the day.

"'Freight Trains Sporadic. Still No Passenger Service!'" calls the newsboy as I exit the door.

Tommy is waiting for me on the porch, his hands in his pockets, and frost from his mouth. It has to be below zero with no moisture in the air, save what we breathe. Somewhere Tommy has come up with a green knit cap that covers most of his ears. "Morning, Stella."

"Good morning to you, too. How are you fitting into life as a dishwasher?"

"I like Mr. O'Flynn. He bellows and shouts a lot, but he don't mean nothin'. I do as I'm told, and he does me right. I forgot how nice a bed can be 'specially on frozen nights like this."

A cot in a basement is a bed? Well, considering before this, Tommy must have been sleeping under newspapers or in used stable hay. *Remember*, I tell myself, *you can't save the whole world.* "What did you come up with yesterday?"

"Well, that Quarrels fellow went out for breakfast 'round eleven. Then he walked to St. James Theatre on Washington Street. I didn't go in, but he came out about five. Had dinner at his pub and went home. Unless he met someone at the theatre, he didn't talk to nobody saving playing some billiards with my friend."

"Good report, Tommy. What did George Feller, your billiard hustler, have to say?"

"Yup. He thanks you for your business, ma'am. Wanted to make sure you understand how appreciative he is."

"Angling to do more work for me, isn't he?"

"Not so much that, Stella. Feller is just a nice mick if you ain't playing pool with him. Even then, he is polite. Anyway, he tells me that Quarrels couldn't put a ball in the ocean, even if he were on the beach. George said he had a hard time losing to the scrod."

"Interesting. What about the baron?"

"George played him 'round lunchtime. Said the baron was a full-up shark. Let George win a couple of games and then upped the stakes and took him for twice what George had already won."

I now have something I feel solid about. Quarrels beat the baron at a high stakes game of pool? What a load of fish entrails. It was a payoff, pure and simple, made to look like something else. "Tommy, that is exactly what I needed to know. Now, I want you to stop following Quarrels and start following the baron. His home is…"

"I know, Miss. Everyone knows to stay away from the baron's place. He done hurt some of my boys for sleeping out behind his coach house."

"In that case, be very careful, Tommy." I give him four bits.

"You ain't need to do that, ma'am. I already got my pay for this week."

"Call it a bonus for doing so well. Now off with you."

"Yes, Stella."

# # #

Ice on the roads engenders a slow walk to church in order to maintain my footing. I climb the steps just as the doors are closing. I start when I see Baron Cardiff sitting in the back pew being fawned on by a couple of the older female witches.

"Good Sabbath, Mrs. Ochoa," he says with enough sugar to make the greeting pleasant. "Can I offer you this spot?" he says, pointing next to him. The woman sitting there gives me an evil glare but moves aside.

"Thank you, sir," I say. *Am I sitting with a snake?* Unlikely even a serpent would do anything foul within the Lord's house.

"Learned anything new on your little investigation?"

The condescension in his tone and the words just grate on my soul. I can't let him know I'm focusing my attention on him. At the same time, lying in church seems at best sacrilegious, and at worst blasphemous. "Only a little," I fudge. "Found some salt contamination in one installation. Not sure if it has anything to do with escapes." I feel as "Liar!" is emblazoned on my forehead for all to see.

The baron nods without replying as services start. My eyes bore into him. All I can think about is if the baron is truly guilty, how can he possibly sit there as if butter won't melt in his mouth? Christ himself should strike him down with fire and brimstone, visit a pox on him, or something equally Old Testament.

So intense is my righteous indignation that Father Juan's service, normally so enthralling, fails to pierce my miasma. I don't remember two things about the service even as the closing hymn breaks through my emotions.

Automatically, I get in line for confession. The baron slips in behind me as he deflects the attention of several young women. "An inspiring service. My priest doesn't have the forthright manner of Padre Dubois y Cantonio. I wish I could get here regularly on Sunday. You are lucky to have him."

I nod in response. I am not sure what to say. "Thank you," seems trite, especially considering the direction my analysis is taking. I take my turn to confess my sins to save me from any further interaction. My emotions, still frayed, calm as the ritual overtakes me. I offer up my catalog of sins without any true thought. The padre gives me penance and absolution.

I break form by not leaving the confessional. I kneel there with my thoughts still jumbled. "Father, what happens to those who deliberately hurt others? I mean, not in the 'I forgot close the barn door,' type of thing, but those who knowingly perform acts that will cause death and mayhem?"

"My daughter, there are many scriptures that call out what will happen to those damned souls, but they all mean the same two things: They are forever kept from God's love; they are punished in hellfire for all eternity."

"They cannot be redeemed?"

"Not unless they repent and choose the path of righteousness."

I kneel there, realizing that if the baron is guilty, then his downfall will be his own pride. He will never debase himself before anyone. His beautiful skin would bake, crack, and char in the inferno of hell itself. "That's good enough for me, Father."

I find the baron on the steps of the church outside his carriage. "Can I offer you a lift, *señora?*"

"I'm sorry, Franklin, but I have to meet with the padre over provisions for the orphanage." *Not quite a lie,* I tell myself. I do need to talk to Father Juan, but we had a meeting scheduled for Thursday evening around six bells.

"Another time, then. I have an important set of business meetings on Monday. Could we possibly meet Tuesday evening to go over your findings in detail?"

"Absolutely. Why don't you send your man around seven, and I'll catch you up on my investigations?" *In a pig's eye,* I think to myself.

"Very good. Thank you, Mrs. Ochoa. Until Tuesday, then." The baron mounts his coach, barking something at his driver. As his team pulls him away smartly, I notice Tommy's familiar gawky form clinging to the back of his carriage. Tommy winks at me as they pull around the corner.

I'll give the youngster his due. He does nothing by half.

# # #

I'm getting spoiled. Without Lordship Helms's coach, it takes much more time to investigate the installation sites on my list, and the bunions on my feet are paying for it. I know I said it before, but never again will I buy store-made shoes. As I walk between each demon-powered site, I even think of splurging on a pair from the cobbler, job or no job.

For today, I focus on those specifically done by John Quarrels. While I'm intruding on Sabbath evening, few make even a token objection when I share Lord Helms's warrant. The only places where I fail to gain entrance are commercial sites closed on the Lord's Day.

With absolutely no surprise, I find salt contamination in one, two, and in the end, fourteen in all. I discover so many that I run out of my own personal cache of chalk to amend the sites. I start making notes on my list of sites Lord Helms will have to visit earlier than others.

Some of Quarrels's early installations aren't subtle at all. It looks as if someone dumped a whole bottle of crystals in the chalk. In later chalk imprisonments, I find smaller streamers of the circular salt and water depressions radiating out through the powder.

What little guilt I still have about those people I didn't save fires my anger, not depression. My teeth clench hard enough to hear them grinding. My rage has a focus. Quarrels certainly, and by concatenation the baron as well. I couldn't believe that humans could, with forethought and malice, cause such destruction and woe upon their fellow man.

People part out of my way. Many cross the street. Then I feel why. Tendrils of earth reaching up in sympathy to cover each of my feet as they land. The last time I'd felt such an all-encompassing emotion of hatred, a spire of rock sixteen feet high lifted out of the earth. My mother dismissed the stone and then beat me with a switch. She whipped me again and again. "Witches have a stronger need than most to control ourselves," she said, punctuating her stinging stripes. "When we lose control, we destroy. You must learn to keep your emotions deep inside."

Knowing I had to control myself for the love of everyone near me, I walk over to a remaining snowdrift. I scoop up a handful of the gray, soot-covered crystals and dump them down the front of my dress. As my eyes snap fully open with the cold, the supple stone fingers return to their earthen state. I dance about as the snow makes its way inside my fundamentals, melting against my skin.

With damp undergarments, but a calmer demeanor, I continue my walk home. It gives me time to think. I probably have enough proof to go to the constabulary. But as I walk by the Bell in Hand, I realize I might be able to test the waters for certain.

My luck holds. Inspector Second Antonio Guizzetti sits at his usual table. I ignore the *Dos Campanas'* customary table, currently vacant, and walk up behind the man. For the first time, I'm not thinking about the tightness of his slacks over his arse. He guffaws at something one of his other boys in blue says.

"Inspector?" I ask.

"Huh? Oh, hi, Stella. Did you hear that one? Terribly perfect joke."

"No, sorry. I was wondering if I could have a word with you."

One of his bushy eyebrows raises. Even in a pub, a woman doesn't usually ask a man for a date, especially a lady with any semblance of morality. "Certainly. Gentlemen, if you would excuse me."

He follows me over to my regular table. "I know this is unusual, but I have a crime to report and don't know how to go about it."

"Well, you tell me or go to the constabulary and tell the desk sergeant. Not difficult, Stella."

"I don't think I've said this correctly. I want to see if it is a crime…I mean, I want to know if I have enough…Oh, to hell with it. I don't know what I mean. Can I just tell you what is going on and let you give me advice?"

I'm sure he thinks I've been drinking.

I give him class and verse of what I've been looking into—a demon escapes, perfect supplies, salt contamination, billiard payoffs, coal profits, Quarrels, Helms, Cardiff, and Jasperson. His face gets darker as my story spills into its second half-hour. By the end, his normally jovial expression is now in a professional scowl.

"Stella, this is fantastic. Part of me wants to go over and arrest Quarrels right now. But the professional part of me knows it would be a mistake. A king's bench would release him within a fortnight.

"You have no real evidence. You have a remarkable story that makes me take notice, but no one can prove that Quarrels, or any other of those witches, put the salt within the chalk. Any first-year barrister would get it thrown out on that alone.

"As far as the baron goes, no one could prove he didn't just have an off day at billiards. We can't prove conspiracy without one of the installing witches cooperating with us.

"And as far as Bruce Jasperson and the Coal Syndicate goes, they are untouchable. You have nothing but speculation—oh, good speculation, but unless Cardiff confesses and gives up Jasperson, then you have nothing."

My heart sinks. All this work has been for naught.

"Oh, don't despair, *señora*."

"Huh?"

"Your face fell so far I thought I was going to have to go to the basement to pick it up," he jokes. "A prosecutor can take your testimony as an expert witness on the installation AND escape of demons. If we can prove that Quarrels is actually salting paths for them, we may have the nit that will allow us to unravel the entire ball of yarn.

"However, I have a problem. I couldn't take this to my chief inspector. With just what you've given me, he'd throw me out of his office. So we need to give him a reason to listen."

"And how do you suggest we do that?"

"Funny you should ask."

# # #

Riding in a police wagon is a new experience. Not that it is any different than a civilian one, except for the cage in the back and the Royal Constabulary marking. "Are you absolutely certain we can trust Viscount Helms?" Inspector Guizzetti asks over the trotting horses and the squeaks of the metal bars moving around behind us. "I mean, on the surface, I don't see any reason he would be, but couldn't he still be part of the plot?"

"Not a chance, Inspector." I decide to use his formal title to keep his caramel color skin and broad chest out of my mind. I'm only partially successful. "He has nothing to gain and everything to lose. But Lady Helms, that's a different kettle of fish." I offer my potential theory revolving around His Grace and Karie's regular assignations versus my experiences with her ladyship's jealous streak.

"Well, definitely worth keeping in mind. I suggest we meet only with Lord Helms."

"Agreed." His strong hands control the team with the skill of a teamster. I wonder what those fingers would be like under my still damp underthings. They now become damper for other reasons. I am troubled about my inability to keep my body in check lately. I have no need for a man in my life, especially a staid policeman. "So, how do you know horses so well?" I ask. *Great line, woman. He'll see right through that.*

"My father hauled beer for Boston Ale Company. I helped him from knee-high until I chose to put a badge on and walk a beat. Always had a way with them almost as much as I can't stand those trolleys. Gives me the shivers to use those windup things. All that energy coming from nowhere."

"Makes as much sense as any of the arguments I've heard against them. What do you do for fun?"

"I feel like the conversation has turned."

Fortunately for me, he doesn't turn as I feel the heat coming to my cheeks. "Not trying to create an inquisition. It's just that I've known you for at least two years, and all I know about you is your profession and that you tend to hang out at the Bell in Hand."

"Football, when I get the chance. I play sweeper or, in a pinch, goalie for our local constabulary team, the Blue Coats. I'm something of a fanatic. Had the chance once to scrimmage with one of the professional teams. Never forgot it. Wish I was good enough to do that for a living, but I love being a policeman as well. So what's good for the goose is good for the gander. What about you?"

"I love to garden. I don't seem to have much aptitude, though. My backyard garden never seems to give up any produce at all. I got one cucumber and a mouthful of peas."

"I'd never have picked you as a gardener. Maybe someone who does ceramics or throws pottery." His tone is playful.

"I've done both, but I don't have the artistic temperament. My vases turn into lopsided abstract sculptures. My abstract sculptures fire into nothing more than solid lumps of dirt."

"You can't be good at everything. I understand you are quite a good witch."

It is an odd statement. "Better than average."

"Do you have a witching rank?"

Definitely not where I have been heading with this conversation. "I never bothered. I saw my mother go that stuffy route and didn't want to have anything to do with it. After I passed my practicing witch examination in front of five ranked members, I turned my back on it."

"No desire to put Mistress in front of witch?"

"Never."

"Stella, you are an odd duck," he says, maneuvering his team around a disabled wagon having its wheel replaced.

"Oh? Why do you say that, Antonio?"

"Well, probably the most important quality of any constable is his ability to notice things going on around him. I hear you and your Two Bells troupe talking and teasing one another. I've gleaned more about you than you would probably be comfortable with."

"Oh? Amaze me, Mr. Inspector."

"Alright, but I did warn you." He clucks the horses into a trot as we exit the Canal Bridge, and the three-mile-per-hour speed limit no longer applies. "First off, I know you are a widow and that your husband, Aaron, died in the Irish Liberation. From some comments and your relative youth, I assume that you had not been married long."

"Nothing there a secret, Constable. You will have to do better than that."

"Oh, I'm only getting started. You are either estranged from your parents or have a very strained relationship. I've only heard your mother mentioned. I'm assuming your father is deceased."

"My father left while I was young. My mother is the only source of information on this topic, so I take it with a grain of salt. And yes, I don't exactly get along with my mother."

"Correction noted. Unlike many witches, you care about people."

I turn to look at him. His statement puzzles me. "Witches care. Many of their tenets have to do with doing no harm."

"Stella, that is much different than doing good. Most witches are as selfish as the winter is long."

"I don't necessarily agree, but why do I care, and they don't?"

"This little investigation is one thing. You are flooding your own gold mine by doing this. You could make a fortune just capturing demons that escape. Instead, you try to prevent it from happening." He holds up a hand before I can object. "Another case in point is that cutpurse, Tommy. I've hauled him in more than once. Yet you treat him as a real person, and he responds to you. Not even one of those tambourine do-gooders could make that happen. I've heard more, but I'll stop there."

"I still won't concede the point, but I will accept the observation."

"You also are the most infuriatingly chaste woman I've ever met."

"Excuse me???"

"I mean, butter wouldn't melt in your mouth on a hot summer day in a whorehouse, not that you would be caught dead in one. No need to play coy, Mrs. Ochoa. More than once, I've given you a smoldering glance that usually melts women in their tracks. Oh, I'm not vain, only observant to what impact I have on the ladies."

"But—!"

"No need to keep your mouth open, Stella. I'm not trying to court you. In fact, you really aren't even my type. I have to assume you are either the most asexual young woman I've ever met, you are more cunning at hiding your liaisons than I suspect, or that your friend, Miss Karie Taylor, has something to do with your calm outward demeanor. My guess is the latter, although I would have expected you to go all the way with a Boston marriage or at least move in with her if for no other reason than to get away from that slum lady you currently pay rent to."

Now I'm sputtering. The inspector is right. He does know things. I don't know how to refute it as everything I think to say to deny it seems to all but confirm his opinions. He speaks again before I can come up with an appropriate righteously indignant response.

"I also know you almost certainly could be classified as Mistress Witch with your powers. Also, that you wield more than one field of witchcraft."

"OK, stop it right there, buster. I've never claimed more than one magic skill."

"I know. I told you, I'm observant."

I try hard to think of anything we might have said at the Bell in Hand that could have even hinted at my extra gift. I wrack my memories for a full minute before something else pops into my head. "What do you mean, I'm not your type?"

He chuckles. "I wondered when you would catch that one."

"I mean, I know I'm not every man's cup of tea, but I thought most men fawned all over themselves if any broad even flashed an ankle."

"I'm not most men," he says with a haughty lift of his chin.

"*Vete a la mierda.*"

"You, too, Mrs. Ochoa. Seriously, I have a girlfriend right now. She has a thing about the morality of pubs, but I'm going to drag her down to the Bell in Hand one day anyway. You two couldn't be more different. You are like a big ole coon dog, persistently chasing your prey. She is more like a terrier, tiny and yipping at everything."

Now it is my turn to laugh. "Inspector, I'll give you a powerful piece of advice. Don't ever compare your lady, or any lady for that matter, to a dog. You just might find out how hard we bitches bite."

# # #

"Mrs. Ochoa…glad you could call again so soon," Lady Helms chirps with a smile three sizes too large on her face. There may even be a slightly vacant expression, and the back of her dress doesn't fall neatly to the floor. "And you brought a constable with you. Does this mean you have good news?"

"It is to be determined, viscountess. We need to speak to His Grace again.

"Oh, and where are my manners. Lady Helms, this is Inspector Second Guizzetti of the Royal Constabulary."

"Pleasure to make your acquaintance," Lady Helms says.

"And yours, Lady Helms."

"Lord Helms will be down momentarily. Can I offer you refreshments?"

"I'm sorry, Lady Helms, but we are in a hurry. We need the viscount's assistance to move forward."

"I see. Well, if you would wait in the library, he will be there forthwith."

"Thank you, Lady Helms."

As she turns away, I detect a smudge of lipstick on her earlobe.

"Fifty to one against," Antonio offers in a whisper as our hostess leaves our presence.

"Huh?"

"You said Lady Helms was a possible suspect in the conspiracy. Very unlikely. I mean, we will investigate, but it won't turn into anything."

"How do you know?"

"Whenever a constable, especially an inspector, gets involved with a case, suspects act differently. They either guard themselves, become overly brazen, tease, or just act as if they don't have a care in the world. I didn't detect any such artificial signs with Lady Helms. In fact, she seemed distracted."

"Probably because of the young woman she has in her bed-chamber."

"Excuse me?"

"My turn," I say, with no little smugness. "Lipstick on the viscountess's fingers, neck, and earlobe. Her dress had been thrown on in haste, not letting it fall properly. I also caught a whiff of lilac water; a cheaper scent Lady Helms wouldn't be caught dead wearing. I also noted a dreamy-vacant expression as if she'd just climbed the mountain and skied down in a satisfying avalanche. Also, notice that she didn't try harder to be a hostess. She had somewhere...or should I say someone to be with."

"With your powers of observation, maybe you should join the constabulary. Probably would outrank me in a fortnight."

"Unlikely, Inspector. Witches aren't allowed on the normal force, only the Royal Inquisitor staff."

"True. But I can't help but think we have missed an opportunity in your case."

My response is interrupted by Lord Helms coming into the room. "Stella!"

"Henry, I'd like to introduce you to Inspector Second Guizzetti of the Royal Constabulary."

To his credit, the viscount extends his hand. "It is a great pleasure to meet you, Inspector."

Antonio shakes it. "My pleasure, Your Grace."

"So, Stella, what do you have for me?"

"First, I have confirmed fourteen cases of salt contamination in Quarrels's installations alone. All of them are high profile locations."

"So, I was right. That bastard needs to be sacked. I'll need to send people over to reinstall each one."

"I have a list for you, Your Grace," I say, handing him a crisp bit of stationery that I'd copied each location on. "I also patched each of them save the last three. I ran out of chalk."

"Thank you, Stella. You are a lifesaver, literally."

"Thank you, Your Grace. The second reason I'm here is that I shared my suspicions with my friend, Inspector Guizzetti. I know I technically broke my pledge to silence, but I know this man, and he wouldn't betray our trust."

Henry takes the time to give Antonio a lengthy inspection. "Well, Constable, what do you think?"

With a straight back and sober demeanor, Antonio says, "Inspector, Your Grace. I spent many years earning my title."

"My apology, Inspector."

I try to decide if this is one of those male macho things or a socialist verses royalist viewpoint. Antonio defuses my concern with his next statement.

"I only wanted to clarify because it shows I have some small authority within the constabulary."

Henry nods. "Pray, continue."

"Yes, Your Grace. I listened to Stella's story. I am inclined to agree with you both about the guilt of John Quarrels. That being said, I'm not a magistrate. They don't take the gut feeling of anyone but themselves into account. They want evidence. With Stella's testimony, we would have proof of a crime, but not a perpetrator. Any barrister could get it thrown out."

"I guess I could see that," Lord Helms says, looking down at his own feet, searching for some answer.

"As it stands, I don't even have enough to take to my chief. At best, he would have me investigate Quarrels. In the process, we would almost certainly lose Baron Snowdonia as the instigator."

Henry's eyebrows draw together, and he purses his lips. The set of his jaw says enough. "I can handle that filth Quarrels. I can make him wish for being shanghaied."

"Your Grace, I can't listen to you planning anything illegal."

"Who said anything about illegal, Inspector?"

Antonio harrumphs. "I'm sorry for any implication, sir."

"No offense taken, sir," Henry says with stiff formality.

I am quietly observing but need to intervene to keep this from driving off the rails. "Will you two bandy roosters get your feathers down? We are here to save lives, not butt heads." I ignore my own mixed metaphor.

"Stella is right. I apologize again for my manner, sir," Henry says with flair and an offered hand. "Can we please start over?"

"By all means, My Lord."

"OK, so if we can't successfully bring these villains to heel, what can we do?"

"We trap them like rats," I interject with glee before Antonio can answer. If I had been in different company, I think I might jump up and down like a can-can dancer.

"Yes, we offer these scum a target that they can't refuse," the inspector offers.

"Oh? What? The Royal Constabulary itself?"

"No, sir," he replies, "but what about the home of Boston's most notorious lady, Miss Karie Taylor?"

I expect Lord Helms's gaze, so it doesn't surprise me as he snaps to face me. I give a tiny shake to my head to answer the question he is dying to ask. He turns back and manages to keep his voice calm. "Do you have reason to believe that such a high-profile person would be willing to support this effort?"

"Mrs. Ochoa is a close friend of that lady. I believe that friendship and the prospect of a free demon installation would be more than enough inducement," Antonio offers.

I nod in agreement when an absurd thought comes to mind. I wonder what Lord Helms would think to know that he and I had both partaken of the charms of Miss Taylor. If it weren't so deadly important, I might smile.

"Hmmm. That probably is likely. OK, I agree. I assume I need to have Quarrels assigned for the installation?"

"Yes, my lord. That and one other item."

"Oh?"

"Yes, I need you to talk to my chief and demand this action. If it comes from someone of your prominence, he couldn't dismiss it as the fancy of a second inspector."

Henry smiles. "I can see that. Consider it done. In fact, why don't we go for all of the culprit installers at the same time? I can set it all up for emergency installation on Monday afternoon."

"We only have one install site planned."

"Don't worry about that, inspector. I can come up with some high profile customers that are on our waiting list. If you think your chief can supply the men, I can supply the opportunity to grab them."

# # #

"Karie, it is in your best interests," I say in the sitting room of *Casa de* Taylor. Inspector Guizzetti occupies the cushion next to me on the pastel-green, brocade sofa.

Karie sits court in an oversized stuffed chair the color of evergreen trees. "To have one of those demons in my basement? I don't think so," she says, pulling her loose kaftan tighter around her. "Ewww."

"I never thought you were afraid of anything."

"Mrs. Ochoa, I may not have much in the way of Christian values, but I do fear hell. With my profession, just about everyone assumes that I will be going there. If that is true, I don't want any part of it close to me before my fateful death." She pulls her feet up into the chair, wraps her arms around her limbs, and buries her face into her knees.

Karie has never, ever called me by my married name. I'd seen her eagerly engage with men known to hurt women, and now she balks at this. A new side to my friend.

"Miss Taylor," the inspector says, "We could ensure that no demon is ever summoned and your home is restored to normal afterward. My chief inspector and His Lordship Helms have given us a good deal of resources."

"Why does it have to be here?"

"We want to pull this off quickly, so no more people are hurt, and we don't scare away any involved in the conspiracy," Antonio offers. "We pretty much have to have your decision immediately, Miss Taylor."

Karie sits in a fetal position for several seconds. She looks directly at me and doesn't engage with Antonio at all. "No demon?"

"I'll make sure one is not summoned or is banished immediately," I reassure her.

Several more seconds pass. "Mr. Guizzetti, will you please give us a minute to confer alone?"

Antonio looks at me. I nod. "*Absolutemente, señorita.*"

Karie just sits there quietly after the inspector leaves the room.

"I didn't know this would bother you so much, Karie. I didn't mean to cause you pain. I can call this off."

"No, it is important, but I am going to need comforting tonight," she says, peeking coquettishly over her knees. "It is part of my price."

I sigh in fake exasperation. "Wench, you are turning me into a woman for hire."

Jumping up from her chair, she all but leaps into my arms. "Good!"

"So this fear business was all for show?"

"Oh, not entirely. I hate the idea of a demon in my home."

"Well, in that case...I'll keep my word." Karie kisses me on the lips. "Hold up, Miss Eager," I say. "We have a problem. You still have a guest."

"ALEJANDRO!" Karie bellows, quite unladylike.

"Yes, miss?" says the man entering the room from a servant's entrance.

"Would you be so good as to tell Inspector Guizzetti that I agree to his proposal? Then work out the details with him and send him on his way."

"Yes, miss."

"Is the Blue Room ready?"

"As always, miss."

"Then bring up a hearty dinner in say..." she says, looking into my eyes, "two hours."

Karie doesn't wait for Alejandro to leave, pushing my few loose hairs back and nibbling my neck.

"Very good, miss."

11—Monday, February 13, 1888

I feel a rasp across the pleasure centers of my mind and the scent of menthol dragging me into consciousness. Karie is massaging my feet, ankles, and calves with a cream that makes them tingle as much as her hands alone are doing. For me, feet are far more sensual than even the nape of my neck or the underside of my breasts. The sensations as she weaves her fingers between my toes, make my center go gooey. Waking up through this fog of sensuality is the blurry sweetness of chocolate-covered caramel.

Parting the curtain of sensation, I notice I'm not in my nightdress. I must make quite a sight with only a blue satin sheet draped across my body. This would normally send me into a panic of shame, but right now, all I can do is enjoy my lover's ministrations. I can't even tell how long this lasts. Each moment stretches out into an infinity of pleasure. Some eons later, Karie's caresses travel higher up my legs, kneading my thighs, tickling the back of my knee, and teasing my...well, my pubic hair. I must be lying in a puddle by this point. Every part of me down there slides against one another like they have been greased more than the pistons of the Philadelphia Flyer. I guess five times last night wasn't enough.

The gentle caresses and sharp fingernail rakes continue up my body, merging into my overall glow. Suddenly, by comparison, my right breast aches in a delicious way as I find Karie's lips fastened onto the nipple. Her hands explore my bottom alternating stroking and squeezing.

"Hey, now," I whisper. To aid the process, I roll closer, pressing myself against my lover's mouth. I add an arm around her head and intertwine my fingers into her auburn hair. Karie makes little mewing noises as her tongue swirls around my hardened nipple and, in the process, strokes the little bumps on my areola. The sensations are too strong. *Not so quickly*, I think.

I pull her face back and plant a kiss on her lips. She squirms a bit up my body to put her in a more comfortable position to more easily explore my mouth. She doesn't force her tongue in me, but traces across my lips, darting and teasing. Her hand that I don't have trapped beneath me sneaks up and again tickles the hair in my nether regions. It doesn't touch anything but my tuft. This causes me to moan. Like a good general,

Karie wastes no time exploiting my open mouth, darting her tongue in to share that intimacy.

I try to take her away by pulling on her hair. I want to please her again, too, but she doesn't stop. In fact, the hair tugging seems to intensify her efforts. She uses the palm of her hand to press down on my mound. Too much sensation. I start squirming my hips beneath her. I want to tell her to go inside, but my tongue and lips are engaged.

After what seems an eternity of bliss, Karie releases my mouth and attacks my breasts with dozens of tiny nips alternating with sucks. The palm on my mons venus begins to rotate around in big circles without letting up on the pressure, trapping it against my pubic bone.

She manages to snake her other arm from beneath me. Without stopping anything, she straddles my leg, where she starts rubbing her own wetness across my thigh. *Too much!* "Karie!" I keen. The world drifts away, and my body gives in, again, to my lover.

As my world comes back to me, I feel Karie, her face buried in my neck, shaking with her own sloppy spend all over my thigh.

I let life go out of focus again. I don't fall back to sleep but just float in that bliss of being happy, sated, and, most important, knowing your partner is satisfied. Her slim body doesn't bother me even three quarters on top of me. I feel Karie's ragged breathing against my chest and her breath against my ear. *I can lie this way forever.* The thought throws a cold bucket of snow on me. It startles me into full wakefulness.

I'm not thinking of actually making this permanent, am I? Would I give up everything only to share her with her clients? Now I can't wait to get out from under her, to put on my clothes, and leave. I need to get away! I try and slide her off of me, but she wraps an arm around me, just under my breasts and clings. She gives a little whimper.

I think about how to extricate myself when a cacophony of noise from somewhere outside our room jolts both of us upright.

"*¡Dios!* I'm going to skin Alejandro," Karie growls, untangling herself from me and the bed linens. She throws open the door and storms out, naked as the day she was born. I take the opportunity to gather my clothes, currently all over the floor, and start dressing.

"What in the bloody hell is going on down there," I hear her bellow.

I hear her butler's voice but not enough to understand what he is saying. My hostess continues her loud rant with, "Well, I don't give a damn if they need to get in here early enough to set up. Keep *los cabrones* quiet, understand?"

I hurry up, trying to get fully dressed before my hostess and lover returns. But as with most tasks, hurrying only makes it harder. I manage only my bloomers and start tying up my brassiere when she comes back.

"*¡Hostia! ¡Tócate los cojones!* Hey! Why are you getting dressed?"

"I…" I stammer, struggling to get my slip down past my oversized behind. "I have to go check out the quality of the materials they are going to send with Quarrels." I sit down and pull on my stockings.

"You shouldn't need to do that for hours yet," Karie says, sitting down next to me.

Thinking fast, I add, "I also have to get home to get a report from Tommy, and there is the job hunt I need to start on." There is a pause long enough for me to get my stockings and boots on.

"What's really wrong, Stella?" she says, leaning back to give me the distance I need. At the same time, I don't think she realizes just how distracting she is, wearing nothing and smelling like a woman who has been freshly pleasured.

I pause with my skirt in hand looking at the floor before doing my best to lie to my best friend, "It reminded me of a time with my Aaron. It made me embarrassed that I wasn't living up to his memory."

Karie scoots in closer and wraps her arms around my shoulders. "Stella, I may not understand fully, but I can empathize. I'm here for you to cry on my shoulder anytime you need."

She is making my internal conflict worse, not better. But I told the lie and have to live with the consequences. "Thank you," I say softly.

"And *mi amor*, I think I can say categorically that you have surpassed any expectations that your husband might have had for you."

"Thank you. I just need to get out to think."

"Go. I will never keep you from your needs, *querida*."

# # #

I lied to my best friend and ran away from her like she has smallpox. I still don't know why. I leave Karie's boudoir with no destination other than home in mind. Home. Love. Forever. Freedom. All of these keep bouncing around in my head and multiplying. *Am I unable to commit? Would I have ever lasted with Aaron? Why does the air here taste so much more refreshing than that of the Blue Room? It has no bars. It isn't a cage.*

Yet, I don't want to go near it ever again. The thought sends my stomach sinking and a shiver of dread all the way up to my scalp.

The morning air, so cold it makes my lungs hurt with every deep breath, couldn't taste sweeter. *I am free, but of what? Myself?*

"'False Arrest. Edison Sues New Barcelona.' Read about it here."

Oh, that is going to get messy, I think, grasping at any straw to stop from examining my own thoughts. Edison has a long reputation for successful court actions. While I dislike many of his inventions, I respect the man's legal intuition.

Seven bells peal out over the town as I walk briskly south. I have to put a good foot under me if I'm going to make it back to the boardinghouse before Tommy leaves. Being honest with myself, there is no way I can reach my home in time, even with a hired coach trotting full out, but escape from my lover is still foremost on my mind. Any excuse to cling to in my storm of emotion.

I've spent more nights in Karie's arms than I ever had the chance to spend with my Aaron. Just because I don't exactly agree with her profession isn't enough to stop something more permanent—*is it?* I was even jumpier when Aaron took me out for the first time. I was so nervous that to this day I don't remember what we talked about, and only barely remember that we attended the Boston Museum.

With Karie, it was always friendship until I received that letter from Aaron's commanding officer announcing his death. I spent two weeks in our tiny apartment, sobbing. When Karie came to collect me, I couldn't tell her the day of the week, how long the bread on the counter had been molded, or when I'd eaten last. I'd not even gotten out of my coffee-stained night dress since the letter's delivery. She took me to her home and nursed me back to physical health and a slightly better mental state.

Our friendship morphed months later. I'd been chastely mourning my husband's death, but even with the dark emotions, my body wouldn't let me forget the sexual hunger that stirred in my breast.

I answered her weekly invitation to dinner, the event that usually ended up with me as a snotty, bleary-eyed mess. She comforted me with an arm around my shoulder. I looked up to ask her forgiveness for blubbering. Without any conscious thought, I kissed her full lips. She kissed me back. The next thing I knew we were—

"MRS. OCHOA!" A shout breaks through my musing.

I look up to see Inspector Guizzetti, in the civilian attire of a tradesman, sitting in a buckboard older than the monarchy. Realizing this is some form of anonymity from the people walking around me, I follow along. "Hello, Mr. Tony."

"I be thinking you be deaf. I done called your name like six times."

"Lost in thought, mister."

"Your friend said you'd left the house early and might need a lift. Can I offer you a seat in my carriage?"

"How chivalrous of you, Mr. Tony," I say, climbing up onto the bench next to him, pulling the warm lap blanket over my limbs.

"And where might you be headed?" he asks.

"Honestly, I hadn't exactly decided. I probably should check on the material for your work."

"Thank you, mum. I could rightly use the coin." He set his tired horse off, making listening in on us difficult to impossible. "You really would make a tremendous inspector, Mrs. Ochoa. You fell into that without even a hint from me."

"Native cunning?" I joke.

"Then I'm certainly glad you aren't my partner. I'd ever be trying to catch up."

I laugh. "*Mierda de toros.* You are smarter than that, Mr. Guizzetti."

"And the mouth of a sailor. Didn't your mother ever wash your mouth out with soap?"

"Often, until I learned not to say it in her presence. I was a slow learner. I still have the hint of Ivory flavor in my mouth every time I curse."

He chuckled. "So shall we head over to Forever Power and certify the materials? I have a guardsman waiting to sit on them until they are sent to Miss Taylor's home."

"Certainly." I mulled it around in my head. Why not ask this man who isn't involved in my mess his opinion. "Can I ask you a couple of questions, Antonio?"

"I reserve the right not to answer."

"They may be personal."

"Oh, the best kind, Stella."

"Have you ever thought about marrying your girl?"

He darts me a severe glance. "That is a bit personal. But I'll answer. Yes, often."

"Why? Is it just so you can get a look of and touch her legs? Maybe get into her bloomers?"

"Goodness, but you ask some rough ones."

"I warned you."

"Yes, you did. No, actually, that isn't the reason. The reason is that I see Carmen making my flat a home. I see her on my arm as we go to church. I see her scolding our children for making a mess. I can envision her crying when the Christmas tree gets knocked over by the dog chasing the cat. And to dissuade you from your other thoughts, Carmen and I are as intimate as possible without the church's direct blessing."

"Thank you, Antonio."

"Are you thinking about getting married?"

I don't answer for longer than is polite. "It passed through my head briefly, but I don't see that same future for me. I see only bouts of intense passion interspersed with pain."

"Then I suggest he isn't the man for you," he answers.

I am glad he is obtuse at least this once. "I think I have to agree with you."

# # #

"Stella!" Patty squeals as I enter with the plain-clothed inspector. Her red curls bob as she bounces on the balls of her feet. "I hoped you'd come back soon so I could invite you and your husband to dinner."

"I'm sorry, Patty, but I'm a widow. My husband was lost in the War of Irish Independence."

"Oh, I'm daft. I'm sorry. Maybe your boyfriend here?" she says, giving the inspector an appreciative examination.

"Wrong again, Patty. But I take no offense—"

"Maybe I do!" Antonio says with a tease in his voice. "I wouldn't be caught dead with such a plain woman."

"Be careful there, Inspector. I'll tell your lady you were flirting with me. I'm sure Patty here would back me up!"

Patty looks a bit confused but nods.

"Peace, ladies. I was only joking."

I give him a glare with a raised eyebrow before turning back to Patty. "I'd be happy to attend your home whenever you find it convenient—with or without a partner at my side," I say, once again giving the inspector a glare.

"Excellent. Sunday next? I promise I'll try to keep my foot out of my mouth."

"Definitely. Seven PM?"

"Perfect. Now can either of you tell me why I have a policewoman parked here and insisting I can't leave until the final bell? She even threatens to attend the outhouse with me."

"Well, no, Mrs. Smith," the inspector offers before I can speak. "Patty, this is Inspector Second Guizzetti."

"Nice to meet you, Mrs. Smith," he says, bowing over her hand.

"I'll decide if I'm as enchanted after you explain," she tosses back.

"We assure you it is vitally important that you not do anything other than set up the four kits for installations today. Interact with no one."

Patty looks at me dubiously, but I nod. "I promise, Patty, that I'll tell you everything as soon as I can." Now it is Antonio's turn to give me a look. "With the inspector's blessing, of course." I roll my eyes back into my head. *Some men.*

"Actually, the kits have already been assembled. I received notice in a memo directly from Lord Helms."

Antonio screws his brows together. "Is this normal?"

"On rush orders it is, Inspector. About every third Monday I find a personal memo from Lord Helms."

"I see. Thank you for setting my mind at ease, Mrs. Smith."

"Patty, we need to inspect your kits. Again, we trust you—"

"But we need independent verification," the inspector butts in.

"Antonio, if you are going to keep interrupting me, then you better put a ring on my finger to give you the right to do so," I tease.

"My apologies, Mrs. Ochoa. I wouldn't dream of it."

"Which, butting in or marrying me?"

"I'll leave that as an exercise for the student," he says with a mischievous grin.

Patty gives her own grin at the byplay. "All four kits are over here."

While the inspector, Patty, and a dour female constable watch on, I sample each item. The silver-nibbed pens are well above the minimum quality, as is the paper and incense. The chalk is of especial importance, so I actually use a silver comb to spread it all out in a fine layer, scrutinizing it through a magnifying lens.

"I can certify that each of these four kits is free of salt contamination or anything that would prevent a successful capture and internment of a demon," I say to the small group.

"Guardswoman Kelly, I give these kits into your charge to ensure they remain inviolate until they are sent to the installation sites."

"Yes, Inspector."

# # #

I manage the rest of the morning without falling into a pattern of self-destructive thoughts about my prison break this morning. I change into my ragged, barely presentable work dress. It is dark and more forgettable, should someone, namely Quarrels, accidentally see me. I add a hat outdated ten years ago and a bit of soot from my fireplace to become a working drudge that no one would look twice at.

Ducking into the narrow alleys between the brownstones, I arrive at Karie's tradesman entrance just as eleven o'clock's three-quarter-hour bell sounds from several church bells in town. Quite thankfully, Alejandro answers the door. I don't know what I'd do meeting Karie with my mind in such a jumble from our last meeting. Before I can even exchange greetings, he shoves a sandwich into my right hand and a mug of warm cider in the other. "Please go down the back stairs, Mrs. Ochoa."

I'd never been in Karie's kitchen or belowstairs of her home. A cheery affair, the kitchen is arrayed in mostly white ceramic tile with a bright-yellow mosaic of a blazing sun. Bright copper cookware hangs efficiently near the stove. There is an actual water faucet over the porcelain sink rather than a pump out of doors.

I discover the steep back stairs and, with care, take them down. I find myself in an earthen-walled cold cellar where meat hangs, vegetables are stored in bushels on the ground, and canned produce fills one entire wall. The portion that held the household wine is no longer as composed as the others. The wine racks from the south wall have been moved, and bottles of wine rest on potatoes, nestle in a bushel of carrots, and even lie on their side trapped by cloves of garlic. I'm sure Alejandro has more than one curse word, closely-held to himself, about the chaos. I give myself a mental note to remind the constabulary to return the cellar to its normal state.

Within the small space, I find Lord Helms, the inspector, and a gentleman I've not had the pleasure of meeting. The unknown man's bulk, Sunday-best suit, and Antonio's deference leads me to believe that this may be the chief inspector. "Good morning, gentlemen."

"Welcome, Mrs. Ochoa," Antonio says to me in very formal address.

"Chief Inspector, this is the witch I mentioned in my report. She has already been vital in her evaluation of the materials to be used and pointing out possible perpetrators."

"Absolutely, Chief O'Hara," Lord Helms chimes in. "If it weren't for Stella here, we would still be in the dark."

Chief O'Hara looks at my disreputable state up and down with darting gray eyes. It feels as if his eyes take in my attempt at disguise, sums up my bank account, determines my intelligence, and plans my usefulness all in that one brief examination. He holds out a hand that would have looked natural on an enormous bear. "It is nice to meet you, Mrs. Ochoa." After juggling my sandwich and cider into the same hand, I do a dainty shake of his hand.

"Likewise, Chief O'Hara. Have Lord Helms and Inspector Guizzetti filled you in on our adventure here?"

"Yes, quite, Mrs. Ochoa. I look forward to a successful conclusion one way or the other."

That is so carefully said that I would peg him as a judge trying to make sure he isn't prejudiced to one side in a case. "Agreed."

I look over our blind. A narrow slit has been cut through the earth of the bare southern wall. It looks down over a lower basement where workers seemingly prepare for a typical demon installation. While we can look down quite easily, the slit is up within the floor joists. If we douse our candles and remain quiet within our cellar, there is no way we can be detected from the other side.

"Lord Helms, when is Quarrels scheduled to arrive?"

"Three PM. I try to get my installers to arrive fifteen minutes early, just in case. I'd expect him no earlier than half-past two."

"So, we have a couple of hours to kill. Anyone up for some cribbage?" Lord Helms offers, pulling out a board and cards. While I can't say everyone is eager, it is a way to while away the hours.

We agree to play for a penny a point. It is hard-fought and keeps our minds off of things we can no longer change or influence. After two hours, I am up six pennies. The chief is up four bits, but I only think so because I believe the inspector keeps throwing him cards for his crib. Helms is down a dime or so.

One of Karie's other servants tosses a potato down the stairs, our signal that Quarrels is here. Dousing the light, we all cuddle up to the wall, four abreast. We have an agreed-upon sign. When, or from the chief, **if** I see Quarrels do something to the installation, I am to tap the shoulder of the inspector and the chief.

We watch as Alejandro leads Quarrels down the stairs. "Workmen have been here all day making a mess and more noise than you can fathom. Do you know when all this will be finished? Mistress is expecting to entertain in the early evening."

"Actually, my portion of this will be done in a short hour, sir. There may be some minor tweaks to the boiler; however, they should not be lengthy."

"Good. The mistress will be pleased. I'll leave you to your work."

John set about making a picture-perfect installation. Every phase is flawless. I doubt my mother could have done a more excellent job. The demon, a massive brute that looks more like a locomotive than anything living, arrives roaring his challenges but quickly settles to his helpless situation. I begin to wonder if I've led us onto a fool's errand until Quarrels pulls a silver snuff box with the image of the Crown inlaid in mother-of-pearl from his waistcoat.

"Let's see how daring you are after this, Miss Karie," he says, spraying a tiny pinch of the box's contents onto the chalk ring. I smack the inspector and the chief immediately. Even in the ghostly light cast up from below, I can see their nods.

The demon looks down in some surprise. "WHY!" the hellspawn says. John says nothing. He packs up his tools and walks up the stairs.

Inspector Guizzetti dashes up the stairs three at a time. Lord Helms follows but only manages two at a time. I go up next, but in skirts and heeled boots I have to hit three times as many steps up the steep incline.

I get to the front door just in time to hear, "By the power vested in me by the Royal Constabulary, I arrest you, John Quarrels, on the charges of murder, attempted murder, and conspiracy to murder."

# # #

I arrive to see Quarrels's eyes wide in surprise.

"I'm sorry, but this has to be some kind of absurd joke. I've done nothing wrong."

While I expect Lord Helms to attack the man, he remains passive except for the glare he directs at Quarrels.

Antonio doesn't hesitate to move forward. "Guardsman Hennessy, if you will be so kind as to search the subject and place every object on the table next to him. I will not touch him, as I am a direct witness." Antonio is making sure this arrest has absolutely no holes in it.

"While our constable is searching your person, I must advise you that you have the right to remain silent. This means you do not have to say anything, answer any question, or make any statement unless you wish to do so. However, if you do say something or make a statement, it may later be used as evidence. Likewise, should you not say something that you later use in your defense, it may prejudice the case against you. Do you understand?"

"I tell you this is absurd. I'm not a murderer!" Quarrels says as Guardsman Hennessy empties the man's pockets. One of the items that is on the table is a silver snuff box.

"Will you witnesses confirm that I've read the accused of the rights provided to him by King Frederick the Second?"

"I will," or its equivalent is echoed by everyone in the room, now including the chief.

"Hennessy, would you please open that snuff box and tell me what is inside?"

"I use that for my lunch," Quarrels says without waiting for an answer.

"Salt, Inspector. By the by, Inspector, if ya look into his lunch pail, you will see he has a whalebone salt shaker. I seed him eat'n earlier."

I see the man's dark face turn a pale gray. Tears well up in the corners of his eyes. *Stupid, and quite brittle little niñita*, I think.

"Would you like to revise your statement, Mr. Quarrels?"

"Inspector, we should examine the installation for evidentiary purposes," I add, now noticing more uniformed guardsmen traipsing through Karie's home than I have ever seen in one place.

"Quite right. Inspector Third Left Bear, please accompany Witch Ochoa to the cellar and witness her inspection."

"Yes, sir, Inspector."

Together the constable and I go down to face the demon. "I'm going to dismiss the creature, and then we can get at the actual site of the contamination."

"You, Mrs. Ochoa, are the expert. I'm only here for confirmation."

"Right." I sit down and take off my boots and stockings. Standing, I feel the preponderance of smooth clay within the dry, gritty soil. It can't hold water if it tried.

This isn't my best thing. I need to concentrate. Closing my eyes, I reach beyond the soil for the taut, slick fabric of our world. I feel the holes, like that of a block of Swiss cheese in our existence, and disparate ones in other layers. I mold the layers like sheets of parchment, twisting but not folding them until the holes intersect, right under the demon. I feel his evil pass through along with some of the dirt. Before releasing my tension on the sheets, I open my eyes to confirm he is gone. Only the constable and I are in the basement. Only a shallow divot remains where there had once been a beast. I take a deep breath and let go.

The snapping back of reality makes me dizzy. "Whoa, there, Mrs. Ochoa." I feel the policeman's arm steadying me. "Are you alright?"

"I never was very good at that," I say, feeling the earth solidify beneath my feet again. Now, shall we have a look at the installation?" I get down on my knees, ignoring the mess it is making of my dress. "There—see the tiny, rock-like things in the powder?"

"Yes, ma'am, I do."

"How do we preserve this as evidence? Would varnish work?"

"I believe so. Maybe we can dig a thin slab of wood underneath and coat it with varnish. To seal it."

"I'll leave that to you, Inspector. It's your evidence. I'm just an unbiased witness," I say with a smug smile. I have earned a pint at the Bell in Hand.

"Thank you, Stella," Lord Helms says. I hadn't even heard him come down the stairs. "I owe you a debt of gratitude bigger than you can imagine."

"Well, I'm sure we can come up with something. I could use some new shoes."

Helms laughs heartily, I'm sure for the first time in weeks. "I'm certain I can be more appreciative than that."

12—Tuesday, February 14, 1888

I moan as I sit up in bed. My temples throb to the beat of a cha-cha. My stomach threatens to stay in bed, with or without all its contents. At this time, I realize that there is a banging on my door. "Mrs. Ochoa! Mrs. Ochoa! Wake up."

I look at the window, and dawn hasn't even lightened the darkness of night. The pounding in my head matches that at the door. In defense, I bark in frosty little puffs in the moonlight, "Stop. I'm coming."

Thankfully, the banging stops. By touch alone, I find my dressing gown and slip it on. I strike a match and light the candle by my bedside and squint at the visual abuse.

As I struggle toward the door, I bang my toe on the nightstand. "*¡Hijo de la chingada!*" I snarl. Even my own voice tears sheets of pain through my aching head. What did I drink at the Bell in Hand last night? I limp to the door, and after two attempts to unbolt it, I fling it open. "What!" I hiss, compromising between a shout and a whisper.

Janice Potsdam, one of the girls of our boardinghouse, stands there in her nightshift. "Mrs. Ochoa. Your young man is at the front door."

"What? I don't have a young man!" I snap at her. I reach up to hold my head as if it might fall off or explode.

"The young waif you see every morning. He came banging on the front door and wouldn't stop. Mine is the closest to the front door, so I answered before it woke up Mrs. Chapman."

"Wise. That bitch is a handful at the best of times," I say, letting my mouth just pour out what my mind dredges up. "What the bloody time is it?"

"A bit after five."

"Well?" I ask, my head as dense as my tongue feels.

"Well, what, Mrs. Ochoa?"

"Why did you wake me up?"

"The young man, named Tommy, insists that he speak to you now. He says it can't wait."

I shake my head—a mistake. Someone puts a garrote around the top of my head and tightens mercilessly, or at least, so it feels. It doesn't make me charitable toward either Janice or Tommy.

"Let's go," I say. Each stair down to the ground floor is an exercise in torture. Someone sets off one of those Chinese New Year firecrackers between my ears with each step.

"Stella," I hear Tommy's voice muffled through the door. *In for a penny*, I think. Bracing myself for the pain to come, I unbolt and open the door. I've never seen Tommy look worse. The knees of his breeches are torn, he is covered in mud and in some places, blood. His cheeks are white as milk, snowflakes perch on his eyelashes, and his lips are blue. Were it not for his new clothes I believe he might have frozen to death.

Setting aside my ire and pain at least until he is ministered to, I say, "In close to the fire, boy." I pull him in and push him to the parlor. I close and rebolt the door. I rest my throbbing head against the nearby wall.

I find him shivering in front of the fire, his scraped hands close to the banked coals. "Janice, a slug of brandy for this boy to warm him up." The young woman throws me a worried look, so I continue, "I'll settle with Mrs. Chapman later." I take an afghan from the couch and throw it over him, pausing only long enough to brush the snow off his shoulders. Tommy shudders.

"Ma'am, I got to tell you—"

"This first," I insist, pointing to the brandy. He snatches the goblet and tosses the entire thing down in a rush. His eyes go wide, and he blows out an oath in a language I think might be Turkish. "It's meant to be sipped, not gulped, Tommy."

"I see that now, Stella. But I got to tell you about the baron."

"Really, this couldn't have waited until the morning?"

"It is the morning," Janice adds helpfully.

"OK, at our normal time in the morning?"

"I don't think so, miss. You see, he done run off."

"What? I don't understand. Start at the beginning," I say, motioning for him to sit down on the couch.

"I'm all wet, ma'am. If'n you don't mind, I'll sit on the hearth.

"See, I followed the baron just like you said. It seemed like any normal ole day until a constable knocked on his door. They talked for a bit, and the baron gave him a pouch o' coins before closing the door."

"What time was that?"

"'Bout three-thirty, maybe four in the afternoon."

"Go on."

"Ten minutes later, the baron left in his carriage with two big trunks on the back. I followed him to the English Bank of Boston. He went inside. The bank guard wouldn't let me in, so I hadta wait. He were inside about fifteen minutes and left with a big, I mean really big, leather case.

"Him and his carriage went south. I knew it were important, so I grabbed a cab and followed him with the money you done given me. I followed as long as the money held out. The cabbie finally had enough at Mount Hope and kicked me out. I watched the baron's carriage keep going south until I couldn't no more. I then ran back to tell you. Took all night."

"How did you get all banged up, Tommy?"

"It's slick out there. As fast as I was going in the dark, I kept falling arse over akimbo. It's nothing. I had worse playing stickball, Stella. The warmth lets me know I'll be right as rain after some sleep."

"Tommy, you did exceptionally well. Janice, will you please get the boy another brandy. I need to change. And Tommy, sip this time."

"I won't be making that mistake again, Stella."

# # #

My bank accounts wouldn't thank me, but I didn't hesitate. I gave Tommy a doubloon and stood him a meal at Mrs. Adveries Restaurant. I also didn't want to waste any time and so hired the first cab I could flag down to take me to Boston's Royal Constabulary.

I arrive just before the sun peeks over the horizon. The streets only contain wagons of butchers, bakers, and greengrocers, making their deliveries to restaurants and other stores.

I push open the constabulary's front doors to find much more industry inside than out. Guardsmen are moving around like bees in a hive. A sizeable oaken desk separates me from them. Perched in the middle, looking particularly starched and pressed, is a middle-aged sergeant. He wears more ribbons and braids than I've seen on an entire marching band.

"May I help you?" he asks in a friendly way that still manages to come out gruff. Maybe it is just his rough voice.

"Yes, Sergeant, I need to speak with either Inspector Second Guizzetti or Chief Constable O'Hara. It is quite urgent."

The man maintains his air of calm. "Chief Constable O'Hara isn't in and wouldn't see you without an appointment. Would you care to make one?"

"Not if Inspector Guizzetti is available. Truly, Sergeant, the information I have is time-sensitive and relates to the demon case he just made an arrest for."

Again, with no particular haste or perturbation, he offers, "If madam will have a seat, I will inquire if he will see you. Your name?"

"Stella Ochoa."

"Very good." He writes something on a piece of paper. He hands it to a runner before returning to what I notice is a patrol schedule in development.

I wait for the count of forty-two Mississippis before Antonio shows up, quite a bit more worse for the wear. His clothes, which still bear some cellar dirt, are rumpled, his hair is askew, and he has the wide-eyed look of someone who's had one too many coffees. The last is confirmed as when he offers me his hand, it is quivering. "Stella, what are you doing here so early this morning? Did you know that the three installers we caught are all busting open like *piñatas*? They have all implicated the baron."

"That's what I'm here about. The baron has taken it on the lam. He skipped out last night."

"Tell me about it."

I give him chapter and verse as close to Tommy's discourse as I can.

"Do you think young Tommy would point out the guardsman?"

"Maybe. That might be pushing him a little hard, but I can try to convince him."

"OK, that is for later anyway. For now, come with me." Despite the hoary look the sergeant gives me, the inspector leads me back to an interrogation room where Quarrels sits, looking even worse than the inspector. His face is red from sobbing, and fresh snot is on his upper lip. To my surprise, Lord Helms is present, glowering from a dark corner.

"Is this OK? I'm a witness. I shouldn't be with the accused."

"Don't worry about that now," Antonio whispers. "With his written confession, he is done. But he managed to get the Royal Prosecutor to agree to twenty years hard labor, rather than death, for being so gracious in sharing his information."

"Quarrels!" Antonio barks. "Where is the baron going?"

"Huh?" the wretch mumbles. "Going? I don't understand."

"You said the baron hired you to undermine the demon restraints. He has run away. Where is he going?"

"I don't have a molly."

Antonio glares at the prisoner, and his voice takes on a more authoritarian tone. "Don't lie to me, pig. You better get an idea," he says, picking up a sheet of paper from the table. "I can just tear this deal into little shreds and see you in the dock for multiple murders.

"Bart," he says to another policeman, "how did the Crown decree that the last murderer die?"

"I think they tied each of his limbs to four skittish horses and then fired a pistol."

"No. Really. I don't know," Quarrels blubbers.

Antonio tears the sheet cleanly in half. I happen to catch that the paper is only a blank schedule sheet.

"Nooooooo." He fully bursts into tears. "I don't know. Please, I'll tell you anything, just give me back my deal."

"Then you better come up with an idea."

Quarrels suddenly brightens up. "Wait. The baron has an estate down near Hartford. That is where he went. It must be. Please give me my deal back."

"I'll think about it. Bart, take over."

Quarrels sobs and his chest wracks with his wheezing. I almost feel sympathy toward him until I envision all of the people who've died at his hand.

The inspector grabs Lord Helms by eye and leads us both from the room. "Don't worry about that worthless worm."

"Oh, I'm not," I say. Henry shakes his head, matching my sentiment.

"Well, if he is on his way to Hartford, then he is in Connecticut or soon will be. The Dukedom of Connecticut is well outside our jurisdiction. I can telegraph the constabulary there, but multi-jurisdiction cases often have lessor priority to the guardsman on the beat."

"Telegraphs are down anyway," Lord Helms offers in additional bad news.

"Yes, and likely will be weeks before they are fixed. And if the baron takes it on the lam as you suspect, Mrs. Ochoa, he will likely head to the Freeport of Baton Rouge.

"And then he might as well be on the moon as far as we are concerned," I growl in frustration.

"That's right, Stella."

"If we had any chance of catching him inside of the monarchy, I could claim hot pursuit to any other duchy," Antonio says. "But with the storm, icy roads, and the fact that he has a fourteen-hour lead on us, we have basically no chance."

Lord Helms's eyes go wide. "How is he traveling, Stella?"

"Last I heard by coach."

"How many horses?" Lord Helms asks with a certain incongruity.

"I seem to remember Tommy said two."

"Inspector Guizzetti, would you like at least a chance to catch the bastard?"

"I'd eat slugs for just the chance, Lord."

"I think I can beat the baron to his home if it is just the two of us."

"I don't see how. The trains aren't moving, and even if I could requisition a dirigible, the winds are too bad."

"How about the poderabile?" Helms asks, looking at me.

"Brilliant," I say. "That will vastly outpace any horse."

"Yes, and if I carry extra pressure tanks, we won't have to stop to rest our horses, only swap out bottles when they are played out."

"I don't know what you are talking about, but I'm game. But if we are going after a powerful witch, I think we need one of our own. Can you bring Stella, too?"

They both look at me, and I smile. It hurts my head.

"Oh, yes. I was counting on it," Henry says with a smile like a jackal. "If you all are willing, meet me at Forever Power at noon, and we will hunt down that bastard. Dress warm."

#

Not knowing how long I will be gone, I pack my carpetbag with my extra pair of undergarments, a nightdress, my Sunday clothes, and some feminine supplies. As an afterthought, I grab one of my bankbooks.

My head continues to throb as I walk quickly. It keeps my attention. Someone must have slipped me a shot or six of absinthe. I dodge an entire group of bicyclists up to who knows what before I end up in the Bell in Hand. "Michaeleen!" I wince again at the sound of my own voice.

"Stella, I was thinking to myself that you'd be still sleeping it off after the one you tied on last night."

"I should be, Mick, and that is a fact. But I have business out of town to take care of. Would Tommy be here?"

"I should say. After I rounded on him for not being here last night, he told me a tale of following the Baron Snowdonia for you. I woulda thrashed him for a liar, but he showed me the doubloon you give him."

"Yup. He did both of us proud. But can you have him come out for just a second? I won't keep him long."

Tommy doesn't wait to be fetched. The scamp probably overhears every word we say. Wiping his hands on a towel, he comes out wearing his leather dishwashing apron. "Yes, Stella?"

"Tommy, I'm going to be out of town for an unknown amount of time. Don't bother to come by to see if I have chores until I seek you out. I'm going to give Michaeleen your pay for the next three weeks just in case. Mick, would you see that he gets one dollar every Friday."

"Certainly, Stella."

"Thanks, Mick. I already gave you a monetary reward for doing a good job, but I wanted to tell you that you did great. You have done beyond well." I swear that the boy blushes four shades of pink and three of red. I can probably use him as a night-light.

"I only done my job best as I knew, Stella."

"Keep it up, Tommy. Now get back to work!"

"Yes, ma'am."

"Michaeleen, can you throw me together six of your big trencher sandwiches to go, please."

"No problem. Picnic?"

"I wish. I'm off to capture a witch." Anyone else would ask a million questions, but Michaeleen has seen me go off to imprison demons. Capturing a witch must seem like nothing. "Oh, and a gallon jug of your stout."

I pull my own glass of ale from the tap, leaving my coin on the bar. I sip on it with worries swirling, mixing with the aching through my head. I've never confronted another witch. It isn't something we are taught. I can't ever remember it happening, at least anyone my mother has ever talked about. There are always rumors of how the Royal Inquisitors are trained, but they seem more like fairy tales meant to scare kiddies.

I don't want to fight the baron. I want him to give up and face a

Royal Magistrate. Both my head and my heart says I will have to fight him, and that fills me with dread.

Mick delivers a large paper bag and a clay jug. I thank him and make way to my next stop. Earlier I picked up the passbook of the English Bank of Boston, it being on the way to Forever Power. I am one of many in line. I wait my turn with my odiferous sandwiches making several people look in my direction. Finally, I make it to a teller with not a little grumpy in my mood.

"Good day, madam. What can I do for you on this day?"

"I'd like to withdraw two hundred dollars, all in gold doubloons if you please."

The teller looks down his nose through a pair of nose pinchers. "I show here that you have only ever made deposits. May I ask why you would be withdrawing such a large sum?"

"No."

"No, what, madam?"

"No, you may not ask."

"Just one moment, madam," he says and walks over to one of the bank managers. They return together, where the manager takes over the inquisition.

"Madam," he pauses to look at the passbook, "Ochoa. I understand you wish to make a large withdrawal."

"I don't know about the definition of large, but yes, I'm making a withdrawal."

"Well, it is the business of our bank to protect the interests of our clients. We would like to know what the purpose is of withdrawing the large percentage of your account."

I still have the remnants of a hangover. I've yet to have anything to eat. The smell of Michaeleen's lunch is driving me almost batty with hunger. Add to that, I hate officious *pendejos*. "What purpose did your bank use my deposited money for?" I ask.

"Excuse me, madam?"

"It is my business to protect those I entrust my money to. What did you use it for?"

"That is the business of the bank, madam!"

"And why is it any different for me?"

"Well, you are a woman. Have you maybe a letter from your husband explaining this withdrawal? We wouldn't want this to be used frivolously."

I swallow a good deal of anger before speaking again. "What is your name, sir?"

"Maximilian White."

"And your position here at the bank?"

"I am Executive Senior Floor Vice President," he says with some inflation of his chest beneath his expensive suit.

My experience is that the more words in someone's work title, the more of a *gilipollas* he is. He wears his minuscule power like Napoleon did before Wellington's troops put a bullet in him.

In soft words, I deliver my response in a slow, measured cadence, "Mr. White, I am a widow. I am only beholden to myself."

"In that case, we have an even larger responsibility to protect your interests in place of your husband."

The manager must not notice the increasingly bland façade I put on my expression. He may not be aware of the danger he faces. "Yesterday, Baron Snowdonia came in and made a massive withdrawal, well in advance of my paltry two hundred royal dollars. Did you question him thus?"

"No, of course not, madam. We don't pry into the affairs of our customers."

"Then why are you prying into my affairs?"

"I've already explained, Mrs. Ochoa—"

"Mr. White, are there any bank officers of higher rank than you on the premises?"

"Yes, madam, but I don't see—"

"Please send for them. And while you are at it, you might summon your bank guards."

"Why would I do either of those things? This is really a simple matter to resolve."

Continuing calmly, I add, "Because I'm about to rip this cage apart because of two bloody obnoxious idiots. Do it now."

Both men back up half a pace, and the teller waves frantically for the guards. "Madam, threatening a bank official is a crime."

"So is theft. I'll put my threat against your theft in court and see what the magistrate thinks."

"Madam," says one of the two large guards I now have flanking me, "I think it best you leave now."

"Gentlemen, perhaps you are unaware, but I am a hellfighter." The teller doesn't waste any more time and bolts. The manager takes another step backward. "I've faced down more demons than you have decades in your combined lives. Don't think you will be intimidating me.

"I have been calm. I've been patient to your blatant abuse because I do not stand to pee. I've asked to obtain my own money. When turned away, I asked to speak to an officer, a real officer of the bank," I say with a look at the Executive Senior Floor Vice President. His already pale face blanches further. "I've been rebuffed at every turn." I now raise my voice loud enough that the entire lobby can hear. "Now you will either give me my money, every last bit and penny, or I will turn your beautiful lobby into a pile of rubble. Your choice."

The other customers now seem to be deciding whether to run or to get their money as well. Most of them choose the latter. There is a sudden crush to get to the windows and demand funds.

The two beefy guards reach for me but find that the marble floor yanks from beneath their feet. They both land with the dignity of a sack of potatoes thrown over a wall. I look at the manager. "I've put up with this enough. I'm assuming you no longer want to keep me from my own money?" He shakes his head. I look at the passbook. "Two thousand five hundred sixty-four dollars and ninety-four cents. Now, please."

"There isn't that much in the tray. I'll have to send for it."

"Do so." The bank guards threaten to stand. I use the tiles of the floor to pull them far across the room.

A runner comes back with a carefully arranged tray of coins. I give the manager credit. He isn't shaking, and he hasn't peed himself. He just finally realizes the futility of standing up to me. "If madam will count your money."

I do. It is as accurate as only a bank can make it. "It is correct."

"Then, if madam will sign this ledger, I will take and destroy your passbook."

"Perfect," I say, signing where indicated after dumping the coins into my carpetbag.

"Then, is your business complete here at the Bank of England?"

"Absolutely. I will never allow you to trouble me again." I put the floor tiles back into place, leaving the lobby unscathed, save the mayhem of people trying to obtain their money. The chaos spills out into the street. *Too bad for those English dicks.*

I'd only planned on two hundred dollars in gold doubloons, just in case. I have assumed that the limitations of the poderabile mean we will be going on a one-way trip. I will need some living and traveling expenses. I now have over ten times that much.

I wish I had the time to go home for another passbook so I can deposit the excess, but the old saw says if wishes were horses. I guess I am just unusually flush.

#

The dock of Forever Power looks like someone has stirred a nest of ants. Thousands run around doing tasks only they themselves understand. Almost all of the activity focuses on the poderabile and a four-wheeled wagon attached behind. The wood of the cart looks new as if it has been built just this morning. Metal fastenings are all shiny without the slightest hint of corrosion. Six-foot-long and maybe eight-inch-across metal cylinders are in a high stack within the wagon. Wide leather straps hold them into a roughly rectangular shape.

The tradesman's boxy shape has been modified to hold more of the cylinders upright around its middle. It looks like the waist of a Western gunslinger with dozens of extra cartridges.

"Stella!" Lord Helms yells and waves from the roof of the poderabile. He motions to one of the workers. "Fasten that down." He climbs down the back within the grid of bottles like a bighorn navigating the face of a cliff.

"We didn't have time to make a special cart to carry the extra canisters, so we had to improvise."

"I see that. Will this thing move?"

"Definitely. My engineers made a few modifications since our last trip. Even with the load, it still should go as fast as the other morning. We estimate forty miles an hour at the top end."

The rest of the workers clear out, leaving us almost alone near the monstrosity.

Forty? That's almost as fast as a dirigible, I think.

"Forty?" Inspector Guizzetti asks incredulously as he walks into the area. "I've seen racehorses that didn't reach that speed. Are you sure it's safe?" Antonio asks, his Adam's apple bobbing up and down. If it weren't for the cold, I bet he probably would be sweating.

"Safer than any trolley," the viscount offers.

Oops, I think. *Way to make it accidentally worse.* Closing his eyes, Antonio works his jaw as he swallows several times. "How much longer before she is ready to go, Henry?"

"She? Well, I guess it's a vessel like any other. I'm sure I can scrounge up a bottle of champagne. Arthur, go up to my office and fetch the San Cristobal in my filing cabinet.

"I hope neither of you has much in the way of luggage." The inspector, still looking a bit green in the face, holds up a tote no bigger than my purse. My bag is somewhat larger.

"Which reminds me, Lord Henry, can I borrow your safe?"

"Excuse me?"

"I had a little trouble at the bank this morning. I seem to have more cash on me than necessary, a lot more cash." I jingle my duffle.

The young runner Arthur comes pelting out of the dock to Lord Henry's side, holding an oversized magnum of champagne. "One more thing, Arthur. Hop over to accounts receivable. Bring back a single depository bag. When Mrs. Ochoa seals it, I want you to take it back and ask that it be held in our vault separately."

"Thank you, Lord Helms," I say.

"Not at all...now, what is that wonderful smell from that paper bag?"

"Lunch!"

"Excellent!" Henry chimes in. "A quick picnic lunch before we trundle off?" he says, taking down a buffalo-skin lap blanket from the cab of the poderabile and spreading it out on the cold ground.

I break out the butcher-paper-wrapped sandwiches and pickles and put the jug between us. "No steins, so we will have to share."

In the frigid breeze, it isn't the most comfortable picnic ever. But not the worst, either. I remember a summer luncheon where my school class had chosen to set up on top of a mound of fire ants. We all had welts for a fortnight.

Antonio is the only one that doesn't dig in with an appetite of three. I did because I have not broken my fast. I assume Henry has been working hard all morning if the calluses on his hands have anything to say. I like Henry. He is a member of the aristocracy who pitches in and pulls his weight.

I pass the growler around. The stout complements the crusty bread and the sharp pickles. Somewhere in the middle of lunch, Arthur shows up to take my coin into safekeeping. He brings two bags just in case. I count one hundred ten gold royals: two thousand, two hundred dollars, into the first stout canvas and woven steel bag with lettering proclaiming it the property of Forever Power. It also has a wax seal that I clamp as tightly as possible and scrawl my initials upon. Before I let it go, I look at Henry. He nods and smiles around some mustard at the corner of his mouth. I reluctantly release the small fortune to his runner.

As we wrap up, Lord Helms jumps up. "Cecilio!" Lord Helms bellows toward the dock, his voice still muffled with the last crumbs of his second sandwich. "Where is that man? Cecilio!"

"*Si, jefe*," Delgadillo says, appearing almost as by teleportation.

"I need some black paint and a small paintbrush."

"*¡Absolutamente, jefe!*"

"Shall we christen this land yacht?" Helms asks as he picks up the champagne.

"What's her name?" Antonio asks, still holding over half his sandwich. Helms provides an evil grin. Cecilio returns with the materials to solve the problem. The neat hand Henry uses painting the letters on the side just behind the seat leads me to believe he has spent some time as a draftsman.

"Very appropriate, viscount," Antonio says, nodding.

"I agree, Lord Helms."

Henry picks up the champagne and hands it to me. "Mrs. Ochoa, would you do the honors?"

"Thank you, Henry. I would be pleased."

I walk up to the front of the poderabile and aim at the metal corner brace. "By God and his son Jesus Christ, I christen thee 'Lady Justice.'" The bottle explodes, spraying foam and liquid everywhere. The gentlemen clap, as do some workers looking on from the dock.

"Well done, Mrs. Ochoa. Shall we see if she can live up to her name?" Henry scrambles up onto his invention. I gather up the fur from the ground and shake it clean, folding it over my arm twice.

Inspector Guizzetti, who has been uncharacteristically quiet, just stands looking at Lady Justice. "Antonio, you should get in on the other side." Antonio gives me the look of a sick puppy dog but sets his jaws. Before he can leave my side, I offer him the other depository bag remembering Baron Snowdonia's severe reaction. "Just in case."

We climb up to bracket Lord Helms in the cab. I notice that the levers now have handgrip controls on them. "Henry, did you make a change?"

"Yes, ma'am. It was your discovery. Remember when you pulled back to slow, and you were thrown forward, causing us to shoot forward again?"

"Yes, all too well," I say, rubbing the spots where I'd gotten bruises.

"Well, the grips are such that the levers won't move forward unless you squeeze them. So to brake, you let go of the grips and pull back." He demonstrates. He then shows me how it wouldn't move forward even to a determined hit of the heel of his hand. He then squeezes the grips and slides them forward.

"Excellent. Nice safety feature."

"I'm always looking for a way to improve. I also padded the front bar in case a passenger is cast forward. Antonio, are you ready?"

The inspector clenches his jaw again and nods. The viscount reaches above his head to turn on the air lines. "Here we go!" he shouts, pushing forward both levers. The poderabile doesn't leap forward like it had without the trailer, but it still moves forward with more dispatch than an unspurred horse might.

"This isn't so bad," Antonio says as if trying to convince himself.

Henry turns into the lane with a massive thump and metallic jangle as our trailer drops off the sidewalk instead of exiting the carriageway. A squeal of indignation in Spanish accompanies Henry's driving of limited skill.

"Sorry," Henry calls out to the woman he nearly runs down.

"Lord Helms, I might offer that all wheels will travel inside the front wheels. This means you have to turn late and wide," Antonio says, with renewed wits.

"Thank you, sir. I will definitely take that advice in the future direction changes. In the meantime, let's get some speed on."

"It goes faster?" Antonio says.

"We're just getting started." I wonder if Lord Helms is sadistic, playful, or just hasn't realized the inspector's qualms. I am leaning toward the latter, but don't rule anything out just yet. Henry eases the levers forward about half the way. "Stella, one thing you have to keep in mind is that you don't want to go faster than this will stop, just like a normal wagon."

The jostling manner we receive from the cobblestones seems more like an energetic laundress over a new washboard. It makes me want to check to ensure my teeth are in one piece. Bundled up, children chase after us cheering and yelling. Adults just stop and stare. We must make quite a sight in a double delivery wagon without a team of horses in front. The wind is still stiff enough to chill me. I unfold my buffalo fur and wrap it around my limbs and torso. I button the top button on my coat and pull my scarf tighter around my neck and head. I'm very glad two seasons back that I'd splurged to purchase sealskin gloves. My hands are one of the few places on me that are actually warm.

"Are we going to freeze before we get there?" I ask, my voice wavering with the rattling we are receiving.

"We will have to stop in four hours or so to change air bottles. I brought a warming stove. We can defrost then," Lord Helms offers in a bouncing voice of his own. He skillfully navigates a pothole in the road.

"If we aren't blocks of ice by then."

No one answers. *What can't be cured must be endured. I almost wish I were a fire witch right now.*

Before I even notice, we have been swept out west of the city where our poderabile wrangler pushes his control levers to the three-quarters mark. With only gravel roads, the washboard jostling is gone. However, there are intermittent potholes and rocks whose jars more than make up for the more regular rough ride in the city. "Ah, Henry, shouldn't we be going south?" I ask.

Antonio perks up at this.

"Your young friend said that the baron went south. That means he will be traveling through Westwood, Uxbridge, Thompson, Ashford, and Manchester before he can turn south toward his family estate," Henry says. "And that is assuming he doesn't divert even further south to Providence. The Uxbridge path is the most direct route, but the roads aren't so great for us. We'd have to slow down to almost a team's speed. If we take the good roads east through New Seville and further to Springfield, we can turn straight south. We can keep the speed high almost the entire way."

"What if he stops along the way or goes straight south on his way to Baton Rouge?" Antonio asks. "We might miss him then."

"Inspector, this chase has always been predicated on catching him or waiting for him at his family's estate in Hartford. If he chooses any other intermediate destination, then he will escape."

Antonio goes quiet. I can't read his facial expressions as he is on the other side of the viscount.

"The other thing is that if we want to get in front of him, we are going to have to travel all night. My energy from our success against those butchers is waning. Stella, I'm going to need you to spell me when the time comes."

"Absolutely, my lord."

"You might try and get some sleep."

"Yes, sir."

I wrap myself as best as possible in the wooden seat, laying my head into the crook between the back and the side wall. Even with the bright western sun in my face, I close my eyes, and I try to sleep. Every time I finally get to a point where I'm dozing off, we hit a hole or rough patch in the ground. It slams my head against its hard support and wakes me up. I'd pad my head, but all of the soft materials I have are going into keeping me from freezing. My efforts don't amount to much by the time the sun sets behind the horizon. What finally brings me to full wakefulness is the poderabile slowing to a stop.

"What's wrong?"

"First air bottle change," Henry says as he turns off the bottle's air supply. "Stella and Antonio, if you would be so kind as to get the lanterns out of the trade box in the back. I'll fire up the heater so we can defrost a bit."

Without much discussion, the inspector and I bring out and light seven lanterns. Henry totes out a box no larger than a hound dog but with more copper tubing than a still. He opens it and lights something inside before closing it back. I bring one lantern closer to inspect it. The box has a white, fibrous exterior and a boiler on top. "It will take a few minutes for that to warm the boilers. Then the tubing will provide radiator type heat that we can move around."

"What's inside?"

"Another of my inventions. I figured out how to make a safe, semi-solid cooking fuel. I put it in an asbestos insulated box to prevent stray energy loss. It turns out about eighty percent efficiency in delivered heating."

"Very nice. Why not put it in our cab?" Antonio asks. "Even with a double woolen layer under my winter uniform, I think I'm about one step warmer than ice cream."

"I'm not sure yet that it is safe."

"It might be worth the risk."

"I also only have about three hours' worth of fuel," Henry says, shooting down that plan.

"Oh, well. It was worth a try."

We wait silently, cupping our hands over the boiler. Small tendrils of heat escape until we hear the steam coming through the copper tubes. We stand next to them, and it amazes me just how much heat they radiate. I even open my coat and lean over them to luxuriate in temperatures likely still colder than Mrs. Chapman's kitchen icebox.

We gobble up more of my sandwiches. I barely notice the taste. It is only to stoke our body's ability to keep itself warm.

"We need to swap bottles out. They are threaded at one end. I'll deal with that part of it as they are delicate. One mistake and it will severely impact our trip. Lay the empties by the roadside and then hand me up the fresh ones, pointed side first, from the trailer."

"Leave them by the road, Henry? They must be valuable."

"They are, but really only to me, Stella. I have a team coming along behind us to collect them." He points at the side of one of the metal canisters. It bears stenciling on its side proclaiming, "Not abandoned. Property of Forever Power." "Besides, the lack of weight will allow us to go faster, in theory. In reality, the roads are bad enough, and it is getting dark. We likely won't be able to take the opportunity to push much faster."

Henry arranges the lanterns to give maximum light on the rear of the trade's wagon and the grid of twelve bottles. It takes only two bottles before we become an efficient team. Henry unscrews the empty and slides it back into my waiting hands. Anthonio gets on the front end of the bottle and takes the weight as it finally drops off the edge. We carefully stack them next to the road.

When we pick up a full one, I take the front, and Antonio bears most of the weight as we lift it into Henry's hands. He glides the container into the cylindrical hole with the care of a watchmaker. When it is fully inserted, Henry first rotates it slightly left and then right, eight full turns.

Moving the great bottles is more difficult than I expect. They are quite heavy, even empty. They must weigh as much as a slightly built woman—maybe as much as Karie does. I'm not sure if they are heavier full. It is, after all, only air. The empty bottles are considerably colder than even the ambient temperature with ice formed on the outside. I don't know why. It makes me once again thankful for my sealskin gloves.

When we finish, twelve bottles later, we have a neat semi-pyramid between two fence posts with five on the bottom, four on the next layer, and three on top. The whole exercise takes us close to twenty minutes.

"We need four lanterns for the front of the poderabile," Henry says. "Inspector, if you would douse the rest and put them away."

Henry motions for me to carry the other four to the front. He opens special glass lens front boxes made for the lamps. "These are designed to focus and shine the light farther ahead so we can see the road better.

"Stella, if you will get up and get ready to drive, I'd appreciate it. I'm going to put away the heater."

I am being thrown into the deep end of the pool. The fate of our endeavor and our lives is in my hands. I've been confident in other life and death situations but because I'd trained and exercised my skills. Here I'm a neophyte. I swallow my own bile as the inspector and viscount climb up next to me. "We all strapped down back there?"

"Yes. Let's go," Henry says.

I squeeze on the handles and push the levers forward. Nothing happens. I push further, but the poderabile doesn't move. I then mentally kick myself. I let the levers move back to their resting state. I turn partially within my life belt and open the valves for the air tanks.

Henry says nothing. When I look at him in the reflected light of the forward lamps, I realize he probably is already asleep. Antonio's eyes are also closed.

This time the vehicle responds as I press forward. We are off again, much slower, but we are moving. I experiment at a slow speed. The gravel road makes steering a bit slushier than in the town. The water on the surface in what had been puddles are solidified ice. They provide no grip at all, not even as much as an ice skate. Like in town, when I see them, I mentally reach out to push tendrils of frozen earth to pierce the freeze. But I have to see it. At least once going around a blind corner, I encounter a frictionless surface in the tracks. I panic, but the sheer sides of the ruts themselves keep us from flying off the road.

It takes several minutes for my heart to return to its normal rhythm and settle into driving—at a much-reduced speed.

Henry's lighting system pleases me. One lantern on either side looks down at each track of the road out about forty feet. The other two cast beams out at seventy and a hundred feet or so. It gives me some idea of what's coming. The two longer ones aren't very bright, but they provide enough illumination to catch the red eyes of a herd of deer in the road. I slow down to almost a stop as they take their time traipsing across our path. The buck doesn't want to leave and keeps staring me down. I decide that we are bigger than he is. I push forward slowly. While it may not be bright, the deer decides the wagon isn't worth broken antlers and walks out of my path.

I drive into Springfield with only the sounds of our wagon wheels again on cobblestones. We get a look by a constable as we trundle under a streetlamp. As I continue, he just watches. I have a feeling had we stopped, we would have been questioned, at least until he saw the inspector's uniform. I've never been to Springfield, so I'm driving even slower to see if I can catch some sign of a turn.

"Take that road there, Stella," Henry says softly in the dark, startling me that he is even awake. "That's Springfield-Hartford road."

"Thanks, Henry," I reply with my head facing him to try not to rouse Antonio.

"I figure the air bottles will play out soon. I'll drive the rest of the way from there."

"Did you get any sleep?"

"Surprisingly, yes. I'm used to grabbing fifteen-minute catnaps as necessary as I tend to work late into the night. I believe Edison does something similar."

The conversation gives me a much-needed jolt of energy. "Are you saying you emulate Edison, sir?"

"Posh, no. I've only met him twice at parties. But once I looked at doing a business deal with him. A double team of horses couldn't have made me sign that contract. His method for getting his way has nothing to do with the law, the spirit, or the letter of the agreement. He just waves enough lawyers at you until you give in from frustration and your purse is drained. I find the man reprehensible."

"What about Tesla?" I say, more to keep the conversation moving than caring what it is about.

"Met him three times, twice at parties and once at a convention of inventors. Brilliant man but a bit of a nut. Of course, many say that about me and even the contraption we are riding in."

"Well, on that last part, you can be assured that they are wrong. Lady Justice, this self-propelled wagon, is *genial.*"

"Thank you, Stella. I know I always think they are great and the people working for me think so too, but I pay their salary. There are times I do wonder."

"If I were rich enough, I'd have seven of these...one for every day of the week." I pull the right lever to swerve around a patch of ice I see late.

"I think that might be laying on the mustard a little thick."

"Maybe, but this is a wonderful invention, once you figure out how to keep us warm," I say, using one hand to pull my scarf up over my chin.

"Trust me, next thing on my list," he says, chattering between his teeth.

The throttle levers of Lady Justice stop giving her thrust just as light peeks out over the eastern horizon. The three of us pile out and change the bottles again, more like zombies than people who are consciously being effective. Antonio and I empty the trailer. "Last from the trailer," Antonio says as he lifts his end into the empty slot.

"Start taking them from around the sides. You will have to carefully unstrap each one. Be careful," Lord Helms says.

"Damned right, we'll be careful. Bloody things weigh a ton. Stella, I'll hold it in place, and you unstrap it. Then I'll ease it down."

"Yes, Antonio."

I unbuckle the leather straps and then bend over to ensure the bottle doesn't slide off its little metal shelf as the inspector lowers it onto his shoulders. I then take the upper end. As before, Antonio carries a good two-thirds of the weight by being nearer to the center of the cylinder's length.

"*¡JODER!*" Henry barks.

"What happened?"

"I stripped the threads on this bottle, Stella. We will have to move this one out before I can take another." We are forced to jockey our full one to the ground and lean it against the wagon before taking the other out.

"Just place it with the other empties. It is useless until it is rethreaded."

"That means we don't have another full replacement set," Antonio says, huffing and puffing. I don't really have the breath left to speak.

"I know. We shouldn't need to charge again, knock on wood," Lord Helms says with a superstitious rap on the wagon's wooden exterior. "I figure another ninety minutes to Hartford and thirty minutes beyond that to the baron's estate.

We finish the work, sweating as much as we were cold before.

"Antonio, would you unhook the wagon while Stella and I collect the lanterns?"

"Not a problem, sir," the inspector says as he starts immediately. Antonio's uniform, usually so neat, is rumpled. Sweat stains the underarms and in a V down his neck and back. The viscount isn't much better. His smart suit is covered in tiny wood splinters from climbing up and down the back. Two buttons on his vest are torn, and his heavy coat has somehow been splashed with mud across the left side. It also bears a fist-sized tear under his right arm. I don't even want to imagine what a figure I cut.

As we get to the front and start removing the lanterns, Henry whispers to me, "Are you sure we can deal with Cardiff if he becomes belligerent?"

I look at him and answer as honestly as I can with a shrug.

"If you aren't sure, I can invent a breakdown. You needn't lose face."

"Henry, if we don't at least try, I think we are as bad as he is. While I am not sure about my abilities, I take comfort in the biblical passage, 'Put on the full armor of God, so that you can take your stand against the devil's schemes.'"

"Agreed. I just wanted to give you an out if you felt you needed one."

"No, Sir Henry, I'm quite committed, no matter the outcome." I get a shiver, and this one not from the cold, as I realize I really mean it. Mentally I interpose the dead faces from Prince Street over Snowdonia's convivial image. He may not have salted the spell, but he definitely killed every one of them. I decide right now that I will not leave until Snowdonia answers to justice or to the Almighty himself. "I am quite committed, no matter the outcome," I repeat, taking out one of the lanterns and blowing it out with the breath of my words.

Not much of a Saint Valentine's Day.

13—Wednesday, February 15, 1888

"Stella, wake up. We're here," Henry says into my addled brain.

My neck is stiff from leaning up against the side of the poderabile. My head rings from the bruise just above my left ear, where it rattled against the wood. As my brain reconnects with my body, I remember where I am. The sun is midmorning high behind white, fluffy clouds. I see no homes, only that we are in a small bowl with a plowed field behind a barbed wire fence to our right. "We are where?"

"The Cardiff home is just over the rise in front of us." Lord Helms says. "Antonio reports that the baron's coach is in front of the house. It got there recently as the horses are still steaming. He's watching the house up there now."

"Do we have a plan?"

"I'm not sure you'd call it a plan, but our thought is that the inspector will go to the door to make the arrest with you as backup. I just sit here and look pretty." The viscount coughs at his own disheveled state. "If things go sour, you take down Cardiff with Antonio covering the household staff for you. I make sure that the baron can't leave by coach or horse."

I think for a moment as I unwrap hair that has tangled around my neck and caught in my mouth. "I guess that is the best we can do without knowing anything more."

"What more do you want to know?"

"Be nice to know the house layout."

"I know some of that. It is a three-story home. The main foyer splits the house in half. Immediately to your right is a ballroom. To the left is an ornate staircase that goes up to the billiard room and library on the second floor and the family rooms on the upper. Behind the stairs is another set that goes down. Further into the foyer and to the left is the dining room in the center of the house. At the back of the house on the left is the parlor. All of the rooms to the right of the ballroom are for the servants—kitchen, pantry, and quarters."

I just look at him with my mouth open. "How in the name of all that is holy do you know that?"

"Baron Cardiff has a cousin who had a coming-out party I attended. That's also how I knew to stop in this little hollow instead of just topping the hill and let everyone see us."

"Well, that isn't nothing, Henry. Thanks for the information."

Returning, Antonio's steps crackle as they break the thin film of icy mud. "Are you two ready?"

I remember my own fears and deflect attention from myself. I ask, "Are you?"

Antonio pulls out a gun and cracks the round, spinny thing away from the handle. I see the ends of six bullets there. Closing it, he places the pistol back into a prominent waist holster leaving the flap loose. As an afterthought, he reaches around to touch glass manacles, the ones specifically made to hold witches, hanging from his waist. "Yes, I'm ready."

I reach down and pull up a bit of the nearly frozen mud, crushing it between my fingers. I lick my thumb—loam, clay, degenerate shale, mulched hay, horse droppings, among other constituents. I alert the earth that I may be calling on it. The mud ground into the knees of Antonio's breeches calls out for help. With a wave, I cause all of the dirt to drop off of his uniform. He doesn't look pressed, but he no longer presents as a hobo. "Let's go. Are we sneaking in?" I ask.

"Nope. We are the law. We don't sneak."

I personally don't think that is a good idea, but Antonio is our authority. We might be able to use the viscount's title in a pinch. I have zero right to demand someone surrender. I follow the leader.

We walk over the hill and right past the carriage. It is empty, I note with a quick glance. The horses have been ridden hard. Sweat on their flanks is steaming, and rime still rims their noses. Based on the footprints in the frost across a grass lawn big enough to play soccer on, the driver must have gone inside with the baron.

I take a deep breath as we approach the door. Inspector Guizzetti takes the first step to make the arrest—he knocks.

A butler, from his regalia, opens the door. "May I help you, Constable?"

"I'm here to talk to Franklin Cardiff, Baron Snowdonia."

"If you will come into the foyer, sir, I'll get him. Whom shall I say is calling?"

"Inspector Second Antonio Guizzetti of the Boston Constabulary," he says as we both enter. The inside of the building is significantly colder than the world outside.

"One moment, sir."

The butler walks up the stairs on our left, just as Lord Helms had described. Henry hadn't mentioned the railing and balcony with a view from above. That's a weakness for me, especially with the extensive basement the earth beneath me reports.

"Inspector, I'm not sure I can affect anything up on the balcony."

"Understood."

The butler is gone so long I wonder if he has skipped out the back of the house. I am just about to look for a chair to snooze in when the butler comes out from behind the staircase, not down the ones he'd mounted. I joggle Antonio's elbow.

"I saw it," Antonio whispers.

"The master will see you in the solarium. Please follow me."

The butler walks toward the back of the house in the stiff, measured manner of a man in service for many generations. He doesn't seem concerned. He doesn't hurry. Just before we reach the midpoint of the long foyer, my head spins like I'd been too long on a merry-go-round. I stagger.

"You alright, Stella?" Antonio says, grabbing my arm.

"Dizzy." I reach out for the earth to steady me. The home has wooden floors, walls, and even ceilings, the paranoid bastard. Even the dirt in the basement floor has ice covering it. I can feel it, but it is trapped.

"Of course you are dizzy, Mrs. Ochoa," Baron Cardiff says in his deep baritone that reverberates in the hall as he strides in. "Most witches lose their equilibrium when the planes are moved around near them. I, on the other hand, have spent years inuring myself to those effects."

"Franklin Cardiff, you are under arrest for conspiracy to murder," Antonio says, drawing his revolver. He aims with the steadfastness of a rock even though I can't tell which way is up.

"Come now, Inspector Second," the baron says with the cordiality as if he is at a garden party. "You know that weapon isn't viable against me, and your pet witch is incapacitated. Despite the bind you've put me in, I don't like killing. Just walk away."

Antonio fires a shot. The water in the air solidifies into ice in front of it, deflecting it away from the baron's body.

"Now that wasn't very friendly. I don't want to be forced to kill you, man. Take Mrs. Ochoa and walk away. Last chance."

STONE! my brain screams. A marble, tabletop-copy of the Venus de Milo. There isn't much to work with, but it is near enough the wall that if I send a spike out in the right direction, I can send it flying...but at which of the three barons I see?

Any action is better than none. If I miss, maybe it will distract Cardiff. I teeter over onto the floor. My stone statue hurtles across the room. It slams into the baron's forehead. My dizziness begins to clear. The inspector fires. Cardiff spins as blood sprays. From my side, I look up, seeing only two of everything.

Two identical French doors open into the solarium. Two identical Franklin Cardiffs stagger through them. "GAZZUNREEP," he calls with a gurgle in his throat.

What the fuck? What does Gazzunreep have to do with anything? I think, struggling to my knees. My mind is still muddled. *How does he even know Gazzunreep's name?*

"I've got him, Stella," Antonio says. I'm trying to tell if there is one or two of him when the floor explodes. Literally explodes. Antonio disappears in a mass of splinters, flying floorboards, and fire.

Floating over the hole, where just moments ago Antonio sprinted across a floor toward our quarry, is a demon whose likeness is burned into my mind and into my flesh. Vaguely humanoid, his three horns mark him as no animal of this world. All of them stick straight out of his skull—one out of his forehead like a unicorn and one more each corkscrewing out of either side above where his ears should be. Fangs stretch out far enough to make the hinged mouth necessary. Two beady sources of flames flicker out of his eye sockets. He spreads his bat wings wide showing his narrow, red, and black-furred body—Gazzunreep.

"I TOLD YOU I WOULD COME FOR YOU, STELLA," he shouts into my mind over the constant roar of the conflagration that he brings with him.

Even though it is only a foot tall, I can feel the waves of heat flowing off of him, warming even in this frozen house. My head is clearing, but my heart starts beating like that of a hummingbird staring down a cat. I manage to stand. Baron Cardiff escaping is minor—I worry about surviving.

"Why?" I ask, trying to buy myself even a few more seconds of life.

A shaft of red light, not gout of flame, lashes out from its open mouth. I dive behind a heavy oak console table. The ruby beam ignites everything it touches. The sideboard table erupts in flame. I realize that the dress between my legs is burning. Whacking it with my gloves, I extinguish it.

"BECAUSE YOU TASTE SO GOOD, MY LOVE."

"Taste?"

I hear a sizzle and pop just before the ray burns through the table. The beam stops. "YEARS AGO, YOU CALLED ME AND LET ME TASTE YOUR SOUL. YOU WEAR MY MARKS."

I'm casting about for anything I might do. It takes a full team to bind a lesser demon, much less a ranking lord. It sometimes takes dozens of witches to destroy one. One could send a demon back to hell, but it requires time and most of all their concentration.

Years ago, during my first attempt to pass my witchcraft test, my mother stood proctor. She had prepared to send any demon I might summon back before it could do much damage. I don't have her preparation time. My only hope is time.

I bolt back out the way I came. The beam licks at my feet as I go, melting my boots' heels so that I have to stumble about on uneven soles.

"I WILL SNACK ON YOUR PHYSICAL BODY BEFORE TAKING YOUR ESSENCE WITH ME TO SAVOR FOR ALL ETERNITY."

With no other witches present, I have only one hope. I need to buy time. "Only God can have my soul," I say as I hide behind an evergreen bush. I begin reaching out to the planes of existence. *Concentrate*, I beg myself.

That damnable beam cuts my bush cleanly in half, top and bottom both erupting in flames. I flatten down.

"THAT IS WHY I ATE YOUR HUSBAND, WOMAN."

"My husband died liberating Ireland." *Concentrate! You will only get one chance at this.*

"OH YES, THAT PETTY HUMAN CONFLICT. TRUTH. BUT I CORRUPTED THE ENGLISH TO CALL UPON ME AS AN INSTRUMENT OF WAR—ALL TO ENJOY HIS MEAT."

"But that wasn't me, filth."

The smoldering remains of the bush are sliced down again further. I roll across the ground to another shrub, anything to buy me a few seconds. I know he is just playing with me, but I need those seconds.

"HA! YOU CALL YOURSELF A WOMAN OF GOD. DO

YOU NOT KNOW YOUR BIBLE? GENESIS 2:24—THEREFORE
A MAN SHALL LEAVE HIS FATHER AND HIS MOTHER AND
HOLD FAST TO HIS WIFE, AND THEY SHALL BECOME ONE
FLESH. THUS, I TASTED YOU THROUGH HIS MEAT. I SUPPED
ON HIM FOR HOURS WHILE HE SHRIEKED AND PLEADED."
Don't be distracted, I tell myself. *You have already mourned your
husband's passage to the next world, and the worm may be spinning yarns to
torment you.* I reach my mind out wide. I can feel the weakness in each of
the planes like a child's toy that I need to align right under him.

"I WILL RELISH YOUR SWEET AGONY, STELLA OCHOA. I
WILL LAP UP THE BOILING MARROW OF YOUR BONES. YOU
TOO WILL BEG TO BE KILLED, BUT I SHALL JUST FEAST
FURTHER ON YOUR PAIN."

The beam of death cleaves the plant hiding me in twain and rips
open one of my sleeves. With no more cover, I roll out into the open.
Gazzunreep floats over the scorched remains that had once been the
front lawn.

"COME, MY LOVE, SO THAT WE MIGHT SHARE IN THE
SWEET STENCH OF YOUR BURNT FL—"

The earth beneath my feet is eager. I entice it to action. It reaches up
in four grasping claws to engulf the demon in an earthen tomb. The ball
of stone stifles his boasts, at least for a moment.

Before the planes can shift away from where I've aligned them thus
far, I grab them with my mind. They don't move easily. It's like dragging
a heavy bureau across a rough wooden floor. It's disorienting, but at least
I know in which way.

The sphere of rock glows in front of me as I tug and drag the universe
itself with all my mental powers. For Gazzenreep, the ball now parts
easier than a warm piece of taffy might for the teeth of a young child.

"ENOUGH ANTICIPATION, STELLA. IT IS TIME FOR YOU
TO EMBRACE ME."

Hold off just another—

The red beam strikes me dead center of my chest. My clothes ignite,
and all I see is red and yellow flame. I prepare to meet my maker.

There is no pain. My skin isn't bubbling and charring under the
intense heat. I feel warm, but not injured as my dress and underclothes
turn to ash.

"WHAT TRICKERY IS THIS?"

I'm as shocked as my opponent, but I return to my task. The beam repeatedly lashes over my skin. It fires directly into my eyes, which briefly blinds me as a bright light in the darkness might. Still, it causes no pain. I can feel the planes of existence sliding into place. *Just a few seconds more—*

An explosion underneath my feet throws me to the ground. I can feel the pain and shock as bits of rock and blackened twigs tear into the skin of my feet and legs. Once, as a girl, I'd been accidentally shot by rock salt from a shotgun. It feels very similar. The pain slips away, and I feel like I am detached. The floating feeling seems to ease the movement of planes like putting grease between them.

The red maw of hell opens up directly beneath Gazzunreep. He claws upward and flaps his wings. "NO. NOT YET. I HAV—" and just like that, he is sucked down out of our world.

I realize there is no longer the fire's roar from the demon's presence. It is quiet and still for a moment as I lie on the cold ground. I try to decide if I have enough energy to move. Pain from my feet sucks at that spirit that keeps me conscious. A random thought strikes me. I hope there is enough ash of my clothes left to cover my nakedness.

Footsteps crackle through the remaining char of the grass. I don't even have the will left to look. I can't even summon the earth to move me. "Almost," Baron Cardiff's confident voice says. He walks into my view holding something as archaic as a sword. Blood drips down his arm and even more soaks into the legs of his breeches. He holds the weapon in both fists like a stake to drive through the heart of a mythical vampire. "You almost pulled it off, but not quite, *puta!*" His arms raise up the blade.

A loud report matches the gout of blood and brains out the front of Snowdonia's head. The man's lifeless body falls on top of me, the sharp sword, pushed by the corpse's weight, slices across one breast and down my ribs.

"Stella!" I hear Antonio calling. The baron's body is rolled off of me. "Are you alright?"

"Fuck, no," I whisper, with all the vehemence of a marshmallow before my mind shuts off.

14—Later

I hear birds calling outside the window like it is spring. I don't want to open my eyes. My feet and legs throb painfully with each beat of my heart. My left side stings with every breath.

"Drink this, Stella," I hear a sweet, female voice say.

I try to see what is being fed to me, but I can't as something is keeping my eyes shut. Just thinking about my situation drains enough energy for me to lose focus. I just open my mouth. I cough and spit at the bitter concoction I recognize as laudanum.

"Sorry," the voice says. "Now, some soup."

The discomfort eases as beef broth is spooned into my mouth. It soothes my throat and warms my center.

"You haven't eaten anything in a week. We worried you might not live." For whatever reason, I still can't place the woman's voice, but my lack of will and the fog of the drug don't help.

15—Thursday, March 8, 1888

The room I wake up in is not one I recognize. The twenty-foot ceilings and massive windows are enough to classify it as an expensive home and not my boardinghouse. The brocade print curtains, window treatments matching an obverse wallpaper pattern, rule out a hospital. The silk and lace bed linens speak of wealth. Nothing of this room speaks of Karie's style. I don't know how to describe it other than Karie's use of money is ostentatious with the intent to impress. This room is meant to be comfortable and practical in its wealth.

I smell like I've not bathed in a fortnight.

Then it hits me. When was last night? For that matter, what is the last thing I remember? A minor terror overcomes me when I remember Gazzunreep. I pull up the cover and find myself in my old nightdress, patched holes and all. My feet are still there, but uniformly yellow bandages cover them. Pulling up my gown, the dressings make their way up to mid-thigh. They have lemon-colored stains the size of a quarter over most of their surface as if they have smallpox that are yellow.

The door opens beside my headboard, and Lady Helms comes in carrying a tray full of jars and strips of new bandage. She starts, almost dropping her load. "I'm sorry, Mrs. Ochoa. I didn't mean to leave you, but it was time for your bath and bandage change. I didn't expect you to awaken."

I open my mouth to speak. Nothing comes out but a croak. My throat and mouth are as thick as if someone had poured glue down them.

"Hold on. Let me get you some water."

I try to say that I can get my own bloody water, but it comes out closer to Russian than anything intelligible. I try to swing my legs off the bed, and Lady Helms goes berserk.

"NO! Don't do that. Your feet have been badly damaged. It will take some time for them to fully heal." She looks directly into my eyes, "Please!" Then she asks much more softly, "Please, Stella, stay off your feet."

I give her a scowl and put my limbs back under the covers. "Thank you, dear. Let me get you some water so you can speak."

"Do I hear the warrior princess has arisen?" Henry's voice says as he saunters into the room in his nightclothes. The top of his head and arms are swaddled in their own bandages, but he still wears a broad smile.

I wrinkle my eyes at him and point to his injuries. "Well, my dear, that is what you get when you lie unconscious too near a reigning prince of hell. You basically cook from the outside in. Oh, don't worry. I'll be right as rain in another week or two, but our mutual jail-keeper is making certain I'm not disfigured. I'm getting much the same treatment your legs are getting—garlic-infused honey as a poultice."

Lady Helms comes in with a crystal pitcher of ice water and matching glass. "Here, Mrs. Ochoa. Drink it slowly and not too much."

The water lubricates my mouth to a point where it now only feels sticky instead of cemented. The rest of the water gives me a healthy glow radiating from my middle. "How long have I been out?"

"Which time, dear?" Mrs. Helms asks rhetorically. "The last time you were conscious was two days ago. Before that a week and before that, almost two weeks since you saved everyone at the Cardiff Estate."

"I saved my own skin, not everyone else's."

"Well, think that if you wish, but had you not put that creature back where it belonged, both my husband and Antonio would have both perished, and likely Baron Cardiff would have escaped."

"I don't understand—"

"How about I let Antonio tell you himself. He saw most of it. I saw almost none," Henry says. "I made a wrong choice and ended up pretty much out of it from the start."

"Antonio will be along presently," Lady Helms barks at him. "For now, I want your ugly face back in bed before I sic the dog on you."

"Henpecked, and I don't even get the good part of marriage."

"Off with you now."

"When will Antonio be here? Is he alright?"

"I'll send for him if you behave yourself and manage well enough this evening. He can be here in the morning along with that group of ruffians you call a team.

"In the meantime, if you will eat, I will bring one of your friends, although I'd use that term loosely, who refused to be kept away. He broke into my home four times before I gave him a list of chores and a bed."

I'm not sure whom she could be referring to until Tommy's mop of sandy hair precedes a peek around the corner. "Miss Stella!" he says, bolting around the corner. "You are OK!" He runs up to the side of the bed but then gently leans over and gives me a soft hug.

"Damn you, Tommy," Lady Helms barks at him. "I told you I'd call you when she was well enough. Oh, I don't know why I bother with you! See if you can get her to eat. I'll come back and change her bandages later."

"I'll get her to eat, Lady Helms."

"If you don't, I'll skin your hide."

"Yes, ma'am."

Lady Helms leaves the medical supplies and storms out of the room in a swirl of petticoats. By the purse of his lips and roll of his eyes, I can only assume Tommy is suppressing a giggle.

"She sure barks loud, don't she?"

Ignoring his slur on the viscountess, I lay into him with, "I'm asleep for a day or two, and the world goes and gets crazy. What's going on, Tommy?"

"Well, it weren't just a day or two, Stella. Lord Helms weren't kidding when he said that you was laid up for nigh on a month. You wouldn't wake. Your limbs done swolled up like balloons with infection. If it weren't for Mr. Parker, a doctor woulda had to take both of 'em off. Mr. Parker done lanced the puss out of them in many places. He done spelled them, and wrapped them up with garlic and honey."

I blink. My legs ache, but they don't seem sore enough to require amputation.

"Add to all that, you wouldn't eat none. We had to force soup down your throat. You damned near wasted away."

"I could stand to lose a few pounds."

"Not no more, Miss Stella." I can see I'm going to need a mirror, but that is for later.

"So, how did I end up here?"

"Well, I have strict instructions only to let Mr. Guizzetti tell that story."

"You little brat! I'm paying your wages, you scamp."

"Not no more, Miss Stella. Lady Helms done hired me away from you and Mr. O'Flynn. Sorry."

"You rat," I say with a broad smile. "Is her ladyship paying you well?"

"Yes, ma'am. I got my own room, my own bed, and ten dollars a week, and all I gots ta do is keep her stables up. I like horses." He lowers his voice to a near whisper, "I mighta paid her to let me."

"That's quite a nice arrangement, Tommy. I'm glad this is working out for you. Tell me one thing. What happened to Baron Cardiff?"

"Deader than a doornail, ma'am. I thought you already knew it. The copper blew a hole out his head bigger than the hoof of a Lipizzaner."

"You saw the body?"

"Splashed all over the papers, Stella. You are quite the celebrity now."

"*Dios*," I whisper at the uneasiness of what my world holds for me when I do get out of my velvet prison.

"Yup. Lots of reporters done tried to sneak in to take your picture and get your story, but I taught Lady Helms where they was gonna try and sneak in. Dogs done got some free meat from some of those snoops."

I hang my head in fatigue. I've only been up a few minutes, and I feel like I've done without sleep for several nights in a row.

"I done saw that, ma'am. You are tired, and I won't be answering no more questions, but if'n I don't get this soup in you, Lady Helms is gonna box my ears from here to Sunday."

I wink at him and open my mouth like a little bird.

16—Friday, March 9, 1888

My spacious room seems crowded with more people in one place than the last Friday night I'd spent at the Bell in Hand. My friends and team, the *Dos Campanas*, and Inspector Antonio Guizzeti stand on one side of the bed. Tommy sits on the foot. Chief Inspector O'Hara, Father Juan, and Henry sit in chairs on my other side. And as had been her habit since I'd been awake, Lady Helms fusses about me and my comfort like a hen missing a chick. As notable exceptions, my mother and Karie are not in presence. I can understand the unique problems of Karie not attending, but despite our estranged state, my missing mother shocks me.

"I'm sure you have as many questions as we do," Henry says. "Only Chief Inspector O'Hara has heard most of it, at Inspector First Guizzetti's insistence of secrecy."

"Wait a minute," I jump in. "Inspector FIRST?"

"That's right, Mrs. Ochoa. After hearing the facts and seeing the scene, I was forced to promote this miscreant," O'Hara offers with a fake grimace. "I mean, this whole episode hasn't hurt my chances at the superintendent post that just opened."

"I don't doubt that, sir," I reply, hiding a smirk, but likely letting my amusement out in the tone of my voice. Maxwell, who holds my hand, titters.

"If I may continue in my own home as host," Henry says, with some fake testiness.

"By all means, my lord," O'Hara says.

"Thank you. As I was saying, Antonio has held out on everyone until you were well enough to hear the story, and you could tell your side as well. Now I will release the floor to the inspector first."

"Thank you, Lord Henry. I'm going to shorten our travels, not to take credit away from the viscount and his wonderful machine," Antonio says, giving our host a tiny bow, "but it was a long, bumpy trip at a speed that would make a horse ill." This gets several giggles from the assembly. "Needless to say that even with almost a day's head start, we arrived at Cardiff Estate virtually at the same time as he did. Mrs. Ochoa and I knocked on the door. We were invited inside by a servant who then went upstairs to announce us to the baron.

"He returned from downstairs letting Stella and I both know that there was another passage from the upper floors to the basement. This became important to me later.

"The butler took us toward the solarium in the back when Cardiff appeared, causing Stella some kind of distress I couldn't see."

I jump in with, "Oh, I know this may not make sense, but when our world aligns with that of another plane, like hell, it causes witches disorientation. The baron had placed our worlds close so he could call forth a demon, not summon one, but rather to allow one that is willing to come through. Most aren't, but he made a deal with one who has a grudge against me. So, in short, I was too dizzy to do anything."

Antonio continues, "With Stella incapacitated, I draw my revolver and fire once, but his witchcraft spelled my shot away. I didn't know what to do until some strangely shaped object flew across the room—"

"A marble statue that I managed to fling."

"Yes, and it clipped Cardiff across the head, breaking his concentration. I shot for a second time. Unfortunately, the statue's impact moved him away, and I only got him in the upper arm." There are a few boos in the peanut gallery. "Agreed. I saw the baron run out back, calling out some odd word...Gazeep?" Antonio says, looking at me.

"Gazzunreep. It is the name of the demon who wants to, for want of a better word, eat me."

"Little chance of that," Raquel tosses in with a bit of false bravado.

"Don't be so quick, Raquel. Gazzunreep is a ranking prince. What I could have spelled at him would be like a popgun in response to what he could do. Anyway, back to the story. I saw Antonio chasing the baron when all of a sudden, Gazzunreep explodes through the floor from the basement below. I didn't know if Antonio was even alive."

Antonio picks it up. "The explosion threw me through the glass wall of the solarium. I picked myself up and saw both the demon confronting Stella and Franklin running up the back stairs. As neither fisticuffs nor a bullet would affect so powerful a demon, I pursued the baron.

"He had a head start and knew the layout of the house. I cautiously checked each room, finding no trace of my quarry. I even wasted a bullet on a lock to give me access to one room. Out the window of one room, I could see Stella burst out onto the lawn. I couldn't stay as the entire house was being involved in the fire." The entire audience is in rapt attention. "I should let Stella catch up to where I am now."

"Good grief. That sounds so much more heroic than my cowering. I knew I couldn't beat Gazzunreep. I knew I was dead the moment he got me with that flaming mouth of his. My only chance to live was to dismiss him back to his own plane, but I couldn't. He wouldn't possibly give me the time I needed. But I kept things between him and me while I tried. I needed earth to give me another chance, so I ran outside."

"Stella, why not from under the house?" Carlos, who has been silent up to this point, asks.

"Large, deep basement. I didn't think anything I could get up through the floor would be viable."

"Fair enough."

"Back to the inspector first's story," I goad.

"Witch," Antonio says in good-natured teasing.

"Smile when you say that."

"Anyway, by now, the house is filling with smoke. I'm coughing, but I see a figure going out a back window. I take two shots at it. I rush over to see Cardiff pulling down some scaffolding that had been there to do repair work. I take another shot but miss as he dives around the corner of the building lugging a sword. I don't relish a jump from the third floor, so in one of the earlier rooms, I had found a narrow staircase down. Holding my breath, I climb down probably five flights of stairs until coming out in a vast basement. It is hazy and hot there, too. I took off my uniform shirt to breathe through it. I don't want the house to burn down on top of me, so I look for another exit. Luck would have it, I find a trap door out onto the front lawn.

"I climb out just in time to see Stella struck by not just one fiery beam of light but several, and not be hurt. The demon tries more than once, but she just shrugs it off. Finally, it aims its maw at the ground at her feet, causing an explosion, but she lives."

"Why is everyone looking at me?"

"Demons don't leave people alive, Stella," Donny says to me. "Especially hellspawn with a taste for human flesh."

"What did you do, Stella?" Raquel asks. I can even see the question in Carlos's eyes.

The room falls silent enough to hear the cook, three floors down, working on lunch. *When in doubt, tell the truth.* "I don't know," I say with an upward handed shrug. "I honestly have no idea. I expected him to fry me like a single bean dropped into a skillet of hot oil." The blank looks and scowls tell their own story. My explanation hasn't fulfilled everyone's curiosity or even concerns. "I intend to find an expert on demonology to find out myself."

"Shall we leave that point and move on," the padre offers after a pause, saving my mind this time rather than my immortal soul.

"Well, yes," Antonio continues. "Next I know, the screaming demon is sucked down into some kind of hole in the universe. I figure at this point that with Stella and I both alive, I'd call it a win, even if Cardiff got away.

"And then, almost like I'd wished it, the bastard appears over the top of Stella. He meant to impale you on his family sword while his estate burned down in front of him."

"What took you so long to shoot? I still wince whenever I breathe."

Antonio blushes. "Somewhere I'd brushed against something on fire, and it burned my holster. It took me four tries to draw my gun. And then I only had one shot left; I had to make it count, or he might kill you."

"Despite its less than timely appearance, I thank you, Inspector," I say, giving him my hand. The man bows down and kisses it.

"OK, if that is all, I want this herd out of my house," Lady Helms snaps. "The patient needs her rest. You'll be seeing more of her soon enough." The gathering grumbles but starts to leave.

"Wait a minute! What was Lord Helms doing during all of this?"

They look at the hostess. "If you must," she says with enough vinegar to ensure the story will be abbreviated.

Everyone returns to their previous position. "Oh, I did little enough," Henry says with a smile. "We'd agreed that I'd make sure that Cardiff didn't leave by coach or horse. I originally planned on nothing more strenuous than pulling the cotter pins on the coach's wheels and blocking the barn with the poderabile. But like any business plan, this one started falling apart the moment it started.

"I heard an explosion, which I assumed was not a demon, but rather a firefight between two witches. I drove up over the hill and see someone climbing into the carriage. Based on what the inspector has said, I have to assume that it was one of the servants, but I didn't see the person well enough to know. I wasn't about to take chances, so I crashed the poderabile directly into the coach at full speed. I underestimated the energy involved, and I wasn't wearing my driving harness.

"I saw the mess later when Antonio woke me up after the conclusion of the tussle. I had flipped the baron's carriage, splintering the back axle and shattering three of its wheels. I also injured two of the horses, not severely, thankfully. The poderabile had its front driving compartment reduced by a serious dent but took no other damage."

"OK, that is more than enough. Everyone out, now!" Lady Helms says.

I find myself saying thank-you's to everyone wishing me a speedy recovery as they leave the room. The viscountess acts like a shepherdess with her crooked staff switching along a flock of sheep. I give Maxwell a warm smile for his work on me. It seems I promise no fewer than twenty people a drink upon getting up on my feet again.

Somehow the padre remains behind. "Stella, I've asked for special dispensation to talk to you alone."

"I could probably use a confession, Father."

"I doubt it, daughter. I mostly stayed behind to give you a message from your mother. She is away on critical business."

Probably some royal party, I whinge to myself.

"She will visit you again as soon as she returns. She did visit you while you were ill. She also made me promise to tell you that she is proud of you."

"Thank you, Father Juan."

"I wanted to tell you that I am also proud of you. And that if you ever pull a foolish stunt like that again, I'll excommunicate you!"

I giggle for the first time in a long time. It hurts across my ribs and breast where the sword cut. "I hear my confessor and obey like a good daughter of the Church."

"Thank you, Stella. I don't think you know just how special you are to me."

"You are a good friend to me also, Father."

"One more thing you should know that you wouldn't likely hear from another source. Lord Helms, despite his own burns and injuries, drove you into Hartford for a doctor else you may not have lived. It damaged his hands so badly that he may not get the full use of them back again. He definitely will wear scars on them for the rest of his life despite my prayers."

"I don't know what to say, Father."

"Just don't forget that you owe a debt to this man."

"I won't, Father."

"If you aren't up for church on Sunday, I'll come by to give you a special prayer."

"Thank you, Father Juan."

"*In nomine Patris et fillii et Spiritus Sancti*," he says, crossing me as he leaves.

# # #

Lady Helms slathers the daily honey and garlic across my legs and feet with the gentleness of a newborn chick's down. For the first time, I take an interest. From the knees down to the ankles, my limbs look like they've been scarred badly by the pox. Each mark is still pink.

"I think these will actually fade in time, Mrs. Ochoa."

"Lady Helms, with your care, you know more about me than I hoped anyone would ever know. Can you please just call me Stella?"

"If you don't think I'm being disrespectful."

"Are you kidding? You have a title and are married to a magnificent, rich man. You could call me *puta,* and I should be honored."

She flashes me a smile while keeping her attention on my limbs. I wince a bit as she starts unwrapping my feet. "Sorry...Sorry, Stella."

"Just a little twinge."

She remains quiet as she concentrates. The skin on my feet, on the other hand, looks like someone put it through a sausage grinder. In fact, I can still feel tiny bits of rock and earth inside the scabs and muscle. I mentally will them out. I hiss as they burrow through my skin with pains like drawing a dull blade across your palm. I hear the patter as tiny and larger bits drop out onto the cloth under me.

"Now, aren't you a help! I wish you were awake earlier. Maybe we could have skipped most of that infection."

"Doubt it was only rock and soil. I can't affect twigs or other things."

"Any little bit helps.

"I do have a condition," Lady Helms says, not in flow with our conversation or her ministrations.

"Excuse me?"

"I'll call you Stella if, at least in private, you call me Adrianna."

"If you feel it is proper, then I will, Adrianna."

"Thank you, Stella. It is so hard being stuffily formal with someone you are caring for."

"Have you ever done this before?"

"I nursed my mother before she went to her reward. My father wouldn't let anyone else touch her. At eleven, I learned both through mistakes I made with my mother but also through reading. The more I learned, the more I knew what the final outcome of her illness was to be. My father got more and more distant until after Mother's death, he wouldn't see me any more than absolutely necessary. He packed me off to boarding school just twenty-two days later."

"I'm sorry for bringing up bad memories, Adrianna."

She wiped her eyes. "No, Stella, good memories. I was close to my mother. We spent many a quiet hour just talking as she got so ill she couldn't even get out of bed. On the other hand, my father never was close. In his journal, after his death, I learned he believed my mother cuckolded him, and I wasn't his daughter. I've read Mother's diaries, and if there was another man, she never mentioned him, not once, not even in her private journal. She clearly loved my father."

"That still must have been hard."

"I wouldn't call it hard, Stella. My life definitely has had advantages. I never worried about my next meal or if I had a roof over my head like that Tommy boy."

"Oh, yes, that reminds me," I begin, a bit indignant.

Adrianna raised her messy hands as if to defend herself.

Before she can say anything, I say simply, "Thank you."

My nurse and host looks around her hands, raising one darkly drawn-on eyebrow. "You aren't angry?"

"Not at all, Adrianna. That boy needs a family, even if it is a surrogate one. From what I've learned about your husband, and what I hope to learn about you, I think this is an excellent place for him." One thing you learn about blonds is that they have difficulty hiding emotion. Her fair skin blushes to the color of a ripe peach, all the way down to the neckline of her blouse.

"*Gracias, señora,*" she replies.

"*De nada.* So when can I get back on my feet again?"

"Assume you will be off of them for a week. Maybe tomorrow we can let you get into a wheelchair, if you eat!" Lady Helms says, wrapping my feet and legs up loosely in bandages.

"Yes, ma'am," I say, snapping an open-palmed salute.

"Maggie!" Adrianna yells as she is washing the sticky honey off her hands in the basin. "Maggie! Send up Stella's dinner."

"Yes, ma'am," I hear from down the hall.

Two minutes later, Tommy walks in with a bed tray with soup, toast, orange juice, and a sliced-up apple. "Your dinner, *señora*," he says, offering me a napkin to tuck into my nightgown. "And for your after-dinner entertainment..." He places a copy of the *Boston Herald* into a side tray.

"You are training him to be a butler, too?" I ask my hostess.

"Not a chance. He breaks more china than his work is worth. But he does do a darned good job polishing silver," Adrianna says, still trying to get the sticky stuff off her.

Tommy leans forward and offers in a conspiratorial whisper, "If there is anything else you be wanting, I'll get it for ya."

"Thanks," I whisper back.

While simple, the meal looks like a feast, and I don't come close to finishing it all.

# # #

One of the downsides of convalescing in bed is the lack of access to the outhouse. I understand that the Helmses' home has something I've only heard of, a water closet. Regardless, my jailer won't let me stand, so both options are out for me.

Adrianna waits patiently for me to do my business and then takes the chamber pot out to empty it. Something in this doesn't sit right. Why is a society lady waiting on me hand and foot? I can't roll over without her right there to adjust the covers and pillows. Every wince prompts her to inquire about my health. I get a thermometer shoved in my mouth at least every waking hour, sometimes more. She also has a disturbing tendency to measure my pulse at both my wrist and neck.

When she returns, I put the question to her. "Why all this attention, Adrianna? Don't get me wrong, I'm delighted with the way I'm being treated, but it doesn't add up."

"What do you mean, Stella?"

"Lady Helms, don't—"

"Back to Lady Helms, Mrs. Ochoa?"

"Alright. Adrianna, don't think I'm ungrateful for all of the care and support you and Henry have showered on me, but I don't understand it. You could have just hired a nurse to care for me in my own home. It's the personal level of attention that has me flummoxed."

Lady Helms sits on the edge of my bed. She stares into my eyes with those big green eyes that could swallow a ship of the line. "Stella, do you have any idea what you are or what you have done for us? For me? I grant you that my husband and I don't share a traditional marriage, but I love him nonetheless. You saved his life. You saved his business. You saved our fortune, and maybe most important of all, you saved our family honor. The Helms name will not be looked at as some vile money-grubbing filth who put profit ahead of the people's safety. If you've read that paper that Tommy brought you, it calls out the praises of Forever Power at rooting out the evil and punishing the wicked. Personally, I think they go too far, but the papers seem effusive enough in their praise for everyone involved.

"But if you are so thick-headed as to not see the enormity of the personal service you have done for my husband and me and accept our thanks in kind, I will ship you off to that hovel of a boardinghouse with a pair of nurses to hover over you."

Chastened, I swallow hard before saying, "Thank you, Adrianna. I am happy to be in your charge and will say no more on this matter." I realize how wrong I've been about my hostess. She is exhibiting all of the positive things of the aristocracy, not being a leech to her station in life.

"Oh, I will say more on this matter, you can be assured of it. But that is for later."

17—Tuesday, March 13, 1888

A week as a patient is interminable. No matter how good-natured your nurse is, no matter how posh and comfortable the bed and room, no matter how excellent the food, no matter how many friends and well-wishers show up, being a patient is being locked up in solitary confinement. Even when I'm given a wheelchair and taken out onto the grounds, I can barely tolerate the forced inactivity. Attending dinner in the hall is an improvement, but I am still wearing my bed jacket, not real clothes.

I am not a good patient. I fuss. I kibitz. I grumble. Each tiny barrier to normalcy seems like a personal affront. I have to take deep mental breaths and accept how close I came to dying. Only in the fifteen or so seconds after that rationalization do I accept the limitations of my jailhouse.

One additional torture of this is that it gives me far too much time to think. What could I have done better? Why didn't I get torched by Gazzunreep? How could I have kept from being blown up? How could I have kept anyone from getting hurt on Prince Street? Why did I run away from Karie? The latter receives an excessive amount of my attention, especially as I've been unable to ask her here.

My feet are getting better. Out of sight of my prison matron, I put them on the floor, slowly increasing the weight until I feel pain. They are toughening up every day. Tommy has been my secret partner in helping me get back together. He shows up several times a day and lets me use him as a crutch.

"Tommy, I wonder if you could manage a big favor for me," I ask him as I stumble around with a fair amount of grimacing.

"If'n I can, Stella."

"This is big and might cause you trouble if you're caught. I'll understand if you can't."

"Miss Stella, if'n you don't tell me what it is, I can't know if I can."

"Do you know Daring Karie?"

The boy's cheeks become seven shades redder. "No, ma'am. I heard stories, though."

"Well, she is a friend of mine. I would like you to sneak her into the garden for a visit when I'm out there myself, all without letting Lord and, especially, Lady Helms knowing. The Helmses have...reasons for not wanting her here or her presence noted."

Tommy gives me one of his impish grins. "If'n the lady is a fair hand at keeping her mouth shut, I think I can get her into and out o'here without anyone seeing."

"Tomorrow?"

"Sure. Where does your friend live?"

18—Wednesday, March 14, 1888

She waits for me near the frozen fountain. I've never seen Karie look so proper. I didn't even know she had a dress that would make her look like any other wage slave in the city.

I roll up in my convalescent cart, as I'd taken to calling the wheelchair. In a flash, less than a second long, I see eighteen different emotions play across her face, including worry, love, elation, anger, and friendship. I can tell she wants to run up and throw her arms around me but settles for a more ladylike gentle hug. She sits on the edge of the fountain and takes my hand. Questions play across her face, but she says nothing. I've never seen her so quiet.

"I'm sorry," I say as a starting point. Karie squeezes my hand. "I didn't know you would be excluded from visiting."

"I was so worried. The papers talked about the explosion and carried a picture of you, almost dead in that Hartford doctor's office. It nearly scared me to death. I had to go find out from your demon hunting buddies at the Bell in Hand where you were and after that how you were doing. I knew I'd never be welcome coming to the front door."

"I'm sorry, Karie."

"You should be, you one-bit tart. Don't you ever, ever do anything like that to yourself ever again. My heart can't handle it."

I give her hand a squeeze back. "I think you can be assured that I'll avoid it like the plague."

"It is so good to see you almost healthy, Stella. When will they let you out of here? Now that those bloody police are done returning my house to normal, I can entertain again. I mean, I don't want to rush you, and we could just cuddle. I want you well!"

I take one deep breath. *Waiting won't help anything.* I expose my soul. "Karie, that is the second reason I asked you here. I have to apologize a second time."

"Huh? I'm confused."

"Remember our last morning together?"

"Yes, I do. I thought you got out of bed like a cat doused with a bucket of ice water."

"There was a reason for that, and it had nothing to do with the constabulary operation or my husband's memory."

"Hell, girl, I knew that. You had panic painted all over your pretty forehead. I just don't know what it was about."

"When we woke up, everything just seemed so right. Dread settled into my chest of being tied down, of being your wife."

Karie just looks at me. She doesn't say anything. After four heartbeats, she puts her hand over her eyes, lowers her head, and begins laughing. Not in a ladylike giggle, but rather guffawing like some deranged mule. I am glad the Helmses' garden is large enough to hold her merriment. After thirty seconds or so, she calms down. She looks at me again and then bursts back into hysterics.

I try to understand what is so funny. I think it is tragic. I've let down my friend and lover. I've cheapened what has been so perfect between us. I expect shouts and belligerence, not laughter.

"I'm sorry, Stella," she says after she gets herself under control. "You didn't deserve that, but I realize that we have never been clear on that part of our relationship. I honor and cherish our friendship. You are the one person I can share anything with. But I don't want you as my spouse."

My face falls.

"Don't get me wrong, darling. If there would be anyone I'd consider for my life mate, it would be you. If you took me at my offer of the blue room, I'd maul you like a newlywed, but you would remain one of many.

"I'm honest, at least to myself. I am too wanton for any one person. I couldn't live in that world. I couldn't subject anyone else to me as a partner."

"Oh," is all that comes out of my mouth. Part of me is relieved. Another part seems like I've been told I'm superfluous, that the engagement is off, that I have leprosy.

"Don't be like that, pet. I love all of you. You are welcome in my bed anytime, darling. You make the earth move, and the universe turn—just not as my wife."

"Looks like I worried for no reason."

"Friend Stella, I appreciate that you love me strongly enough that you felt distressed in this way, but I assure you that it is unfounded."

"Well, piffle. Mother always said I was a worrier."

19—Friday, March 23, 1888

There is something decadent about the stiff feel of any new dress. This deep-green silk and high bodice make me feel like a queen as I admire myself in the dressing mirror. It is even cut such that it gives me a waist, without a corset, something with which I have a problem. My chest and hips are always trying to meet in the middle. The silver and jade *peineta* and matching bracelet are definitely over the top. I grant the splendor is out of place in my boardinghouse quarters, but I revel in them anyway.

The Helmses continue to shower me with gifts. Along with the dress, new underpinnings, and padded, cobbler-made boots waiting for me on my bed, I found out this morning that they had kept the rent paid on my room here. If that isn't enough, they are throwing a party in my honor tonight.

It may seem silly to some that I left their home this morning, in a coach they hired for me for the day, just to return this evening. Both Henry and Adrianna understand my need for independence. And while my home is less than the mansion I've spent so many languid days within, it is mine. The air seems so much cleaner and easier to breathe here.

A knock interrupts my preening. I open the door. Mrs. Chapman is standing in attendance. She has been no less sour to me since my return, but she has been keeping it to herself.

"Mrs. Ochoa, there is a gentleman to see you downstairs. I left him waiting in the parlor." She hands me an introduction card with the name Marcus James Carlton on it. I would become angry, but why ruin such a lovely day.

"I'll be down directly, Mrs. Chapman. Please have the gentleman cool his heels without any refreshment."

"Yes, Mrs. Ochoa."

I take my time with a light touch of the makeup I do own. I smooth down my hair in the few places the unruly stuff escapes from. Finally, I can think of no other good reason to delay any further. Carlton has been kept waiting long enough to make my point. I take up my handbag and go down the stairs. My new dress, under the pressure of umpteen petticoats, swirls into the parlor before me.

Carlton stands there in a freshly pressed dark gray suit, checked vest, and shined shoes. His hair is slicked down, and he holds his jet black top hat in his hand. I can't decide if the expression on his face is one of concern, contrition, or indigestion.

I decide to rub it in a bit more. The papers had been full of my exploits for the last week. "Yes, Mr. Carlton? I am terribly late to get to a party in my honor at the Helms Estate. Please make it brief."

"Yes, ma'am. I'm sorry to trouble you, Mrs. Ochoa, but I've come to apologize for my bad behavior."

"Acknowledging one's failings is always a good place to start improving one's self," I say, wondering if I am bearing down on his privates too hard with my heel.

"Yes, ma'am. I've come in hopes that you would allow me to plead for your return to work at the Coal Syndicate. We are in desperate need of you."

I stand there and look at him as one might a flea crawling up your foot. "You do know that the Duchess of Massachusetts has offered me a position in the new Royal Demonology and Installation Over-Watch Ministry?" I am not dissembling, at least not directly. Lord Helms and a telegram from Duchess Kincaid of Massachusetts did give me just such a marvelous offer. I'd thanked them both and turned it down. Henry hadn't been upset but felt he had to at least offer it to me. I told him that I couldn't give up the *Dos Campanas*. If I stayed with them, taking his job would be like eating my dinners in the outhouse. There would always be questions if I'd falsified my reports to facilitate more demon releases for the reward of their return.

The man swallows hard. "No, ma'am, I wasn't aware."

"What are you offering, as the duchess has given me a very generous offer."

"What would it take, ma'am? I'm somewhat at your mercy."

I think about that for only a moment as I've contemplated this scene since Jasperson mentioned that his distant relative had to meet the royal soot removal quota. "I will require a public apology to me at the same venue where you fired me." I watch his face as I deliver my demands. He flinches slightly but says nothing. "Next, every witch, male or female, that works in your department receives a fifty percent pay raise. And if it ever drops, then I walk out and leave you holding the soot bag."

"Mrs. Ochoa, I don't think I can get fifty percent. I can probably get the company to increase the department's pay by thirty percent."

"Then, you will have to pay the remaining twenty percent out of your prodigious salary, Mr. Carlton, or you can spell down the soot yourself."

I can see the calculations in his head.

He nods.

"Then we have an agreement?" I say, offering my hand.

I can see beneath the hat in hand meekness that he will find a way to make me pay for this humiliation. He shakes my hand gently. "Yes, ma'am."

"I'll be in Monday morning for my apology and to start our new relationship."

# # #

"I thought this was a party of maybe twenty folks, not a free-for-all that includes the entirety of Boston," I whisper to Adrianna.

"The guest list was under three hundred," she assures me.

"Ladies and gentlemen," Lord Helms orates on a small stage in his resplendent tuxedo. The formal wear, unfortunately, makes his slight form and unruly red hair look more like a lit candle. "I want to thank you for coming tonight to honor the woman who saved not only me from financial ruin," this earns a few gentle laughs from a throng of probably two hundred people, "but also the lives, livelihoods, and property of uncountable thousands of people in Boston alone. I give you the heroine of the hour, Stella Ochoa!"

Loud enough to even startle a demon, applause crashes down around me.

"Take your bows, dear," Adrianna, in her bronze-colored gown, whispers. When I don't move immediately, she gives me a nudge toward her husband and the tiny stage at the front of the room. Fortunately for me, I have such dark skin that likely the crowd can't see the heat I feel in my cheeks and chest. At least I look as good as I ever have standing up there. I pick my mother, Father Juan, the Campanas out of the audience.

"Speech!" some well-meaning idiot calls out as the tumult dies down.

"Wait until we give her something to give a speech about," Henry says. My head snaps around to look at him. "Since I am host, I'm going first, and to hell with our mayor's seniority." The crowd likes Henry and laughs at his little joke. The mayor, Erin Williams, in a severe gray gown, gives him a friendly scowl from the throng. "Stella has done so much that I can never repay. She will always be welcome in my home as a friend and even sister. But I wanted her to have something a little more concrete than a bit of nursing. If you will bring it in, boys." The big French doors on one side of the ballroom opened and in chuffs Lady Justice, the poderabile, parting the crowd and all but filling the space. It has the damage repaired and has been decorated in a deep green that accents my dress. "I present to you, Stella, a gift from my very own hand. May it keep you moving faster than the demons!"

Tears well up in my eyes. I look toward Henry and shake my head back and forth. "No."

"Yes, Stella, with all my heart."

"Thank you, Henry. Thank you very much!" I go over and caress its bowed front where Henry's hand-painted name, Lady Justice, remains. There is a bright flash, and I realize now that there are reporters in the audience. I pull out a handkerchief and daub at my eyes.

"Oh, we aren't done yet," Henry says, taking my arm and leading me back to the stage. "I'd now like to introduce Stella's mother, Senior Mistress Witch Stella Romero."

The crowd claps enthusiastically as my mother, wearing a maroon velvet dress over her svelte frame, climbs up on stage. I look like a grapefruit next to her elegance. She waits patiently as the applause dies off. "I believe my daughter finds me cold as I've sometimes pushed her to excel. Yet I have always been proud of my daughter. Tonight I'm even a prouder parent. Normally advancement in witchcraft is dealt with by rigorous examination and practice. Sometimes, under extreme situations, covens can and do recognize that the skill displayed by a practitioner is well above their current status. It is in this light that I have been appointed by the Massachusetts Coven of Witchcraft to convey upon my daughter the title of Mistress Witch." She reaches out to me with a silver pin in the shape of a capital M with a hackneyed brimmed, pointy hat perched on top. Without my help, she manages to get it on my dress right at my waist.

Tonight is a kaleidoscope of images and shocks. I never sought out a title. I'd never tested for it. I never yearned for it like some.

"Speech. Speech. Speech," the crowd starts to chant.

"Wait a moment," Henry interjects. "We still have the mayor. Let's give Mrs. Williams the floor."

The cheers aren't quite as obstreperous but still worthy of her position. Her voice is as tinny and piercing as I remember it from one of her campaign speeches.

"I will forgo a long speech—" The crowd erupts. The mayor smiles. "I'll remember that for my reelection speech next year." Laughs interspersed with some good-natured boos respond.

"I just want to say that Stella Ochoa exhibits all that is good in our citizens. She puts them before herself. She has sacrificed so that others may have the wonderful life we have here. Because of that, we have several gifts to bestow on this young lady. First of all, we have the bounty for subduing the demon in Boston." Erin hands me a pouch with some coins in it. "We have a similar bounty from the Duchy of Connecticut that I've been empowered to bestow." Yet another pouch. "Then we have the matter of the forfeiture of the Cardiff Estate—"

There are many boos and hisses within the audience. I wonder if they are all ruffians from the local pub rather than the cream of society.

"The Duke Lopez y Martin has assigned to Stella Ochoa the deed to the baron's entire six hundred acre physical estate south of Hartford." She places in my hand a rolled scroll with a ribbon. "Unfortunately, in the Duchy of Massachusetts, the Cardiff Estate amounts to very little with no real property. But with the help of Duchess Kincaid herself, we have boosted the normal ten percent prize money to one thousand dollars," she says, placing a much larger bag in my arms.

"To this, we add the key of the city and the thanks of a grateful populous," Mayor Williams says. She adds a gilded metal skeleton key weighing thirty pounds to the top of my stack. Another photography flash catches me just before I drop the key onto the floor.

Following some laughs, as I try to juggle the load in my arms, the chant starts again, "Speech. Speech. Speech."

"Oh, bloody hell," I say. That earns me a chorus of laughs. Tommy, in a waiter's uniform, appears at my elbow.

"I'll take this to a safe place, Stella," he whispers. He gently collects all of my burdens, waves to the crowd, and disappears.

I smooth my dress, catching a finger on the exposed pin of my new witching honor. Without thinking, I stick it into my mouth. I blush again. "I had no intention of speaking. Personally, I find all of this too damned much for me. I really am a simple woman with simple tastes. I thank you all for these honors, but I hope like anything that you never need anyone to be your heroine again.

"Now, will someone strike up the band and get some dancing going so I can slip back into obscurity?" The crowd applauds.

Inspector First Antonio Guizzetti appears at my shoulder. "May I have the first dance, Mrs. Ochoa?"

"Absolutely, Inspector." He invites me into his embrace and directs me expertly across the floor. "But won't your girl be jealous, it being the first dance and all?"

"Not at all. She tossed me over for a big, burly teamster. I could see us in a life together, but she couldn't."

"Her loss," I say.

"Yup. I'll find the right one yet."

"I'm sure you will," I say with a level of distraction. Lady Helms isn't dancing. She is watching me in Antonio's arms, with a scowl on her face.

Author's Note

I can hear all my fans out there already. "What on earth led you into steampunk?"

Well, that is quite simple—my spouse. For those paying attention, I dedicated one of my first books, *An Eighty Percent Solution*, to my wonderful wife. She is an avid reader. It is a rare week that she hasn't plowed through at least one book, often more. She's read many of my books. I'm ashamed to say that as of the writing of this book, she still hasn't read past about the third chapter of the book dedicated to her. Cyberpunk isn't her thing.

With all that in mind, I know she does enjoy the steampunk genre. I decided to write something with those tropes in mind. I had already considered an alternative history where the USA becomes a monarchy instead of a republic. Merging these two brings me to this novel.

As I'd never written steampunk before, I made sure I got a great deal of advice. I did a full alpha and beta review, and had sensitivity readers around my lesbian sex scenes. I didn't want to miss the dirigible on any of it.

I've never done nearly as much research or note-taking as I did with this novel. I can't count the number of times I was writing along and said, "Did they even use that word in that year?" This would be followed by searching the etymology of a phrase and, often as not, changing the wording. One of the more difficult research issues was period costuming for Spain. Unlike most steampunk, where Victorian England rules, in this world, America gets most of its fashion sense through Spain. I engaged several people who are experts in period costumes. I got a blank stare when I mentioned Spain. England, loads of material. France, reams of data. Spain (screech, crash, tinkle.) I ended up spending a good deal of time investigating photographs that have survived from that era to make my own decisions.

Oddly, the single most challenging thing in this book wasn't the costuming, or the different tropes, nor even the extended sex scenes. It was (is) the present tense. I tend toward writing past tense, even if in first-person. Changing that inbred bias is like telling someone who likes Pepsi that they have to drink Coke from now on, even if Pepsi is in the cooler. Good grief! Even after all my rewrites, I am STILL finding places where I accidentally slipped into the past tense. "So why did I do it?" I hear you ask. Partially because of multiple requests to have a first-person, present-tense offering, and partly...well, professional vanity. "I can do this!" I said to myself more than once. In the end, I believe I did it well and true.

All the above being said I loved writing this novel. Every day I'd wake up eager to type out the next scene (which I usually dreamed about the night before). If I didn't have commitments to write the next Toy World novel and the next CorpGov Chronicle, I'd be writing on the next Monarchy of America book already. Fear not, fair reader, more will come. I've already sketched out plots for six more books. The second book, tentatively entitled "Power Plays," is already more than a sketch. Hold on, folks. This one is going extra innings.

Thank you for being part of our world. Without your imagination, none of this would be exciting nor worth it.

Translations (and other odd terms)

<Alphabetically>

absolutamente—absolutely
aether—a parallel universe touching but not seen by our world; mythical
    and theoretical only
amiga—female friend; not girlfriend
amigos—friends
arroz—rice
arroz a la marinera—seafood over rice
diablo—devil or demon
bien—good
brujo—warlock
buenos—good
buenos dias—good morning or good day
cabrón—stubborn goat
cabrones—fuckers
cacafuego—shit fire or also braggart
cocina—kitchen
campana—bell
capullo/capulla—like *gilipollas* but with a certain amount of evil
    intentions, aka wanker
chimpancés—chimpanzees
chocho/chocha—senile person, also cunt
coqueto—flirtatious
de—of
de nada—you're welcome; literally "of nothing"
dias—days
Dios—God
¡Dios Mío!—Oh my God!
dos—two

dubloon—old Spanish currency that equals sixty-four reale or approximately eight dollars

dulce—sweet

duro—a five peseta coin where four pesetas equal one dollar

en sotto voce—in a soft voice meant to be overheard

genial—brilliant

gilipollas—jerk, or stupid in their own right, often through social ineptitude

gracias—thank you

Gracias a Dios—Thank God

¡Hijo de la chingada!—Son of a bitch

hostia—literally wafer, specifically communion wafer. When used as an exclamation it means the same as "God damn"

jefe—boss or chief

¡Joder!—to fuck or colloquially just "Fuck!"

Madre Dios / Madre de Dios—Mother of God

marinera—sailor

mi amor—my love

mierda de toros—bullshit

mujer—woman

murió—died

muy—very

niñita—little girl

noches—night

Okeus—Powhatan American Indian god of war

pan—bread

pan dulce—similar to American donut

papas—potatoes

peinetas—Spanish hair comb

pendejo—fool, idiot, asshole

peseta—Spanish coin equal to a quarter

pinche—fucking

puta—whore

querida—dearest or mistress

reale—old currency where eight reale equals one dollar

salchicha—sausage

semana—week

señor—Mr.

señora—Mrs. without the implication of marriage, a mature woman

señorita—miss

serpiente—serpent or snake or demon

si—yes

tardes—afternoon/evening

¡Tócate los cojones!—What a surprise!

tortilla—flatbread

vdo—widow

veinte—twenty

vete a la mierda—literally "To go to shit" translates as "Go fuck yourself"

y—and

The Alternative History of the Monarchy of America

Like all good alternative histories, there has to be some event or events that have drifted this world away from our own past. In the case of the Monarchy of America series, there are several. If you haven't picked it up from the writing itself, let me share.

Napoleon brings the battle of Waterloo to a draw but is severely wounded, becoming a broken man. France continues to be a thorn in the world's side. Still, without Bonaparte as a driving force, it no longer threatens world domination.

Germanic tribes wrest themselves free of the French grasp but never become a world power.

Spain, with the aid of the Catholic pope, holds sway throughout a good deal of the world and never leaves her golden age. Charles II has several heirs who continue the line, maintaining a strong and united Iberian peninsula. Charles III and IV never seek any world conquest ambitions but rather domination by exploration.

England, with her smaller, more widely diverse empire, is forced to play a much more aggressive and smarter world view game rather than the massive hammer it was in our world. As a result, there are many clashes with the powerful Spanish. Most of these end with a bloody nose for the English. The Brits choose to bide their time.

In the mid seventeen hundreds, King George decides to honor the troubled American colony's desire for representation. He appoints his son, Frederick, as hereditary Prince of America.

In 1843 Queen Victoria wants to replace Frederick with her son, Edward, as Prince of America. Frederick and the Americans take exception to this and declare America a monarchy of its own.

Over the following forty-plus years, tensions between England and America are at the point of war. Spain has declared that it will side with this new country if England intervenes. The pope himself presided over Frederick's coronation as the first King of America, which includes modern-day Canada as well.

England bides its time but seethes at the humiliations it has had to endure. It continues to find ways to incite incidents with Spain and America while looking for allies.

Because of the smoother overall political landscape, the Industrial Revolution kicks off earlier. There is no fight for states' rights (there are no states, only duchies of similar shape and size), so no Civil War. In an ironic twist to previous policies, the King of America declares slavery to be an abomination, and all African Americans are forcibly shipped to Cuba.

The "Louisiana Purchase" becomes the "Caledonia Purchase" from Spain. Later, after Lewis and Clark's fateful trip, America and Spain enter into the "New Cadiz Purchase." It includes modern-day Oregon, Washington, Idaho, Montana, Wyoming, and parts of British Columbia, giving America her ports on the Pacific Coast. By that time, the Bonapartes in France have grown powerful again and are threatening to take back the Germanic countries, which are Spanish protectorates. Spain does this transaction not only to be a good ally and to bolster America's ability to withstand the English aggression but also the New Cadiz sale helps Spain with the finances it needs to blunt French hostility.

By fiat, America annexes northern Canada and all of modern-day Alaska.

Native Americans are not kicked off their lands or slaughtered but rather convinced to relocate into the Oklahoma territories. They are given this land "until the sun grows cold." For once, a deal with the natives is kept. Eventually, the Native Americans ask to become colonies of the Crown as the region Ysa, named after the Shoshone creation god.

Catholic Irish are persecuted by the Protestant English. They eventually plead to Spain and the pope himself for aid. In 1877 the Spanish publicly condemn the English for their meddling in Irish affairs and order them to withdraw from Ireland entirely.

Queen Victoria has the Spanish ambassador beheaded, returning the head in a gilt box as a response.

Spain can ill afford a war on two fronts, so it beseeches King Frederick II to send their army to Ireland. In America's first flex of her fledgling might, she lands thousands of troops, tons of supplies, weapons, and ammunition in Galway, Ireland, sparking off the War of Irish Independence, June 14, 1878. Many more soldiers would cross the

Atlantic, and tens of thousands of Americans would be buried in Irish soil.

By November of 1884, the remains of the English army, outnumbered by the Irish Nationalists and their American allies, are forced out of Ireland. The native Irish rejoice for a few short months. But, before Ireland can even get organized as a country, the Potato Famine strikes (forty-one years later than in our world). Many flee to America as their ally in the war and others to Spain.

England eyes the weakened country a mere twelve miles away, but knows to pounce would likely cause a world war. Victoria bides her time and casts about for allies.

In 1888, the date of our first book, there is growing tension between England and America. Spain and France are on the verge of war.

As with most steampunk, petroleum products just never take off. From a scientific point of view, I've made the assumption that it has approximately a quarter of the chemical potential energy of what it has in our world.

Thus coal-heated steam is the power of choice. It is relatively cheap, mobile, and an infrastructure exists for it. But coal has a new rival. As the education of magicks has increased, a fusion between technology and magic has led to captive demons coming into their own as a power source. They are summoned to a fixed location where their inhuman bodies heat boilers providing the steam to run homes and industry. No one has been able to hold a demon on a mobile platform.

www.ingramcontent.com/pod-product-compliance
Lightning Source LLC
Chambersburg PA
CBHW051340020726
47501CB00007B/2191